Just One More
A Psychological Thriller

Tamara Merrill

CALI Press

CORONADO, CALIFORNIA

CALI Press
PO Box 2213
Coronado, CA 92118
www.TamaraMerrill.com

Book Layout © 2017 BookDesignTemplates.com

Cover Illustration © 2022 Teresa Espaniola
Edited by Lisa Wolff

Just One More/TamaraMerrill -- 1st ed.
ISBN 978-1-7338555-7-0 Hardback
ISBN 978-1-7338555-4-9 Paperback
ISBN 978-1-7338555-6-3 eBook
ISBN 978-1-7338555-8-7 Audio

DEDICATION

To everyone who faces a bully and says, "Stop It!."
To everyone who communicates with crows.
And, to Theresa One and Teresa Two, who believe I am not crazy.

CONTENTS

One for Sorrow is an Old English counting rhyme
used throughout the United Kingdom.

One for sorrow.

Two for joy,

Three for a girl,

Four for a boy,

Five for silver,

Six for gold,

Seven for a secret, never to be told.

Eight for a wish,

Nine for a kiss,

Ten a surprise you should be careful not to miss,

Eleven for health,

Twelve for wealth,

Thirteen beware, it's the devil himself.

One for sorrow,

"I used to think that the worst thing in life was to end up all alone. It's not. The worst thing in life is ending up with people who make you feel all alone." —Robin Williams

These are ten things I know about me:

1.   I am ten years old.
2.   I am smart. I can read anything.
3.   My feet are size six, that is large but not too large for my height, which is four feet eleven inches. My grandpa says I am a "firmly rooted string bean".
4.   My name is Penelope Jane, that is not true. It is only my name today. My real name is too horrible to write on this list.
5.   My father doesn't live here anymore.

"Girl, get down here!" Jerry's voice always sounded mean, and sometimes he was. She leaped off her bed, snapped her notebook shut, and ran for the stairs.

The hall was dark, but she knew better than to turn on the light. Jerry hated what he called "wastin' 'lecticity" almost as much as he hated her. She stumbled and stubbed her toe. "Damn, damn, damn," she muttered.

"What did your mama tell you 'bout swearin', girl?"

The creep can hear like a bat. "Sorry, sir." She slid to a stop in front of the worn recliner where Jerry lay sprawled. She dropped her eyes to avoid seeing him scratch his private parts. *Mama wouldn't like that any better than me swearing.*

She stood frozen, afraid to move or catch his eye. When he was like this, she didn't know what to expect. The TV cast a blue light across the room. Music surged from the TV, louder and louder. She wondered what he was watching but didn't dare sneak a peek. *Crescendo, C-R-E-S-C-E-N-D-O, a gradual, steady increase in loudness or force.*

"Cat got your tongue?" Jerry brought the recliner to upright with a load bang. She jumped. "I ast you a question."

She cleared her throat, brought her thoughts back to Jerry, and managed a whisper. "Mama said nice girls don't swear."

Jerry threw back his head and laughed a horrible laugh, rough and mean. "Guess you don't need to worry, then. You ain't no nice girl."

He grabbed her arm and pulled her close to his chair. She nearly gagged on the odor wafting from him. She pictured his breath as a putrid green cloud of gas. *Mama,* she wanted to scream. *Mama, where are you?*

"Don't stand there gawkin' like a retard. Git me a beer."

Jerry dropped her arm. She scurried away, keeping one eye on the big hand to be sure it wouldn't grab her, or pinch her.

The inside of the refrigerator smelled almost as bad as Jerry, rancid with mold and damp. The light was out, but she could see the beer in the faint glow from the TV. She carried it back to Jerry and pulled the tab. He grunted as she placed it next to his chair. His eyes stayed glued to the TV.

She walked backwards out of the room and climbed the stairs to her bedroom, where she opened her notebook and picked up her pen. She resumed her list.

6.   I am the best speller at Exeter Charter School.

7.   My mama is very beautiful, and she loves me very much.

Tears fell on the paper. She brushed them away impatiently. Tears never helped anything, she reminded herself. She ripped the page into tatters and began her homework again.

Ten things about me:

1.   My name is Harriet Blimm.
2.   I live at 1436 Main St.
3.   Our house is yellow.
4.   My bedroom is mostly green and pink.
5.   My favorite book is Heidi.
6.   I look like my mother.
7.   I do not have a grandpa.
8.   I do not like to play volley ball.
9.   I have a red bike.
10. My favorite subject in school is spelling.

***

"Hey, Hairy Fairy, what you got in your lunch today?" Toby snatched her creased and tattered brown bag from her hand and tipped it over. The sandwich she'd carefully constructed using the heel of bread and the small amount of peanut butter still in the jar slipped from the plastic wrap she'd covered it with and lay in the dirt. Her small, hard orange rolled away and came to a stop. Toby kicked the orange under a bush and stepped on her sandwich.

"You're an asshole." She opened her eyes wide and blinked rapidly, forcing her tears not to fall.

"Harriet Blimm!" Mr. Comstock's voice jerked her around. He grabbed her shoulder and pulled her away from Toby and his gang. "We do not use language like that. Apologize to Toby, then march yourself to the office."

Harriet said nothing.

"Now, Miss Blimm."

"But…" Harriet started to protest.

"But nothing. Apologize."

Harriet turned to Toby and squinted her eyes, hoping she looked mean. With her back turned to Mr. Comstock, she extended the middle finger of her right hand and muttered, "Sorry, Toby."

Toby nodded, pretending to accept her unfelt apology. He locked eyes with Harriet and mouthed, "Fuck you."

She held her head high as she walked across the asphalt, keeping her eyes straight ahead, ignoring the giggles and whispers that accompanied her departure. She pulled the heavy metal doors open and entered the school building.

***

"Hello again, Harriet."

Harriet recognized that voice, Miss Charles, the school counselor. Harriet avoided eye contact but nodded her head in acknowledgment of the greeting.

"Come on in. It sounds like we need to talk."

Harriet glanced around the small office. The morning sun slanted through the open blinds and created a striped pattern across the carpet and up the far wall. Miss Charles seated herself in one of the soft blue chairs arranged around a low table and gestured to Harriet to take a seat. A sigh escaped from Harriet as she settled into her chair.

Miss Charles smiled. "Do you want to tell me about your morning?" She waited. Harriet kept her eyes on the carpet. The sounds of students, passing in the hall, whispered into the room.

Harriet took a deep breath and forced herself to look at Miss Charles. "Nothing happened." She shrugged her shoulders.

"I heard that Toby Meyers was talking to you and that you called him an inappropriate word."

Silence.

Harriet kept her hands still and silently spelled, *A-S-S-H-O-L-E.* *Factual, not inappropriate.*

Miss Charles cleared her throat and tried again. "Is that true?"

Harriet raised her head and glanced out the window. The schoolyard was empty. Classes were beginning.

"You need to answer me, Harriet, or I will have to keep you after school for detention."

Shit. Harriet almost said it out loud. She couldn't be late. Jerry would kill her. She turned to face Miss Charles. "I did not call Toby an inappropriate word. I called him an asshole. 'Asshole' is a vulgar word, but it is very descriptive of Toby's behavior."

Miss Charles bit her lip to keep from laughing. She covered her mouth to hide her grin. "Harriet." She shook her head. "What am I supposed to do with you?"

"I imagine you are supposed to reprimand me and send me back to my classroom."

Miss Charles nodded. She gazed out the window for a long moment before returning her eyes to Harriet. "Allow me to ask you a different question." She kept her words as formal as Harriet's own. "How may I help you?" Harriet stayed completely still. "Can you tell me what you need that will ensure your ability to comply with the school rules?"

Harriet squeezed her hands tightly together under the desk. *Mama, I just need Mama.* The clock clicked loudly in the silent room. No one moved. A fly buzzed and settled on the windowsill. Miss Charles adjusted her skirt, pulling it farther over her knees.

Harriet stayed motionless.

Miss Charles sighed. "Harriet, go back to your classroom and stay away from Toby. You are a smart, beautiful child and you need not resort to name calling." She reached out and touched Harriet's knee. The child stiffened. She pulled her hand back, aware of the school protocol stating it allowed no touching. Ever. No matter what.

Harriet stood and moved toward the door. She hesitated a moment; tilted her head as if to speak, then opened the door and slid out of the room.

The counselor opened Harriet's record and wrote; This child needs to be loved.

***

"Mom," Harriet shouted, opening the front door. "Are you home?"

"Shut up, brat," Jerry snarled. "Your mother ain't here." His dark eyes blazed as he glared at her from under a hank of greasy hair.

Feeling his anger, Harriet paused in the archway between the living room and the hall unsure if she dared to ask more, but she couldn't stop herself. "Do you know when she'll be back?" Her voice trembled. She swallowed hard.

"You goin' to cry?"

Harriet shook her head. "No sir." She cleared her throat and continued, "I was just wondering. Mom's never been gone this long before."

"Your mom's a working girl. She'll be home when she's good'n ready." Jerry pulled the lever and his recliner snapped upright. He stood, unzipped his jeans and tucked his shirt in. He used the opportunity to scratch himself.

Harriet turned away.

Jerry grabbed his jacket from the back of his chair. "I'm goin' out."

Harriet nodded. "Okay."

The door slammed behind him. Harriet breathed a sigh of relief. Sometimes it was scary to be home alone, but it was better than being home with Jerry. *I wonder why Mama chose him to stay with me.* She dropped her backpack at the foot of the stairs. She was hungry.

The kitchen looked exactly the way it had this morning when she'd made her lunch with the last of the bread and peanut butter. Harriet was aware there would be nothing in the cupboards. But she opened each battered, chipped door, hoping she had overlooked something. The refrigerator still had that sour, awful smell, but the beer was gone. A lone bottle of ketchup stood on the shelf. She pulled it out and held it up to the dim light penetrating the kitchen through the filthy window. A meager quarter inch coated the bottom. She tipped the bottle upside down and shook it. The ketchup didn't move. Harriet shrugged. "Better than nothing," she muttered and turned on the hot water faucet.

The water trickled out. She waited, testing it with her finger, hoping it would get hot, or at least warm. Nothing happened. The gas must have been turned off again. Without gas or electricity, the water heater wouldn't heat, and the stove top wouldn't work. Harriet removed the ketchup lid and filled the bottle with the tap water. She screwed the lid back on and shook the bottle until, finally, the ketchup loosened from the bottom and the liquid turned a pale red. "Bisque," she said. "B-I-S-Q-U-E, a creamy soup, traditionally made with seafood, but often made with tomato."

Harriet carried the bottle back to the stairs, picked up her backpack and went up to her room to do her homework. Her stomach growled. She flicked the light switch. Nothing happened. *Maybe Jerry has gone to pay the bill and the lights will come back on before dark.*

When Mama comes back, I need to ask her why Jerry really lives here, Harriet speculated *If she believes he's taking care of me, he's not.* Jerry wasn't really her brother, even though she was supposed to tell anyone who asked why he lived at her house, that he was.

Harriet stood in her window, looking out at the neighborhood. All the houses looked alike, different colors and different trash in the yards, but still they were all the same. *Mama called them ticky-tacky boxes.* A few people hurried down the street, their heads ducked against the rising wind. A gust rattled the window and caused the thin curtains to stir. "Draft, D-R-A-F-T," she spelled aloud, "a current of air in an enclosed space."

The sun set, taking the light from the room. As the house grew darker and colder. Harriet huddled by the window, her blanket wrapped around her. She tried to read her book. The streetlights came on. Their glow fell short of the page. She closed her book, lay her head on her knees. Her stomach rumbled. Harriet began to count aloud. "One thousand, nine hundred and ninety-nine, nine hundred and ninety-eight, nine hundred and ninety-seven..." Her eyes drooped, and she drifted to sleep.

***

A door slammed. Harriet jerked awake. The book hit the floor with a bang. She shivered and tugged her blanket closer. The moon was high in the sky, caught in the branches of the pine tree in the yard. For a second, Harriet noticed how beautiful the moon looked.

"Girl, git down here."

She could tell from his tone that he was drunk. Harriet scrambled to her feet. She stumbled. Pins and needles shot up her legs. *How long was I asleep?* she wondered. Harriet held onto the windowsill for a minute to allow her legs and feet to wake up.

"You sleeping, girl?" Jerry bellowed again. "Get your ass down here. This place is a pigsty."

Harriet hurried. When Jerry was drunk, she never knew what might happen. "Hey," she called from the stairs, trying to keep her voice light and welcoming. She could see him silhouetted against the window in the hall. He swayed side to side, obviously very drunk. He lifted his arm and took a long drink from the bag he held in his hand. *Whiskey,* she mused. *Hard liquor is always worse than beer.*

"Hey, Jerry," she said again. Harriet stopped at the bottom of the stairs, keeping her distance from him.

"Why ain't there no light in here?" he slurred.

Harriet wanted to scream, *because you spent the money on booze!* Instead, she said carefully, "The power must be out. The gas isn't working either."

"Oh, yeah." Jerry took another long drink. "Forgot about that." He seemed to take a sober look at Harriet. She froze; it was never good when Jerry actually noticed her. "Cold in here."

Harriet nodded.

"I saw your mama today."

Harriet's mood lifted instantly. Any news was better than no news. "Is she okay? Will she be home soon?"

Jerry chuckled. "Soon as the drugs run out, I imagine."

"Did she..." Harriet knew she shouldn't ask, but she needed to know, "Did she ask about me? Where did you see her?"

Jerry took another long drink. His face changed, and he shook his head a bit. "Well, she didn't exactly ask. She was kind of busy." He reached his hand out as if to touch her.

Harriet stepped back and felt her heels bang against the bottom stairs.

"Go to bed, girl." He grinned at her. "Don't do no good to worry about your mama."

"But..." Harriet's voice shook. She stammered to a stop.

Jerry dropped his grin. His face darkened and became even uglier. He squinted at her. "Don't whine, girl. It's colder than shit in here. I'm leaving." He swung around, pulled the door open and slammed it behind him.

Harriet sank down onto the stairs. She swiped angrily at the tears that threatened to overflow. Her whole body trembled. She hugged herself and began to count —"Two, four, six, eight..." When she reached "twenty-eight," the tears were gone. Harriet locked the front door and went back upstairs. Instead of going to her room she turned to her mother's room, and without undressing crawled under the covers and continued counting until she fell asleep.

***

Harriett woke, shivering. She looked around, unsure of where she was. Light poured in through the crack between the drapes and, with a deep sigh, she recognized her mother's bedroom. She turned her head and buried her face in the pillow. The slight hint of her mother's perfume reassured her. She thrust the pillow aside and sat up, refusing to let herself cry. A spiderweb stretched from the drapery to her mother's dressing table. It stirred and quivered. Harriet narrowed her eyes, hoping to make the web go away. *How long has Mama been gone?* she wondered. She peered closer, not wanting to see the spider that lived in the web, but afraid not to find him. *Arachnid,. A-R-A-C-H-N-I-D, a class of arthropods; including spiders, scorpions, mites, and ticks.* She stayed perfectly still, eyes wide as they searched the room and found nothing.

She sat up and listened carefully. The house was silent. If Jerry had come home last night, he was asleep. "No surprises," she murmured. "No spider. No Jerry. It's safe."

She needed to be quiet. Bothering Jerry when he had a hangover was never a good idea. Her stomach growled loudly. She stood up, surprised to feel the room sway. Harriet steadied herself against the nightstand and waited for her stomach and the room to steady.

She wondered about the time. Without electricity, the clocks weren't working. In the hall, the light was brighter. With one hand on the wall, Harriet made her way to the bathroom. She flipped the switch. Nothing happened. "Damn," she muttered. "The lights are still off." She splashed her face with ice-cold water and considered her situation.

She needed to get to school in time for the free breakfast. Her stomach erupted again in agreement. If she arrived in time, she might be able to sneak in and get something to eat. Her mom hadn't signed her up for the program, and she had no ticket, but with any luck the lunch lady would be too busy to notice one more kid.

Harriet contemplated her clothes. Everything looked dirty. The jeans would do. The torn sneakers were her only shoes, but she needed to find a clean top of some sort. She had worn her own clothes multiple times. It had been weeks since anyone gave her money for the laundromat. "I need a shower," she said aloud. Her voice echoed in the small room. With nothing but ice-cold water, the idea of washing more than her face was not appealing. "Perhaps, Jerry really will get the gas and lights turned back on today." She nodded to herself. "I'll shower tonight."

Harriet opened her mother's closet. She'd done this a million times and knew there was nothing she could wear to school. The shoes were all spiky heels, and the dresses were covered in sparkles and beads. The dresser drawers held nothing but bras and panties. A robe hung behind the door. "I need a clean T-shirt," she said, and left the room, carefully closing the door behind herself. There was nothing clean in her room, and she was afraid to check in Jerry's.

"I'll just brush my hair and wear my red sweater again." She picked up the sweater and sniffed it. Not bad. The stain on the front didn't appear too noticeable. She pulled it on, found her hairbrush, and tried to draw it through her thick, curly hair. The brush caught and pulled in the snarls. Her hair was tough on a good day when she'd washed it and used conditioner. This was not a good day. Harriet divided her hair with her fingers and managed to twist it into two loose braids.

She grabbed her backpack and hurried downstairs, more worried now that she'd miss the free breakfast. Her stomach let out a loud growl as if to remind her to hurry. Jerry's navy-blue hoodie hung from the newel post. It would cover the stain on her sweater. Harriet snatched it and ran toward the school.

***

"Aw, here comes, Stinky." Toby pointed. His friends laughed and held their noses as Harriet approached. "Pee-ew," Toby said loudly. "Something smells awful." His friends hooted and took exaggerated sniffs.

"Smells like something died."

"Nah, I think it's a skunk fart."

Harriet kept her expression blank and pretended not to understand that they were making fun of her. *Imbecile,* she thought. *I-M-B-E-C-I-L-E, a stupid person.*

"Hey, Stinky," Toby caught Harriet's arm. "I'm talking to you."

Harriet shook his hand off. The world grew dark and began to spin. Toby's voice faded away. She fell to the ground. Toby ran.

"Miss Blimm, what is going on here?"

Mr. Comstock's voice came from a distance. Harriet struggled to focus.

"Are you hurt? You need to get up."

Harriet opened her eyes. The world spun again. She closed them. *I'll just stay here,* she thought.

"Harriet, Harriet. Can you hear me?" Mr. Comstock sounded irritated.

How strange, Harriet thought. She opened her eyes again and tried to focus. "I'm okay," she managed.

"What happened?" Mr. Comstock demanded, his fear replaced by irritation.

Miss Charles knelt down beside Harriet. She placed her cool, soft hand on Harriet's forehead. "Hi, Harriet." She smiled directly at her. "Mr. Comstock, I'll take care of this. Why don't you move the rest of the students along to class? The bell will ring any second."

Harriet stayed quiet. She kept her eyes closed until the schoolyard grew still. Miss Charles waited, one hand on Harriet's arm. At last, she said, "Do you think you can sit up now, Harriet?"

Harriet's stomach let out a massive growl. She placed her hand over it, hoping she could keep Miss Charles from hearing. She opened her eyes and managed to nod. "I think so." Miss Charles slid her arm around Harriet and helped her to a sitting position. Harriet stiffened. She knew Toby was right; she did stink. The world tilted again. She trembled.

"It's okay, Harriet. Just go slow."

Harriet sat, her knees drawn up to her chest, her head bent down. Her stomach rumbled again.

"Can you stay right here, Harriet? Everyone else is gone. I want to get you something."

Harriet nodded without lifting her head. Miss Charles patted her back as she rose to her feet.

"I'll be right back. It'll only take a minute."

Harriet sat huddled in the middle of the concrete yard. An empty McDonald's bag blew across her feet and she caught the aroma of french fries. A crow cawed from the roof and flew down to land not far away. It cocked its head and hopped closer. Harriet watched. Footsteps approached. The crow cawed again and flew off.

She turned her head and opened her eyes. Miss Charles smiled and handed her a can of V-8 juice. "I hope this is okay. The vending machine was out of everything else." Harriet nodded. "Sip it slowly. I think you fainted."

The V-8 was the best thing Harriet had ever tasted. She wanted to gulp it down and ask for more.

"Harriet," Miss Charles asked, "did you forget to eat breakfast this morning?"

Forget, F-O-R-G-E-T, fail to remember. "Not exactly," Harriet said, drinking the last of the juice.

Miss Charles thought a moment, then said, "Harriet, do you think I should call your mother so that you can go home?"

Harriet shook her head. "No, my mom's at work. I just need to go to class. I'll be alright." Her stomach made that horrible sound again. She sat up straighter, then stood. "Thank you for the juice."

"You're welcome, Harriet." Miss Charles studied her for a long moment. "I think before you go to class, you need to get cleaned up." Harriet blushed, but Miss Charles ignored her and continued, "You fell on the dirty pavement and you've torn your jeans. I'll get a key for the teachers' shower room. I can borrow some clothes for you from the lost and found. Would that be okay?"

***

The hot water gushed over Harriet. As she stood, face lifted and head thrown back, the tension eased from her body. She leaned her back against the wall, dizzy and afraid she might fall again. She scrubbed her hair and every inch of her skin. Feeling clean at last, she turned off the water and wrapped herself, and her hair, in the towels Miss Charles had provided.

Harriet found clean underwear, jeans, and a bright T-shirt emblazoned with a unicorn prancing under a rainbow folded on the bench. A pair of sandals and Jerry's hoodie completed the ensemble. *Ensemble,* she thought, *E-N-S-E-M-B-L-E, a group of items viewed as a whole instead of individually.* Harriet moved to the mirror and combed her fingers through her wet hair. It was already starting to tangle and curl.

A tap sounded on the door. "May I come in?"

"Okay."

"If you sit down on the bench, I can help you with your hair," Miss Charles said. "I don't have a brush but I do have this big comb." She waved a large, broad-tooth comb. "Do you want a ponytail, braids, or just to let it hang loose?"

Harriet considered the options. "Mama likes me to wear it loose."

"Okay, loose it is."

Miss Charles stood behind Harriet and carefully worked the comb through her wet hair. When she hit a snarl, she slowly and patiently separated the knots. Harriet relaxed and allowed herself to daydream. *Maybe,* she thought, *mama will come home today.*

"There." Miss Charles's satisfied tap on her shoulder brought Harriet back to the present. "You look very pretty."

Harriet considered herself in the mirror. *I do look better than usual,* she conceded, *but not pretty.* "Thank you."

"It was my pleasure." Miss Charles tucked the comb in her jacket pocket.

Harriet's stomach roared again.

Miss Charles laughed. "Come on. Let's get you some food."

***

Harriet gazed out the classroom window. The crows looped across the sky, chasing one another in what looked like a game. *Corvus, C-O-R-V-U-S, genus composed of crows, ravens, and rooks.* She smiled slightly. Everything seemed better now that she was wearing clean clothes and had a full stomach.

"Harriet." The teacher's voice pulled her out of her daydream. "Please, calculate the mean of the numbers Toby has written on the board."

Toby looked over his shoulder and smirked. Harriet avoided his gaze and answered carefully. "Three plus four equals seven, plus nine equals sixteen, plus seven equals twenty-three, divided by four equals five-point-seven-five. The mean is five-pont-seven-five."

"Excellent, Harriet."

"That was an easy one," Toby declared. "Bet she can't do this one." He sprawled numbers on the board: 123, 76, 1167, 894, 5, 109.

"Toby, since you like a challenge," the teacher said, "see if you can find the mean."

"But..." Toby protested.

"But, nothing. You may show your work."

Toby screeched the pen across the whiteboard.

"Three hundred seventy-seven-point-on-seven," Harriet murmured, and looked out the window again. The crows were gone.

***

At last the dismissal bell rang. Harriet lingered by her desk. Toby had been whispering with his friends and she was sure he was planning to do or say something mean. Her teacher noticed the loitering and asked, "Do you need something, Harriet?"

Harriet shook her head no, adjusted her heavy backpack and joined the other students in the hall. She dawdled, keeping an eye out for trouble. When she did not catch sight of Toby or his cronies, she pulled the heavy schoolhouse door open and stepped outside.

The wind whipped the fallen leaves into a frenzy of color. Harriet noted the whirlwind and reached out to snatch a brilliant red oak leaf.

"What you gonna do with that, Hairy Fairy?" Toby taunted.

Harriet dropped the leaf. She'd thought it would be a nice present for her mother, if she came home tonight. But now, it just seemed stupid to believe that her mom might appear.

"If you're so smart, what's a million times a million?" Toby demanded.

She wished she could ignore him, but it was such an easy question. Harriet narrowed her eyes and said, "A trillion."

Toby considered the answer. He tapped his fingers together as if to count. "Yeah," he drawled, "everybody knows that."

"Bet you didn't," Harriet said

"You calling me stupid?"

"If the shoe fits." Harriet grinned.

"Get her, Toby," someone yelled.

Harriet froze. Toby reached out and grabbed her arm. She shoved his hand away. Toby raised his fist.

"Toby Meyers!" Miss Charles's voice rang out. "You are not about to hit Harriet, are you?"

"No, Mam." Toby shuffled backwards. "I was just going to pick a leaf out of her hair."

"I doubt that. You boys get on home now."

Toby murmured, "Tomorrow, Hairy Fairy," as he turned away.

Harriet shot him the stink eye and turned to face Miss Charles.

"I have something for you, Harriet. Could you come back to my office for a moment, please?"

Harriet nodded and counted backwards from one hundred. *One hundred, ninety-nine, ninety-eight...* She hoped she wasn't in trouble.

"It'll only take a moment. If you need to call home and tell them you'll be late, you can use my phone."

Harriet shook her head. "It'll be fine." *As if anyone cares when I get home,* she thought.

Miss Charles turned and walked toward the school. Harriet followed. In the counselor's office, she sat perched on the edge of the visitor chair holding her backpack on her lap to conceal her shaking legs.

Miss Charles sat next to her instead of behind the desk. She smiled gently at Harriet and adjusted her skirt to cover her knees. She folded her hands and waited.

Harriet held her breath. *One hundred, ninety-nine, ninety-eight...*

"Harriet," Miss Charles laid her hand on Harriet's arm. "Look at me, please."

Harriet forced herself to make eye contact. She allowed her eyes to open wide, tilted her head down, and smiled slightly, exactly the way Mama had taught her to gaze at the man in the store when they didn't have enough money to pay for what they needed.

"Is everything all right at home? I can help you if there is a problem," she hesitated, "of any sort."

"I'm sorry my clothes were dirty today, Miss." Harriet let her eyes fill with tears. "The washing machine's broken and Mama has to wait for payday to get it fixed."

"I understand, Harriet." Miss Charles stood, then moved to her desk. She picked up a neatly folded pile of clothing. "I washed your clothes and added a few things from the lost and found. Put these in your backpack."

Now tears gathered for real. Harriet didn't want to admit how much she needed the clean clothes. "Jerry says we can't take charity."

"It's not charity, Harriet. These are your clothes, and you can return the extra things when the washer gets fixed."

Harriet squinted her eyes, and bit her lip, as she considered the offer. Jerry had told her that people who give you something for nothing want something, but she couldn't see that Miss Charles wanted anything. "It might be a long time," Harriet hedged.

"That's okay." Miss Charles picked up a paperweight from her desk and studied the flower trapped inside. "This is just between you and me, Harriet. If you drop your dirty clothes in my office, I'll wash them for you until your washer is working."

"Every day?"

"Yes, every day. I'll take them home with me and bring them back the next day. This time I used the washer here at school, but I suppose it would be better to take your laundry home with me."

Harriet stayed quiet. Jerry would be mad if he found out. *But,* she reasoned, *he never looks in my backpack.* "Okay." She nodded. "Just until Mama gets the washer fixed." She stuffed the clothes into her pack.

"One more thing: I have some school cafeteria breakfast and lunch tickets. I want you to take them. They will just be wasted here in my desk drawer." She opened the drawer and withdrew an envelope.

Harriet shook her head.

Miss Charles thrust the envelope into the outer pocket of the pack. "You need to eat, Harriet. Every day." She laid her hand on Harriet's hair. "I didn't tell anyone that you fainted from hunger this morning and I won't, as long as I see you eating breakfast and lunch every day."

Harriet studied the counselor.

"Harriet, you are a smart girl with a lot of potential. I understand that things are hard at home, but it will get better."

Tears threatened again. Harriet blinked and forced them away.

"You may go now, Harriet."

Harriet turned to the door and twisted the knob. She looked over her shoulder and mumbled a thank you.

"If you ever need help, remember you can tell me."

Harriet stumbled out the door and hurried down the hall. Miss Charles moved to the window and watched as she exited the building and ran out of the schoolyard.

***

"Where have you been, brat?" Jerry greeted her from the living room. "You do something bad and have to stay after school?"

"No, sir." Harriet started up the stairs.

"The kitchen's a pigsty. Get it cleaned up."

"Yes, sir." Harriet took another step. "I was waiting for the hot water to come back."

"Don't talk back to me. There's plenty of hot water."

Harriet could smell his rank beer breath and recognized his mood. She decided not to argue. "I'll just put my homework upstairs and be right back."

Jerry mumbled something. Harriet didn't wait to hear more. She ran up the stairs and glanced toward her mother's room; the door was still closed. Harriet went into her bedroom, dropped her backpack on the bed, and ran downstairs. In the kitchen, she turned on the tap. Hot water gushed out. She squirted soap over the pile of dishes and opened the refrigerator while waiting for the sink to fill.

Maybe if he's paid the bill, he bought food, she thought. No such luck. A six-pack and two loose cans of beer sat on the shelf. Nothing else. The refrigerator light was still out. She flipped the switch for the overhead light and smiled her satisfaction when it came on. Waiting for Mama to come home wasn't as scary when there was hot water, heat, and light.

She pushed up the sleeves of her hoodie and plunged her hands into the bubbles.

***

Jerry came into the kitchen. Harriet heard him and squeezed her shoulders together. She kept her back to him and continued to scrub the cast-iron fry pan. *Adumbrate, A-D-U-M-B-R-A-T-E, to darken or conceal partially,* she spelled silently.

Please, let him take a beer from the refrigerator and ignore me, she prayed. The refrigerator door opened and closed. *He'll be gone in a minute.* Her hands kept moving.

"What the fuck!" Jerry grabbed her shoulder and spun her around. "What are doing wearing my hoodie, you little creep." He let go of her shoulder and clenched his fist. His arm lifted.

Harriet reacted. She swung the frying pan and connected with his uplifted arm. Jerry screamed and lost his grip on her shoulder as he clenched his arm.

"I'll kill you," Jerry swore, reaching for her again.

Harriet whipped around him and fled up the stairs. Jerry stumbled after her, holding his arm tight to his side and screaming obscenities. Harriet scrambled from one step to the next. At the top, she paused and looked back. Jerry was a few stairs below. She grabbed the handrail and kicked out. Her foot connected squarely with his stomach. He bellowed, grabbed for the railing, and missed it. Harriet kicked again, hitting him in the knee. She pushed with all her might. Jerry seemed to freeze for a second. He wavered and fell back. His head hit the railing, and a gash appeared in his forehead. A hand reached toward Harriet and grasped only the air.

Jerry screamed, "Bitch!"

Harriet covered her ears. She stood, vigilant, and observed him as he fell, tumbling head over heels, until he landed on the rug at the bottom. She sat down on the top stair and waited. The blood pooled around and under his head. He made strange gurgling sounds. His hands opened and closed. Then he lay still and became silent.

When Harriet was sure he would never move again, she ran down the stairs and out the front door, yelling "Help, help, I need help!"

***

Harriet sat sideways on the back seat of the open police car, face streaked with tears. Her legs dangled off the seat, not quite touching the ground. A young policewoman, crouched down in front of her, watching closely. Each time Harriet sobbed, the woman patted her knee and said, "Hush now, it will be okay." But Harriet didn't think it would be. Tears rolled down her cheeks. Someone handed her a Kleenex.

"Okay, sweetheart." A tall gruff-looking man wearing a wrinkly suit replaced the policewoman. "I'm Detective Williams."

Harriet glanced up for an instant, then dropped her eyes to her feet. *Circumspect. C-I-R-C-U-M-S-P-E-C-T. Be careful,* she told herself.

"I just need to ask you a few questions, sweetheart." He placed his heavy hand on Harriet's shoulder.

She winced.

"It's okay, no one wants to hurt you. We just need to understand what happened here."

Harriet gulped, "I want my mom." She kept her head down and didn't look at the man.

The policewoman spoke. "I'm sure you do and, if you can tell us where she works, we'll send someone to tell her you need her."

Harriet closed her eyes and counted silently. *One, two, three, four, five, six.* Perhaps if she never opened her eyes everything would go away. *Stop this,* she told herself and opened her eyes. She brushed her tears away and straightened her shoulders. She forced herself to look directly into Detective Williams's eyes and lied, "Mom will be home at five thirty. I'm not supposed to call her at work."

He glanced at his watch. "Okay," he said. "She's probably on her way right now. We can wait." He leaned against the patrol car and gazed at the house.

Harriet's thoughts scrambled from one worry to another. She'd need to come up with an excuse when no one appeared. She pulled the hoodie sleeves over her fists and counted backwards from one hundred.

"Harry!"

Harriet jumped up and ran to the woman coming down the block. She flung her arms around her mother's waist and burst into real tears. "Mama, Mama, Mama," she cried.

"Harry, honey." Stacy Blimm tipped her daughter's face up and wiped away the tears. "What's happening here? Are you alright?"

"Mrs. Blimm?" Detective Williams approached. "Harriet is fine. There's been an accident."

Stacy moved Harriet away, held her at arm's length, and looked at her carefully. "What kind of accident?" She brushed the hair from Harriet's forehead and smiled at her. "Don't worry, sweetie. I'm here and I'll fix it. Where's Jerry?"

Harriet caught her breath and blurted out, "He fell down the stairs, Mama. I think he's dead."

Stacy turned to the detective, who nodded in confirmation. "Oh my God! How did that happen?" she asked.

"We need to ask Harriet a few questions, Mrs. Blimm," the detective interrupted her before she could ask more questions.

"Call me Stacy, please. Yes, of course." She pulled Harriet in for another hug. "No matter what happened," she tilted Harriet's chin up and looked her in the eye, "I'm home now and I'll take care of it. Okay?"

Harriet blinked back her fear. "Okay."

"My team is still working in the living room. Perhaps we could talk in the kitchen."

Stacy nodded. "Got it. Come on, Harry, let's use the back door." She held her daughter's hand and led the way.

Harriet stumbled along. *I'm surprised she remembers we have a back door,* she thought. *But I'm glad I did most of the dishes before Jerry...* She stopped her thoughts. *Conceal, C-O-N-C-E-A-L, hide the truth,* she reminded herself.

Stacy pulled Harriet close and whispered, "Just tell them Jerry is our friend. Nothing else."

She turned to the policemen and asked brightly, "Could I get you a cup of tea?"

No! Harriet screamed silently. There hadn't been a tea bag in the house for at least a month.

"No thanks, Mrs. Blimm." Detective Williams, motioned toward the table. "Let's all just sit down and we'll ask our questions and be done with this."

Stacy pulled a chair close to Harriet's and kept one hand on her daughter. "Are you ready, Harry?" Harriet nodded. "Tell the policemen what happened."

Harriet took a breath, clenched her fists, and closed her eyes for a moment. Then she began, "I'm not sure why he fell. I was scrubbing that frying pan." She nodded toward the sink. "Jerry yelled something that sounded like..." She looked at her mother.

Stacy nodded encouragingly.

"Sounded like 'fuck.'" Harriet took another deep breath. "Then there was a lot of banging and thumping and I dropped the pan and ran into the living room." She let a tear escape. "Jerry was lying on the rug and there was blood, a lot of blood. I tried to wake him up."

"When he didn't wake up, what did you do, Harriet?" the detective asked.

"I think I ran outside and yelled for help. I think I was screaming." Harriet looked directly at Detective Williams. "Should I have done something to help him?"

"No, Harriet." He smiled at her. "You did exactly the right thing. I'm sorry you had to witness Jerry's accident. I want to talk to your mom for a few minutes. Can you go outside with Officer Banks?"

Harriet looked at Stacy. She shook her head. "I want to stay with my mom."

Stacy smiled at her and pulled her close for another hug. "Go ahead, Harry. It'll be okay."

Officer Banks placed her hand on Harriet's back and propelled her outside and away from the open door. Harriet strained to listen to what the detective was asking her mother.

The policewoman smiled. "Is there anything else you want to tell me, Harriet?"

Harriet forced her attention back to Officer Banks. She frowned. "About what?"

"Oh, anything at all." She waited a minute and when Harriet said nothing she asked, "Tell me about Jerry. Is he your dad?"

"No, he's my mom's friend. When Mom has to work, he stays here to take care of me." *Careful, C-A-R-E-F-U-L, avoid danger,* Harriet reminded herself.

"Does your mom work a lot?"

Harriet shook her head. "Just regular, like everybody else."

"How about Jerry? Does he work?"

"He takes care of me after school. I don't know what else he does."

"Is Jerry your mom's boyfriend?"

Harriet considered this for a second. Her mom had said. "Tell them Jerry is our friend." "You mean like kissing and stuff?" She wrinkled her nose.

Officer Banks laughed. "Exactly, like that."

"No, of course not," Harriet declared. "He's just our friend."

The front door opened. Harriet glanced over as a gurney was rolled out. The body was covered. "Is Jerry dead?" she asked.

"I'm afraid so, honey."

The policewoman squeezed her shoulder. She forced herself not to shake it off. Harriet turned away to cover the relief shining in her eyes. Jerry was gone. Mama was home.

***

Two for joy,

"It is better to listen to a crow that lives in trees than to a learned man who lives only in ideas." —Kate Horsley

The smell of bacon woke Harriet. She pulled the covers over her head and wiggled down, content in the feel of clean sheets and homey sounds from the kitchen. Mama, she thought. Mama's still here. She threw the covers aside and scrambled out of bed. Her clothes were clean and folded on a chair, her new sneakers carefully aligned beneath the seat. Harriet dressed and grabbed her hairbrush as she headed downstairs. With her mother there to help with her hair, she no longer had a rat's nest on the back of her head.

"Hi, sweetie, I'll do your hair after breakfast." Stacy smiled at her daughter and flipped a perfect pancake onto a plate. She arranged a smiley face of bacon strips and placed the plate in front of Harriet. "Eat up. I start my new job today, so we need to get going."

Harriet's hand paused in her reach for the syrup. She spoke carefully without looking at her mother. "Will you be home tonight?"

"Yes, Harry. Stop being such a worrier. I'll be home by six. We talked about this." Harriet managed a nod and poured a stream of syrup over her pancake. "Look at me, Harry."

Harriet turned and lifted her eyes. Stacy stood at the stove, a spatula raised in her hand. The sun poured through the window and highlighted her shiny, blond hair. She turned and moved to the table, where she reached out and cupped Harriet's chin. "I promise that I will stay clean and sober today, Harry. I love you and I want to be a good mother." Harriet gulped back a sob. "I know I screwed up," Stacy continued. "I should never should have left you with Jerry. My friends told me he was reliable. But I can't change the past. Someday I hope you will forgive me."

A mother comes home. She doesn't send a stranger to take care of her child. Forgive, F-O-R-G-I-V-E, stop blaming.

Harriet wanted to believe it, but Stacy had said all of this before. She managed a slight smile before she dropped her eyes to her plate and carefully ate her bacon.

***

"Hey, Hairy Fairy. Kill anybody last night?" Toby taunted as he passed Harriet in the hall. Harriet shot him the finger and kept walking. Even though the police had declared Jerry's death an accident, Toby wouldn't let it drop. He acted like he knew something that no one else knew just because his dad was a policeman. He'd made sure that everyone in the fifth grade knew that she'd been there when Jerry fell. Toby's friends laughed and slapped him on the back.

"Good one," they whooped.

Harriet followed them into the classroom and settled into her desk. Later, when Harriet received a summons to the counselor's office, Toby tutted as she left the room. "Mr. Meyers," the teacher said, "mind you own business."

Harriet allowed the door to slam. *One hundred, ninety-nine, ninety-eight, ninety-seven...* she counted as she calmed herself and walked toward the office.

Miss Charles met her at the reception desk and greeted her with a smile. "You look very nice today," she complimented Harriet and waved her to a chair. "Do you and your mom have vacation plans for the summer?"

Harriet slipped her hands under her legs to keep them from trembling. "Mom hasn't been at her new job very long, so I think we're just staying home."

"What will you do all day while your mother is working?"

Discreet, D-I-S-C-R-E-E-T, cautious, be very careful, Harriet thought. "Mom was talking about day camp."

"Would you like that?" Miss Charles asked.

"Maybe."

"Have you been to day camp?"

Harriet shook her head.

"What did you do last summer?"

An image of Jerry, yelling and scratching, flitted through Harriet's mind. She shrugged again.

"Did your mom work last summer?"

"I guess so," Harriet said.

"If you didn't go to camp, who took care of you while she was at work?"

Harriet wanted to say, *I took care of myself,* but she knew better.

"Did you go to someone's house?"

"No. Jerry came to live with us. He took care of me."

"Are you sad that Jerry is gone?"

Dead, you mean, Harriet thought. A crow landed on the windowsill and cocked its head, waiting for her answer. She pulled her hand from beneath her leg and pointed. "Look."

Miss Charles turned. Her sudden movement startled the crow, and it flew off. "Do you like birds, Harriet?"

She nodded. "Especially crows."

"Why crows?" Miss Charles asked. She jotted "Jerry" with a question mark on her desk blotter.

Harriet gazed out the window, watching for the crow. "I just do. Crows are very smart."

"Yes, they are, and so are you. That was why I called you in today. I think you might like to go to a special class this summer."

"Isn't summer school for the dumb kids?" Harriet protested.

"Harriet, you have the highest test scores in the fifth grade. There is a summer program— rather like a day camp—for students who would like to learn more about a subject." Miss Charles handed Harriet a brochure. "The community college offers eight-week classes and activities for sixth and seventh graders. It's called Summer Campus. I thought you might find it more fun than a regular day camp or than staying home all summer."

Harriet glanced at the shiny brochure that showed a picture of kids gathered around what looked like a science experiment. "I don't think my mom can pay for this." She laid the brochure back on the desk.

"It's a free program for gifted students, Harriet. I'd like to know if you'd be interested and, if you think you might, I'll call your mother and we can set up a time for her to come in and do the paperwork. School will be out in three weeks, so we need to make a plan."

"Will I need special clothes?"

Miss Charles shook her head. "Your regular clothes are just fine. Maybe a swimsuit, but you'll need one of those for the summer anyway, right?"

"What kind of classes? Like homework and all that?"

Miss Charles handed her the brochure again. "Take a look. You have quite a choice—mostly in the areas of math and science—and all presented in fun ways. I don't think you'll have any homework at all."

"Are you telling Toby about this?"

"No, Harriet. You are the only student invited from our school." Miss Charles wrote "Toby Meyers" on the blotter and underlined it twice.

Harriet flipped the brochure open and took a quick look. "Does my mom have to pay for the bus?"

"No. The bus will pick you up and bring you home. Everything is free, even your lunch and snacks."

"Sounds too good to be true." Harriet shook her head. *Valid, V-A-L-I-D, on the up and up, genuine,* she thought, considering the brochure.

Miss Charles shook her head. "It's real, Harriet. What do you think?"

The crow returned to the windowsill and tapped the glass with its beak. Harriet laughed. "Okay, I'll take this home and talk to Mama." The crow cocked its head and looked straight at Harriet. She cocked her head back, and the crow flew away.

Miss Charles looked stunned. "I think that crow wants you to attend the summer program."

"I know," Harriet agreed. The bell rang. She tucked the brochure in her backpack and left without saying goodbye.

***

Harriet loved the Summer Campus program. Nobody knew her or her mother. She was just one of the smart kids. The very first day she'd introduced herself as Ari, and no one questioned her choice of nicknames. Harriet had cut off a pair of jeans that were too short and carefully fringed the legs. Each morning she pulled her hair into a ponytail and dressed carefully in clean underwear and a T-shirt. She wore the cut-offs most days and she looked like everyone else. The counselors encouraged independence. No one teased her.

Stacy was home every evening by 6:30. Some nights she went to a meeting. She invited Harriet to go along. After a experiencing a couple of the kids' group sharing sessions, Harriet declined and stayed home. On the Fourth of July they attended a carnival and stayed for the fireworks. Harriet relaxed; maybe this time rehab had worked.

In August, the temperature was in the high 90s every day and the house stayed hot all night. One night Harriet heard voices and got up to see who was talking. Stacy sat on the front step. She was wearing pajamas and a short robe, her hair twisted up in a sloppy knot, and a cigarette dangled from her fingers. A tall man stood in front of her.

Harriet couldn't hear all the words, but it was obvious Stacy was enjoying the conversation. Harriet watched as the man sat down on the step and her mother laughed. *Suitor,* she thought, *S-U-I-T-O-R, one who desires another.* She went back to bed and fell asleep to the soft sound of their voices.

By the end of the week, Stacy introduced the tall man to Harriet as their neighbor Bob, and invited him to stay for dinner. Over KFC, Bob asked where Harriet had gotten her name and Stacy quickly jumped in to tell the story of how she'd read a book about a girl named Harriet who was a spy and decided to name her daughter after that brave child. Bob laughed and admired her imagination.

Harriet smiled and thought, *Bullshit, B-U-L-L-S-H-I-T, stupid or untrue.* She'd heard that story before, but she'd never seen her mother even pick up a book, much less read one. "I found that book in the library and read it," she told Bob. "I'm nothing like that dumb girl and my friends call me Ari."

Stacy frowned at her and gave her a small head shake.

Bob laughed. "A much better choice. I'll call your Ari, too."

Maybe this guy is okay, Harriet thought, and took a big scoop of the mashed potatoes.

Camp ended and Ari returned to school. It had been a good summer.

***

Despite Toby Meyers being assigned to the same classroom, and his continuing harassment, Ari found sixth grade to be tolerable. Her mother had taken her shopping for new jeans and tops. She now looked like all the other kids. Miss Charles commented on her appearance and her new level of confidence. After she told Miss Charles about her new nickname, her teachers called her Ari, too. When her mother called her Harry, she didn't answer until Stacy said Ari. Most days her mother remembered to give her lunch money, and when she forgot, Ari found food in the house and was able to pack a lunch. She

JUST ONE MORE · 31

never thought about Jerry or the blood on the carpet. When she woke from a dream about him, or his hairy hands, she pushed it down and away and went back to sleep.

never thought about Jerry or the blood on the carpet. When she woke from a dream about him, or his hairy hands, she pushed it down and away and went back to sleep.

Ari's worries eased.

***

Stacy went out with Bob, or to a meeting, most nights. But, even when Ari fell asleep before she returned, her mother was always there in the morning. And, usually, she was up and had made breakfast. She helped Ari with her thick hair. Everything felt right.

On Thanksgiving, Bob arrived with a bottle of wine. Stacy accepted it with a laugh and opened it at once. She caught Ari's look and said, "It's a holiday. One glass isn't going to signal the end of the world. Don't be such a Debbie Downer."

Ari turned away in disgust.

"Ah, come on, Harry. You can have a glass, too." Stacy smiled flirtatiously.

Bob chuckled.

Ari turned back and glared at the two of them. "My name is Ari. I'm eleven years old, Stacy. Your daughter. Not your friend."

Stacy took a deep drink from her glass and squinted at Ari.

One hundred, ninety-nine, ninety-eight, ninety-seven, ninety-six... Ari counted as she left the room. *I don't give a shit if I hurt her feelings. She promised she wouldn't drink.*

One bottle became two. Bob and Stacy left to go for a walk. Ari pulled the overdone turkey from the oven and ate alone.

***

Now when Bob came over he always brought a bottle, and he always spent the night. Stacy stopped going to meetings. Ari came straight home from school and did her homework as she waited for Stacy. Ari watched and listened. Sometimes she thought about telling Miss Charles, but she didn't want to a make her mother go away again. *It is better than having Jerry here,* she told herself. *At least Bob is nice to me.* In December, Stacy and Bob brought home a Christmas tree. A tree that was much too big for the tiny living room. They laughed uproariously as they struggled to squeeze it through the door.

The commotion brought Ari out of her room. She looked over the railing. It didn't look fun. It looked familiar. "Buzzed, bombed, blitzed, drunk. "D-R-U-N-K," she spelled under her breath and went back to her room. She slammed the door, but no one cared.

***

Returning to school after the winter break, Ari knew she was in trouble. Her mom hadn't been home since New Year's Eve. The heat and lights were still on, but the food was running very low. She'd searched everywhere for cash, but the meager eleven dollars and thirty-two cents she'd being able to find hadn't lasted long. *At least my clothes are clean,* she thought as she tucked a peanut butter sandwich into a bag, along with the last apple. *If Miss Charles calls me in for one of her nosy talks, maybe she won't notice anything.*

At lunch, everyone was buzzing about their gifts and holiday adventures. Ari read a book and tuned them out. She kept her head down and avoided eye contact. All morning she'd half expected to be called to the counselor's office, but no one seemed to notice her at all. Even Toby ignored her. It felt like a good day.

She crumpled up her lunch bag and tossed it away. Her stomach rumbled. *Miss Charles might not want to talk to me,* she thought, *but I need some of those meal tickets.* She screwed up her courage and headed to the guidance office.

"Good afternoon, Miss Blimm." Mr. Comstock's unctuous tone caused Ari's toes to curl. "Are you in trouble again?"

I should smack him, Ari thought. *Smack, S-M-A-C-K, a sharp slap, or blow.* "No, Mr. Comstock. I just wanted to talk to Miss Charles."

"Did she send for you?"

"No, sir." Ari fixed her gaze on the countertop.

"Then may I inquire as to what this request pertains?"

"No, you may not." Miss Charles spoke from the doorway, her voice coated in ice. "Any student may ask to see me, at any time, without saying why. I believe you are aware of that, Mr. Comstock." She turned to look at Ari. "Come into my office and keep me company while I have my lunch." She placed her hand on Ari's shoulder, gave it a slight squeeze, and turned her toward the office. "Have you eaten?"

Ari stumbled after the counselor. *Jerk, J-E-R-K, contemptible, obnoxious person. I hate the way he makes me feel.*

"Sit." Miss Charles waved to a chair and plunked herself down behind the desk. "The first day back from a vacation is always crazy." She opened her carryout bag and pulled out a thick deli sandwich.

Ari's stomach rumbled loudly.

Miss Charles handed her half. "Let's share. There isn't any way I can eat all of this."

Ari's mouth watered. The sandwich smelled so good. She took a bite and then another.

Miss Charles bit into her half and watched Ari. The girl was scarfing down the sandwich. She passed the chip bag to Ari. "Help yourself. Want a bottle of water?"

Ari nodded.

They finished the sandwich and chips in companionable silence. Miss Charles crumpled the wrappers and tossed them in the trash. She avoided looking at Ari, as she asked, "What's up?"

Ari didn't answer.

Miss Charles broke an oversized chocolate chip cookie in two and handed the larger portion to Ari.

Ari looked at the cookie, and then wrapped it in her napkin and placed it in her hoodie pocket.

Miss Charles waited.

One hundred, ninety-nine, ninety-eight, ninety-seven, ninety-six, ninety-five, Ari counted. She took a deep breath and blurted, "I need some lunch tickets."

"No problem," Miss Charles opened her desk drawer and withdrew a packet. She handed the bundle to Ari. "There are breakfast and lunch tickets in here. Breakfast is at seven-thirty—will you be able to get to school that early?"

Ari nodded. "I can get there. It's just for a little while. My mom will," she caught herself, "will get a new job soon."

The child had dark circles under her eyes, but she looked clean. "You look a little tired, Ari. Did you have a busy holiday?"

Ari thought about the long days and nights. Most nights she slept in the living room, leaving the TV on all night for company. It made the house seem less spooky. Her mother had been gone five days and nights; surely she'd be home soon. *Masquerade, M-A-S-Q-U-E-R-A-D-E, disguise, hide behind.* "It was just the usual tree, presents, food, you know," she lied.

"Sounds lovely." The guidance counselor handed Ari the rest of the cookie. "Here, you better eat this. I think I gained ten pounds over the holiday, and I don't want to gain any more."

There was definitely something going on that Ari wasn't telling. Her experience with kids cautioned her to wait it out. "I understand you're competing in the final round of the school spelling bee championship."

Ari smiled slightly.

"Does your mom help you practice?"

The smile vanished. "Sometimes," Ari muttered.

"If you need someone to drill you, I'd be happy to help. What with jobs and things, parents don't always have time." Ari kept her eyes downcast. "We could use your lunch break and do it here in my office. Would you like that?"

"Maybe." Ari's feet kicked against the chair legs.

"Why don't you talk to your mom tonight and if she says it's okay, we can start tomorrow." Ari still didn't look up. "If you'd rather have lunch with your friends, that is fine, too. This isn't a requirement. You are already an excellent speller."

Friends! Ari thought. *I don't have any friends. One hundred, nine-ty-nine, ninety-eight, ninety-seven.* She took a deep breath. "Okay."

"Great. Just pick up your lunch and bring it here. I'll get a copy of the word list tonight and we'll start tomorrow."

Ari nodded.

"You better head for your classroom now. The bell will ring in a minute."

Ari stood and pulled her hoodie sleeves over her hands. She opened the door, glanced back over her shoulder, and blurted out, "Thanks."

***

The January nights were long and cold. The house grew gloomy by 4:30 and there was nothing to do. Ari lived in the living room now, surrounded by the detritus of her daily struggle. Every day she feared would be the last day there would be electricity. She was able to wash her clothes in the bathtub. It took two days for her jeans to dry, so she had to remember to wash them on Friday night. The meal tickets from the school, supplemented by the snacks that Miss Charles provided each day, were enough to keep her hunger at bay. *I wonder how long this can last before someone finds out,* she thought.

The spelling practice sessions became the highlight of her life. The only time she wasn't afraid.

Each day, Miss Charles continued observing Ari carefully. She spoke to her teachers. No one reported seeing bruises. They did call her skittish and uncommunicative. The teachers assured Miss Charles that Ari was just being Ari.

However, concern nagged at Miss Charles. Ari's clothes and body were clean enough. She appeared well-groomed. She wrote a note in Ari's record reporting the spelling sessions and her concern that Ari always saved some of her lunch "for later." Miss Charles added that she could identify no telltale signs of an eating disorder; Ari was thin, not emaciated.

***

"Shall we get to work?" Miss Charles asked.

Ari nodded and brushed the crumbs from her jeans.

"Okay. Let's begin with a hard one, 'feuilleton.'" Miss Charles carefully articulated the word.

Ari grinned. "May I have the definition, please?"

"Feuilleton, a part of a European newspaper or magazine devoted to material designed to entertain the general reader."

Ari looked puzzled. "Feuilleton," she repeated. "F-A-I"

"This is one of those words that is not spelled the way it sounds. Try again." Miss Charles shook her head as she spoke.

Ari gazed out the window. A crow perched in the tree, staring at her. Ari cocked her head to the side. The crow did the same.

Miss Charles turned to see what had caught her attention. The crow cawed once and flew away.

"Feuilleton," Ari began again. "May I have it in a sentence, please."

The counselor consulted her list. "His fame as a journalist was based on the feuilleton he wrote." She laid the word list down. "Wow, that really is a hard word. I don't think I've ever heard it before. I wouldn't even be able to guess how to say it if this list didn't show the correct pronunciation." Ari's laugh caught Miss Charles by surprise, and she laughed with her.

"Well, I just hope I don't have to spell anything like this during the spelling bee." Ari twirled her finger in her ponytail and caught her lower lip between her teeth. She shrugged. "Feuil—whatever, is probably a word for national finals and I'm only a sixth grader. I won't get that far."

"Think positive, Ari. You have two more weeks to practice. You're a great speller and anything is possible."

Ari's face fell as she thought, A*nything…but my mom showing up.* She shrugged again and said, "Give me the next one."

Miss Charles complied.

***

Ari trudged home through the sleeting rain. She wore an old wool jacket, that used to belong to Jerry, over her hoodie. She jammed her hands deep into the pockets, but she was still cold. Very cold. It was 2,546 steps from the school door to her front door. She knew because she counted them every day. *Two thousand four hundred sixty-nine, two thousand four hundred seventy...almost there.* Ari allowed herself a glance at the kitchen window. It was dark. "No one home but me," she said aloud. "Just me."

Something moved on the porch. She stopped and peered through the sleet. *Not big enough to be a person,* she reasoned. *Probably a cat.* Ari approached carefully. With a flutter of dark wings, a crow flew up and over her head, cawing loudly. She turned to watch its flight but instead of going far, the crow landed on the gutter and continued to caw. "What's the matter with you?" Ari asked.

An answering caw came from the porch. Ari hurried the last few steps and dropped to her knees, regardless of the cold puddle that quickly soaked her jeans. Another crow, its wing hanging, was huddled by the door. Ari moved slowly, stretching a hand toward the frightened bird. "Is your wing broken?" she whispered. "I think I know how to fix that. You stay right here, and I'll be back in a flash."

Ari unlocked the door, flung her backpack down, and hurried to the kitchen. She grabbed a ragged dishtowel and ripped off a strip. Ari returned to the porch and found both birds waiting for her. She knelt again and spoke quietly. "I saw a man do this on TV once. I don't know if it will hurt, but I'll try to be careful."

The crows didn't move. They observed her; their bright eyes seemed to understand she meant them no harm. Ari stroked the injured bird's head with her index finger, then gently lifted the wing back into place and wrapped the cloth around the crow, carefully binding the wing to its side.

The healthy bird kept its eyes on Ari, cawing softly, seeming to encourage both Ari and its mate.

"There now. Is that better?"

The injured bird closed its eyes and for a moment Ari was afraid. The crow made a soft clicking sound and settled down, roosting on the floor.

"You're tired, aren't you? Mama always says you need to sleep when you don't feel good." She continued to stroke the crow's head. "You need to come inside and stay warm for a few days while your wing gets better. I'm going to pick you up, okay?" She slipped her hands under the crow. Its mate cawed loudly and flew up to the roof, continuing to protest. Ari laughed. "Come on. You can come in, too." She left the door open and carried her injured friend into the living room.

Glancing back, she saw what she decided was the male crow land in the doorway and look around. "Don't worry," she said to the bird in her hands, "he'll be with you in just a minute."

Talking to the birds felt right to Ari. The house seemed less empty. She put a blanket in an old cardboard box and placed it close to the sofa. With the box on its side, the birds were able to walk in and out of their new home. "You're safe," Ari told them. They responded, making quiet sounds. Ari lay down and fell asleep, hungry but happy.

***

The sound of cawing pulled Ari from her dreams. The morning light revealed the crows. Ari sat up and rubbed the sleep from her eyes. She grinned, happy to find that they were still there. *Wow,* she thought, *I slept all night.*

"Okay, I'm awake. What do you want?"

The larger bird strutted toward her and flapped his wings.

"I take it you want me to let you out. Come on, then." Both crows followed her across the room. "No one would believe this," she said, and opened the door.

Ari watched as the uninjured bird flew away. The smaller bird stood quietly, unable to use her bandaged wing. "Don't worry," Ari said. "He'll be back, you'll see." With nothing on but the clothes she'd slept in, Ari was cold. "I'm going inside," she told the bird. "But I'll leave the door open for you."

In the house, Ari glanced at the clock, changed her T-shirt, and put on her hoodie. She had forgotten to wash clothes last night and these would have to do. *I have to hurry or I'll miss breakfast. Now, what do I do with the crows while I'm in school?* she pondered as she washed up, ran a brush over her hair, and pulled it back into a ponytail. *They will be happiest outside,* she decided. Ari carried the makeshift, cardboard bird bed out to the porch. The injured bird walked right in and settled down. "There you go. I have to go to school, but when I get home, I hope you're still here." The crow looked at her and cawed softly.

Ari grabbed Jerry's old wool coat and ran.

***

All morning, Ari kept one eye on the classroom window. She knew her crow looked just like all the other crows, but she was sure she would recognize him. At lunch, she hurried to Miss Charles's office and ate quickly. "Could I have a library pass, instead of practicing?" she asked.

"Of course." Miss Charles was surprised by the request. Ari never asked for anything but lunch tickets. She wrote out the pass and handed it to the girl. "Have fun. I'll see you tomorrow." Ari waved and smiled as she exited the office.

"I wonder what's got her all stirred up?" Miss Charles murmured. She made a note in her record book.

Ari went straight to the librarian's desk, waved her pass, and asked, "Where do I find a book about crows?"

The librarian smiled and reached for her computer mouse. "Fiction or nonfiction?"

"Facts. I need to look up facts about crows, like what they eat and stuff."

"Nonfiction," she said, clicking and typing. "That would be in section 598.864. Come, I'll show you where to look."

Ari trailed after the librarian. She looked at the bright displays, wanting to read everything she saw. The librarian paused and pointed. "Here you go. Any book with the number 598.864 will be about crows. You may also find relevant information in other bird books. Let me know if you need more help." Ari sank to her knees and pulled a book from the shelf. The cover depicted a shiny, black crow cocking its head to one side, its bright, button eyes glittering. She opened the book and began to read.

Ari found a list of the best foods to feed a crow: fruit, nuts, snails, eggs, worms and grubs, bread or pasta, popcorn, grains, cat food, and hot peppers. She closed the book on her finger and approached the desk again. "May I take this book home?" she asked politely.

"Of course. Tell me your name and your classroom. You may keep the book for two weeks."

Ari recited the requested information and carefully tucked the book into her backpack. *Where can I get food for my crows?* The question consumed her as the afternoon dragged by. *If it were summer, worms and grubs might be easy to find. Tonight, they might have to eat the bread from the half sandwich I saved at lunch.* Her stomach made an awful sound at the thought of sharing the bread. *We all need food,* she thought.

When the final bell rang, Ari hurried out of the classroom but found her way blocked by Toby.

"I hear your mom's boyfriend is in jail," he taunted. Ari stopped trying to get past and glared at him. "Guess your mom didn't tell you, huh?"

Ari shook her head. "What'd he do?"

"That's for me to know and you to find out," he teased.

When Ari didn't ask again, Toby added, "He's a dirty drunk. Dad caught him peeing in the street."

She squinted at Toby. Her fingers curled into fists. Ari bit her lip to keep from crying and squeezed her hands tighter. Her nails dug into her palms.

"What'cha going to do? Hit me?"

Ari shook her head and forced her fingers apart. "You're a dumb, stupid, liar."

"Am not."

Ari drew herself up as tall as she could and forced herself to look directly into Toby's eyes. "You are beneath my contempt. Step aside."

Toby took a step backward, surprised by the force of her defiance. Ari walked away, refusing to look back when Toby yelled, "I'm not a liar. Your mom is a slut."

Ari pushed the school door open and escaped into the cold, rainy afternoon. Her tears overflowed. She brushed them away and started walking. *One, two, three, four, five, six…*

***

Ari sat on the floor next to the injured crow and read the library book from cover to cover, twice. When she read aloud, the birds listened.

"I think I will call you Morrigan." Ari stroked the bird's head with gentle fingers. "And," she turned to the larger male crow, "I will call you Nevermore."

The crows cawed softly and cocked their heads as they looked at Ari.

"It's from a book I read," she explained.

Nevermore flew to the newel post and cawed happily.

Ari laughed. "I'm glad you approve." She opened the book again. "Now, it's says right here that crows like popcorn. I'm going to walk past the movie theater on my way home tomorrow and see if I can find you some in the dumpster. Okay?"

Nevermore bobbed his head and Morrigan chirped in agreement.

Late that night, with the lights off and the curtains tightly drawn, Ari stared up at the ceiling from her makeshift bed on the sofa. "I'm not afraid," she said aloud. "I just like to sleep down here with you guys."

Nevermore cooed and clicked quietly.

"Toby called my mom a slut," she whispered into the dark.

Nevermore clicked his soft night noise.

Ari pulled the blanket over her head and fell asleep.

***

If any anyone had noticed, it might have seemed strange to see the girl and the crows together. But in Ari's neighborhood everyone kept their heads down and ignored each other. Each morning she moved the box to the porch and each day, after school, she brought it inside and shared her food. At school the spelling contest drew closer until, at last, it was time.

"Are there any other words you'd like to practice today?" Miss Charles asked.

Ari shook her head.

"The school-wide contest is tomorrow. Will your mother be coming?"

Ari looked down at her feet. "She has to work," she mumbled.

"Oh dear, that is too bad. I'm sure she would like to be here." She extended her hand, then stopped her movement just short of Ari's shoulder and said, "I have a surprise for you."

Miss Charles turned her back and pulled open her cupboard.

Ari took a deep breath, counted *one hundred, ninety-nine, ninety-eight, ninety-seven,* and slumped farther down in her chair.

Miss Charles turned with a gift-wrapped box in her arms. "I'm so proud of you, Ari."

"It's not my birthday."

Miss Charles chuckled. "I know. This is because you've worked so hard and because I've enjoyed working with you."

Ari accepted the box but made no move to open it.

"Go ahead, Ari."

Ari peeled off the ribbon and slid her finger under the tape. The paper fell away. She lifted the lid and gazed at the bright red hoodie, emblazoned with the school's name and logo. Tears threatened and she didn't dare look up. She touched the soft fabric with one finger.

"I thought you might like to wear it tomorrow."

Ari managed to nod. She patted the bright sweatshirt. "I might not win."

"Win or lose tomorrow, Ari, you're a winner either way." Miss Charles wiped beneath her eyes. "Consider this a good luck present."

"Thank you." Ari patted the hoodie again and closed the box. "I'll pick it up after school."

"You can take it with you now, Ari. It's yours."

"I don't," Ari drew a circle on the floor with the toe of her shoe, and stammered, "I don't want Toby Meyers to grab it."

"Of course." Miss Charles nodded. "It'll be here, ready for you, after school."

***

Ari woke early the next morning. Morrigan and Nevermore were nestled together in the box. She stretched out her hand and the birds allowed her to stroke their heads. "You are so pretty. It's been two weeks. According to the book, I can take off your bandage today, Morrigan. Would you like that?"

Morrigan stood up and walked closer.

"You guys understand everything I say, don't you?"

Morrigan cawed loudly.

Ari laughed. "All right, I'm getting up." She sat up on the sofa and swung her feet to the floor. The new red hoodie hung on the newel post. She smiled again. "Today's the spelling bee," she said to the crows and headed to the kitchen to retrieve the scissors.

Morrigan followed at her heels. Nevermore stepped out of the box and flew ahead of them.

Ari picked up Morrigan, stroked her head and back, and placed her on the kitchen table.

"Good thing there are no adults here," she told the birds. "Adults would have a fit about a bird on the table."

Nevermore cawed loudly and landed next to Morrigan.

"I agree. Birds should be allowed everywhere."

Morrigan and Nevermore cawed in unison.

Ari giggled. "Right. Not all birds. Just crows." She picked up the scissors. "Okay, stay still. I'm going to cut this away and then you can try your wing."

Morrigan stayed quiet as the bandage was removed. Ari dropped it on the table and asked Morrigan, "How does that feel?"

Morrigan didn't move.

"Does it still hurt? Do I need to put it back on?"

Nevermore cawed to his mate. Morrigan, tentatively, moved her wing. She cawed back to Nevermore, looked at Ari, walked to the side of the table, and stepped off. Her wings spread as she dropped. She flapped them twice and rose, flew once around the kitchen, and headed to the living room.

Ari clapped her hands in excitement.

Nevermore cawed as he flew after his mate. They flew together, cawing happily, circling through each room, and then landed by the front door.

Tears filled Ari's eyes. She brushed them away. "Do you want to leave already?" She placed her hand on the knob. "Will you come back?" she asked.

The birds stayed silent. Ari open the door and they flew away.

Ari stood in the doorway for a long time, watching the sky and hoping. When they didn't return, she closed the the door and went upstairs to take a shower.

Deserted, D-E-S-E-R-T-E-D. "Everyone always leaves," she whispered to her reflection in the mirror. "I don't care. It's no big deal."

***

Ari tapped on Miss Charles's open door.

"Hi, Ari. You look very nice." She smiled. "What can I do for you this morning."

"Um…" Ari hesitated.

Miss Charles waited.

"My mom had to go to work early today and—" She took a deep breath. "I couldn't reach the back of my hair. I brought my brush with me. I guess I thought, maybe, um, maybe you could help me."

"Of course—come on in."

Miss Charles rose from her desk and crossed the room. She pushed her door shut. "Turn around. Let's see what I can do."

Ari pulled the brush from her backpack. The counselor took it and began to stroke through Ari's thick, curly hair. The top layer, and the sides were smooth, but the back was a mass of snarls. "Does your mom have to go to work early a lot?" she asked casually.

"Just sometimes. When she's home she always brushes my hair." Ari sounded defensive.

"That's nice. I'm glad you asked me to help today. I know you want to look nice up on stage."

Ari nodded. The brush caught and jerked her head back.

"Sorry," Miss Charles apologized.

"It's okay. It didn't hurt."

Miss Charles continued to work the brush through the snarls. "Are you worried about today?" she asked.

"Worried about what?"

"Anything?"

"Well…" Ari started to tell her about the birds flying way but then realized that Miss Charles didn't know about Morrigan and Nevermore. She caught herself. "Maybe a little about which words I'll get."

"You'll do great, Ari. You've practiced every word on the list. Just remember to take a deep breath before you begin to spell." The brush pulled again. Miss Charles used her finger to untangle a difficult knot. "And, as soon as we get these snarls out, your hair will be perfect."

Miss Charles finished. "I'll be cheering for you this afternoon, Ari."

"Thanks." Ari glanced out the window—no crows. "Thanks for helping with my hair." She slipped out of office.

Miss Charles made a note in her planner. *Schedule home visit - Ari.*

***

Ari sat quietly, her hands folded in her lap, awaiting her next word. She silently spelled each word as it was given to one of the other students. When only four students remained in the competition, the principal called for a break. Ari stayed in her seat. The others left the stage.

"Hi." Miss Charles approached and handed her an apple juice. "You're doing great."

Ari nodded. "I spelled much harder words in our practice session." She grinned up at the counselor. "That kid, Jess, is only in the fourth grade, but he's the one I'm going to need to beat."

"I think you may be right. Don't you want to stretch your legs?"

"Nope, I'm fine." Ari glanced toward the entrance to the auditorium. "I just want to sit here." *And stay away from Toby Meyers,* she thought.

"Okay. Drink your juice. They'll start again in a minute."

Ari passed the time counting. She'd made it all the way to 549 when the spellers were called back to the stage.

Four more words and two more spellers were out.

Now it was just Ari and Jess.

They sat side by side. Rising and spelling and then sitting again. *Polemic. Framboise. Rheumatic. Predilection.* Jess stumbled over the word, replacing the second "e" with an "i." He was excused. Ari rose to spell her word. The pronouncer said "Corvus." Ari asked for the definition just to be sure she hadn't imagined the word.

"Corvus, the Crow, a southern constellation between Virgo and Hydra."

"Thank you." Ari spoke carefully following the protocol she'd learned from Miss Charles. "Corvus, C-O-R-V-U-S, Corvus."

"That is correct. Congratulations, Harriet Blimm." The judge spoke loudly and firmly. "You are the new Exeter Charter School Spelling Champion and will represent us in the regional spelling meet next month." He handed her a trophy and shook her hand.

The watching students applauded and stamped their feet. A few called Ari's name and cheered. Ari shook hands with the judge and the pronouncer, spoke to Jess, and exited the stage. Behind her, she heard the principal dismissing school for the day.

Miss Charles stood in the wings. Her face broke into a wide grin. "I knew you could do it! I'm so proud of you."

Ari grinned.

"I'm sorry your mom couldn't be here, but maybe she can get the day off for regionals."

Ari nodded.

Miss Charles handed Ari an envelope. "Please, give this to your mom."

"Okay." Ari tucked the note into her hoodie pocket.

"See you tomorrow. Congratulations again."

"Thanks," Ari mumbled and hurried away.

***

Ari tore open the note as soon as she was safely away from the school. She scanned it quickly. "Shit!"

I don't want to think about that. She crumpled the note and stuck it back in her pocket. *I'll figure that out later. First, I have to get some popcorn from the alley in case the crows came back.*

She walked quickly, keeping watch for trouble, and hoping to see her mother. The theater was quiet as slipped around to the alley, opened the dumpster, and scooped popcorn into her backpack.

As soon as Ari reached her house, Nevermore and Morrigan cawed a raucous greeting to her from the rooftop.

She looked up and grinned. "Hi, guys. I got you lots of popcorn today."

The birds flew down and walked beside her as she entered the house. Ari spread the popcorn on the filthy carpet and sat down with them. Nevermore watched her closely. He hopped closer and then onto her knee. Ari stroked his head.

"I won the spelling bee," she told him.

Nevermore flapped his wings and cawed loudly. He and Morrigan lifted into the air and swooped through the small rooms, cawing and clicking. Ari laughed aloud and clapped her hands. The birds settled down to their snack. Ari said, "I have some bad news, though."

Nevermore stopped eating and came back to her knee.

"Miss Charles sent a note home, asking Mama to come in for a meeting."

Nevermore bobbed his head up and down.

"What should I tell her?"

The bird stayed quiet.

"She knows Mama works a lot. Maybe I could write a note back and pretend to be Mama. I could say I don't have time."

Nevermore seemed to consider this a moment, and then bobbed his head and hopped back to the floor.

"I know, it's wrong. But I can't think of anything else." Ari stood up. "I have to wash some clothes and do my homework. Then I'll figure it out."

Morrigan followed her to the kitchen. Nevermore pecked at the popcorn.

***

Ari couldn't sleep. She lay in the dark and stared at the ceiling. *I hated Jerry*, she thought. *But mama is worse. Mothers are supposed to take care of their kids.* Tears threatened. She dashed them away. *Somebody once said crying never solved anything, and they were right.* Ari got up and put on her shoes.

Nevermore stirred in the box. She bent and stroked his back. "I'm just going to walk around down by the theater, where those bars are, and see if I can find Mama. I won't be gone long." Morrigan tucked her head deeper under her wing. Nevermore stepped out of the box and followed Ari to the door. "You don't have to come with me." Nevermore cocked his head and waited as Ari pulled on her coat and gloves and wrapped a scarf around her neck.

They stepped together into the cold, black night. The wind whistled. Ari shivered and took a deep breath. She looked down at Nevermore. "Mama will come home if I tell her I need her."

Nevermore stayed quiet.

"Right? Mothers have to help."

Nevermore lifted into the air and flew toward the movie theater. Ari followed after him, keeping to the shadows in case anyone was out and about at this hour.

A few porch lights were on. Here and there, a blue glow showed in an otherwise dark house. The theater was closed, all the lights off, and the parking lot empty. Nevermore flew ahead and circled back, always staying close. Ari could hear music from a bar on the next block. Light spilled onto the sidewalk from the propped-open door. She scurried along, staying close to the buildings. Someone yelled out a good night and was answered with words Ari couldn't understand. A woman stumbled out of the bar. She lurched, grabbed the wall for support, and headed toward Ari.

Nevermore swooped low over the woman's head. She screeched and batted the bird away. "What the hell? Get away from me, you crazy bird."

A man stuck his head out of the bar. "You're seeing things, Stacy. Ain't no bird out here at this hour of the night. Go on home now." He withdrew and the bar door closed behind him.

Ari stopped in the shadows and stood still, watching her mother.

Stacy reached the corner and turned down the block.

Ari crossed the street and moved more quickly.

Stacy reached the alley.

Ari was close now.

Nevermore swooped low again.

Ari laughed.

Stacy turned and glared. "What do you want? I don't have any money!"

"Mama. It's me, Ari."

Stacy didn't respond. She shuffled faster and turned into the alley.

Ari followed. "Mama." Ari reached out and touched her mother's sleeve.

Stacy backed away, swatting at her. "Get away," she snarled. "Leave me alone."

Ari stepped closer. "Mama," she pleaded, "I need you to come home."

"That's not going to happen, Ari." Stacy suddenly seemed completely sober. She glared at her daughter. "I never wanted to be a mother. And I don't want to be one now." She turned to walk away.

Ari yanked the back of her coat. Stacy jerked away and turned. She swung her purse at Ari's head.

Ari grabbed the purse and pulled.

Stacy stumbled toward her. "Leave me alone," she snarled.

Tears flowed down Ari's face. She let go of the purse, looked up at her mother and whispered, "I hate you. I really hate you."

Stacy shrugged.

Ari reached up, placed her hands on her mother's shoulders, and pushed as hard as she could. Stacy staggered backwards, out of control. Her heel caught in the rough pavement.

Her mother fell, and her head hit the brick wall. She crumpled to the ground; her head bouncing on the pavement. She jerked once and lay still.

Ari looked over her shoulder. The alley was still empty. She gazed down at her mother, brushed the tears from her cheeks, turned and walked away. "'Bye, Mama."

Nevermore flew rapidly to the end of the alley and back. He stayed quiet as he escorted Ari home.

***

Three for a girl,

"If you say that a place is a particular distance away as the crow flies, you mean that it is that distance away measured in a straight line." —Collins Dictionary

The raucous sound of the crow's cawing pulled Ari from a deep sleep.

She stretched, sat up on the sofa, and rubbed her eyes. The pillow and blanket lay crumpled on the floor. A headache throbbed in her temples. She was still wearing the jacket she'd worn last night.

Nevermore flew to the arm of the sofa and cawed loudly.

Ari stood up. "Matricide," she said aloud. "M-A-T-R-I-C-I-D-E. I think I killed my mother last night."

Nevermore flapped his wings and circled through the living room, into the kitchen, and back to the sofa. Morrigan followed close behind.

"It is time for us to leave," Ari told the crows. "You are my only friends but I don't think we can live like this anymore." Ari moved to the front door and opened it wide. The crows left the house and mounted the sky. Ari kept watch until they disappeared. "What happens now?" she asked aloud.

I need to tell someone that I'm living here alone. I love the crows, but they can't pay for anything. I guess I have to tell Miss Charles that Mama is gone, but I don't have to tell her about the crows.

***

Ari climbed the stairs and entered her mother's room. She pulled open each drawer and found nothing she wanted to take with her. She dropped to her knees and peeked under the bed. A single gold bangle sparkled in the dust bunnies. Ari brushed it off and slid it on her wrist. In her own room, Ari changed clothes. She took the book of fairy tales her mother used to read from and pushed it into her backpack, along with a few clothes. Nothing else in the house mattered. She started out the door, then turned back and took a small, framed picture from the windowsill.

***

School was in session by the time Ari reached the building. She took a deep breath and looked up at the sky, hoping to see her crows. Nothing. She pulled the heavy door open and walked straight to the counselor's office. Ari swallowed hard and knocked on the door frame. *I can do this.*

Miss Charles looked up. "Ari! Is everything okay? Why aren't you in class?"

Ari stepped in and pulled the door shut; her knees shook. She stepped close to the desk, clenched her fists to stop their tremble, then reached for the edge of the desk and hung on. Her knuckles turned white. She forced the tears to come. "I need help," she whispered.

"Oh, honey." Miss Charles rose, walked around the desk, and guided Ari to a chair. "Whatever it is, I'll help you."

Ari sobbed into her hands.

Miss Charles waited, handing her one Kleenex after another.

At last, her sobbing slowed. She blew her nose and wiped her eyes on her sleeve.

"Can you talk now?" Miss Charles asked.

Ari nodded and allowed another ragged sob to escape. She drew in a breath and looked toward the window before dropping her eyes to the floor.

"I think I have to tell you something." Ari kept her head down, her eyes focused on her shoes.

"Whatever it is, you'll feel better if you tell me. And, whatever it is, I'll help you. I promise."

Ari slipped her hands under her legs to stop their shaking.

Miss Charles waited.

"I think my mom is using drugs again." Ari drew in another deep breath. "Like all the time."

"Oh, Ari." Miss Charles placed her hand on Ari's leg. "Why do you think that?"

"She doesn't come home at night."

"You mean she didn't come home last night?"

Ari shook her head. She stood and walked to the window.

"How often are you home alone, Ari?"

She kept her back turned and searched the sky, hoping to catch a glimpse of her crows.

"Ari, you need to tell me. When was the last time you saw your mom?"

Ari shuddered and squeezed her eyes tight shut. "They went out on New Year's Eve, and they didn't come back."

Miss Charles gasped. "What?"

Ari turned around and held herself perfectly still.

"But that's over six weeks ago, Ari."

"I know." She watched Miss Charles think about what it meant that Stacy had been gone so long. *Circumspect, C-I-R-C-U-M-S-P-E-C-T, be careful, don't say anything else.*

"Are you sure?" Miss Charles shook her head as if to clear it. "Sorry, of course you are. I just never suspected."

"I thought Mama would come home. Every day, I thought she'd come home." Ari pulled her hoodie sleeves over her fingers.

"But, Ari," Miss Charles hesitated and then continued, "have you been alone in the house all that time?"

"Yes."

"Really? All alone?"

"Well, the crows keep me company." *I shouldn't have said that.*

Miss Charles reached for her phone and then let her hand drop. She tried to smile. "Ari, come and sit down. We need to talk about this."

Maybe she didn't hear me say "crows." Ari crossed her fingers and returned to her chair.

Miss Charles took her hand. "I need to ask you some questions."

"Can I have something to eat first? I got here too late for breakfast."

"Yes, of course, honey." Miss Charles jumped up. "You sit right here, and I'll be back in a flash."

Miss Charles stepped out of the office and pulled the door shut behind her. Ari waited until the counselor's silhouette was no longer visible through the frosted glass panel. She moved to the desk and pulled open the center drawer. Nothing but pens and pencils. *I need cash,* she thought, and closed the drawer. She looked around. *If Miss Charles has a purse, it must be hidden somewhere.* She tried to open a tall cupboard, but the door was locked.

A large crow landed on the windowsill. "Nevermore." Ari quickly approached the closed window and pushed it open.

Nevermore cawed loudly and shook his head.

"I know," Ari explained, "it's wrong to steal, but I don't know where I'll be sent, and I might need to ride a bus to find you."

Nevermore looked her directly in the eye. He made a lengthy series of clicks, cawed again, and shook his head.

"Okay, I get it. I won't steal, but you have to come find me."

Nevermore gave a soft rattle, then lifted his wings, and flew away.

Ari shut the window and sat down to wait for Miss Charles.

***

Miss Charles stayed quiet while Ari wolfed down her breakfast. When Ari wiped her mouth, she asked, "Do you have electricity at your house?"

Ari nodded. "Yes, but the overdue notice came a few days ago."

"What about the rent? Who's paying the rent?"

"Um, I don't know. I don't know anything about rent."

"I have to call Child Protective Services, Ari." Ari stayed quiet. "Do you understand what that means?"

Ari nodded. She sucked on the straw stuck in her milk carton. The satisfying noise of air, as she sucked the last drop, sounded loud in the small office. "I know. It means I have to go to foster care. I did it once before when I was little."

"I didn't know that."

"It was in another town." Ari set her empty carton on the edge of the desk, then stood and walked to the window. "Mama said I'd never have to go again, but I guess she lied."

"I'm going to call CPS now. It will probably take them a while to get here and then, I think, they will want you to leave with the social worker. Do you want to go to class while we wait, or stay here?"

She kept her back turned and watched the sky. "I might as well stay here."

***

When Mr. Comstock announced the arrival of the police, Miss Charles excused herself and left the office, pulling the door closed. Ari stayed at the window. *Surrender. S-U-R-R-E-N-D-E-R. To give oneself up, submit, yield.*

A few minutes later, the door reopened. "Ari," Miss Charles said, "the police and your social worker are here. She wants to talk to you, and then the police will need to ask you some questions."

Ari nodded but didn't turn around.

Miss Charles crossed the office and placed one hand on Ari's shoulder. "It'll be all right," she said in a quiet voice. She gave Ari a gentle squeeze and turned her away from the window. "Ari, this is Mrs. Jenkins."

Ari glanced first at the police. She breathed easier, relieved to see they were not the ones that had come to the house the night Jerry died. She shifted her eyes to look at the woman. Gray hair, glasses, a long hippie dress, and a big purse.

"Hello, Ari. No need to call me Mrs. Jenkins. Everybody just calls me Jenks." The woman smiled, showing all of her teeth. She sat down and motioned Ari to the other chair. "My paperwork shows your name as Harriet Blimm, age eleven. Is that correct?"

Ari gave a quick nod.

"I have some questions you need to answer. The police need to be here, and you should have an adult family member with you. Who would you like us to call?"

Ari shrugged.

"I understand that your mother isn't available, but how about a grandparent?"

Ari shook her head.

"An aunt?" Jenks kept her eyes on Ari's face, waiting for an affirmative response. "An uncle? Your mom's best friend?"

"It's just Mama and me."

Jenks stood, moved to the officers, and conferred with them in low whispers. She waved Miss Charles over to join the conversation. Ari shut them out. She walked back to the window and scanned the sky. *Valiant. V-A-L-I-A-N-T. Courageous, brave, unafraid.*

The voices behind her stopped. Ari turned to see that only the younger policeman was still in the room. "Where'd everybody go?" she asked.

"Your social worker needs to get a special court order so she can place you in emergency care."

"Does that take a long time?"

"Usually it's just a phone call. What are you looking at out that window?"

Ari glanced over her shoulder and shrugged. "Nothing."

The policeman nodded. "Jenks is one of the good ones. You'll be okay."

Ari took one more quick look out the window and returned to her chair. She seated herself and tucked her hands under her legs. Her feet swung just above the floor. She kept her eyes on her shoes. They waited in silence until Miss Charles returned with Jenks. Miss Charles sat at her desk and Jenks took the chair next to Ari.

"I need to explain a few things," Jenks said.

Ari stiffened but didn't lift her eyes.

"Because you are in immediate danger, I am removing you from your home effective right now. This afternoon we will talk to a judge and seek an emergency order to place you in the care of Child Protective Services. That means that the court will decide where you will live and when you may return to your home."

Ari nodded her understanding and Mrs. Jenkins continued. "These policemen have some questions they need to ask about your mother. It's their job to try to find her and notify her about the hearing. I'll stay with you while they ask their questions and if you'd like, Miss Charles can stay, too."

"Okay."

Miss Charles rose from behind the desk. "Let's go into the conference room so we can all sit down." She moved to Ari's side. "Come on, honey. Do you want a juice box or something to eat?"

Ari shook her head.

They filed out of the room. Mr. Comstock, who was lurking by the desk in the outer office, came to attention. "May I help you with something, gentlemen?" he asked.

"Nope, we're good," the policeman said. He led the small parade as they walked past Comstock and entered the conference room. Miss Charles shut the door with a firm click.

That'll teach him, he's such a busybody, B-U-S-Y-B-O-D-Y, a person who pries into or meddles in the affairs of others. Ari suppressed her grin and forced herself to pay close attention.

The older policeman pulled a notepad and a pen from his pocket. He cleared his throat, picked up the pen and opened his notepad. "So…" he began. "Ari, huh? I like that name. Nice sound to it." He shifted in his chair and tapped the pen on the table a few times. "Okay, let's see what we can do to find your mom."

Look in the alley, Ari thought. She kept her eyes on the policeman.

"Is your mother Stacy Blimm?" He didn't wait for a response. "When was the last time you saw your mother?"

Last night. Ari pushed the thought away and mumbled, "New Year's Eve."

"That's a pretty long time, more than two months. Are you sure?"

"Of course I'm sure," Ari snapped.

"Tell me about that. Was she upset when she left?"

"I don't think so. They were just drunk."

The policemen exchanged looks. "Who did she leave with?"

"Bob. I was kind of mad, so I was in my room with the door shut."

"Bob, huh? Do you know Bob's last name?"

Ari frowned and looked toward Miss Charles.

Miss Charles smiled encouragement.

"I'm not sure. I think it's just a normal name."

"Is this Bob your mom's boyfriend?"

"I guess so. He was at our house a lot."

"Is he a nice guy?"

Ari shrugged. "I guess."

"Did Bob and your mom fight a lot?"

"Not a lot."

"But some?"

"Some," Ari mumbled. "Not like hitting and stuff, just yelling."

"How about your mom's other friends. Does she have a best friend?"

"I don't think so. Mostly she just has boyfriends."

Mrs. Jenkins made a tutting sound.

The policeman ignored her and continued, "Boyfriends, huh? Know any of their names?"

"They didn't live at our house," Ari explained, shaking her head. "I just heard them on the phone sometimes."

"So, you've been living in your house all alone since New Year's. That's a long time for a kid to take care of herself. Why didn't you go to a friend's house?"

Idiot, I-D-I-O-T, a foolish or senseless person. "Because I don't have any friends except..." Ari caught herself.

"Except who, Ari?"

Ari squirmed. *I can't tell them about Nevermore and Morrigan.* She glanced around the room. "Except for Miss Charles," she finished quickly. She shifted her eyes to look at the counselor to be sure she hadn't said anything wrong and was surprised to see Miss Charles wipe away a tear.

"Your mom has a history of drug addiction."

"I know."

"Got any idea if there are drugs in your house or who she buys her drugs from?"

"Officer!" Jenks spoke sharply. "Is that line of questioning appropriate?"

He shrugged. "We need to find the relatives, ma'am. You'd be surprised what kids know."

"I have worked with children for thirty years. I am fully aware of how children behave and think. Let's finish this up. We'll go before the judge in a couple of hours. I'm sure he'll give you a search warrant for the house."

"Yep, I'm sure he will. Ari, I want you to think really hard and try to remember any names or places that your mom ever mentioned. Like, maybe, a bar she likes to drink at or a club where she goes to dance. If you think of anything, Jenks will know how to reach us. Got it?"

Ari gulped. "Yes, sir." She drew in a deep breath. "How about AA? She used to go to those meetings, sometimes."

"We'll check that out." He placed his notepad in his pocket and buttoned the flap. "Thanks for your help, Ari. We'll be in touch." The two men rose together. The younger one winked at Ari and gave her a little salute as they left the room.

Jenks placed her own stack of papers back into her large purse. "Ari, I'm going to drive you to the courthouse now. We'll have a little bit of time, so we can get a sandwich in the cafeteria before your hearing. Do you understand?"

"Can Miss Charles come to the hearing?"

"I'm on your side, Ari," Jenks said.

"I know, but I…"

"Of course, I'll be there, Ari," Miss Charles interrupted. "A familiar face seems like a good idea. Don't you think so, Mrs. Jenkins?"

***

The police, Mrs. Jenkins, Ari, and Miss Charles sat at a long, oak table facing the unsmiling judge, who sat behind his own table. Ari's eyes wandered to the high window. *Nothing to see. It's weird in here, not at all like a courtroom on TV.* She glanced at Officer Gonzales. *I wonder if he knows I saw my mother last night? What if someone saw me in the alley?*

"I don't have a foster home available tonight." Jenks spoke directly to the judge, not including Ari in her comments. "I have someone trying to find a temporary group home placement."

"That is not the best-case scenario, Mrs. Jenkins." The judge tapped his pen a few times. He turned to Ari. "You've done nothing wrong, young lady. We are simply concerned for your safety. You are much too young to live alone. I'm going to issue a warrant so Officer Gonzales can search your house. It may help them locate your mother.

And, when the police locate your mother, we may be able to resolve this situation." He pulled his glasses off and chewed on the arm. "Are you sure you can't think of a friend or relative you could stay with for a few days?"

The door opened. Everyone turned to the sound. It was Officer Banks, the policewoman from the night Jerry fell. Ari ducked her head.

Banks walked quickly to Officer Gonzales and spoke quietly.

He rose. "May we approach the bench, your honor?"

"This is an initial emergency placement hearing, not a trial. I have no bench."

"Yes, your honor, but I have some relevant information."

"Alright, alright." The judge waved Mrs. Jenkins and Officer Gonzales forward. They began to speak softly.

Ari held her breath. *One hundred, ninety-nine, ninety-eight, ninety-seven, ninety-six.* She blew out her breath. *Ninety-five, ninety-four, ninety-three, ninety-two.*

Miss Charles squeezed her hand.

The judge looked at Ari and shook his head.

"Why is he looking at me like that? What do you think they are talking about?" Ari whispered.

"I have no idea." Miss Charles placed her other hand over Ari's. "We just have to wait and see."

Mrs. Jenkins and the policeman returned to the table. The judge cleared his throat, fiddled with some papers, and then sighed. "Harriet, I have some news about your mother."

Ari gasped and covered her mouth. Dread flooded her body. She wanted to run. *They know!*

"She's had an accident, Harriet."

"Is she hurt? Where is she?" Ari's heart thumped in her chest. *Maybe I didn't kill her.*

"Sometime last night. It appears she fell in an alley and hit her head. Someone found her this morning and called the police. They took her to the hospital."

Ari stood up and walked toward the judge. Mrs. Jenkins extended her hand to stop her, but the judge motioned that it was okay.

"Can I go to the hospital now?"

"I'm sorry, Harriet. There is no easy way to tell you this." He sighed. "Your mother died a few hours ago."

Tears rolled down Ari's cheeks. She reached out and clung to the edge of the judge's table, trembling from head to toe. Miss Charles hurried to her side and hugged her close. *Dead! She's really dead. Do they know I was there?* Ari managed to demand, "Are your sure it was my mom?"

"Yes, Ari," the judge said. "We found her purse in the alley. Her identification was still in the wallet."

"Can I see her?" Ari swiped the back of her hand across her nose. *I need to be sure she's dead.*

"Mrs. Jenkins will make that decision. Right now, I need to ask you a few more questions."

Ari accepted Kleenex from the social worker and blew her nose loudly. She allowed Miss Charles to help her to her feet and accepted one more hug. The judge waited.

When Ari was seated at the table again, the judge said, "Are you absolutely positive you don't have any relatives that can help you?"

"I think I'm sure." *Orphan, O-R-P-H-A-N, a child whose parents are dead.* "Maybe I have a father somewhere."

"Do you remember anything about your father?" The judge scribbled something and so did Jenks.

Ari shook her head. "Mama just always said he was gone." She thought a minute. "I don't know if she said dead. I guess I just thought 'gone' meant dead."

"Do you know the lady that owns your house?" the judge asked carefully.

"You mean my mom?"

"According to the court record, your house is owned by a woman named Harriet Ilene Blimm."

"That's not me!"

The judge chuckled. "I'm sure it's not, but since the name is almost the same as yours, I have to wonder if she is a relative." He allowed the thought to sink in before he asked. "Did you ever go to visit someone older with your mom?"

Ari began to count as she slowly shook her head from side to side. *One, two, three, four, five, six. "I..."* She hesitated. "I think I went to a house where the lady had a lot of cats. But I think she was a babysitter. It was in another town. Where I had to go to foster care."

Mrs. Jenkins was jotting furious notes now. The judge tapped his pen a few times and watched her scribble. "What town would that have been, Mrs. Jenkins?"

"We have no record of prior foster care in this state, your honor."

"It sounds to me like there is the possibility of a grandmother. Ari, for tonight, and most likely for a few days, you will need to become a temporary ward of the court. That means that Mrs. Jenkins here," he tipped his head in her direction, "and I will make some decisions about where you will live and go to school."

Ari nodded.

"May I have a minute, Judge?" Mrs. Jenkins asked.

She beckoned to Miss Charles to lean forward and spoke just above a whisper. "If Ari could stay with you for a few hours, maybe overnight, I may be able to find a better placement than the group home."

"Absolutely. I'd be happy to help." Miss Charles turned to look Ari in the eye. "If it is all right with Ari, and the judge, it is all right with me."

Ari smiled her approval.

The judge agreed and the arrangements were made.

"Now, remember this is just temporary," Jenks warned Ari. "The police will go to your house and search for any information they can find about your mother and the mysterious owner of your home. I will find you a foster home and you will stay with Miss Charles until I come to get you. Do you understand?"

Understand, U-N-D-E-R-S-T-A-N-D, to perceive the meaning of words or actions. "Got it," Ari said. She watched the social worker as she gathered her notes and paperwork. "Do you think it will be to-night?"

Jenks looked at Ari. "Will what be tonight?"

"All that stuff you said about searching and finding."

Jenks glanced at the clock on the wall. "It's after three, so probably not. However, sometimes things move very quickly. Miss Charles has graciously agreed to watch over you until I find you a place." Jenks turned to Miss Charles. "You do understand that you are responsible for Ari until I am able to place her in a home, don't you?"

"I do and I am delighted." Miss Charles grinned at Ari. "Come on Ari. Let's go." Ari stood up and grabbed her backpack.

"You be a good girl, Ari." Jenks said. She turned to Miss Charles. "If you have any trouble, you have my number, call any time."

"We'll be just fine. Won't we, Ari?"

Swinging her backpack over her shoulder, Ari nodded and fol-lowed Miss Charles from the courtroom.

When they arrived at Miss Charles's small apartment, Ari stood just inside the door and looked around. She ran her finger around a glass bowl on the entry table. "Everything is so pretty," she said.

"Thank you. Now come in and make yourself comfortable. You can leave your backpack and hoodie on the bench." Miss Charles pointed. "If you want to freshen up, the bathroom is through that door," she pointed again. "Please, watch TV if you like or come join me in the kitchen. I'm going to see what I have for dinner." Miss Charles disappeared though an archway.

One hundred, ninety-nine, ninety-eight, ninety-seven, Ari counted slowly. *I am not afraid. Ninety-six, ninety-five, ninety-four, ninety-three.* She She twisted the bangle on her arm and followed Miss Charles to the kitchen. The setting sun shone through a cobalt blue vase filled with yellow roses and cast a rainbow across the wall. Ari touched a petal. *Roses, R-O-S-E, showy-flowered shrubs of the genus Rosa.* She felt the counselor's gaze and dropped her hand.

"Everything okay?"

"Do you think Jenks will be back tonight?"

"I'm quite sure she will. Mrs. Jenkins seems like a nice woman." She opened the refrigerator door and looked in the bins. "How does Pasta Primavera sound?"

"I don't know what that is," Ari admitted.

"Then you are in for a treat," Miss Charles said. "Want to help me cook?" Without waiting for an answer, she continued, "You wash these veggies and I'll chop. Do you like garlic?"

"Hm, maybe." As she washed the vegetables, Ari kept her gaze on the darkening sky, hoping to see the crows. When they didn't appear, she turned off the water, dried her hands, and asked, "Couldn't I just stay here tonight?"

"I don't know. It depends on how long it takes them to find a licensed foster home. Kids can only stay with relatives or in licensed foster care. The court has lots of rules that must be followed. Especially when it comes to kids." She handed Ari a box of pasta. "Please, dump this in the boiling water."

Ari was quiet as they finished cooking and ate. Miss Charles watched her but stayed quiet also. When Ari's plate was empty, she offered her a second serving of pasta.

Ari nodded to accept and said, "I didn't know that vegetables could taste this good."

"What is your favorite thing to eat?"

Ari considered carefully before admitting, "I guess pancakes. When I learn how to cook, I'll make pancakes a lot."

"Not a bad idea. You can make a lot of different kinds of pancakes. Almost every country has a variety of their own."

"Maybe when I'm older, I'll travel around the world and eat nothing but pancakes." Ari grinned widely.

"Sounds like fun, but I think you'd miss out on a lot of really great food."

The doorbell rang. Ari froze. The animation dropped from her face.

"Stay here." Miss Charles rose. "I'll get it."

Ari clenched her hands and closed her eyes, *One hundred, ninety-nine, ninety-eight, ninety-seven, ninety-six.* She heard Miss Charles greet Jenks and waited to be summoned. *Ninety-five, ninety-four, ninety-three, ninety-two, ninety-one.* The voices moved toward the kitchen. Ari opened her eyes and concentrated on her plate. *Ninety, eighty-nine, eighty-eight.*

Jenks sat down at the table and sighed as she eased her feet out of her shoes. "Ari, I've found a place for you to stay for a few days. The family usually only takes infants, but since this is an emergency, they have agreed to take you."

Ari didn't respond or even look at Jenks.

"It's actually a stroke of luck. The judge wasn't happy with the idea of a group home and neither was I. The Wallaces are really nice people and they've agreed to drive you to your current school for a few days until we get this situation settled." Jenks rapped her knuckles on the table. "Harriet, I need you to look at me."

"Don't call me that!" Ari looked at Jenks and narrowed her eyes. "When do I get to see my mom?" she demanded.

"When I say so," Jenks said, "and not until I say so. That's what being a ward of the court means and unless we find a relative that wants you, that's what you are. Got it?"

Ari nodded and glared at Jenks her lips pressed tightly together. *Do not cry.*

"That's more like it." Jenks frowned and continued, "As I was saying, the Wallaces are expecting us, and you and I need to get some
things straight before we drive there."

Jenks pulled a file folder from her big purse and opened it to a
form. "Do you have adequate clothing for tonight and tomorrow?"

Ari nodded.

Jenks made a check mark. "Do you have any valuable items in
your possession?"

The bracelet seemed to burn on her wrist. Ari shook her head.

"What about that?" Jenks pointed at the golden bangle.

"It's my mom's."

"But is it valuable? Let me see it."

Ari slid the bangle off and passed it to Jenks, who studied it a minute and handed it back.

Ari slipped it back on. *Bitch, B-I-T-C-H, a mean, unpleasant person, especially a woman.*

"I don't see a stamp. It's most likely plated. You can keep it with
you, but you need to remember that things turn up missing in foster
families." She made another check mark and moved to her next question.

"You are required to behave with respect toward the foster family
and you must not leave the home, at any time, without permission."

Ari nodded.

Jenks placed a third check mark. "Now, about your mother. The
coroner has received an identification from her friend Bob. Tomorrow
I'll pick you up after school for a viewing. Perhaps by that time the
police will have searched your house and found evidence of a relative."

"How did Bob know she was," Ari hesitated, "hurt?"

"The police showed her picture in the bars close to that alley where
she was found. Bob came forward." Jenks closed the file and stuffed it
back into her purse.

"Oh." Ari stopped herself from saying more. *One hundred, ninety-nine, ninety-eight, ninety-seven, ninety-six.*

Jenks placed her pen behind her ear and patted her hair into place. "Say thank you to Miss Charles, and then we have to go."

"May I speak to Ari alone for a moment?" Miss Charles asked.

Jenks considered the request. "Sure, I don't see any harm in that. But make it quick." She moved toward the front door and left them in the kitchen.

"Ari." Miss Charles placed her hand under Ari's chin and tilted her face up. "I know this has been a terrible day. You've been very brave. You did the right thing coming to me. I want you to stop in and talk to me anytime at school and," she pulled a card from her pocket and handed it to Ari, "this card has my cell phone number so you can call me if you want. I'll always be willing to help."

She smiled. "You are a very special girl, Ari. Don't ever forget that." Miss Charles leaned forward and kissed the top of Ari's head.

Real tears welled in Ari's eyes. She rubbed them away impatiently. "Will you keep this safe for me?" Ari twisted the bangle off her wrist and handed it to Miss Charles.

"I will." Miss Charles brushed away her own tears, tucked the bracelet into her pocket, and walked with Ari toward Jenks. "See you at school tomorrow, okay?"

"Okay." Ari shrugged on her bright red hoodie and picked up her backpack.

"Ready?" Jenks asked.

One hundred, ninety-nine, ninety-eight, ninety-seven, ninety-six. Ari took a deep breath and blew it out. "Ready."

Ari kept her hands tightly folded in her lap and watched the sky as Mr. Wallace drove her to school. *Maybe,* Ari thought, *I can do this foster care thing.* Mr. and Mrs. Wallace seemed nice enough. *My room is clean and comfortable. Mrs. Wallace made French toast for breakfast and Mr. Wallace didn't bug me on the way to school.*

The car braked in the drop-off lane. She swung the door open and moved to step out.

"Mrs. Jenkins will pick you up this afternoon, okay?" Mr. Wallace said.

"Okay, thanks for the ride."

"You're welcome, Ari. It was a pleasure meeting you. I hope everything goes well for you."

Ari stopped halfway out of the car and looked back. "Won't I see you again?"

"I don't think so, Ari. We were just your emergency placement. At your hearing, this afternoon, the judge will decide on the next step for you. Mrs. Jenkins will explain it."

"What about my stuff?"

"The social worker will pick it up and make sure you get it. You be a good girl. If you follow their rules everything will be fine. You'll see."

Right, Ari thought as she slammed the car door shut. She ignored his lifted hand, checked out the empty sky, and dragged herself across the schoolyard. *So much for thinking positive.*

"Hey, Hairy Fairy!" Toby shouted from the basketball court. "I didn't think you'd be back after the cops hauled you away yesterday."

Ari spun around and glared at him. *Fat fuck.* "Why don't you mind your own business, Toby Meyers?"

"Ya, Toby," someone taunted, "mind your own business."

Toby whirled around, hands on his hips, looking for the unknown challenger, and declared, "If she killed someone else I just want to know."

Ari clenched her fists and held her breath. She felt her classmates turn to stare at her. *One hundred, ninety-nine, ninety-eight, ninety-seven, ninety-six...* The bell rang. She avoided all eye contact as she stumbled up the stairs and through the school doors. *I hate him, I hate him, I hate him.*

***

Sitting by herself at one of the lunch tables, Ari pretended to read her book. She kept one eye on Toby and his friends. Ari couldn't hear what they were saying but, from the way they were looking and pointing, she was pretty sure she was the object of their conversation. She ate her meal and refused to acknowledge them.

When lunch ended, Ari hung back making sure she was the last one to dump her garbage and place her tray on the rack when the others exited the room and headed to the schoolyard. *Hide, H-I-D-E, to conceal from sight, prevent from being seen. Maybe I can hide in the...*

"Get a move on, Miss Blimm." Mr. Comstock's order interrupted her thoughts. "You need to get outside with the rest of your class. Unless," his eyes swept over her, "you have an appointment with someone. Do you?"

"No, sir," Ari managed to say, "I was just going to check with Miss Charles to see what time Mrs. Jenkins will be here."

"No need for that. If she comes before the end of the day, you'll be contacted."

Ari nodded once, scurried around the vice-principal, and hurried toward the building doors. They swung open and Mrs. Jenkins entered.

"How convenient," Jenks said. She ran her eyes over Ari and her lips turned up, but her smile didn't reach her eyes.

She turned away from Ari and continued, "Good afternoon, Mr. Comstock. I've come to check Harriet out of school. We have an appointment with the court."

"Very well. Harriet, go get your things and meet Mrs. Jenkins in my office." When Ari hesitated, he clapped his hands together, once. "Go on now, you don't want to keep the lovely Mrs. Jenkins waiting."

Ari scurried away.

When Ari was out of earshot, he turned back to the social worker. "A most unfortunate turn of events."

"Events?"

"The death of her mother, of course." Mr. Comstock shook his head sadly.

Jenks nodded.

He continued, "Will Harriet be returning to our school?"

"I can't answer that until a permanent placement is found."

"Right." He shook his head again. "That won't be easy with a girl like Harriet."

"Oh, why do you say that?"

"She's quite disruptive you know, always picking on the Meyers boy." He dropped his voice to just above a whisper. "She's bright enough, but breeding will always show. The mother is—*was*—rather vulgar. I don't imagine there is much chance of success with her." Mr. Comstock frowned. "In my experience, by the time a child is twelve they have become set in their ways. She'll most likely turn to drugs and drop out soon."

Jenks pursed her lips and raised an eyebrow. "Miss Charles seems to think quite highly of Harriet's capabilities."

"True, she does. But our Miss Charles has never married and is most idealistic. I, on the other hand, am a realist." He tugged at the lapels of his suit jacket and straightened his shoulders. "Shall we adjourn to my office? As the vice-principal, I am in charge of discipline."

He turned, opened his office door, and waved Mrs. Jenkins to a seat.

"I keep notes from my interviews with potential problems." Mr. Comstock pulled a file from his cabinet. "This is Harriet's file. I think you may find it interesting."

Jenks accepted the folder and flipped it open. She scanned the topmost document and looked up at Mr. Comstock. "Oh, my! This is not good." Her eyes returned to the folder. She shook her head and flipped page after page. "There is certainly a pattern of belligerence."

Mr. Comstock pursed his lips and agreed. "I've done my best. You can see that I've talked to Harriet about her behavior at least once a month, and sometimes many times a month. In almost every instance the precipitating event involved Toby Meyers."

"How does Harriet explain her behavior?"

"She doesn't bother. She refuses to give any explanation."

"And how does she react to consequences?"

Mr. Comstock sat back in his desk chair and placed his hands behind his head. "I have tried to contact the mother. There has been no response, despite repeated notes and phone messages. Harriet has been given detention and extra assignments. She always apologizes to Toby, but it is not sincere and it has no lasting effect."

"Does she have friends?"

"Well," Mr. Comstock brought his hands back to his desktop and shook his head, "I'm afraid not. The girl isn't very clean and there is often an unpleasant odor."

Jenks closed the folder and placed it on the desk with a firm tap, as she asked, "If the school suspected neglect, a social services report should have been filed."

"That would be up to Miss Charles and as you noticed, she has a soft spot for Harriet." Comstock clicked his tongue against the roof of his mouth. "I can't imagine why, but she does." A tap sounded on the door. Comstock winked at Jenks. "Come in, Harriet."

Ari slipped into the room and stood silent, her eyes on the window.

The adults rose. Jenks offered her hand to the vice-principal, and said, "Thank you for your help."

"Please be in touch." He looked down at Ari. "Good luck, Harriet. I'm sorry about your mother. Remember everything we've talked about and try to be a good girl." When Ari didn't respond, he caught Jenks's eye and raised his eyebrows as if to ask, did you see that?

Jenks gave a brisk nod, gathered her belongings, and moved to the doorway. "Come along, Harriet. We don't want to keep the judge waiting."

***

Rainbows danced across the courtroom from the sunlight entering through the high windows. Ari placed her hand on the table, allowing a rainbow to cross her palm. A shadow caused the light to disappear. Ari looked up and saw the outline of a large bird on the windowsill. "Nevermore," she whispered.

"What?" Jenks asked.

"Nothing," Ari muttered. She looked up again and watched the crow walk back and forth. *I knew you would watch out for me.*

The judge's gruff voice interrupted her thoughts. "Do we have a report on the search for the missing owner of the house?"

"Yes, your honor." Officer Gonzales glanced at his file of papers. "We were able to locate, Mrs. Harriet Ilene Blimm. She stated that she is the girl's maternal grandmother."

Ari jumped in her seat. She focused her attention on the police officer. "Really?" she blurted.

Jenks put a restraining hand on her arm. "Just listen."

"But—"

The judge smiled at Ari and turned back to Officer Gonzales. "Ari and I want to know about this person. Tell us what you learned."

Gonzales cleared his throat. "Mrs. Blimm is a seventy-eight-year-old woman, living in Fresno, California. When contacted, she stated that she is the mother of Stacy Blimm, and the grandmother of Harriet Blimm, and the owner of the house in which they reside. Mrs. Blimm stated that she and her daughter had a falling out about eleven years ago. She confirmed that Stacy has a history of substance abuse and neglect. She has not had contact with either her daughter or granddaughter for more than eight or nine years."

"Get to the point," the judge directed.

"Approximately four years ago, Mrs. Blimm was confined to a nursing home. She is aware that Stacy then moved into her former home and has continued to live there. Since the home is paid for and was to have been Stacy's inheritance, Mrs. Blimm has ignored their occupancy of the premises."

"But why don't I know her?" Ari interrupted again.

"Families are very complicated," Jenks said.

"Families are complicated," the judge agreed. He looked back at Officer Gonzales, "Is the grandmother able to care for this child?"

"No, your honor. She would like to be allowed to meet her grand-daughter, but it will need to take place at the nursing home."

"I see." The judge tapped his pen against the desk blotter. "Do you have anything else?"

"Yes. We also conducted a search of the premise where Harriet, the younger, was living. We found no sign of drug paraphernalia or criminal activity. It would appear that the minor child has, in fact, been living alone in the house for some time. The neighbors report no strange activity and were unaware of the girl's situation." He paused and looked at Ari, before he continued. "Oddly, the lower level of the home contained bird droppings, feathers, and what appeared to be a roosting box."

I should have cleaned up, Ari thought. She twisted her fingers together, forcing herself to stay still. *One hundred, ninety-nine, ninety-eight, ninety-seven, ninety-six...*

"I believe I'd like to speak to Ari in my chambers." The judge stood up and stepped down from his bench. "Ari, please come with me." Ari stood and Jenks rose with her. "No need to come with us, Mrs. Jenkins. We are just going to take a little break. We'll be back in a few minutes."

***

"Ari, this nice lady is my clerk, and I'm going to ask her to stay with us while we talk. Okay with you?" the judge asked.

Ari knew it wasn't an actual question. She nodded. *Scrupulous, S-C-R-U-P-U-L-O-U-S, I must be very careful, precise, and exact.*

"Make yourself comfortable. I just want to get to know you so I can be sure that we are making good decisions."

Ari sat and tucked her feet beneath her chair. There was no window in this room. *I wonder if Nevermore is waiting on the courtroom windowsill. Two, four, six, eight, ten, twelve, fourteen, sixteen, eighteen.*

"Do you need a soda?" the clerk asked.

When Ari didn't answer, the judge rubbed his chin and began. "You must be a very brave girl. Didn't you get lonely?"

Ari raised and lowered her shoulders in a shrug.

"Tell me about your mom."

"She's beautiful, and she knows how to French braid my hair."

"That sounds like a nice mom. How did you feel when she didn't come home?"

One hundred, ninety-nine, ninety-eight, ninety-seven, ninety-six, ninety-five. Ari looked down at her shoes and then up to the judge. He was watching her closely and not speaking. Ari squirmed in her chair.

The judge waited.

"I wasn't surprised," Ari whispered.

"But why do you think she didn't come home?" The judge removed his glasses and placed them on his desk next to a framed picture of a woman and three kids.

"Is that your family?" Ari asked.

The judge glanced at the picture and smiled slightly. "My daughter and grandkids." He touched the picture frame and adjusted its position with one finger. "I need you to talk to me, Ari. I want to help you, but I need to get to know you."

I don't think so. If you know me, you won't help me. "I think my mom was just having too much fun to remember to come home. I'm sure that if she hadn't..." Ari stumbled over the words "gotten hurt she would have come home soon. She always does. Maybe she was on her way when she fell."

"Perhaps, but the truth is you were living alone in that house a long time, weren't you?"

"Yes, but the crows..." Ari stopped in mid-sentence.

The judge waited.

"Okay." Ari lifted her eyes to look directly at the judge. "It was lonely, and it was kind of scary, but it was better than when Jerry lived at our house. My mom is an addict. I know how to take care of myself."

She glared at the judge. *Three, six, nine, twelve, fifteen.*

The judge didn't flinch. He flipped open a folder and carefully scanned a page. "Jerry Switzer. Died about nine months ago." He looked up. "At your house, when you were alone with him."

Cautious, C-A-U-T-I-O-U-S. Be careful! "Mom came home right after. I wasn't really alone."

"But you were the only two people in your house when he died?"

He's testing me. Ari nodded. "Yes, I was doing the dishes, and he fell down the stairs." She let her eyes go wide and fill with tears. "That was pretty scary. There was a lot of blood. I think he was drunk."

The judge crossed one leg over his knee and leaned forward. "Ari, I want to do what's best for you. It would help if you will talk to me. I need you to answer my questions so that I can do my job. Do you understand?"

Ari managed a nod.

"Tell me about the birds."

Wary, W-A-R-Y, be on your guard against danger. She twisted her hands together and studied the floor. *I need to tell him something.* "Is it against the law to have birds in your house?"

"Of course not." The judge chuckled. "But it sounds like the birds at your house were allowed to be free. That's a bit unusual."

"But not illegal," Ari protested. "Lots of people have birds for pets."

"Not illegal," he conceded. "But not sanitary, which means—"

"I know what it means," Ari interrupted. "Birds poop. They can't help it, you know. I let them go outside every day. It's just that they like to sleep in the house with me." Ari clamped her hand over her mouth. *Damn, damn, damn! Stupid me. I'm talking too much!*

"What kind of birds are they?"

"Crows," she whispered.

"How many and how long have they lived in your house?"

"What does it matter? I can't live there anymore, and they can't either." She crossed her arms defiantly and glared at the judge.

"Try to remember that I'm on your side, Ari. Now answer my question."

"Two. I found them on the spelling bee day. Morrigan had a broken wing. She couldn't fly. I fixed it, but it took a while to heal."

"Interesting. Go on."

"Crows mate for life, you know. So, Nevermore had to stay with us, too." Her eyes wandered to the bookcases. "I got a book from the library and learned what to feed them and stuff. They're my friends."

"Do you know where they are now?"

"I let them out yesterday morning and told them I wouldn't be back to that house." Her lower lip trembled a bit. "I think they'll be all right."

"I'm sure they will," the judge said kindly. "You are a unique child, Ari. Most impressive."

"Unique isn't always good. Usually, it just means different."

"True, but I think, in your case, it means uncommon." He stood up. "Are you ready? Let's get this done."

***

"Mrs. Jenkins, during the time that this child…" he paused and smiled at Ari. "This remarkable young lady is a ward of the court. I expect the system to function in her favor. She deserves a decent, safe home, preferably in the same school catchment zone. Through no fault of her own, Harriet has come into our care, and," he looked sternly at each person in the room, "the circumstances of her prior living situa-

tion are not to be discussed with the press. Do I make myself clear?"
Everyone in the room nodded.

"Of course, your honor. Social Services never discusses our clients
with the media." Mrs. Jenkins rifled through the papers in front of her.
"I've contacted the nursing home, and Mrs. Blimm, would like to
meet the girl ASAP."

"The girl is Harriet Blimm, Mrs. Jenkins."

Jenks flushed and resumed. "Fortunately, the Wallace family," she
glanced toward Ari, "—where you stayed last night—have agreed to a
temporary placement. They are only certified as short-term care pro-
viders. However, we have worked with them in the past and, since
they are willing to open their home to Harriet, we consider this to be a
good solution. Harriet will be able to finish the school year, and it will
allow time for a complete assessment."

"Ari," the judge looked directly at her and ignored the others in the
room, "what do you think?"

Not a choice. "Sure. They seemed nice."

"All right. That's settled, then. Ari, you are now a temporary ward
of the court. As such, Mrs. Jenkins will assure that you are well cared
for and that a full assessment of your case is completed in a timely
manner. If no relative is found able and willing to provide for you during this ninety-day assessment period, you will come before the court
again. At that time, you may be made a permanent ward of the court.
Do you understand?"

"I think so."

"Do you have any questions?"

"Um — maybe, just one." She dug her fingernails into her palms
and then forced herself to look at the judge. "Doesn't permanent mean
forever?"

The judge chuckled and shook his head. "Not in this case. It means
until your eighteenth birthday."

Ari bit her lip and nodded. *Seven years. That's a long time.*

***

Pulling away from the curb in front of the Wallace house, Mrs. Jenkins asked, "How are you doing, Ari?" She glanced at the slumped figure next to her. "Are you settling in?"

Settling, S-E-T-T-L-I-N-G, derived from "settle," to adjust, to establish residence. Ari bit her lip and tapped her fingers against her denim-clad knees. Mrs. Jenkins reached over and stopped the tapping.

"Is there a problem at the Wallaces'?"

Ari shook her head from side to side and moved her knees away from the social worker's touch. "No. It's fine."

"How's school?"

Ari shrugged.

"Is Mr. Wallace still giving you a ride each morning?" Jenks waited a moment and then continued, "Ari, I need you to answer my questions."

"Why? What difference does it make?" Ari twisted in her seatbelt as far as she could and stared out the window.

Jenks sighed loudly. She tried again. "Are you worried about meeting your grandmother?" She waited a minute and continued, "She is quite excited to see you."

"Right!" Ari shoved her hair out of her eyes and shot a glare at the social worker. "Like where has she been all my life, if she's so happy to see me?"

"There are two sides to every story, Ari. I think you need to let your grandmother tell you hers."

"How long is this going to take?"

"The nursing home is in Baron. About an hour's drive."

Ari pulled her backpack onto her lap and extracted a book. "Okay, I'm just going to do my homework." She opened the book and dropped her eyes to the page.

Mrs. Jenkins stayed silent as she drove. She watched as Ari chewed a fingernail and seldom turned a page.

***

They checked in at the reception desk and were escorted to a small living room area.

"Mrs. Blimm," their escort said, "your visitors are here."

The elderly woman who sat in a wheelchair lifted her hand as they approached. "Hello, Harry," she said. "I don't suppose you recognize me, but I'd know you anywhere."

Ari stopped a few feet from the chair and studied the woman. She seemed very small and frail, scarcely bigger than Ari herself. The woman's cropped white hair stood around her face in a soft halo of curls. Her dark eyes shone with tears. Ari considered her carefully and then stepped closer. "You had a cat, a big white cat."

The tears overflowed. "I did. Duchess. I can't believe you remember that." She brushed the tears from her cheeks. "You were such a little, bitty thing, that cat was almost bigger than you."

"I don't think I really remember you, just the cat."

"That's enough, Harry. Duchess was a memorable cat." She wiped a tear from her cheek and blew her nose. "I'm sure they told you, I'm your grandmother, your mother's mother."

Mrs. Blimm turned her wheelchair and rolled toward a sofa. "Come sit next to me, over here. I want to get to know you."

Ari looked toward Mrs. Jenkins, who waved her forward. She shuffled after the wheelchair and sank down in the farthest corner of the sofa. Sliding her hands under her legs to still their shaking, she closed her eyes and counted, *One hundred, ninety-nine, ninety-eight, ninety-seven, ninety-six.* Opening her eyes again she examined her grandmother. "You don't look like Stacy," she declared.

"Stacy took after her dad's side of the family," Mrs. Blimm agreed. "You look more like me than your mother did."

Ari stared at the old woman. "I do not!" she blurted.

"I wasn't always old." Mrs. Blimm chuckled a bit. "Don't worry, you don't look the way I do these days." She took a ragged breath. "Do you always call your mother Stacy?"

Trap, T-R-A-P, any device, trick, or the like to catch a person un-aware. Ari stood and walked to the window. She kept her back turned to her grandmother as she answered. "I do now. My mother is dead, you know," she sneered.

"Ari," Jenks spoke sternly, "there is no need to be rude."

"She has a right to be angry." Mrs. Blimm hushed Jenks. "Life hasn't exactly been easy, has it, Harry?"

"My mother called me Harry, too. I don't like it."

"Did she? She never really liked the name Harriet, but you were too old to change it when she took you away."

Ari whipped her head around and glared. "What did you say? What does that mean—took me away?"

Mrs. Blimm took a deep breath and let it out in a long sigh. "When I learned that your mother was dead, I didn't cry. Did you?"

Jenks widened her eyes and started to speak. Mrs. Blimm waved her to silence.

Ari considered her response and finally shook her head. "No. Not really."

"I wasn't happy to hear of her death. Stacy was my daughter and I loved her, but her actions have hurt so many people, I was relieved to hear that it was over and that you were alive and well." She closed her eyes for a moment before continuing. "You are very young, but I am your only living relative. However, I am quite ill and unable to take you into my home and raise you."

Ari stayed perfectly still. She kept her eyes locked on the old woman's hands and refused to meet her gaze.

"I think you should hear what I have to say." Mrs. Blimm turned to the social worker. "I'd like to be alone with Harry, Mrs. Jenkins. If you don't mind? Just for an hour or so; the nurses will call you when we are finished."

Jenks sputtered a bit about inconvenience and legality, but in the face of Mrs. Blimm's calm determination, she agreed to leave the room after assuring Ari she would be right outside.

***

"The most important thing I can tell you is that I love you very much, Harry."

Ari glared at her grandmother. "I told you, I hate being called Harry!"

"I understand you are quite angry. And that's okay," Mrs. Blimm said quietly. "What would you like me to call you?"

"Ari." She squinted her eyes as if she expected to have to fight for her choice.

"Okay, I can remember to do that." Mrs. Blimm coughed and wiped her mouth with a Kleenex. She took a moment to catch her breath. "Did your mother tell you about us, your grandparents?"

"She told me you were dead." Ari watched as the old woman bit her lip and then nodded slowly.

"She didn't like you much," Ari added.

"That's certainly true." She took in a deep breath. "She was our daughter, our only child, and we loved her but, in the end, we didn't like her much either."

Ari shifted and kicked her feet against the coffee table. Curiosity overcame her reticence to know this blunt woman. "Why? What did she do?"

"Your grandfather and I waited a long time to have a child. Your mother was born when I was forty. She was a beautiful baby, but—looking back—I know that she was never content or happy unless she was getting her own way. Stacy knew exactly how to get what she wanted. I suppose we spoiled her. But at the time, we just wanted her to be happy." She paused and shook her head slightly before continuing, "This is not a conversation I'm comfortable having with my twelve-year-old granddaughter, but I'm afraid you need to know a few things and I don't have much time."

Ari watched her grandmother closely as she said, "I already figured out that Stacy mostly loved Stacy. I mean, when she was home, she was a lot of fun and we did all sorts of stuff, but I know she used drugs and drank too much. They said she was drunk when she died."

Mrs. Blimm stretched her hand toward Ari. "Sit closer and allow me to tell you a few things."

Ari waited quietly. She didn't move closer.

"Stacy struggled in school. I don't know exactly what was wrong. Now, I look back and I think she must have had a learning disability of some sort. Perhaps if we'd recognized that, things would have been different." She shook her head again and continued, "Instead, by the time she was in high school she was running with a wild group. First it was just skipping school and talking back. That quickly escalated into drinking and then drugs. We tried to make rules. However, our rules had no effect on her behavior. She began to stay out later and later." She sighed and shifted in her wheelchair. "At fifteen she disappeared. Your grandfather and I reported her missing. The police knew her and the crowd she ran with and were sure she'd simply run away." Mrs. Blimm wiped away a tear. "Eight months later she appeared one night. Just walked into the house and sat down at the dinner table as if she'd never been gone."

Mrs. Blimm coughed again. A nurse opened the door and looked in. She waved him away, saying, "I'm fine."

She pointed at a water cooler in the corner. "Ari, please get me a drink of water from the cooler over there."

Ari complied and sat down, just a bit closer than before. She stayed quiet, waiting for the old woman to resume her story.

"Your grandfather said, 'You're late for dinner.' I just stared for a moment and then blurted out, 'You're pregnant!'"

Ari recoiled. "Pregnant with me?"

"Yes. Stacy laughed and told us she was due soon. It was obvious she was still using. We knew that. You could see all the signs." She motioned toward her glass of water and Ari handed it to her again. "I took her to the doctor the next day and he confirmed that you were due to arrive any day. On the way home, we stopped at the mall and purchased everything I could think of that a new baby would need. Stacy seemed interested, and I remember thinking that was a good sign. We talked about names for the baby and even laughed a little. I didn't ask questions about where she'd been and what she'd been doing. I didn't want to scare her off."

Mrs. Blimm's coughs racked her body.

Summoned by sound of the cough the nurse stepped back into the room. "You need to get some rest now, Mrs. Blimm," he commanded.

"Not yet. I need a few more minutes with my granddaughter." She shooed him away with a gesture. "There will be time enough to rest in my grave."

Ari's eyes widened and she winced.

"Don't worry, dear. That's just an old expression. I'm not ready to die yet, not when we've just found each other." She settled herself more comfortably in her wheelchair. "The very next day, Stacy's labor started. I drove her to the hospital and stayed with her until you were born. You were the prettiest baby I've ever seen. Lots of hair and the biggest eyes." She paused and smiled at Ari. "I fell in love with you instantly."

"Did my mom want me?" Ari interrupted.

Mrs. Blimm pursed her lip. "She was only fifteen, not even sixteen yet for a few days. I'm sure she wanted you, but she was afraid."

"She didn't even hold me, did she?" Ari demanded.

"We placed you in her arms and she looked at you. Then I took you back and she fell asleep. The nurse carried you away to the nursery to be weighed and checked, and I stepped out to call your grandfather and get a cup of coffee. When I got back to Stacy's room she was gone. We alerted security and they searched, but she'd managed to dress and walk out. Her image was caught on the security camera. She just walked out the door of the hospital, turned left, and vanished."

"But…" Ari protested. Then stopped unsure of what she wanted to ask.

"We took you home. Your grandfather insisted on naming you Harriet, after me, and then we called you Harry."

"Stacy said she named me Harriet for that book about the spy girl."

"Your mother was very good at storytelling, Ari."

"I know." Ari inflated her cheeks and blew out her breath, making a puffing sound. "She was a big, fat liar." *L-I-A-R. A bitch that doesn't ever tell the truth.*

Mrs. Blimm looked at Ari and made the same puffing sound. She shook her head. "I wish I could deny that, but you know her better than I did. You may not be old enough to be told your mother's story, but…"

"I'm plenty old enough," Ari interrupted. "I know she was an addict and a terrible mother."

"Yes, she was. We asked the police to search for your mother and even hired a detective. She knew how to hide. They never found any trace of where Stacy went."

Mrs. Blimm hesitated before continuing, "It was lovely having a happy baby in the house. We delighted in everything you did. I started a journal so that when your mother came back, she'd know all about you. The time flew by. Babies keep a family remarkably busy, an exceptionally good kind of busy."

"So, what happened?"

"When you were two years, nine month and eleven days old, Stacy came back."

Mrs. Blimm wiped away a tear and took a deep breath.

She stayed quiet so long, Ari wondered if she would finish her answer.

Ari tapped her fingertips against her leg in time to her thoughts. *One hundred, ninety-nine, ninety-eight, ninety-seven, ninety-six, ninety-five, ninety-four.*

Mrs. Blimm resumed, "We let her in, of course, and showed you off. Your grandfather and I were so proud of what a wonderful child you'd become. I think we expected Stacy to want to be part of our family."

"She didn't, did she?"

"No, she didn't." Tears filled grandmother's eyes. "Instead, she insisted that you were her child and that we had no right to keep you. She had CPS on her side. They gave her custody and allowed us to have visiting rights." Mrs. Blimm dropped her head, slumped over, and allowed her tears to flow. "We saw you one more time and then you were gone, across the state line and away from us. This time the police wouldn't help at all. Legally, Stacy was within her parental rights."

"That sucks!" Ari blurted.

"Yes, it does," Mrs. Blimm agreed.

She chuckled. "I suppose a grandmother should tell you not to use that word, but it does seem like the only appropriate word."

Appropriate, A-P-P-R-O-P-R-I-A-T-E, suitable for a particular purpose, person, or occasion. "Exactly," Ari declared. She slid closer to the wheelchair. "So, how did we end up in your house if you didn't know where we were all this time?"

"You have a good mind, Ari. They told me you were very smart. And that is a particularly good question. I think I can explain. Your grandfather and I have owned that house for a long time."

She looked down at her hands and took a deep breath before continuing, "My mother, Stacy's grandmother, lived there until she died, and then her sister, my aunt, lived there until about four years ago. By that time, your grandfather was gone, and I was in this dang nursing home."

She coughed deeply.

Ari waited for her to finish and handed her the glass of water.

"Thank you, dear." Her grandmother composed herself and returned the glass. "I admit I completely forgot about the house sitting there empty. But I'm guessing Stacy remembered the house. We'd never even cleaned it out, so it was easy for her to move in with you and setup housekeeping. I'm glad it gave you shelter, but I've been kicking myself for not having anyone check on the house. If I'd remembered, I would have found you before your mother died."

"So how did she know it was safe for us to live there?"

"My life has never been hidden; I'm quite sure your mother has been watching and checking on her dad and me all these years. Stacy was willing to do whatever it took to get what she wanted, so even if she didn't care about me or her dad, she'd have wanted to know I wasn't going to steal you away from her."

"Okay." Ari nodded thoughtfully. "I guess I can see that. Stacy was always very worried about what I told anyone. When we moved into that house, I was nine. She didn't want anyone to know where we lived. Stacy even tried to get me to use my dad's last name instead of my own but all my stuff from the other schools had my real name."

"Do you see your dad?"

Ari snickered. "Of course not. I don't really have a dad; that was just one of Stacy's stories."

Ari and Mrs. Blimm smiled at each other. Ari dropped her eyes first.

Mrs. Blimm stretched out her gnarled hand toward Ari. "Is there any chance I can get you to call me Grandmother, or Grandma, or Granny, or something?"

Ari hesitated and then clasped her hands together in her lap. "What did I call you before Stacy took me away?"

Mrs. Blimm let her hand drop and said calmly, "You called me Mama and you called your grandfather Daddy."

Ari narrowed her eyes and studied Mrs. Blimm. She jiggled her legs up and down and fiddled with her hair. "I guess that makes sense. Babies don't know any better. But I used to call Stacy Mama, so I can't use that."

The door opened again. Jenks and the nurse bustled in.

"Ari," Jenks said, "it's time to say goodbye. I need to get you back to the Wallaces before dinner."

"And you need to rest, Mrs. Blimm," the nurse added, stepping behind the wheelchair and placing his hands on the grips.

"Don't be in such a rush, Jason," Mrs. Blimm admonished. "I need to say goodbye."

She held out her hand to Ari.

Slowly, Ari walked forward and placed her hand in the old woman's.

"Thank you for coming to see me and letting me talk. I hope you will come back to see me again soon and often," Mrs. Blimm said.

"I'll try." Ari looked over her shoulder at Jenks and then back to her grandmother. "If they'll let me."

"I'll see to it that they allow it, Ari." Mrs. Blimm fixed her stern gaze on Jenks, who gave an unwilling nod.

She turned her eyes back to her granddaughter and winked.

Ari grinned. "See you soon, Grandma." She leaned in and placed a soft kiss on the woman's cheek. "Thanks for telling me about my mom."

***

At school, everyone knew about the birds. The judge's order to refrain from talking about Ari and the crows had been breached, and Ari was pretty sure it was Toby's fault.

She complained.

Mrs. Jenkins told her to stop fretting about things she couldn't change.

Miss Charles assured her that the other kids would forget soon and move on to something or someone else.

Ari didn't believe either of them.

"Hey, Bird Girl," Toby hissed.

Her shoulders tightened, she clutched her pen and wrote "FUCK YOU" on the paper in front of her. Then, pressing hard, Ari scribbled over the words until they were obliterated.

"Caw, caw," Toby whispered.

Someone on the other side of the room whispered, "Caw, caw."

A snicker ran around the room. Her teacher ignored it.

Ari scrawled "I hate Toby Meyers" on her paper and drew dark circles around the words. She kicked the chair in front of her and hung her head, allowing her dark curls to hide the tears in her eyes.

"Stop annoying the other students, Ari. You need to keep your hands and feet to yourself," the teacher said sternly.

Ari sketched a knife plunging into the word "Toby." *Jackass, J-A-C-K-A-S-S. a stupid person, a dolt.* Ari wasn't sure if she meant the teacher, Toby, or everyone. She added blood pouring freely from the knife and added the word "DIE."

She turned to the window in the hope of seeing her crows.

"Pay attention, Ari!"

The teacher's voice jerked her eyes back to the classroom. Ari swallowed hard to stop the retort that was on the tip of her tongue. *I know Toby told everyone,* she thought. *His dumb dad's a policeman and Toby brags about knowing all the bad stuff all the time.*

She looked at the clock. *Fifteen minutes to lunch. I'll make him pay. If not now, someday soon.*

***

Living with the Wallaces was a pleasant surprise for Ari, not at all what she'd feared in a foster home. It was clean and quiet. Most days, Mr. Wallace gave her a ride to school even though it was only a short walk. Mrs. Wallace was always home after school and always had a snack ready.

The only requirements were that she had to help Mrs. Wallace pre- pare dinner —which really meant help, not cook, make her bed, put her dirty clothes in the hamper, and clean up in the kitchen if she made a snack for herself.

It felt good to have plenty of food. She could pack her lunch, so she didn't have to go through the free food line in the cafeteria. In- stead, she escaped to a quiet corner of the schoolyard with a book and her sandwich. If Toby and the others at school would quit teasing her, life would fine.

Miss Charles encouraged Ari to participate in the Regional Spelling Bee, but Ari refused insisting that she couldn't stand up in front of people who called her "bird girl." Mr. Comstock agreed that it would be for the best if Ari brought no more publicity to the school and Jess was sent instead.

The days crept by. Her ninety-day evaluation period would end with the school year. *Perhaps having to move to a new school would be a good thing. Transformation, T-R-A-N-S-F-O-R-M-A-T-I-O-N, a complete change in form, appearance, nature, or character.*

***

Her history book open, Ari sat at the kitchen table waiting for Jenks. She sighed.

"Everything okay, sweetheart?" Mrs. Wallace asked. "Are you worried about seeing your grandmother today?"

Everything is not okay.

Ari managed to look up and smile at Mrs. Wallace. "I'm fine. I like to visit my grandmother."

I miss Morrigan and Nevermore. I killed my mother. I found a grandmother and she's dying. Nothing is right.

If one more person asked Ari how she felt, she was going to explode. Meeting her grandmother for what had felt like the first time had been hard, but talking about it was impossible.

Strangely, Grandma seemed to understand. She didn't force hugs on Ari or ask stupid questions. Instead, she talked about all sorts of things. She was willing to answer any question and had lots of funny things to say.

Today was no exception. Grandma greeted Ari and asked the nurse to push her chair outside. Once the nurse settled her with a lap robe and gave them each a cup of tea, Grandma turned her face up to the sun and closed her eyes. Ari sat on a bench next to the wheelchair and waited.

"I love the sun, always have. When I was a little girl, all I wanted to do was be outdoors." A loud cawing interrupted her. Grandma's eyes popped open and she scanned the sky. "Crows are my favorite birds, Ari."

"Mine, too! They are so amazing!"

"Look." Grandma lifted a shaky hand and pointed to the hedge. "There are two, right there watching us." She sat with her eyes fastened on the birds. "Will you tell me about your crows, Ari?"

"Did the police tell you I was living with them?" Ari twisted a lock of her hair and chewed it. She glared at her grandmother.

"Among other things, yes. But I'd like to hear your story."

"I wasn't living with them. I just had to take care of her wing." She kicked at the gravel under her bench.

"A long time ago, when I first married your grandfather, I moved to this town and I had no friends. In the afternoon, I'd sit in the yard and read. One day a crow joined me. At first he stayed far away, but after a few visits he would come closer and closer."

Ari listened carefully, still chewing her hair.

"I called him Benedict."

"Why?" Ari dropped her hair and stared at her grandmother.

"I'm not sure. I suppose I'd read the name in a book and I'd liked it. Did you name your crows?"

"Morrigan and Nevermore," Ari admitted.

"Much more imaginative than Benedict."

"It's from a book, too. I didn't make it up."

"It's still an imaginative use of what you read, Ari. A particularly good use, I'd say."

"Tell me more about your crow, Grandma."

"It wasn't long until he'd eat from my hand and follow me around the yard. Then one morning, he dropped a shiny, gold button in my hand." Ari laughed aloud and Grandma smiled at her. "That's probably still the best present I've ever been given."

"What happened to Benedict?"

"I'm not sure. I saw him almost every day for a couple of years and then he was gone. He just stopped coming. I like to believe that he met a lovely lady crow, fell in love, and had a family with her."

"Crows are very loyal. He would have come back to visit you if he could have," Ari said.

"Do your crows come back?"

"Sometimes I see them at the school, but I don't talk to them." She tugged on her hair again, twisting it tight around her fingers. "Toby told everyone and now they all call me Bird Girl. If he knew I wanted to talk to them—"

"This Toby would make your life miserable, right?" Grandma finished.

Ari nodded. "He already does. He's so mean."

"Well, I suppose the thing a grandmother should say is something about understanding him and trying to be nice to him. But I think it is more important that you know that some people are just plain mean and there is nothing you can do to change them."

Her grandmother reached over and took Ari's hand. Ari sat very still. The crows cawed loudly. "I wish that was Morrigan and Nevermore, but crows only fly about fifty miles from their home. This is more than that, right?"

"Yes, but not much more. How do you know it isn't them?"

"They wouldn't hide in the trees. They'd come to me."

"Go to them, Ari' Grandma urged. "Perhaps they are afraid of me."

Ari searched the trees. *One hundred, ninety-nine, ninety-eight, ninety-seven, ninety-six, ninety-five.* "Okay," she whispered. She stood and moved toward the tree line. *Ninety-four, ninety-three, ninety-two, ninety-one, ninety.*

Ari stopped.

The crows cawed.

Ari stepped closer.

The crows burst out of the hedge and flew up, cawing loudly. They circled and dipped, flying around Ari in large swoops.

Ari laughed and sank to the grass.

The crows dropped to the ground and came to her side. She reached out her hands and stroked their heads. "Hello. I missed you," she said.

                                    ***

"Welcome back, everyone." The judge nodded to the group who were gathered to hear the findings of Ari's assessment. He smiled at Ari. "I hear you finished the sixth grade with top marks, Ari. Congratulations."

Ari blushed and kept her eyes on the tabletop.

"I'd like to keep this informal and comfortable. Ari, I'm going to ask you some questions, okay?"

As if I have a choice.

"First, however, I'd like to thank Mrs. Jenkins and CPS for their quick work and input. It is always important to conclude these matters as expediently as possible." He focused on Ari. "Tell me about your grandmother."

"Ah...she's nice," Ari said.

"I'm sure she is, but I need to know a bit more than that. How often do you see her? What do you talk about when you visit? Tell me whatever comes to mind."

"Our reports include a record of every visit, your honor," Mrs. Jenkins interrupted.

"I understand that, Mrs. Jenkins. But I want to hear what Ari is thinking and feeling."

He kept his gaze on Ari and waited for her to gather her thoughts. "Start at the beginning, Ari. When you first met your grandmother, did you remember her?"

Ari narrowed her eyes and shook her head. *Pitfall, P-I-T-F-A-L-L, a hidden danger. Be careful.* "No, I didn't recognize her. I was only like three the last time I saw her."

"Of course," the judge confirmed. "But now you've been to see her a couple of times a week." He flipped the papers spread in front of him. "For a total of fifteen visits. Is that correct?"

"I guess so."

Ari looked at Jenks, who nodded.

"What do you talk about?" The judge tapped his pen on the desk.

"Everything. She tells me about my mom and how to do stuff. Sometimes she tells me stories about herself and my grandfather."

"Does she talk about her situation?"

Oh, now I get what he wants. "Do you want to know if I know she's dying?" Ari glared at the judge. "Yes, she told me."

The judge ignored her anger. "Your grandmother has explained to the court that she is too sick to be made your legal guardian." He looked at Jenks and then focused on Ari as he continued, "Have you discussed what will happen after she dies, with either your grandmother or Mrs. Jenkins?"

Dead, gone, buried.

Ari shook her head, twisted her hair around her fingers, and forced herself to wait.

"You are an unusual girl in a very tough spot, Ari. You are an orphan, and when CPS was contacted, you were living in unsafe circumstances. It is the court's job to assure that nothing like that happens again. Your grandmother, Harriet Blimm, has approached the court with a plan that we are inclined to support."

He looked down, closed the top file, and opened another. "Mrs. Blimm has stated to the court that you are her responsibility and that she has every intention of fulfilling that responsibility."

Responsibility, R-E-S-P-O-N-S-I-B-I-L-I-T-Y, a burden of obligation.

Tears filled Ari's eyes. She brushed them away before anyone could see and drew a trembling breath. "She said I was a blessing, that she loved me," Ari declared.

Jenks took her hand and squeezed it.

Ari pulled away. She crossed her arms and held herself.

"Oh, Ari," the judge said. "You can be sure that your grandmother loves you and cares a great deal what happens next. I only spoke of responsibility in the legal sense. The arrangements your grandmother presented to the court for approval are proof of her love and caring. Allow me to explain."

The judge cleared his throat, adjusted his glasses, and began to read: "In regards to the well-being of minor, female, Harriet Blimm, the court has approved a petition of legal guardianship requested by said child's maternal grandmother. Effective immediately Cedric Danvers, Esquire, shall be designated the legal guardian of the minor child. As the legal guardian, Harriet Blimm will be his ward. He will have full control of decisions pertaining to her well-being, education, living situation, and finances, until such time as the minor child reaches majority."

He removed his glasses and looked at Ari, waiting for her to look directly at him, before he asked, "Do you understand?"

"Who is he, and where will I have to live?" Ari demanded.

"Both very good questions. Mr. Danvers is your grandmother's attorney." His eyes swept the room. "He is a well-known family law practitioner and is an advocate for children's rights. I have known him for many years, as has your grandmother, and I can assure you that he is a good man."

The judge looked at the vacant chair next to Mrs. Jenkins. "I expected him to be with us today. You will reside with him, and he will answer your questions."

He turned to the clerk. "Have we heard from Mr. Danvers today?"

The clerk shook her head. "No, your honor."

"In any case, Mrs. Jenkins, or another caseworker assigned by CPS, will continue to have regular contact with you to assure the court of your well-being."

Jenks spoke up. "If necessary, the Wallace family has agreed to continue as temporary foster parents for a few more days while the arrangements for Ari's care are completed."

"I'm sure this all seems very abrupt and strange, Ari. However, you are a very fortunate child. Not every case has such a fortuitous outcome."

Fortunate, F-O-R-T-U-N-A-T-E, lucky, receiving good from unexpected sources. I don't feel lucky.

The hearing room door burst open and slammed against the wall. Everyone jumped. "Mr. Danvers," the judge said, "nice of you to join us. I was just explaining who you are to Ari."

Ari swung around and took a good look at this person others had determined would be her guardian. *He looks like a chipmunk.* His reddish hair stuck up in a soft tuft. Small dark-rimmed glasses perched on his nose, and his brown suit's pockets bulged with hidden items.

Her eyes locked onto his.

He dropped his gaze first.

Cedric Danvers apologized for his late arrival and assured the judge that the necessary arrangements for Ari's care and housing were complete. There would be no need for additional foster care.

After the judge issued a few more instructions to Danvers and Mrs. Jenkins, he wished Ari luck and banged his gavel. The proceedings were over.

Ari found herself leaving the courtroom in the company of her new guardian. She followed him to the parking lot without speaking.

Ari's mind whirled with questions. Things were changing too fast. She clenched her fists and counted. *One hundred, ninety-nine, ninety-eight, ninety-seven.*

Mr. Danvers opened the passenger door of a big, shiny black car and waited for Ari to seat herself. He walked around and settled behind the wheel.

He sighed. "I'm sorry we didn't get a chance to meet earlier. I'd planned to be there and introduce myself before the proceedings, but..." He glanced at Ari. "Well, it doesn't matter. We are here now. Your grandmother would like to explain her decision to make our law firm, me specifically, your legal guardian. We'll go there now."

The engine purred. Cedric drove out of the lot and headed to the freeway.

One thousand, nine hundred and ninety-nine, nine hundred and ninety-eight... Ari was determined to stay silent for the long drive to the nursing home.

Grandmother was waiting on the front porch when they arrived at the nursing home. She held up her arms to embrace Ari.

Ari hesitated.

"I'm sorry I didn't tell you what I was planning Ari," Grandma apologized. She lowered her arms and watched her granddaughter. "Everything had to be done so quickly and I didn't want to disappoint you if I couldn't get the court's approval. Hear me out; I think you'll approve even though you weren't consulted."

She greeted Cedric with a smile and a warm hug. "Cedric, please push my chair down there where we won't be interrupted."

He moved the chair to the far end of the porch and arranged two wicker armchairs for himself and Ari. They sat.

Grandma coughed once. Took a breath, pursed her lips, and puffed out the air. Ari smiled slightly, remembering when she'd first discovered that she and her grandmother made the same sound when nervous.

Ari reached out and patted Grandma's hand. "Okay," she said. "I'm ready to listen."

"Good." Grandma puffed out another deep breath and began, "If it were at all possible, I'd love to have you come and live with me. But it's not." She dropped her eyes. Her lower lip trembled.

Ari nodded. "I know."

"I told the doctors that I would try anything—new drugs, a new treatment, anything, but they tell me the cancer is too advanced to be halted now. So, I needed to make arrangements. Arrangements that I believed would keep you safe and provide you with stability and a chance to have a happy life. I will not survive to see you become an adult and we have no other family, so I asked Cedric to become your guardian."

Cedric shifted uncomfortably in his chair. Ari turned her gaze on him and then looked back to her grandmother. "Why him?"

"A lot of reasons. I knew Cedric's father and mother. His father was my attorney. He helped us when Stacy took you away. So, Cedric has always known about you and about our family. I have watched Cedric grow up and become a good, caring person. I know he is honest and kind and I'm sure he will always be there to help you, no matter what."

Always, A-L-W-A-Y-S, every time, on every occasion, without exception. Even if he knows I killed two people? Ari could feel Cedric watching her. She kept her eyes on grandmother.

"You should know that the house you and your mother lived in will be kept as a rental property until you are old enough to inherit it. Then it will be yours to do with as you please. There is also a certain amount of money, in a trust, that will be used for your support and education. You will receive whatever is left when you are twenty-five."

"Does that mean you are paying Cedric to take care of me?"

"No, Ari. I would be willing to do that, because I think it is better to be in a loving home than in a foster care situation, but Cedric has declined any payment. He is a successful attorney with resources of his own. He is willing to do this because I am like an aunt to him, and he feels that you are part of his family."

Ari narrowed her eyes as she digested this information.

Grandma smiled at her. "I know you don't feel like he is your family, but I think—I hope—in time you will. You've shown me how strong and brave you are, Ari, and I anticipate that living with Cedric for a few years will—"

A rush of wings filled the air as the crows arrived and settled next to Ari.

Grandma laughed. "Cedric," she said, "meet Nevermore and Morrigan."

The birds turned together and looked at Cedric, who sat mouth agape. "Wow," he murmured, "they really are crows."

Ari and Grandma laughed at him. "I told you, Cedric. Ari and the crows will both be living at your house from now on."

"Cool," Cedric managed.

The birds clicked and cawed. Nevermore lifted himself off the porch floor and landed on Grandma's lap. Together Ari and Grandma stroked his head.

***

Her grandmother's decision had been right; living with Cedric was better than a foster home. Lucy, the housekeeper, was always there in the daytime. When she left at 7:00, Cedric was home. They ate breakfast and dinner together and often watched television in the evening. But his house was large enough that they could each maintain some privacy. They were cautiously friendly roommates.

Ari considered asking if she could go to camp again this year, but her grandmother had requested that they spend as much time together as possible, and so she decided not to ask.

Every weekday morning, a car picked Ari up and drove her to the nursing home to spend the day. Every evening Cedric asked after her day and her grandmother's health but he didn't push for details. On weekends, Cedric puttered around the yard, worked on papers in his home office, and took Ari out to dinner. Ari stayed watchful but she allowed herself to relax a bit.

At first Ari and her grandmother spent their hours together doing jigsaw puzzles and talking. Grandma asked questions about everything, and Ari learned to trust her. She answered any question Ari asked and told stories about her life and Stacy's.

July passed quickly.

In August, their time spent together changed. As her grandmother grew weaker and slept more, they talked less. Often, Ari read aloud from one of the books she found in the small nursing home library. When Grandma drifted off, Ari went into the gardens and waited for the crows.

Most days, they came to join her.

By the middle of August, it was apparent that her grandmother had little time left. She stayed in bed all day now and sometimes didn't wake the entire time Ari visited. On August twenty-seventh, Ari arrived to find her propped up in bed and wide awake. "Hi, Grandma." She leaned in and kissed her cheek.

"Ari." Grandma lifted her arms and pulled Ari in for a hug.

Ari inhaled the soft vanilla scent of the lotion the nurses rubbed into her grandmother's skin every day. She kissed the incredibly soft skin of her cheek and wiped a tear from Grandma's eye. "I'm here."

"Darling girl, I'm so happy to see you. Sit here." She patted the bed.

Ari sat.

Grandma reached for her hand. "I need to tell you some really important things, Ari."

Ari shivered. She accepted the offered hand and stroked her grandmother's delicate, paper-thin skin. *Incredulous, I-N-C-R-E-D-U-L-O-U-S, refusing to believe. I don't want to hear this.* Tears filled her eyes. "I never used to cry," she told grandma.

"I know, child. But tears are good. It means you are feeling something. Feeling something is very important. I know you've experienced more loneliness and sadness than most, but you need to forgive your mother, and more importantly, you need to forgive yourself. Nothing that has happened in your short life is your fault."

What about Jerry and Stacy? I killed them!

"It isn't easy to move on when you are young. But when you do, you will be happier." Grandma coughed and struggled to catch her breath. "Even that horrible boy, what's his name?"

"Toby," Ari supplied.

"Even Toby isn't important." Grandma smiled and squeezed Ari's hand.

"You will never have what others call a normal childhood, but when this part of your life is over, you can be anything you want to be. I promise."

She paused and caught her breath. "For now, allow Cedric to take care of your needs, try to be as happy as you can, get a good education, and allow yourself to enjoy things. Learn to make friends with others. It isn't right to be alone. Create a new family. Fall in love."

She lay back against the pillows and closed her eyes for a long minute. "I'm going to die soon, Ari."

Her eyes opened. She smiled and pulled Ari close in a tight hug. "I loved you since before you were born, and I will love you forever. When things are scary and hard, remember that."

Ari laid her head on her grandmother's shoulder and let her tears flow freely.

***

Four for a boy,

"Love sees sharply, hatred sees even more sharp, but jealousy
sees the sharpest for it is love and hate at the same time."
– *Arab Proverb*

Entering seventh grade felt like a new beginning to Ari. Despite
her grandmother's death, things seemed to be better.

Cedric had instructed Lucy to take her shopping for school clothes,
and for the first time ever, Ari felt that she looked like everyone else
at school. She had the right shoes and the right backpack. Even her
hair had been tamed.

She was relieved to find that Toby had not been assigned to any of
her classes.

Three weeks after school started, Ari sat at the dinner table eating
with Cedric. She felt him watching. *What did I do wrong?* She kept
her eyes down, not wanting to catch his eye. Usually he asked about
school, but tonight the silence felt uncomfortable, dense and heavy.

She cast about for something to say, and finally blurted, "How was
your day?"

Cedric rested his fork on his plate and answered. "Most of my day
was quite ordinary, but…"

Ari held her breath and counted: *one hundred, ninety-nine, ninety-
eight, ninety-seven, ninety-six.*

"This afternoon, I had a call from a Miss Charles." He picked up his fork and resumed eating. "I assume you know who she is?"

Ari nodded.

"And do you know why she called me?"

Damn it. What did I do? She shook her head.

"It seems there is a parents' night next week, and I, although I am not a parent, per se, was expected to respond to the notification and reserve a time with each of your teachers." He studied Ari. "Did you know about this?"

Ari considered her options. *Not worth a lie.* She answered, "Sure."

"Is there a reason why you didn't tell me?"

"I didn't know that you'd want to know about it." She shrugged. "Stacy never went."

Cedric nodded. "Ah, there is that. But, in the future, if you are given a notice for parents, I expect you to give it to me no matter what it pertains to, understood?"

"Sure," Ari agreed. *Intrude, I-N-T-R-U-D-E, to interfere without permission or welcome.* She dragged her fork through her mashed potatoes and nodded.

"All right then, tell me about Miss Charles while we finish our dinner. Then, I do believe Lucy provided us with ice cream for dessert."

***

After parents' night, Cedric began to ask more questions about her homework and her friends. Ari managed to be polite but was careful not to expose her feelings. She made every attempt to disappear as soon as possible, escaping to her room to read or study.

One Saturday morning, in early October, he suggested they go to the farmers' market. Ari tried to find an excuse not to go but failed. She pulled on her new red hoodie and followed Cedric to the car.

Bright red and orange trees shone against a cloudless blue sky. Ari searched for Morrigan and Nevermore. She hadn't seen them since her grandmother died, and she missed their company. *I wonder if they know where I live.*

"Beautiful day, isn't it?" Cedric opened her door and waited for her to climb in. "Are you looking for the crows?" he asked.

Ari's eyes narrowed. *How does he know?* She ducked her head and twisted her fingers.

Cedric half-turned and studied the empty sky. "I met the birds, re-member, and it's in all those court papers." He smiled down at her. "I bet you miss them." He raised his eyes and checked the sky again. "I hope they come back someday. I don't know if they will, but I hope they do. I think it's a remarkable connection you have with them." He chuckled. "But, when they come back, I don't want them living in the house. Deal?"

A giggle burst from Ari as she thought of the beautiful, clean house. Cedric grinned, waiting for her answer. "Deal," she agreed.

Cedric stuck out his hand, and they shook on it. "Okay, let's go buy vegetables." He shut her door and jogged around the car.

They wandered through the market in companionable silence, sampling the produce here and there. The smell of roasting nuts drift-ed on the crisp air. Cedric asked, "You like hot nuts?"

Ari shrugged, unsure of what a hot nut would taste like, maybe like popcorn.

"Come on, let's get a cone." He purchased the nuts and handed the paper cone to Ari. "Careful, they're hot."

The woman in the booth smiled at Cedric. "You've got a lovely daughter there."

"Thanks, I think she's pretty special."

Ari's heart thumped. She wanted to protest the woman's remark. She caught Cedric's wink and decided to let it drop. *Daughter, D-A-U-G-H-T-E-R, a female child as in relation to her parents. Parents, P-A-R-E-N-T-S, a father and mother. Nope, none of the above.*

Loud cawing caused them both to look up at the telephone wires. A row of crows looked down on the crowd. Ari shook her head at Cedric, disappointment shining in her eyes.

"How do you recognize your crows?" he asked.

"I don't know. I just do."

"Ari!" a voice called out. Ari turned and saw Miss Charles walking toward them. Ari waved.

Miss Charles smiled, first at Ari and then at Cedric. "Hi, Ari. Hello, Cedric. How nice to run into the two of you."

"Nicole." Cedric beamed. "How lovely to see you again."

The two adults grinned at each other. Ari looked back and forth. *Collusion, C-O-L-L-U-S-I-O-N, a secret agreement for fraudulent purposes. Obviously, this is not a surprise meet-up.*

Nicole Charles fell into step with them as they resumed their strolling. Ari pretended to be absorbed in choosing precisely the right nut to eat next but listened carefully. After a few minutes, Ari blurted, "Are you guys in love or something?"

Cedric caught Ari's shoulder and pulled her to a stop. "Nicole and I met at your school parents' night. We are attracted to each other, yes. I'm guessing I should have mentioned this to you instead of arranging this pretend accidental meeting."

"It's fine." Ari shrugged and rolled her eyes. "I don't care who you date." Ari increased her pace, crumpled the paper cone with the last of her nuts, and tossed it in the trash.

"I have something for you, Ari." Miss Charles reached into her pocket and pulled out Ari's gold bangle. "Did you forget that I had it?"

"No. I remembered." Ari accepted the bracelet. She traced it with her finger and then slipped it into her own pocket. *I was hoping I'd never see it again.*

Cedric and Nicole exchanged an uneasy look.

"Was that your mother's?" Cedric asked.

"I guess," Ari mumbled. She gestured toward one of the stands. "Are we buying tomatoes?"

"Sure. Want to pick them out?"

***

At first it was strange to have Nicole, as she insisted on being called, around Cedric's house so often. However, Ari soon grew to enjoy the dinners, evenings in front of the television, and the occasional outings they shared. Ari began to believe that she was safe.

Thanksgiving weekend, the crows came back. Ari woke early, confused by the sound of tapping. She sat up, swung her feet out of bed, and reached for her red hoodie before realizing that the sound wasn't someone at the door. The tapping came from the window. Ari rushed across the room and pulled the drape aside. Morrigan and Nevermore stopped tapping and squawked happily.

"Oh," Ari breathed. She pushed the window up. The birds flew away, circled, and returned to the window. "Hello." Ari stretched out her hands and touched her friends. Nevermore strolled across the sill.

Ari remembered Cedric's admonition. "Wait," she cried. "You can't come in. I'll come out."

She ran from the room, leaving the window wide open. Nevermore cocked his head, cawed, and clicked. Morrigan clicked back and flew into the room. Nevermore followed her.

Morrigan landed on the dresser and caught sight of herself in the mirror. She stepped closer and considered her reflection. Nevermore settled next to her. He strolled about, looking carefully at the bits and bobs. A small gilt frame captured his attention; he pecked at it and pushed it over. The noise startled the crows. They lifted off the dresser. Morrigan flew straight through the open window, but Nevermore settled back down. He plucked a shiny gold bauble from the dresser top, looked around once more, and flew out to join his mate.

Ari burst through the front door just as Nevermore sailed out the bedroom window. *Oops!* Ari sank down on the porch step and waited.

He flew to the rooftop, perched on the gutter, and surveyed the yard before joining Morrigan in the branches of a tall oak tree. At last, he cawed a long series of happy sounds and dropped to the lawn in front of Ari. Morrigan followed.

"I missed you so much! Where have you been?" The birds hopped to the porch and settled next to Ari.

They croaked softly as Ari stroked their shiny black feathers.

"I'm sorry you couldn't find me," Ari said. "My grandmother died, and the judge said I had to live here with Cedric until I'm eighteen."

Nevermore clicked back.

"It's okay," Ari said. "He's nice, and Miss Charles, I mean Nicole, is his girlfriend now."

Morrigan cooed deep in her throat.

Ari laughed. "I know, it's pretty weird, but it's okay."

***

"Remember that bracelet, the one Nicole had?" Ari asked.

Cedric lowered his newspaper and looked across the breakfast table. He nodded.

"I wore it the day before the crows came back, and now I can't find it. I…" Ari paused to take a breath and push down the fear of his disapproval. "I know I didn't lose it somewhere because I remember taking it off and putting it on that little tray Nicole gave me before I went to bed. It's where I keep it."

"Then I'm sure it is in your room. Perhaps it's under the dresser or caught on a piece of clothing. It'll turn up." He smiled and lifted his paper.

Ari stirred her spoon through her cereal. *One hundred, ninety-nine, ninety-eight, ninety-seven, ninety-six, ninety-five.* "I think someone stole it," she whispered.

"I find that highly unlikely." Cedric folded the paper and placed it next to his fork. "There is an old proverb that says, 'The very fact that we are looking for something usually stands in the way of our finding it'. Do you know what that means?"

Ari narrowed her eyes and thought hard before shaking her head.

"In this case," Cedric said, "it means relax. You're looking too hard and most likely searching for the bracelet over and over in exactly the same places. It would help if you thought about where it could be in a different way. Now finish your breakfast or we'll be late." He stood. "We need to leave in ten minutes."

She pushed her bowl away and followed Cedric out of the kitchen. "Great advice," she muttered.

"Don't forget to put the dishes in the sink for Lucy," Cedric called back. Ari grimaced. "And don't make that face."

"Shit," Ari mumbled. She returned to the kitchen and cleared the table. Carefully rinsing and stacking their breakfast dishes, she mused about how Cedric always seemed to know what she was thinking.

***

Toby called her "Bird Girl" whenever he got the chance. Ari continued to avoid him and his friends. She read in the library at lunch and didn't attend school functions. When spring arrived and the weather warmed, Ari moved outside with a book and her lunch. She discovered a picnic table at the far edge of the schoolyard partially hidden in a tangle of blackberry bushes. Often, Nevermore and Morrigan joined her and, if no one was close, she chatted with them.

Late in May, Ari sat reading when she was interrupted by the thump of someone sitting down on the opposite bench. Ari jumped.

"Hey. I didn't mean to scare you. I thought you were just ignoring me."

Ari took in the girl who sat across from her. A pale blue headband held the long, bright hair that dropped straight down her back. "You look like Alice in Wonderland," Ari said.

"Yeah, I know." The girl shook her head hard enough to make her hair fly about and frowned. "It's my mom's stupid idea. She thinks if I dress like a magoo, I'll act like a magoo."

Magoo. Ari searched her vocabulary but had no idea what the girl meant. She stayed quiet, watching for clues.

"I'm Angie Layton."

"Ari."

"Cool. What are you reading?"

Ari flipped her book over to show the cover.

"Wow! *Atlas Shrugged.* You must be smart. I wanted to check that out at my last school, but the librarian said it was only available to high school kids. Is it any good?"

Ari nodded.

"Don't you talk?"

"Of course I can talk." Ari's defensiveness colored her voice.

Angie grinned. "Don't get mad. My dad always says I talk enough for two people anyway. We just moved here, and since there are only eight days of school left, I get to wait until September to start. I'll be in eighth."

"Me, too."

"We live over on Lincoln, so I have to ride a bus. I'm not looking forward to that."

A loud cawing filled the air. Both girls looked up and watched a murder of crows circling and spiraling far above the table.

"I wonder what they're talking about," Angie mused.

"It's mating season," Ari answered. "Crows mate for life, so in the spring, the parent crows are urging their offspring from last summer to find a mate."

Angie stared at her. "Is that true?"

Ari nodded.

"How do you know so much about crows?"

"I just like them. I read a lot about them and…" She stopped. "So I know a lot," she finished.

The first bell rang. Ari gathered up her trash and stuffed it back into the brown bag. She stood and took a few steps toward the building, stopped, and glanced back over her shoulder. "Bye."

A grin split Angie's face. Her bright blue eyes twinkled. She lifted her hand. "Yeah, see you tomorrow. Same time. Same place."

***

In the final eight days of the school year, Ari learned to expect Angie to be at the table for lunch.

"What do you do all day?" Ari asked as they shared the homemade cookies from Ari's lunch bag.

"I just ride my bike around town, finding stuff."

"Like what kind of stuff?"

"Just stuff, like where the library is and who sells good ice cream, what movie they're showing—you know, just stuff. My mom is at work, so I'm used to entertaining myself."

"I used to be like that, but now Lucy expects me home after school."

"Who's Lucy?"

V-I-G-I-L-A-N-T, vigilant, watchful, alert to danger. "She's the housekeeper."

"Cool. My mom says we need one. Are you rich or something?"

Ari didn't answer. She stuffed her shaking hands under her legs and took deep breaths. *In through the nose, out through the mouth.* "I'm 'or something,' I guess." Ari didn't look at Angie. She pulled her hand out and twisted a lock of her dark curly hair around her finger as she considered how much to tell.

"Hey, don't worry about it. It's none of my business. I was just being nosy."

Nevermore landed on the table. Ari broke a piece off her cookie and held it out to him. She heard Angie's little gasp. Nevermore hopped closer and delicately took the crumb. He clicked a thank you, cocked his head, and winked at Ari.

"This is Nevermore." Ari broke off another small piece of cookie and gave it to the crow.

"Wow! That is so cool. Do you think he'd take a piece from me?"

"Try it."

Angie broke off a small piece of her cookie and held it out. Nevermore considered the morsel but didn't move toward her hand.

"Just lay it on the table. He doesn't know you, so he doesn't trust you."

Angie did as Ari suggested. She kept her eyes on the crow and asked, "You're the bird girl, aren't you? I saw all about you on the news."

"Don't call me that." Ari scowled.

"Sorry, Ari. I was just repeating what I heard."

"Well, don't. It's rude."

Angie nodded. "Okay. I'll never do it again, and I'll punch anyone who does." She drew a crisscross on her chest. "I promise."

Ari scoffed and cocked an eyebrow. "At this school, you'll have to punch a lot of people."

"I can do that." Angie turned to look at Ari. "So, there's only one more day of school. Do you want to hang out this summer?"

Ari's stomach flipped. She wasn't sure what that meant. "Yeah, I guess."

"Perfect! My mom has to meet your mom, and then they'll let me hang with you."

Dead, dead, dead. "Stacy died."

"Right, I knew that. Sorry again." Angie whipped off her Alice band and pulled her long hair into a ponytail. She secured it with her discarded headband. "Who's that guy I see that gives you a ride to school?"

"That's Cedric. He's my guardian."

"That should do it. My mom just likes to know who I'm hanging out with. Give me your phone number." She pulled her phone from her pocket and handed it to Ari. "I'll have my mom call your Cedric tonight. Okay?"

Ari nodded and punched Cedric's number and her own into Angie's phone. "I'm not allowed to bring my phone to school."

Angie took her phone back and pressed call next to Ari's name. "There. When you get home the call at twelve forty-seven is me. Now you have my number, and we can talk anytime."

***

Ari sprawled flat on the grass, one arm shading her eyes and the other beneath her head. Morrigan was in the evergreen with her fledglings. She cooed and clicked as they waited for Nevermore to return with dinner. Ari smiled, remembering how excited Cedric had been when the birds chose to nest in their tree. Every day, he and Ari had watched from her bedroom window—first the nest building, then discovering the six eggs, and finally the hatching. It wouldn't be long now before the babies made their transition to the ground.

"Hey, girl!" Angie's cheerful greeting caused Ari to sit up and wave. Angie plopped down on the grass. "What's up?"

"Just waiting for you," Ari admitted. "Cedric gave me some money for ice cream."

Angie gave her a thumbs-up. "Good old Cedric. On your feet, girl. Let's go get it."

Only a year ago, I was all alone, Ari thought. How could so much change in only a year? It seemed too good to last, but maybe it would.

When Angie's mom called Cedric, he'd immediately agreed they should meet one another. The Layton's invited Cedric and Ari to dinner, and everyone got along. It turned out that Angie's new house was only six blocks from Ari's. From the dinner on, the girls were together every day. Ari spent several nights at Angie's, and Cedric began urging Ari to return the invitation.

She'd never felt so safe, so surrounded by people who cared. She'd never had a friend before. She'd never been able to tell her secrets to anyone. *I can't tell all my secrets but maybe I could tell some of them.*

"Stop thinking so hard." Angie stood, grabbed Ari's hand, and pulled her up from the grass. "It's summer, and we have only weeks before school starts again."

***

The long, hot days of August arrived. Angie invited Ari to join her family at their lake cabin for a week. "It will be so much fun. You'll see," Angie assured Ari. "My mom said we could take our lunch out to the island."

"Do we have to swim to the island?" Ari asked. "I learned how to swim at camp a couple of years ago, but I'm not very good."

"Nope. We use the canoe. This is the first year I get to take the canoe to the island without my dad," Angie bragged. "I can teach you everything you need to know about swimming. We swim to our float. It's not very far."

Cedric agreed with the plan. "What a lovely idea. You will have so much fun. I'll tell Lucy to take you shopping for a new swimsuit tomorrow."

"She can come with us. My mom is taking me anyway. Let's buy matching suits; then everyone will know we're best friends." Angie giggled.

Ari blushed as she nodded.

"I don't think you need to worry about that," Cedric said, chuckling. "I haven't seen one of you without the other all summer."

FRIEND, F-R-I-E-N-D, someone who has your back no matter what, a person who will never hurt you, who has your best interests at heart. Ari felt her heart beat faster. She hugged her arms tightly around her body and tried not to allow Angie to see that she wanted to cry.

Angie threw her arm around Ari's shoulders. "Come on. Let's go tell my mom that Cedric says okay and that we need to go shopping."

They ran out, waving goodbye as the door slammed behind them.

Nevermore and Morrigan swooped low over their heads. Both girls called out a greeting. Nevermore circled and dropped something shiny on the sidewalk.

Ari slammed to a stop. "What the heck?" She bent down and picked up the offering. "This is my bracelet!"

"Are you sure? Where would a crow get your bracelet?"

"Good question." Ari thought a second. "It was on my dresser, and then it wasn't."

Nevermore perched in the tree over her head and gave a low gargling call.

"Is he laughing at you?" Angie asked.

"It certainly sounds like it." Ari shook her finger at the bird. "I think you stole this! Did you?"

Nevermore gave another caw deep in this throat.

"But how did you get in the house?"

Nevermore hopped along his branch and chortled again.

The girls laughed. Ari slipped the gold bangle over her hand and they ran off, waving again to the crow.

***

The lake was pure bliss. Angie was as good as her word and helped Ari gain confidence in her swimming ability. They used the canoe to take their lunch to the island every day and in the evening swam to the float to watch the stars come out. The week flew by.

On Saturday, they packed their last lunch and headed out in the canoe. When they rounded the far side to pull into their favorite beach, they found another canoe pulled onto the sand.

Angie scowled and put on her best pirate voice. " Arr, Bucko. There be a bilge-sucking scalawag on our shore."

Ari giggled. "Let's roust him out and send him to the briny deep."

"Right-o, there be no reason to share this island on our last day."

The girls paddled to the shallow water and leaped out to pull their canoe onto the sand. Angie shaded her eyes and looked about. "I see the bloke up there by the trees. Come on."

The boy lay sprawled in the sand, sound asleep, one arm over his eyes.

Angie poked him with her bare foot.

He groaned.

She poked him harder. "Wake up."

"Why?" The boy spoke lazily, without moving.

"Who are you? And why are you sleeping on our beach?"

The boy stretched and opened his eyes. "I'm Steve, and it's not your beach."

"Of course, it is. My dad owns this island, and that makes this is our beach."

The boy sat up. His level blue gaze took in Angie and Ari. "I doubt that."

"It's totally true," Angie said.

Ari nodded in agreement.

"Well," the boy said, "even if it is true, this is a beach and no one can own the beach."

"This," Angie pointed, "is a beach on my island, and you are not welcome here!"

"Why not?" He looked puzzled.

Ari watched as Angie narrowed her eyes and considered her response. "Because," she hesitated between words, "we are here to eat lunch."

"So, I'm not stopping you. And, anyway, I'm here to eat lunch, too." He stood up and shook his blond hair out of his eyes. "Are you guys sisters or something?"

"Yes, I'm Angie and this is my twin sister Ari."

"Nice. Why don't you look alike?"

"Not all twins look alike, stupid." Angie winked at Ari. "She's older. That's why her hair is a different color."

"Not true. It doesn't work that way." Steve shook his head in denial.

Ari giggled.

Steve laughed.

Angie looked chagrined and then joined in the laughter.

***

Ari and Angie sprawled across Ari's bed, discussing what to wear for the first day of eighth grade. "I hope we have at least some classes together," Ari said.

"Mom says we will." Angie sat up against the headboard. "I hope we see Steve. I know he's in tenth, but it's all on the same campus, right?"

"Yep." Ari picked up a green T-shirt. "I think I'll wear this with my white jeans. Nicole says it makes my eyes glow."

"If you wear that, I'll wear my white jeans and my pink T-shirt. We'll slay."

The girls slapped a high-five. Angie picked up the small framed picture next to Ari's bed and examined it closely. "Is this your dad?"

Obfuscate, O-B-F-U-S-C-A-T-E, to make obscure or unclear. Ari took the frame from Angie. She rubbed her shirt over the glass and set it back in its place. "I think so," she admitted. "I found it in Stacy's stuff a long time ago."

Angie sat up, crisscrossing her legs, and considered her friend. "He's good-looking. I like the frame. I wish I could call my mom by her first name. She'd kill me if I did."

"Stacy didn't like it either." Ari stood and grabbed Angie's hand to pull her off the bed. *Careful, don't tell too much.* "Come on, let's go see what there is to eat."

***

They rode the bus each morning but skipped it on the way home. Instead, they walked to Angie's house most afternoons to do their homework, and then Angie walked Ari halfway home. In the evenings, they stayed in touch by text.

I'm just like everyone else. BFF—Best Friends Forever.

The first school dance drew near. Their ongoing conversation was filled with Steve Sightings or SS, as they called them. He always waved when he caught them watching and often said, "Hey."

"Do you think Steve will be at the dance?" Angie asked.

"Probably. He's on the football team. I think all those guys go. Maybe he'll bring a date."

Angie sighed dramatically. "I'll die if he does. Mom says I'm too young to date," she complained. "They aren't going to let me do anything until I'm sixteen."

"I don't think I have to worry about dating. No one's ever going to ask me out anyway."

"Stop it, Ari. You're very pretty."

"Hey, lezzies!" Toby Meyers's jeering voice caused them to stop.

Ari spun around. "Shut the fuck up!" she yelled.

"Whoa." Toby raised his hands in surrender. "Just calling it like I see it. Didn't mean to offend you ladies." His friends slapped him on the back and hooted.

"Meyers, what's your problem? Don't you have a puppy to torture or something?" Steve separated from his group of friends and walked toward them.

"Just teasing, Wilson." Toby dropped his gaze and began to move off.

Steve turned his back on Toby.

Ari exchanged finger gestures with Toby.

Steve smiled at the girls. "Hey."

"Hey," Angie and Ari said in unison and grinned back.

"Thanks, Steve," Angie said.

"No thanks needed; it looked to me like Ari could handle that jerk on her own." He grinned broadly. "I gotta get to practice. You two coming to the game before the dance?"

"We wouldn't miss it, Steve," Angie cooed.

"Good. See ya." He turned and trotted back to his friends.

Toby muttered something and slouched away to rejoin his own group.

The girls watched Steve move across the field in silence until Angie sighed. "He's so nice."

Ari rolled her eyes. "And, cute."

"Ya, not like Toby. God! What a creep. Why is he always so terrible?"

Ari shook her head. "He just is. He's picked on me every year, and he gets away with it because his dad is some kind of big-shot policeman or something."

"Well, I hate him!" Angie declared.

"Me, too."

***

On Friday, they rode the bus to Angie's and, after great debate and with much laughter, the girls dressed carefully for the evening. "He probably won't even see us until the dance," Angie complained. She pouted her lips and carefully applied gloss. "Do you think Steve will dance with us?"

Ari's heart skipped. "I hear that most of the boys don't dance. They just stand around and watch the girls dance."

"Even the high school boys?" Angie pulled her hair forward over one shoulder. Ari did the same. "I will positively die if Steve doesn't dance with me."

"Steve who?" Angie's mom asked from the doorway.

Angie blushed as Ari answered, "Steve Wilson."

"Oh, the Wilson boy from the lake. I thought he was older than you girls."

"Just a little bit, Mom. Not that much. And anyway, this dance is for everybody. It's homecoming, remember? Steve's playing in the junior varsity scrimmage before the game."

"Sorry! I had no idea." She grinned and shook her head at the girls. "Daddy's ready to give you a ride to the school. He'll be waiting at the parent pickup at ten to give you a ride home."

"Yes, Mother." Angie rolled her eyes.

Ari took a last look at herself in the full-length mirror. "Do we look okay, Mrs. Layton?"

"You both look lovely. Now grab your jackets and go have a good time." She dropped a kiss on each girl's head.

This time Ari blushed.

***

At midnight, snuggled in bed with the television off, the girls reviewed the evening. "I quite think our evening was a success, Miss Blimm," Angie declared in a fake British accent. "That scalawag Meyers fellow seemed quite out of place."

"Indeed he did, Miss Layton. However, I dare say the young master Wilson was quite charming."

"When he asked me to dance, I thought I'd faint." Angie dropped her pseudo sophistication and giggled. "He is soooo cute!"

"He's really fine," Ari agreed. "His friends are, too. I like it that he introduced us to all of them as the A-Team."

"Marybeth was so jealous I thought she was going to puke." Angie studied her nails in the dim light from the adjacent bathroom. "Did you like dancing with him?" she asked.

"It was okay. That other guy, Cooper, is a better dancer."

"Hmm. Maybe, but Steve is—special. I hope next time he asks me for a slow dance. That's how you really know."

"Know what?"

"How much a guy likes you."

"Because he asks you to slow dance?" Ari sounded confused.

"Not just that," Angie said. "Because of how it makes you feel. And, if you don't want to stop dancing."

"You watch too much TV."

"Maybe. But it's in all the books, too. My mom always says she fell in love with my dad the first time they danced." Angie flipped to her side and punched her pillow into a more comfortable position. "I've got a great idea. Let's get my mom to buy us T-shirts that say A-Team. That place in the mall would do it."

Ari grinned. "Great idea. Maybe we can get black with fancy lettering." *I'm so lucky to have a friend like Angie,* she thought.

Angie let out a soft snore.

Ari realized Angie had fallen asleep. She lay in the dark, picturing Steve. *I wonder what it would feel like if he held me in his arms.*

Ari turned over and buried her face in the pillow. *Yearning, Y-E-A-R-N-I-N-G, a deep longing, often accompanied by sadness.*

***

Angie's mom was easily convinced to buy the T-shirts. The reaction at school was perfect. Marybeth turned green with envy and pretended not to notice their bejeweled shirts. The other girls clustered around them, laughing excitedly and chattering about the dance. Steve noticed and strolled over. He grinned at Ari and Angie and slapped hands, as he declared, "Way to go, A-Team!"

They decorated their binders and pocket folders and signed everything they could with the A-Team name. It wasn't long before even the teachers were calling the two girls the A-Team.

Steve and Cooper high-fived them whenever they passed in the hallways. Only Toby continued to make nasty remarks, and he was easy to ignore most of the time.

The holidays came and went.

Ari loved her new life as one of the 'in crowd' and seldom thought about the time before.

***

Cedric poured himself a second cup of coffee and sat back down at the breakfast table. "Your spring break is coming," he said.

"Duh—." Ari smirked.

"Right. Obviously." Cedric grinned and started again. "What I meant was, I think we should make some plans for your vacation."

Ari scooped up a spoonful of cereal and chewed slowly.

"I was thinking it might be fun to go somewhere?"

"Like where?"

Cedric cocked an eyebrow and mimicked Ari's tone. "Like maybe, Hawaii."

"Hawaii?" Ari laid her spoon down.

"Yes, you know, the island in the middle of the ocean with all the sun."

"Seriously?"

Cedric nodded.

"Wow! Could Angie come, too?"

"I'm not sure that would be a good idea." Cedric picked up his mug and stared down at the contents. "I thought we would ask Nicole to join us."

Ari froze. She inhaled, bit her lower lip, and exhaled with a puff. *One hundred, ninety-nine, ninety-eight, ninety-seven, ninety-six.*

"I asked Nicole to marry me last night."

Ari kept her eyes on the table. *Ninety-five, ninety-four, ninety-three, ninety-two, ninety-one.*

"What do you think, Ari?'

Ninety, eighty-nine, eighty-eight, eighty-seven, eighty-six. Ari picked up her spoon and stirred through the dregs in her cereal bowl. *Eighty-five, eighty-four, eighty-three, eighty-two, eighty-one.* She stood and carried her bowl to the sink.

She inhaled, forced herself to stop counting, put on a bright smile, and turned to Cedric. "Congratulations. I think it's great." She gave him a double thumbs-up. "So, Hawaii would be an engagement trip? Isn't it weird to take a teenager with you?"

"Not if the teenager is my almost daughter, who Nicole and I love very much," Cedric answered."

Almost, A-L-M-O-S-T, very nearly, but not quite.

"Besides," he continued when Ari didn't speak, "Nicole hasn't said yes yet. She wants to be sure it is okay with you."

"Why?"

Cedric frowned. "Why what?"

"Why," Ari challenged, "does she want to be sure it is okay with me?"

"Because..." Cedric paused.

"Because," Ari interrupted, "I'm the weird girl that might do something crazy."

"Whoa!" Cedric held up his hand, palm out. "Where did that come from? You are most assuredly not a weird girl."

Tapping sounded on the window over the sink. Ari muttered, "Oh yeah? You don't think it's weird that I talk to crows?"

She turned and pushed the window open. Nevermore bobbed his head in thanks and strolled across the sill.

"Ari, I don't think it's weird. I think it's cool."

She kept her face turned and stroked Nevermore's head. Morrigan arrived in a flutter of wings and cawed happily, demanding her share of Ari's attention.

Ari heard Cedric rise and go to the refrigerator. She forced herself to breathe slowly. *Why does Cedric need Nicole? He's already got me. Stacy always said, "Rule one, never trust anyone. Rule two, never ever trust anyone." She was right.*

As the birds watched, Cedric placed a small bowl of fruit on the counter. He took a stepped back to give the birds space.

The crows considered his offering and then hopped to the bowl.

"I bought a bag of pine nuts yesterday for your crows. They're in the pantry."

"Thanks," Ari muttered.

"I'll get them." Cedric walked away.

Nevermore selected a strawberry and hopped back to the window-sill with it. Morrigan chose a blackberry and followed.

Cedric returned and sprinkled a handful of nuts over the fruit. He pushed it closer to the open window.

"Ari," he said, "I need you to trust me. I have never lied to you, and I'm not lying now. I promised your grandmother I would protect you and take care of you."

Ari stiffened and kept her eyes fastened on the crows. *But...,* she thought.

"I am forty-five years old. I've never married, and I didn't expect ever to have a family. You have brought a whole new dimension into my life. Your grandmother was a good friend of my father's. I remember meeting your mother, and I've always known about you. I hope you realize how proud I was when I was asked to be your guardian."

Ari shot a quick glance at Cedric.

"I think we are getting along quite well. Don't you agree?" Cedric asked.

Nevermore croaked loudly and bobbed his head.

"I guess," she conceded.

"You do understand that I will always be here for you, right?"

Ari chewed her lower lip and managed a nod.

"When Nicole and I marry, you will have another person in your life, full time. Another person who loves you. You will always have a home with us. Always, no matter what happens."

Guarantee, G-U-A-R-A-N-T-E-E, a promise, an assurance. There is no such thing.

Ari moved the bowl to the outer sill; she stroked the birds again and closed the window. Nevermore gave a long series of clicks and chirps.

"What is he saying?" Cedric asked. "He sounds worried."

"Just that I better hurry up, or I'll be late to school." Ari avoided eye contact as she grabbed her backpack.

"Think about Hawaii. We'll talk more tonight."

***

"What's up with you, girl?" Angie asked. "Are you even listening to me?"

Ari stopped walking.

Angie took two more steps, looked over her shoulder at Ari, and turned back.

"Spill it, girl."

Ari crossed her arms in a tight self-hug. "Cedric asked Nicole to marry him."

Angie's eyes widened in surprise. "Wow!" She watched Ari closely. "That's a surprise, isn't it?"

"It's just stupid. I should have known better than to believe..." Her voice trailed off. She kicked a loose rock and started walking again.

"Believe what? He's always talking about her, and they go out on lots of dates. Didn't you believe they were in love?" Angie giggled. "I think it's romantic. It's like a movie."

"No, it's not! They're both old."

"Yeah," Angie agreed. "Cedric is pretty old, but Miss Charles is only thirty-something. She probably wants to get married so she can have a baby."

A baby! That's all I need. I'll probably have to take care of it all the time.

"Do you get to be a bridesmaid?" Angie rattled on and didn't notice Ari's lack of response. Finally, she came to the end of her excitement and asked, "When are they getting married?"

"Cedric says she hasn't said yes yet."

"What? Of course she's going to say yes. What's she waiting for?"

"My approval," Ari admitted.

"Your approval of what?"

"Cedric says she wants to be sure it is okay with me."

"Really?" Angie considered for a moment. "I guess it's kind of sweet. I mean, you and Cedric aren't like a real dad and kid."

"Right! Fake dad! Fake daughter!" Ari started walking again.

"Come on," Angie pleaded. "You know I didn't mean it like that. It's just not many dads ask for their daughter's permission to get married."

Ari bit back another retort. "I guess. But obviously, I have to say yes."

"You do, but it'll be okay. Miss Charles seems pretty cool, right? Didn't she help you before Cedric?"

Ari wondered what Angie had heard. She knew she'd never told her much about life before Cedric. "True." She changed the subject. "Cedric wants to go to Hawaii over spring break."

"Super! Can I come?"

"I'm working on it. Did you get that answer to the last algebra question?"

***

Ari managed to convince Cedric that it would be better if Angie came with them to Hawaii, but Mrs. Layton said no; Angie needed to attend a family birthday dinner. The girls protested and pouted a bit. However, in the end, Ari was flying to Maui, with Cedric and Nicole, without Angie.

"This is your first long plane ride, right?" Nicole asked as they waited to board.

"It's my first plane ride," Ari admitted. "My first real vacation."

Nicole looked rattled. "Of course. I think I just forgot because you seem so prepared. I always get a little nervous when I fly."

"Angie's been to Hawaii a ton of times. She told me what to bring and what to expect. And Cedric says there is nothing to worry about. He told me this airline flies to Maui every day."

Cedric chuckled. "Relax, girls. It's going to be a great week. Warm sunshine, big waves, giant turtles, maybe whales and dolphins." He stood up. "Come on, Ari. Let's go buy junk food and magazines."

"Go." Nicole grinned, waving them off. "I'll stay here and guard the bags. Bring me a PayDay."

As they walked to the nearest Hudson's, Cedric said, "I'm going to sign up for surfing lessons. Do you want to join me?"

"No." Ari shook her head firmly. "You better take Nicole."

"I think she's looking forward to working on her tan by the pool. Let's you and I try it. I've always thought it looks like fun."

"No way."

"Come on, give me one good reason why?" Cedric cajoled.

"Because," Ari stopped and glared at him, "I can't swim in the ocean."

"Sure you can," Cedric encouraged. "It's just like at the lake, on-ly—"

"Only bigger and deeper and with sharks," Ari finished his thought.

"Okay. Got it. But if you change your mind, let me know."

Is he mad? Ari looked sideways at Cedric, who was whistling a bit while gathering snack food.

"Chocolate or chocolate?" Cedric held up two candy bars.

Ari pointed at the Crunch bar and focused on choosing a magazine.

Back in the boarding area, Nicole approved their purchases and asked, "Did he," she pointing her thumb at Cedric, "convince you to try surfing?'

Ari shook her head, hoping her attitude concealed her fear.

"Told you Ari was too smart to say yes," Nicole told Cedric with a laugh.

Ari sat quietly, watching Nicole and Cedric talk together. *They never seem to fight, and they never drink too much. They never get angry, and no one ever throws anything. If they marry, will it still be like this, or will they change?* She sighed. *Maybe it will be all right.*

***

The hotel was more beautiful than Ari could have imagined. Built right on the sand at Wailea Beach, it seemed like something out of a movie. She sent a text to Angie—**WISH YOU WERE HERE**—adding a sad-face emoji.

Ari put the phone down when Nicole knocked on the open door that connected Ari's room to theirs.

"How's your room?" she asked. "Do you have everything you need?"

Ari grinned. "I have my own balcony!"

"Nice," Nicole laughed. "Change into your bathing suit and come on down to the pool. We are going to make plans and have a cocktail. Do you want us to wait for you?"

"Nope, I can find the pool. You go ahead."

Ari carefully closed the door and looked around. It was like having her own apartment. No one was watching; no one could see or hear what she was doing. No one would know when she was awake or asleep. "This is pretty nice," she told her reflection in the mirror.

Cedric had a list, and he scheduled something every day. Nicole teased him about never having time to relax. They drove the road to Hana and bathed in a waterfall, learned to snorkel, swam with the sea turtles, visited a pineapple farm, zip-lined, went whale watching, and visited a blowhole. The day Cedric took surfing lessons, Ari and Nicole learned to hula and went to the spa for mani-pedis. They all fell in love with shaved ice and ate it every afternoon. The days flew by.

On their last evening, Cedric reserved a table on the beach for the Feast at Lele. Ari and Nicole wore new Hawaiian dresses and tucked snowy white plumeria blossoms behind their ears — Nicole behind her left to indicate she was unavailable and Ari behind her right. Cedric looked handsome in his white linen slacks and Hawaiian print shirt.

They were greeted with orchid leis and Mai Tais and led across the sand. The white tablescloths rippled in the breeze. The scent of flowers was everywhere. "It's so perfect, so beautiful," Nicole said as she was seated.

Cedric smiled proudly.

Ari snapped pictures with her cell phone and sent a few home to Angie. She finished her virgin Mai Tai and watched the crowd. A boy about her age seated at the next table caught her eye. He smiled at her and raised an eyebrow. She started to look away, but then remembered Angie's advice about flirting and smiled back.

The setting sun turned the sky from blue to orange and then to purple. Candles, in hurricane lamps, were lit on every table. The fairy lights came on and illuminated the scene. Waiters moved in and out, serving the guests a lavish five-course dinner.

"I don't know what any of this is," Ari said, poking at a fish wrapped in parchment paper.

Cedric chuckled, "Me, neither. But so far, it's all good. Right?"

Ari took a small bite and swallowed. "I guess," she admitted.

The mournful wail of a conch shell sounded as a softly lit canoe arrived on the beach. Dancers and singers from Hawaii, Aotearoa, Tahiti, and Samoa came ashore to entertain the guests with chanting, singing, drumming, and dancing. Colorful costumes and elaborate headdresses swirled in a bright array of colors.

The night sky darkened, and a bonfire bloomed against the stars. Loud drumming announced the Samoan fire-knife dancers. Their oiled bodies glistened in the light of their twirling flaming war clubs. The crowd responded with cheers of excitement as the drumming intensified.

The dancers threw their clubs high in the air and caught them again and again. They whirled and stomped and rapidly passed flaming clubs through their legs and around their bodies in time to the ever-increasing speed of the drums.

With a final flourish, the drums stopped. In the sudden silence, the dancers dropped to their knees.

The crowd exploded into applause. Nicole and Cedric rose to their feet.

Ari sat spellbound.

Cedric glanced down and caught her eye. "Okay?" he mouthed.

Ari managed to nod.

They gathered their belongings and walked along the beach. Ari slipped off her sandals and allowed the waves to lap her bare feet as they walked in silence to their hotel.

Opening the door to her room, Ari turned to Cedric and Nicole, saying, "That was amazing, thank you."

"You're quite welcome. It's been a good vacation." Cedric slid his keycard into his door lock. "Sleep well, Ari."

He and Nicole entered their room and shut the door.

Ari stepped inside her room and crossed to the balcony. She opened the doors to be able to hear the waves one more night.

Her phone chimed.

She touched the screen. A text message from Angie appeared.

CAN'T WAIT 2 SEE U I HAVE SOOOO MUCH 2 TELL U

A string of happy heart emojis followed.

Ari typed back her own string—Hawaiian dancer, volcano, airplane, a clock face and a heart.

***

During the drive from the airport to the house, Ari sent a text to Angie — **B home in 30 Come over**. Her phone pinged back — **CUS**. Ari grinned.

She settled back and counted only the white cars that passed them as they drove home. *I wonder what Angie's big news is?*

Cedric turned into the drive.

Angie jumped up from the front step and waved frantically.

The instant the car stopped, Ari flew out of the car and ran to Angie. The girls hugged, laughing and talking, at the same time.

The crows arrived, swooping down, cawing loudly, demanding Ari's attention.

"Looks like everyone missed you, Ari," Cedric said.

"You've been gone sooooo long," Angie whined. "So much has happened."

"Tell me," Ari commanded.

"First, come get your stuff out of the car. Then you can talk all you want," Cedric interrupted. He pulled Ari's suitcase from the trunk and set it on the driveway. Morrigan flew to the bag's handle and gave a long series of greeting caws as she bobbed up and down.

"I'm glad to see you, too, Morrigan," Ari said, reaching for the suitcase. "We'll be right back. Come on, Angie. Let's dump this in my room, and then we can talk out here in the yard with the birds."

Cedric stood with Nicole, watching the girls carry bags into the house. "Sometimes, I still can't believe that I live with a girl that talks to birds. Do you think she's happy?" he asked.

"I'd say so. Ari is not like most teenage girls. She's had to overcome a lot in her short life. But she's doing great," Nicole assured him. "She's getting excellent grades, has made friends, and she's about as well adjusted as you can expect with fourteen-year-olds."

"She won't be fourteen until next month."

Nicole laughed and patted his arm. "Don't fret. Cedric. She fine. She'll stop talking to the birds when she doesn't need them anymore."

***

The girls sprawled on the grass in the backyard and shared a bag of pine nuts with Morrigan and Nevermore. The birds stayed close, bobbing and strutting, clicking and cawing. Ari stroked their heads and ran a finger down their backs.

"What's your big news?" she asked Angie.

Angie held out a nut to Nevermore, who plucked it carefully from her fingers. "I like it that Nevermore trusts me now."

"Right. Don't stall around. Spill," Ari said.

"I went to the movies while you were gone."

"Big whoop. That's not news." Ari turned to face Angie.

Angie looked down at her lap and twisted her fingers together. "Steve kissed me," she blurted and quickly added, "We're going together now."

"What?" Ari's eyes opened wide in surprise. "How did that happen? I thought you weren't allowed to date until you turned sixteen."

"I'm not, but I don't tell my parents everything." Angie wrapped her long hair around her fist and twisted it into a messy knot on top of her head. "I didn't lie. I just didn't tell them everything. They know Steve and I are friends."

"I was only gone a week. What happened?"

"Remember, a bunch of kids from school agreed to meet at the movies the Saturday you flew to Hawaii?"

Ari nodded.

"Well, I didn't have anything else to do, so I went. The movie was pretty good. After that, we went to the Taco Bell." Angie dropped her gaze to the grass and fidgeted with the fringe on her shorts.

Ari prompted, "And, then…"

"And then, Steve walked me out to my dad's car and asked if he could come over the next day."

Ari nodded her encouragement.

"And now he comes over every day. And he says he thinks I'm beautiful and he wants me to go with him. I said yes, and then he kissed me," Angie finished in a rush.

"Wow!" Ari held out a pine nut to Nevermore. *One, two, three, four, five, six, seven, eight, nine, ten.*

Angie tapped her fingers impatiently. "So? What do you think?"

I think you're just like Stacy. Ari bit her lip and averted her face as she handed another nut to Nevermore. She took a deep breath, struggled to grin, and forced herself to high-five Angie. "I'm not even surprised that he likes you. You are gorgeous, and he's been flirting with you for months." *I thought he was flirting with me.*

"Not really," Angie demurred.

"Yes, really. What does your mom say?"

Angie giggled and rolled her eyes. "You know the usual junk—Steve is a very nice boy. We like his parents. It's good to have friends, but you're too young to have a boyfriend—that kind of stuff."

Angie stood up and brushed off the seat of her jeans. "Come on. Mom said you could come for dinner and spend the night."

Oblivious, O-B-L-I-V-I-O-U-S, unmindful, unconscious, unaware. Ari shook her head. "I need to unpack and all that stuff."

Angie pleaded, "But I want to tell you everything. Besides, Steve and Cooper are going to come over tonight, and," she paused before adding, "Mom bought all the stuff for ice cream sundaes."

"I'm kind of tired. I'll probably go to bed early."

"The time change goes the other way, Ari. You can't be tired." Angie stretched a hand down and pulled Ari to her feet. "Cooper thinks you're cute. Steve told me."

The crows flew to the big pine tree.

Ari stumbled. "He said what?"

"You heard me, girl. I said I could only do stuff in a group, and Steve said, 'That works. Cooper thinks Ari's cute.'" Angie grinned. "Got it?"

"Yes, I get it." Ari held out her arm to Nevermore.

He flew down to perch on her extended arm. Clicking softly, he rubbed his head against her skin and watched Ari closely. Ari kept her eyes on the bird as she answered, "Okay. I'll come over for dinner. If Cedric says I can, but I have to take care of my stuff now."

"K, see you in a couple hours." Angie grinned and slapped another high-five. She grabbed her bike from where she dropped it on the grass and rode off, waving over her shoulder.

Ari watched her leave.

Morrigan croaked from the tree as Nevermore clicked softly from her arm.

Ari spoke softly to Nevermore. "I know she's not Stacy, but I know what happens when someone gets a boyfriend." Nevermore croaked and crackled. "I told you before: I'm never going to have a boyfriend."

She stroked his head and back, raised her arm, and watched him fly up to join his mate.

"Ari," Cedric called from the house, "we need to go to the grocery. Want to come with Nicole and me?"

"No. Angie wants me to come over for dinner. I'm just going to unpack and then, if it's okay, I'll ride my bike over there."

"Sure. Put your clothes in the laundry and be home before it gets dark."

Relieved, Ari didn't argue or beg to spend the night at Angie's. She'd hoped to find a reason not to go at all, but having to leave early was almost as good. *I don't want to be anyone's pity date.*

***

Steve and Cooper showed up at the girls' lunch table almost every day. Angie walked between classes with Steve. Ari withdrew. Nearly every afternoon, she made an excuse to avoid the couple and rode the bus home alone.

"Hey." Angie grabbed Ari's arm and pulled her to a stop outside the English class. "It's been ages since you spent the night. It's Friday. Come over tonight?"

Ari shook her head.

"Why not?"

"I'm busy. I told Nicole I'd watch a documentary about crows with her."

Angie wrinkled her nose in disgust. "Ewww, that's no way to spend a Friday night."

"I like crows."

"Sure. But you know all about crows. You could probably write the script." Angie tipped her head to the side, causing her hair to fall in a bright cascade. She pouted. "Please? The A-Team hasn't had a meeting in a long time. We never get a chance to talk anymore."

"That's not my fault. I'm not the one that's always busy." Ari pulled her arm loose and stepped away.

"Ari, don't be like that. You're my best friend. I miss you."

Toby shoved past and snickered. "Sounds like trouble in lezzie-land. You two lezzies breaking up?"

Ari whirled around and glared at him. "Shut your fat face, or I'll shut it for you," she hissed.

"I'd like to see you try," Toby taunted.

Angie grabbed Ari's arm again. "Ignore him."

Ari jerked free. "Don't tell me what to do."

"Sorry. Toby's not worth getting in trouble over. Just come spend the night. It'll be like old times." Angie sighed. "I know I've been busy. Don't be mad. I promise it'll just be us tonight. I'll tell Steve he can't even call or text."

Ari nodded reluctantly. "Okay. I'll ask."

Angie threw her arms around Ari and squeezed. "Hurray! We'll have so much fun!"

Ari shut her eyes momentarily and breathed in the familiar citrus scent of Angie's shampoo. *Maybe we are still best friends.*

***

Mrs. Layton opened the door to Ari's buzz. "Hi, sweetie." She pulled Ari into a warm hug. "We've missed you around here. It's so nice to have my two girls together tonight. Angie's up in her room."

Ari smiled. "It smells good in here."

"Cookies," Angie's voice floated down from above. "Mom made your favorites."

"Thanks," Ari whispered.

"My pleasure." Mrs. Layton patted Ari on the shoulder. "Don't be such a stranger."

"K." Ari stumbled a bit. *I'm not going to cry.* She pinched her lips together tightly and stopped her feelings. Then she started up the staircase. *Thirteen steps to the top. Twelve, eleven, ten, nine, eight, seven, six, five, four, three, two.*

Angie seized her in a bear hug. "Were you counting the stairs?" she demanded.

Ari shook her head.

"Yes, you were. You can't fool me. I know you, but I love you anyway."

Angie's enthusiastic greeting forced a smile from Ari.

"My parents are going to the early movie. Mom ordered pizza for us." Angie added, "I got half sausage and half Hawaiian."

"Perfs."

Mrs. Layton called up the stairs, "Angie, we're leaving now. We'll be home before ten. Remember, no boys tonight."

"Yes, ma'am. I remember," Angie called as she crossed her eyes and waggled her eyebrows at Ari.

"I miss this," Ari admitted.

"You don't have to stay away. You're always welcome."

"No," Ari said slowly and carefully, "I'm not. When Steve is around, you only want to talk to him."

"Sometimes, I suppose. But not all the time. You don't need to be jealous. You'll always be my BFF."

"I'm not jealous," Ari protested. *Covetous, C-O-V-E-T-O-U-S, having a great desire to possess something that belongs to another. I'm covetous.*

"Whatever. I can't help it if Steve likes me best. He likes you, too. He thinks you're wicked smart, and funny, and nice and really pretty. Sometimes I'm kind of jealous when we talk about you." She studied her fingernails for a moment. "And, anyway, Cooper likes you better than me. You should give him a chance."

"Angie, I don't want a boyfriend!"

"Of course you do. Every girl does. You just don't know it yet." Angie grabbed a hairbrush from the dresser. "Let's braid each other's hair while we wait for the pizza. I learned how to make an awesome double French braid from YouTube. I'll show you how."

Angie's fingers against her scalp felt so good that Ari began to relax.

"I think we should get new A-Team shirts to wear for eighth-grade graduation," Angie said.

"Good idea. Let's do tank tops." Ari sank back into the comfort of her friend's full attention.

"It's going to be a great summer." Angie twisted Ari's thick, dark hair into an intricate pattern. "We'll be in high school next year. And, if you start dating Cooper this summer, we'll be the cool freshmen girls with the older boyfriends."

Ari admired herself in the hand mirror.

Angie plunked down on the floor and took the mirror. "Okay, now you do me."

"I don't know if I can do anything but a single braid."

"That works. Braid away."

***

The last few weeks of school flew past. Summer vacation arrived. Steve and Angie were always together. Ari made an effort to hang out with Angie, Steve, and Cooper, but it never seemed as much fun as when she was alone with Angie. She missed the time alone with her BFF.

In July, Ari sat on the patio reading. A long, dull summer day stretched before her. Cedric and Nicole had gone out shopping. Angie was busy with Steve. Nevermore perched next to her on the side table. He watched closely as she spoke. "Why don't I have any friends, Nevermore? What's wrong with me?"

The bird clicked deep in his throat.

"I know it looks like I have friends, but I don't, not really. You have Morrigan. Cedric has Nicole. And Angie — Angie's just like Stacy. She doesn't want to be with me now that she has Steve."

Nevermore cawed, flapped a wing, and hopped.

"No, I don't have Cooper. He hangs out with me because Steve told him to. I want someone who wants to hang out with me, someone who thinks I'm worth staying with. Like Angie used to do."

Nevermore cawed and croaked a long series of calls.

"I don't want to wait or be patient anymore. Angie thinks I'm jealous, but I'm not!"

Nevermore shook his head and flapped his wings, clicking and cawing.

"Well, maybe I am. Why should she get everything?"

Nevermore paced quickly, shaking his head and muttering soft calls.

"I know I have Cedric, but he has to take care of me. He gets paid to do it. Angie has a mom and dad and a boyfriend. I'll never have that." She scratched Nevermore's head. "All I have is crows."

Nevermore cawed a long burst of angry-sounding caws and croaks and flew to the roof. He turned his back.

"And, now I made you leave. I'm so dumb."

Nevermore didn't respond.

Ari laid her book on the table.

It's time to take care of this.

She stood and crossed the grass.

I'll give her one more chance to choose me over Steve. But I'll be ready if she fails my test.

Ari picked five oleander leaves from the shrub in the yard. She slipped them into her pocket and walked into the house. In her room, she removed the leaves from her pocket, wrapped them in a Kleenex, and placed them under a book on the bookshelf.

Ari picked up her phone and sent a text. **WYD**

She waited.

The phone buzzed.

"Hey, Angie."

"Hi. I started to text, but it was too much. Let's invite the guys over for TV and snacks tonight."

Ari sighed. She stared out the window and considered what to say. *Excluded, E-X-C-L-U-D-E-D, to be shut out, rejected.*

Angie continued, "I'll have Steve bring some salsa - his mom makes the best."

"Okay, but I can't spend the night."

"No prob. Come anytime. You can help me get ready."

"K." Ari clicked off and searched the yard for Nevermore and Morrigan. They were nowhere to be found.

She removed the oleander from under her book, took it down to the kitchen, laid it on the cutting board, diced it into tiny pieces, and placed the pieces in a plastic bag.

Carefully, Ari scrubbed her hands, the knife, and the cutting board with hot soapy water.

Nevermore cawed from the windowsill. Ari turned and looked at him. He shook his head back and forth and cawed long and loud.

"I don't care what you think," Ari responded. "She's a bitch, just like Stacy."

She turned her back on the crow, wrote a brief note for Cedric, and left the house.

Ari grabbed her bike and headed out. She knew it took exactly five hundred seconds to ride to Angie's. She didn't want to think anymore about her plan. *Five hundred, four hundred ninety-nine, four hundred ninety-eight, four hundred ninety-seven...*

***

"This is going to be so much fun," Angie bubbled, greeting Ari with a big hug. "Come on in. The guys will be here in a few. Do I look okay? I was going to wear those green shorts, but I think this skirt is better. Right?" She didn't wait for a response. "Steve is so sweet." She spun in a circle. "This is the best summer ever!"

I remember when you said that last summer was the best summer ever. Ari forced a smile. "What do you need me to do?"

"Put the chips in a big bowl and get down those cute little dishes from Mexico for the salsa. Steve is going to bring spicy salsa for himself and mild for us. Put the mild in the yellow bowl; otherwise, I'll forget which is which and burn my mouth."

"Got it," Ari answered.

The doorbell chimed and Angie flew to answer it. Ari stayed in the kitchen listening to the greetings and hearing Cooper say, "Knock it off or get a room."

"Yuck," she muttered as the threesome entered the kitchen.

"Yuck, what?" Cooper asked.

"Nothing. What movie are we going to watch?" Ari kept her eyes away from Angie and Steve.

"Don't know. Not a chick flick, I hope."

Steve laughed. "I'm just here for the chips—doesn't matter what we watch." He handed the bag he was carrying to Ari. "Mom labeled the containers. She knows the princess can't handle the spicy stuff."

Angie giggled and slapped him.

Ari removed the salsa from the bag. She opened the spicy first, poured it into the blue bowl, and placed it on the tray with the chips. "You guys, grab the sodas from the fridge. I'll bring this in."

"Doctor P for you, Ari?" Angie asked, her eyes on the contents of the refrigerator.

"Please." Ari opened the mild salsa and poured it into the yellow bowl. The other three trooped out of the kitchen laughing at some dumb thing Steve was saying. Ari slipped the baggie out of her pocket, tipped the chopped leaves into the mild salsa, and stirred it quickly.

"You need help in here?" Cooper popped his head back into the kitchen.

"All done. Just need to wash the spoon and put it away. You can take that in. Remind Angie the mild is in the yellow bowl."

"Will do. We wouldn't want to upset the princess."

Perfect. That was easier than I thought it would be.

***

Ari sat between Cedric and Nicole, on the hard wooden bench, as colorful chips of sunlight bounced around the chapel. A rainbow appeared on the white coffin. Ari heard Angie's mom sob and watched her dad pull his wife close.

The soft organ music changed, and a warm, rich contralto voice floated over the mourners. Ari recognized the lyrics to "Fly."

She squirmed in her seat. Cedric squeezed her hand.

Ari's thoughts drifted away from the chapel. *Angie would hate that song, but she'd love being the center of attention. The sad words are sure to make everyone cry. I guess I should cry, too.* She opened her eyes wide and blinked rapidly, forcing out a few tears.

Nicole handed her a Kleenex.

Everyone stood. Ari followed their movement. The pallbearers picked up the coffin and proceeded up the aisle. The Laytons followed, holding hands, and walking slowly. Ari let her hair fall forward until it covered her face. She kept her eyes down, away from the coffin, avoiding eye contact with anyone.

Mrs. Layton pulled her husband to a stop next to Cedric. She held out her hand to Ari.

Nicole urged Ari forward.

She had no choice. Ari accepted the offered hand and stepped past Cedric into the aisle to walk behind Angie's coffin. She swallowed hard as her tears welled up and spilled over. Real tears. *I'll miss you, Angie. But you got what you deserved.*

Outside the church, it seemed to Ari the whole school had gathered. The girls surrounded Ari, sobbing and hugging one another. Ari found herself the center of their attention.

"Oh my god! I'm so upset." Marybeth gushed. "What happened? I didn't even know she was sick."

The voices of the teenage girls clamored for attention, overlapping one another in their excitement.

"Oh, you poor thing."

"Angie was so pretty."

"She was always so nice."

"OMG!"

"Ari, are you alright?"

"It's so sad."

"What happened?"

Ari searched for a way to get out of the group of wailing teenage girls. She spotted Cooper standing with Steve. Cooper had his arm slung around Steve's shoulder. They were deep in conversation.

"Poor Steve," Marybeth gushed. "They were so much in love."

"It's so tragic," someone else agreed.

Ari pushed her way through the gaggle of girls and joined the boys. Steve was visibly shaking as silent tears rolled down his face. Ari reached out to hug him. He pulled her close.

"I just don't get it." Steve's voice broke. "She was just fine, and then she was dead. How is that even possible?"

Ari couldn't speak. She shook her head, shrugged her shoulders, and stepped back.

"Did she call you that night or anything?" Steve asked.

"Cooper walked me home after the movie. When we left, you guys were still eating chips and kissing and stuff. I thought she would call after you went home, but she didn't," Ari answered.

"We cleaned up the mess and washed the dishes, and I left. She looked happy and beautiful." Steve took a deep, trembling breath and finished, "I kissed her good night, and she waved at me from the doorway. Then the next afternoon, when I called, her dad told me she was dead."

"Unbelievable," Cooper murmured.

Shit, Ari thought. *I forgot about the dishes.* She said, "Her mom told me she woke up about two a.m. and found Angie on the bathroom floor. She told me she'd been vomiting and then collapsed. Her dad called nine-one-one, and they tried to wake her up while they waited." Ari shuddered and counted to ten before continuing. "At the hospital, they pumped her stomach, but it was too late. She never woke up or said anything. They did an autopsy and it was some kind of food poisoning—or maybe an allergy—, since we all ate the same thing, and none of us got sick."

Cooper slung his arm around Steve again and pulled Ari into a three-way hug. "It just doesn't seem possible. Nobody dies from chips and salsa," Cooper muttered.

Cedric stepped up to the group of friends. "It's time to go to the cemetery, Ari."

Ari squinted her eyes against the bright summer sun. It was hot in the graveyard. *A perfect day to go for a swim,* she thought. *When this is over, I'm going to take off this ugly dress and take a long, cool shower.* From the fake grass-covered mound behind the minister, the damp, moldy smell of wet earth rose. Ari wrinkled her nose and breathed through her mouth.

From the corner of her eye, she watched Marybeth reach for Steve's hand. *Bitch.*

Music swelled up from hidden speakers. Ari turned her attention back to the mourners. People were stepping forward and laying flowers on the coffin. *Was I supposed to bring flowers?* She turned to ask just as Nicole handed her two white roses tied together with a pink ribbon. Ari read the gold lettering on the ribbon, "Gone But Never Forgotten."

True enough, Angie. I'll never forget again that you can't trust anyone who says they love you. She laid the roses on the coffin and followed Cedric and Nicole to the car.

Morrigan and Nevermore flew down and walked behind her. *Except for you guys—I can trust you. Can't I?*

***

Five for silver,

"Crows are among the few animals that exhibit a social response to a dead member of their species. Though their caws may sound like heartbroken cries, such funerals aren't so much about mourning their fallen friends as they are about learning from their mistakes." – *mentalfloss.com*

Ari sat, legs crisscrossed, in the middle of her bed, staring at herself in the mirror hanging from her closet door. Her fingers moved quickly, twisting a loop of string in and out of a cat's cradle. She squinted her eyes, tipping her head from side-to-side, as she examined her looks. Dropping the string, she ran her fingers through her thick, dark curls and pulled her hair up into a high ponytail. She twisted her neck back and forth. "Definitely," she told her reflection. "A ponytail is better for high school. No more braids." She secured the ponytail with a pink scrunchie.

Her phone pinged and she glanced at the screen. *Just Cooper.*

She sent back a wave. The three dots appeared, and she waited for his message.

Wana go 2 the movies with us? Last weekend before school starts.

Ari typed back.

I'll ask C

She hopped off the bed, shoved her feet into flip-flops, and headed downstairs to find Cedric.

Nicole and Cedric sat on the patio, deep in conversation. They jumped when Ari pushed the screen door open. "Hey." Cedric greeted Ari with a smile.

"What were you guys talking about?"

Cedric exchanged a look with Nicole.

"Me?" Ari demanded.

Cedric sighed. "Yes," he admitted. "I know you said you wanted to be left alone, but I'm worried about you."

"Well, don't be." Ari's dark eyes flashed in anger. She inhaled through her nose, *ninety-nine, ninety-eight, ninety-seven, ninety-six, ninety-five,* and blew the breath out through her mouth with a small puffing sound. "I really am okay."

"I just thought it might be a good idea for you to talk to a grief therapist," Nicole interjected.

"I know it's your job, Nicole." Ari struggled to keep her voice calm. "But I can handle this. I've handled everything else, and I can handle the death of my best friend."

Cedric said in a soothing voice, "We know you can, Ari, but you don't need to deal with Angie's death on your own."

"I'm fine. Really!" Ari protested.

Nicole spoke up again. "We want you to consider it, Ari. You start high school next week, and it may be difficult to go back to school without Angie."

"Got it." Ari avoided Nicole's and looked only at Cedric. "Cooper and Steve want me to meet them at the mall for a movie. Okay?"

"Sure." Cedric stood up. "Do you want a ride?"

Ari nodded her head.

***

Later, as the boys walked Ari home, three abreast, Ari in the middle, Steve picked up a stick and tapped it against his thigh and then into the palm of his hand before speaking. "I can't believe Angie is gone." His voice quivered a bit. He cleared his throat. "She would have loved that movie."

"I know, man," Cooper admitted.

"Cedric wants me to go to grief counseling," Ari blurted out. *Shit! I didn't mean to tell them that.*

"Yeah, my parents set up an appointment for me to go, too," Cooper said.

Steve wiped a tear and said, "Mine, too. I started on Monday. I've been a couple of times."

"So, you guys think it's a good idea?" Ari asked.

"Maybe," Cooper said.

Steve nodded his agreement. "Can't hurt. Might help. It'll keep the parents happy." He tried to smile, but tears leaked, and he scrubbed them away with his fist.

Provident, P-R-O-V-I-D-E-N-T, providing carefully for the future. Ari said slowly, "Guess I'll have to go, too."

She pulled the scrunchie from her hair and shook her curls loose. A crow called out. Ari looked to the sky but saw no birds. *Deserted, D-E-S-E-R-T-E-D, abandoned, forsaken.*

Cooper took her hand and squeezed. Ari managed a smile and didn't pull away.

Soon Steve took her other hand, and the three moved as one toward Ari's house.

"Did the police come and talk to you guys yesterday?" Steve asked.

Ari and Cooper shook their heads.

Cooper answered, "Not yesterday, right after Angie died."

Steve stopped, pulling all three to a halt. "I think," he stammered, "that, maybe, they think I killed her."

"Nobody thinks that, man," Cooper insisted. "It's probably just 'cause you were the last one to see Angie alive. They're just tying up the loose ends of the case. They do that all the time on television. Right, Ari?"

Ari pressed Steve's hand as she spoke. "It was an accident. None of us, not even her mom, knew that she'd have an allergic reaction to something in the salsa."

"I know," Steve agreed, "but they kept asking the same questions in different ways, like were Angie and I having a fight? Did she flirt with anyone? Did I? Dumb stuff like that." He tossed the stick aside and kicked at a loose rock. "My mom is so upset. She says no one ever gets sick from her cooking. She keeps going over the recipe, trying to figure out what went wrong."

"Weird things happen all the time," Cooper said. "It'll be okay. You didn't do anything wrong."

"Cooper's right, Steve," Ari agreed. "Lots of weird, bad stuff has happened to me."

"I know all that in my head," Steve said, "but in my gut, it feels like something is wrong."

Ari snapped. "Of course something is wrong! Angie died, and that's wrong. There is nothing normal about a girl dying. You can't bring her back. So you have to let it go."

"That's exactly what my therapist said, but I need to know what really happened before I can do that."

I poisoned her! That's what happened. And you'll never know. "Come on. I need to get home. Cedric expects me before ten." They walked on in silence, each lost in their own thoughts.

***

On the first day of school, Nicole presented Ari with a soft pink leather journal and suggested she write her thoughts on its beautiful blank pages, promising that it would be hers alone and no one would read it.

That's not going to happen. I don't trust you. My thoughts are not for sharing. Ari accepted the journal and tucked it away on the top shelf of her closet after writing only one entry: "This journal belongs to Harriet Marie Blimm (Ari)."

***

Toby stepped into the classroom and asked loudly, "What's half an A-Team?" Without waiting for an answer, he finished, "A killer on the loose, that's what!"

Every student in Mr. Zarndt's homeroom froze. All eyes turned to Ari.

She blushed and felt her knees go weak. *What the fuck? I'm going to throw up.*

"Toby Meyers," Mr. Zarndt spoke loudly and firmly, "you will apologize to Ari this instant. We do not tolerate bullies in this school."

"Aw, I was just having some fun," Toby whined. "Ari doesn't mind. She knows I'm just teasing."

"Now, Mr. Meyers!"

"All right, all right." Toby turned toward Ari, rolled his eyes, and mumbled, "Sorry."

"Louder, Mr. Meyers. And make it sound like you mean it."

"I'm sorry, Ari," Toby articulated carefully.

Ari noted the glint of hatred in his eyes and muttered, "That's okay."

Mr. Zarndt glared at Toby. "See that that doesn't happen again." He turned away and raised his voice. "Everyone take your seats."

Ari half-listened to the day's announcements as she doodled in her notebook. *Does everyone think I'm a killer? Or is it just Toby? I need to shut him up.* She pressed her pen down hard and scrawled, "Shut Up! Shut Up! Shut Up!"

When the bell rang, Ari held back to be sure she wouldn't have to walk close to Toby. She found Cooper leaning, one foot on the wall, arms crossed, just outside the classroom.

Ari held up one hand. "Hey."

Cooper came to attention. "What's wrong?" he asked.

"Nothing," Ari muttered.

Cooper cocked one eyebrow and tipped his head to the left.

Ari giggled. "You look like Morrigan when you do that."

"Nice," Cooper said. "Bad enough to look like a bird, but I have to look like a girl bird." He flapped his arms like wings. "So, what's up?"

"Just Toby being an ass," Ari admitted.

Cooper grabbed her free hand. "Come on." He tugged her along as he walked. "It's the first day of a new school year. Don't let the jerk get to you."

Easier said than done. Ari pulled her hand free and walked beside him, without talking, until they reached her second-period class. She half-waved and left his protection.

Cooper said, "See you at lunch."

Ari didn't turn around or answer. Instead, she walked away in silence.

***

On Tuesdays, Ari rode her bike directly from school to Alex Summers's office. The idea of speaking to a nosy counselor was repellent, but after Jenks sided with Cedric, Ari had given in. She often had to wait and amused herself by naming the fish that swam in the large aquarium on one wall.

A few weeks into her appointments, Ari arrived to find a small boy sitting by himself. Silent tears rolled down his cheeks. He did not attempt to hide them or wipe them away. Ari dropped her backpack next to a chair and sat down. The boy didn't move.

"You okay?" Ari asked.

He shook his head, still silent.

Ari pulled a pack of Kleenex from her pocket and changed chairs to sit next to the boy. She tried to hand him a tissue, but he ignored her. Ari sighed. *Everybody's got problems; this is none of my business.* Ari rubbed her knuckles against her pant leg. *Five, four, three, two, one.*

"See that big yellow fish?" she asked.

The boy's head swiveled slightly to look at the aquarium.

Ari didn't wait for an answer. "His name is Walter. That little green fish is his friend Dorothy." She sneaked a peek at the boy. His eyes were glued to the tank, and his tears had stopped. Ari handed him the tissue again. This time he took it. "My name is Ari. Who are you?"

"Jimmy," he whispered.

"Nice to meet you, Jimmy." The yellow fish swam straight toward them. "Look, Walter is saying nice to meet you, too."

Jimmy almost giggled. "Fish can't talk."

"Who says?"

"Everybody."

"Phooey." Ari blew a raspberry with her lips.

Jimmy laughed. "You aren't supposed to do that!"

"You sure know a lot of rules for a kid your size." Ari turned in her chair and looked directly at Jimmy. "Walter and Dorothy talk to each other all the time."

Jimmy squinted and considered her carefully. "Why are you here? Do you know someone that died?"

Whoops! I just wanted to make this kid stop crying. Ari nodded her answer.

"Me, too. My grandma says my dad and I have to come here and tell this guy how we feel, but I don't like him."

"Yeah," Ari agreed. "I don't like him much either, but," she shrugged, "maybe it will help."

The inner office door opened. Jimmy turned to look. Ari kept her eyes on Walter and Dorothy.

"Ready, Jimmy?" a man's deep voice asked.

Jimmy slid out of his chair. He touched the side of the aquarium. "'Bye, Walter. 'Bye, Dorothy," he said and took a step toward the man. He turned back, "'Bye, Ari."

"'Bye Jimmy," Ari smiled and gave him a thumbs up.

"Come on in, Ari." Mr. Summers stood at the door, gesturing her into his office.

***

"Therapy sucks," Ari stormed to Cedric. "He just wants me to feel bad. If I don't cry, he says I'm bottling things up and need to let go. If I get mad, he tells me to control myself and respect others."

"Mr. Summers comes highly recommended."

"By who? Nicole?"

"By *whom*," Cedric corrected. "Yes, by Nicole and Mrs. Jenkins both. Ari, we are all just trying to make this easier for you."

One thousand, nine hundred and ninety-nine, nine hundred and ninety-eight, nine hundred and ninety-seven, nine hundred and ninety-six. Deep breath in. Deep breath out. Ari lifted her chin and looked directly at Cedric. She forced herself not to look away. "And, I appreciate everyone's concern," she said carefully. "I just want to forget about Angie and get on with my life."

"I don't think that is healthy. Nicole says you need to process your grief."

Nicole, schmole. "Right. Whatever Nicole says must be true." She unzipped her backpack and removed her books. "I'm going to my room to do my homework."

"Dinner in forty-five minutes," Cedric called after her.

Ari flung herself on the bed. *This is when it would be good to have a best friend.* She picked up her phone and started a message to Cooper, but changed her mind and opened her history book instead.

I didn't have a best friend before, and I don't have one now. It is better this way. But the questions have to stop. Mr. Summers and Ni-

cole are making me crazy. Ari put her earbuds in and turned on a podcast about serial killers.

***

The school year dragged on, one long day at a time. Without Angie, Ari didn't fit into any of the cliques. She kept her head down and her grades up. She returned to reading in the library during the lunch break, didn't join any teams or clubs, and only occasionally agreed to do something with Steve and Cooper. Cedric and Jenks insisted she continue with therapy, but the appointments dropped to once a month. Sometimes her appointment followed Jimmy and his dad's, and then she'd talk to Jimmy while they waited.

The pink journal stayed empty. The framed picture of her "maybe" father and Stacy's bracelet found a place in the back of her underwear drawer. Morrigan and Nevermore were once again her only friends.

After dinner, Ari went to her room every night, opened her bedroom window screen, and waited for the birds. They never disappointed her.

Cedric and Nicole scheduled their wedding for June. Ari eavesdropped as they made their plans and made her own plan for the summer. She approached them with it. "I've been thinking a lot about summer. I think I need to find something to do."

Cedric started to protest. Nicole laid a restraining hand on his arm.

"Mr. Summers agrees." Ari made eye contact with Nicole. "I'd like to go to that camp I went to when I was a kid. I checked, and I can be a cabin leader, you know, like a big sister." Ari turned to Cedric. "I wouldn't get paid or anything, but it would be free. You'd just have to buy my uniforms — that's just shorts and T-shirts."

"Ari, the cost is not an issue. If you want to go to camp this summer, you can. But why not find a camp where you can meet friends your own age?"

"I don't need more friends my age," Ari lied. "This camp is kind of a camp full of nerds. Since I'm a nerd, I think I can help the girls feel better about themselves." *Take that, Nicole. Perfect use of all your counseling bullshit.*

Nicole beamed. "Ari," she said, "I'm so proud of you. What a lovely idea."

"But, what about the wedding?" Cedric asked. "You're my best woman."

"I thought about that," Ari answered. "School ends on Friday. The wedding is on Saturday and the camp starts the following week. I have to be there on Monday to help with setup and take some training, so we'd only need to figure out what to do with me for the two nights in between the wedding and Monday."

"I was going to talk to you about that," Cedric said. "Grab a Coke and sit down with us."

Ari turned her back and walked to the refrigerator. *This is the tricky part,* she thought. *I think I can get them to let me stay here alone.* She opened the door, took out a Doctor Pepper, and sat, smiling at Cedric. *One hundred, ninety-nine, ninety-eight, ninety-seven, ninety-six, ninety-five.*

"Nicole and I would like to go back to Hawaii for a honeymoon." He smiled at Nicole and then at Ari. "Even I knew you wouldn't want to come with us."

Ari managed to laugh.

Cedric continued, "I talked to Angie's mom yesterday. She suggested that you stay with them while we are gone."

Ari's eyes opened wide. She caught her breath as her lips parted in dismay. "But…"

"I know." Cedric reached over and touched her arm. "That was my first reaction, too. Two weeks would have been too long, but two nights seems just right. I'm sure she'd be willing to drive you to the camp on Monday."

"There is a bus. It picks us up at the school." Ari interjected.

"Perfect." Cedric beamed.

"But Angie won't be there," Ari stammered.

Nicole interrupted, "I understand, Ari. It will be very different without Angie and very sad."

You understand nothing! Ari shoved her hands under her legs and dropped her head to stare at her feet. Her hair fell forward in a thick curtain of tangled curls.

"Mrs. Layton told me how much she misses seeing you, Ari," Cedric said. "She is grieving the loss of her daughter. Spending a little time with you might help her."

What about me? It won't help me. What if she knows I killed Angie? Ari silently shook her head back and forth in denial.

"I know you like the Laytons. They would love to spend time with you. Just think about it, okay?"

Ari nodded and lifted her head, her eyes dark with dread. "Would I have to sleep in Angie's room?" she asked.

***

Ari stood alone on the patio watching, the wedding guests circulate and chat. *This is so stupid. Committing to love someone forever is nuts. Ridiculous, R-I-D-I-C-U-L-O-U-S, absurd, preposterous, laughable. Why would everyone make a fuss about an event that means nothing at all? No one stays married forever!*

Cedric caught Ari's attention and beckoned her to join him on the grass. She summoned a smile and stepped off the patio. From high above, Nevermore cawed happily. Ari glanced up and caught a glimpse of his shiny, black feathers.

"How are you doing?" Cedric asked. "Sorry, there aren't any of your friends here. It must be pretty boring for you."

Friends? Ari Shrugged. "It's fine. Nicole looks beautiful."

Cedric's eyes sought out his new bride. "Yes, she does."

He looked back to Ari. "We'll be leaving soon. The caterer will clean everything up and lock the house. I put your bags in the Layton's car, and you can ride your bike over to Angie's —" Cedric caught himself, "over there — so you'll have it tomorrow if you want to hang out with Cooper and Steve."

Ari nodded and swallowed hard. *Not likely.*

"I'm going to miss you, Ari." Cedric struggled to maintain his usual composure. "We'll be gone three weeks. Then, on the next weekend, we'll drive up the camp to visit you."

"Got it," Ari agreed. "Have fun in Hawaii. Don't let a shark bite you." Ari grinned at Cedric.

Cedric chuckled. "I don't think we need to worry about that."

Nevermore cawed loudly as he swooped down from a tree and then rose high into the setting sun. Morrigan followed close behind.

Ari smiled at Cedric. "I think the birds are telling you congratulations and goodbye."

"Maybe." Cedric considered a moment and said, "Or maybe they are telling us to hurry up and get out of here so they can eat the cake crumbs."

Ari tagged along as Cedric and Nicole thanked people for coming. She allowed Nicole to hug her and let Cedric pull her close in a sideways squeeze. She blew bubbles over the happy couple and waved until the car turned the corner.

That done, Ari kicked off her shoes and hurried into her room to change out of the itchy dress Nicole had insisted made her look beautiful.

She pulled on a pair of shorts, slid her feet into her favorite flip-flops, and pulled her hair into a ponytail. Grabbing her phone, she squared her shoulders and hurried downstairs.

***

Ari cruised through the side streets, taking as long a time as possible to get to the Layton house. She held her head high and pushed all thoughts of Angie from her mind as she rode up the driveway and parked her bike next to the garage. *It's only two nights. I can do this.*

The kitchen door opened and Mr. Layton waved. "Hi, Ari. Come on in."

Taking a deep breath, Ari waved back and crossed the yard. She stepped into the kitchen and looked around. Nothing had changed. Everything was clean and neat. The smell of fresh-baked cookies hung in the air. A vase filled with daisies had been placed on the breakfast bar. Angie's school picture, in a silver frame, stood next to it. Ari took in the image and looked away, pressing her lips together in a hard, straight line.

Mr. Layton, noticing the look on Ari's face, draped his arm over her shoulders in a half-hug. "I know, but we like to see her there." He dropped his arm. "We put you in the downstairs guest room. Sharon thought that would be best."

"Thanks."

Ari turned at the sound of Mrs. Layton's voice. "Hello, Ari. Did you enjoy the wedding?"

Bewildered, B-E-W-I-L-D-E-R-E-D, completely puzzled, perplexed. What am I supposed to say? "Um, ya," she murmured, "it was nice, I guess."

"Angie was looking forward to seeing Cedric and Nicole marry," Mrs. Layton said. "She thought it was very romantic." She drew in a deep shuddering breath before continuing. "I made your favorite cookies. Just help yourself whenever you want. Actually, help yourself to anything."

Ari nodded. She hugged herself and tried to think of anything to say.

A strangled sob escaped from Mrs. Layton.

Ari held herself very still. *One hundred, ninety-nine, ninety-eight, ninety-seven, ninety-six.*

"I'm sorry," Mrs. Layton sobbed again. "It's just so strange to see you here without my Angie."

Ari held her breath. *I need to hug her.* She forced herself to turn and move toward Mrs. Layton's open arms.

They clung together for a long moment. Ari had no idea what to say. *I never meant to hurt you,* she thought. *I was just angry when Angie ditched me.* She pulled away from the hug.

"I know you miss her as much as we do." Mrs. Layton gave Ari a half-smile. "You two girls were so close." She took Ari's hand and gave a light squeeze. "I'm going to bed now."

Mr. Layton sat down on one of the bar stools, slumped, and covered his face with his hands. Ari stood, wanting to run but knowing she shouldn't. The sound of sobbing drifted back to the kitchen.

"It's hard, you know?" Mr. Layton said softly. "It's a cliché, but it's true—children should not die before their parents."

Ari stayed frozen in place.

"It's all so sad." He looked at her. "But, I guess you know that. Children shouldn't lose their parents early, either." He stood up. "Come on. Let's get you settled."

He walked out of the kitchen. Ari followed.

"Stay up as late as you want. The TV won't disturb us." He opened the door to the guest room and waved her in. "I'm going to go out for a walk. Be sure and eat some of those cookies. Sharon will be disappointed if you don't." He paused at the door. "You're a good kid, Ari. We are glad you and Angie were friends."

Ari kept her eyes averted and closed the bedroom door.

***

Ari heard Mr. Layton return to the house and listened as he climbed the stairs. She watched an old episode of *Buffy Vampire Slayer.* When she was sure everyone was asleep, she slipped out of bed and opened the door. The house was dark except for a night light in the kitchen.

Moving silently, Ari traversed the hall and climbed the stairs. She stopped at the top, holding her breath. Nothing moved. She tiptoed past the master bedroom and silently entered Angie's room. In the dim light of the moon drifting through the window, she could make out the familiar furniture. It smelled exactly the same. Angie's Baby Soft bath products lingered in the air. "Angie," Ari whispered.

There was no answer.

Ari shivered. *I don't believe in ghosts.* She crossed to the bedside table, opened the drawer, and pulled out the flashlight she knew was kept there. Covering the lens with her hand to diffuse the light, Ari turned on the flashlight and allowed her eyes to readjust. Angie's diary was not in its usual place. She removed her fingers from the lens and spun around in a slow circle.

Grotesque shadows leaped up the walls. Ari quickly pointed the flashlight to the floor. She examined the room. Everything was clean and neat. It looked as if they expected Angie to come home any moment. Ari opened the closet and found Angie's clothes hanging just like always. Her shoes were lined up on the floor. Nothing was out of place.

She quickly inspected the contents of each dresser drawer, being careful not to disturb anything. A framed picture of Angie and Ari, arms wrapped around each other, sat on the bookshelf next to Angie's jewelry box. Ari flipped the box open and then quickly silenced the ballerina that whirled to a tinkly version of the theme from *Swan Lake*. She held her breath, listening intently to be sure the sound had awakened no one.

The pink satin-covered box held nothing new. Ari slipped a small silver ring on her finger, closed the box, and returned it to its place.

Angie never used to hide her diary. Where is it?

Ari returned to the bed. She lowered herself to the floor and shined the flashlight underneath, back to the far edge and then up toward the mattress. The diary was held securely in place by a bed board. Ari pulled it out.

She opened it to the last page.

It was SOOOO much fun tonight. I think Ari is beginning to like Cooper. That will be good. He is almost as nice as Steve. I

kissed Steve 4 times. I like it. Tomorrow we are going to the mall. My tummy is kind of upset. I better not be getting the flu.

Nothing suspicious. Ari replaced the diary and returned it to its hiding place, then sneaked back to her room. As she reached the bottom of the stairs, she heard footsteps and froze.

Mrs. Layton called softly, "Is everything okay?"

"It's fine. I was just going to get a cookie. Sorry, I didn't mean to wake you."

"It's fine, honey. I don't sleep much anyway. Good night."

"Good night."

Ari went to the kitchen and took a couple of cookies.

***

The sound of voices woke Ari. Somewhere in the house, a door opened and closed. She stretched her arms over her head and listened for other sounds. The house was silent. *Maybe no one's home.* She threw back the comforter and stood up, pulled on her sweatshirt over her pajamas, made her bed, and headed for the kitchen.

Angie's mom smiled as Ari slipped onto a barstool. "Good morning, Ari. Did you sleep well?"

Ari pulled the sleeves of her sweatshirt over her fingers and nodded.

"Are you cold?"

Ari shook her head. "No, I'm fine."

Mrs. Layton lifted her mug using both hands, took a long swallow of coffee, then set it down. Ari could see her hands trembling.

I need to say something nice, Ari thought. But nothing entered her mind.

Mrs. Layton gave herself a little shake and asked, "What would you like for breakfast, Ari?" She gave Ari a slight smile that didn't reach her eyes.

Ari glanced around. A bag of bagels lay open on the counter. "A bagel would be great. I'm not very hungry." She moved to slide off the bar stool. "I'll fix it."

"No, no. You sit still. It's nice to have someone to fix breakfast for." Mrs. Layton turned her back to Ari and swiped at a tear. "Do you have plans for today?" she asked.

"I'm going to meet some of the kids at the river park and just hang out."

"Steve?"

"He'll probably be there," Ari admitted.

"That's good." She pulled the bagel from the toaster and spread it with a thick layer of cream cheese. "Is he doing okay?" She set the bagel on a plate and put it in front of Ari. "How about some juice?"

"Yes, please." Ari took a big bite and considered what to say. She chewed, stalling for time, *Ten, nine, eight, seven, six, five, four, three, two, one.* Then, finally, she placed her bagel in the center of the plate and wiped her lips with a napkin. "I think he's doing okay. He's going to a grief counselor, and I guess that helps. I know he misses Angie a lot." Ari kept her eyes on the bagel. "We all do," she added.

Mrs. Layton nodded. Tears welled in her eyes. She blinked them away. "Did you know the police questioned him?"

Ari nodded.

"They thought he might have—hurt Angie."

Ari's head snapped up. She looked directly at Mrs. Layton. "You don't think that do you?" she demanded. "Steve loved Angie—they were like the school sweethearts. Everybody thought they were so cute together."

"It's just so hard to understand what happened." She poured juice in a glass and handed it to Ari. "I never knew Angie was allergic to anything. We have salsa all the time, and she never gets sick."

Ari picked up the glass and held it to her mouth. *I don't think I can swallow.* She set the glass back on the counter and fiddled with her bagel.

Mrs. Layton noticed Ari's discomfort. "I'm so sorry, Ari. I shouldn't be talking to you like this. Please, forgive me."

"It's okay," Ari mumbled. "But Steve would never have done anything to hurt Angie." Ari stood up. "I'm going to go now."

"Don't you want the rest of your bagel?"

Ari shook her head.

"Will you be here for lunch?" Mrs. Layton picked up Ari's plate and turned to place it by the sink.

"No. If that's all right?"

"Of course it is."

"I think we might have a cookout for dinner and then a bonfire," Ari improvised.

"Send me a message when you know and have fun with your friends. Your bus is at six thirty tomorrow morning, so you won't want to be out too late."

"I'm going to get dressed. Thanks for breakfast." Ari turned to walk away. She glanced back over her shoulder and added, "It's really nice of you to let me stay here."

Mrs. Layton didn't smile, but she nodded.

Ari showered, pulled on shorts and a T-shirt, filled her backpack, and left the house. She mounted her bike, and rode, away from the river, back to her own home. *I'll just read all day, alone.*

By 3:00 p.m., Ari was bored. The crows had come and gone busy with their own lives. She made herself a peanut butter sandwich, using the last two slices of bread in the bread box, and took it out to the yard. She propped up her book on a rock and opened it to where she'd left off. Instead of reading, thoughts of Angie intruded. Ari found herself remembering every moment of their friendship. The sandwich dried out uneaten.

Nevermore landed on the table in a flurry of wings. Ari pulled off a piece of crust and held it out to him. "Maybe I shouldn't have killed Angie," she whispered.

Nevermore accepted the crust and dropped it, keeping his eyes locked on Ari.

"Don't worry. I didn't put poison on it."

Nevermore strutted back and forth, ignoring the crust. He cooed softly and settled himself on Ari's closed book, where he continued to coo and rattle.

Ari stroked his back. "I have to stop killing people that make me mad, Nevermore."

The bird bobbed his head and gave a single affirmative caw.

"What if the police figure out that it was oleander that Angie ate? I wouldn't be able to say it was an accident this time."

Morrigan flew down, grabbed the crust, and flew away. Nevermore didn't move.

"You're right," Ari said. "I'll never kill anyone again. I promise."

They sat together in silence until Morrigan came back, cawing loudly for Nevermore to fly with her.

Ari stood up. "I'm all right, Nevermore. You can fly with Morrigan. I'll ride over to the river park and then go back to Angie's house."

Ari gathered up her belongings and checked the house to ensure everything was ready for Cedric's return. She headed to the park on her bike.

A group of kids was gathered on the beach by the river, laughing and goofing around. Ari noticed Steve sitting off to one side by himself. She considered joining him, but Cooper, holding two red Solo cups, separated from the group and plunked down next to him. Steve accepted a cup and the two boys tapped glasses. Ari shrugged. *Weirdo, W-E-I-R-D-O, odd misfit, unconventional person, psychopath.*

Ari walked her bike up the river path and away from the party. *They aren't really my friends. They were Angie's friends.* She hid her bike off the trail and sat on a flat rock where she could watch the action but not be seen.

Three people in four years. That seems like a lot. Does that make me a serial killer? Ari picked up a stick and traced "Jerry, Stacy, Angie" in the damp sand. She scratched it out, obliterating the letters.

I'll be fifteen by the time I come home from camp. I can't allow death to follow me anymore. Ari lay back on the rock and let the sun calm her thoughts.

"I need to forget them all," she said aloud. "I need to make them go away." Ari dug in her backpack and found the tiny pocketknife Angie had given her to carve their initials on the picnic table at school.

Ari looked around and found three trees growing close together and away from the trail. She stepped to the backside of the first tree. Reaching as high as she could, Ari scratched a "J" in the soft bark. On the second tree, she marked an "S", and on the third tree, she carved an "A" and surrounded it with a heart.

"You all deserved what you got," Ari said, brushing the tree debris from her hands.

Ari counted off the paces from the flat rock to her memory tree cemetery. She picked up her bike and rode back to the Laytons' in the setting sun, sure that she'd be able to find the trees again if she ever wanted to do so.

***

Ari chose Intro to Psychology as her first-semester tenth-grade elective. When the class began with the concept of behaviorism, she was immediately hooked and began to look forward to school again— at least on Mondays and Wednesdays—, when the class met.

She was still being required, by Cedric, to meet with Alex Summers once a month, but even that was more tolerable now that she could engage him in the philosophy of different treatments and avoid talking about herself.

Slumped in the hard, ugly brown tweed chair, Ari defiantly put her feet on the coffee table. *Bullshit, B-U-L-L-S-H-I-T, nonsense, lies, full of crap.* She smiled, cocked her head slightly, and made eye contact.

He's so easy. "I was wondering," Ari began, "if you believe behavior is simply a response to environmental stimuli?"

"Ari, we've talked about this before. You know I'm a behaviorist. And, you know that nothing is simple. Are you worried about a particular behavior?"

Ari crossed her legs slowly, causing her short skirt to ride up and expose her slim thigh. Making Summers uncomfortable had become a game. "Noooo," she dragged out her response. "I was actually thinking about Cedric's response when I tell him I'm finding these sessions to be time-consuming and without value."

Summers pursed his lips and struggled not to show any reaction. "Why do you feel that, Ari?"

Because you're a douche. Ari twisted a curl around her finger and squinted as if in deep thought. She removed her feet from the table and sat up straight. "I'm hoping," she smiled at Summers, "that you will agree with me."

"How are things at school, Ari? Have you made any friends?"

"I know you are deflecting." Ari made eye contact and gave Summers a slight shake of her head. "However, if you are asking if I have a BFF, the answer is no. On the other hand, I do have lots of friends. Everyone knows my name." *The last part's true, at least.*

She embellished her answer. "I'm thinking about trying out for cheerleading, and I'm already on the debate team. I miss Angie, but life is moving on. Isn't that what these sessions were supposed to accomplish? Do you really think there is anything else we need to talk about?"

Ari waited. *One thousand, nine hundred ninety-nine, nine hundred ninety-eight, nine hundred ninety-seven, nine hundred ninety-six. Silence is always effective.*

Summers cleared his throat. "I'll call your guardian and discuss your request with him."

Ari nodded. "Sounds good." She stood up and straightened her skirt. She hooked her backpack over her shoulder and wiggled her fingers in a half-wave as she opened the door. Ari paused, listening for the sound of the click as the door closed before she grinned broadly.

"Ari, Ari, Ari!" Jimmy's excitement caused Ari's cynical grin to become a genuine laugh.

"Hi, Jimmy." Ari opened her arms to accept his excited hug.

A tall man stood and held out his hand. "You must be the famous Ari."

Ari kept one arm around Jimmy as she shook the offered hand.

"I'm Jimmy's dad."

"I figured. I've heard a lot about you, too."

"No secret is safe in the waiting room, huh? I'm Gregg Johnson, and it's a pleasure to meet you."

"I told my dad that someone died at your house, too, and that you're the best storyteller ever." Jimmy slipped his hand into Ari's and hung on.

"Sorry," Gregg said. "I know that's more than I should know."

"It's okay." Ari smiled at Jimmy and ran her hand over his short bristly hair. "I'm sorry for your loss, too." She gave Jimmy's hand a little squeeze and pulled away. "I have to go. See you around, Jimmy."

"Wait, wait, wait! Dad, ask her," Jimmy pleaded. "She's really nice."

The office door opened. "Ari, did you need something?" Summers asked, his voice frosty.

Ari didn't turn. "Nope, just saying hello to my friends."

"Ready, Gregg?"

"In a minute," Gregg said. "Ari, this may sound crazy. Jimmy wants you to come to his birthday party. I actually thought you might be a figment of his imagination since he said you come here all the time, but I've never seen you."

Ari tapped her chest. "Nope, I'm real. We used to see each other when he was waiting for you. But I was gone all summer." She glanced at Jimmy and noted the worry on his freckled face.

Gregg studied Ari for a moment. "You know, I have seen you before, haven't I?"

Ari nodded. "Just once."

"Well, it's a pleasure to meet you, Ari, and to know that you are real."

"Please come, please come, please come," Jimmy interrupted. "I'm going to be five." He held up five fingers. "It's Sunday, in the park, with balloons and chocolate cake. Right, Dad?"

"Right, but I'm sure Ari has grown-up things to do on Sunday."

Alex Summers cleared his throat impatiently.

Surprise, Summers! I do have a friend, even if he is only five. "I'd love to come to your party, Jimmy." She bent to give him a big hug before asking, "What park and what time?"

***

"Do you want a ride to your party?" Nicole asked, flipping a page of the paper she was reading. She lifted her mug and took a sip of coffee.

Ari reached for a piece of toast. "I was hoping you could give me a ride to the pet store and then to the park."

"Pet store?" Nicole turned her full attention on Ari.

"I decided to give Jimmy a fish for his birthday."

"Fish? Why not a toy?"

Ari took a large bite of her toast, chewed it carefully, and swallowed before she answered. "He likes fish. And, little kids should get what they like for their birthdays."

Nicole nodded and shrugged. "I guess you're right. Nobody wants socks or underwear for birthday presents." She looked down at the paper again and turned another page. "Did you ask his dad if it was okay?"

I did not! Ari sipped her juice. "Yep, he said it was fine," she lied.

They stopped at the pet store, and Ari chose a beautiful red and purple beta fish, a bowl, pebbles, and some beta food. "Good choice," the clerk complimented her. "This your first beta?"

"It's a present for a friend," Ari said.

"Cool. Betas are great. Want me to put a ribbon around the bag? Make it look more like a present."

"Thanks," Ari said. "I didn't think about needing to wrap anything."

The clerk smiled at her. Ari found herself smiling back. He tied a bow over the knot of the plastic bag of water and fish and placed it carefully inside the empty bowl. "Here's a little info about how to take care of a beta." He dropped a colorful folder into the bowl. "He's fine in that bag for five or six hours. Tell your friend to read the stuff about getting them acclimated to the bowl water before she dumps them out of the bag."

"Got it! Thanks again." Ari hooked the bag with food and pebbles over her wrist and picked up the bowl. She turned to the door.

"'Bye," the clerk said.

Ari didn't look back. "'Bye."

Nicole held the door open and grinned at Ari as she walked through.

"What?" Ari demanded.

The door swung shut behind Nicole, who glanced over her shoulder to be sure no one could hear. "That boy was totally flirting with you!" she declared.

Ari blushed.

***

It was easy to spot Jimmy's party. A flock of four- and five-year-olds, balloons tied to their wrists, chased each other in a frantic hive of activity. Ari walked across the grass, holding the bowl carefully. Jimmy spotted her and tore across the grass, yelling, "Dad, Ari's here! I told you she would come."

He slammed to a stop; his eyes open wide as he gazed at the fishbowl. "Is that my present?" he asked, reaching to touch the bowl with one finger.

Ari nodded.

"Oh my God!" he whispered. "It's the best present ever."

Gregg approached in time to hear his son, "Jimmy, you know you aren't allowed to say that."

"Grandpa says it's okay if you're praying. I've been praying for a fish."

Gregg laughed, Ari giggled, and they exchanged an amused look.

"Is it a boy or a girl, Ari?"

She handed the bowl to Jimmy. "It's a boy beta fish. He swam right over to me in the pet store and said he wanted to be your birthday present."

"See, Dad! I told you Ari can talk to fish."

***

A few days later, at the dinner table, Cedric cleared his throat and crossed his knife and fork on his plate. Ari looked up, alerted by the pause in the conversation and the click of the silverware. *Uh, oh. Vigilant, V-I-G-I-L-A-N-T, watch for possible danger.* She crossed her knife and fork across her plate and waited.

Cedric leaned back in his chair and watched Ari as he said, "Alex Summers called to tell me that you feel you have completed your time with him."

Ari nodded.

"I discussed this with Nicole, and I called Mrs. Jenkins. We have some concerns."

"Like what? I don't think I need to see Summers anymore," Ari protested.

Cedric frowned at the urgency of Ari's desire to discontinue grief therapy.

"I'm feeling much more confident. I've made new friends," she added. "Even he says I'm doing well. All we talk about now is stuff I'm learning in my psych class." Ari held her breath as Cedric considered his answer.

Cedric nodded. "You have experienced a great deal of loss, Ari. More in your short life than most people experience in a full lifetime." He picked up his empty wineglass, looked at it, and set it back on the table. "We are all impressed by how well you are doing, and we want to do everything we can to assure that you continue to thrive."

Right. Ari rose from the table and began to clear the dishes. *Interloper, I-N-T-E-R-L-O-P-E-R, an intruder, one who butts in where he isn't wanted.*

Nicole caught her arm, giving it a little squeeze. "We are very proud of you, Ari."

Ari forced herself to smile. She ducked her head to avoid eye contact. "Thank you," she managed to say.

Cedric looked to Nicole, who nodded. He said to Ari, "I'll call Alex in the morning and tell him we feel you can stop therapy. But—" Ari's head jerked up. "I want you to promise that if you ever feel you want to talk to him or any other counselor, you will tell me."

"Okay." Ari turned to smile at Cedric. "I promise. Do you want some ice cream?"

***

Ari pulled the pink journal down from her closet shelf. She hummed as she stroked the smooth, soft leather and opened it to the first blank page. She moved to her desk and rummaged for a gel pen. Ari considered each color carefully, chose a green one, and entered the date on the top of the page.

Hesitating a minute, Ari pondered what to write; it had to be believable. She drew a series of small boxes, and then, using all her pens, she filled each box with a colorful pattern. At last, in purple ink, Ari wrote—, "

"Today was a very good day." She closed the journal and placed it in the center of her desk. *There, that will make Nicole happy.*

Each evening, right before bed, Ari added another journal entry. Sometimes a drawing. Sometimes a sentence or two about the crows, or Cedric, or what to wear, but always an upbeat, happy message.

***

Gregg Johnson called Cedric at his office and introduced himself as Jimmy's father. "I know this may seem strange, but I had no other way to get hold of Ari. Jimmy is insisting that I ask her to be his babysitter, and I promised I'd try. So here I am."

Cedric laughed. "The things we do for our kids, huh? I don't know if she wants to babysit, but I know she likes Jimmy, so I'm sure Ari would be fine with you calling her. However, I feel like I should protect her privacy. If you give me your number, I'll pass it on, and she can call you. Would that work?"

"That would be great. I was afraid you'd think I was some kind of pervert asking for your daughter's number."

The men chuckled together and hung up.

Cedric recounted the call to Ari that night and asked, "Do you want to babysit?"

"I don't know," Ari admitted. "Jimmy is a cool little kid. I might try it. I thought they lived with Jimmy's grandma. I wonder why they need a babysitter."

"Here's his number." Cedric passed a page from his old-fashioned call log book to Ari. "He just said that Jimmy was asking for you. I didn't ask for any specifics."

Ari glanced down at the paper. "Okay, thanks." She tucked the number into her pocket and went to her room.

"Should I do this?" she asked her reflection. Getting no answer, Ari punched in Gregg's number and pressed send.

Jimmy answered, "Hi, Daddy's phone."

Ari smiled at herself in the mirror and gave a thumbs-up. "Hey, Jimmy!"

"Ari, Ari, Ari!" Jimmy shouted. "Daddy, Ari's on your phone."

"Calm down, son." Ari could hear Gregg in the background. The phone banged against something, and then Gregg's deep voice sounded, "Hey, Ari. Thanks for calling back."

"Cedric said you might need a babysitter for Jimmy. I didn't know what night, so I thought I should call right away; in case it was soon." *Stop babbling! One, two, three, four, five.*

"Actually, it's more a regular job, not a one-night thing. Jimmy and I are back in our own house, and my mom wants to return to her volunteer work, so Jimmy needs someone to stay with him two days a week. After school, until about seven, when I get home. On Wednesdays and Thursdays."

Jimmy's urgent loud whisper interrupted, "Tell her to say yes. Please, Dad. Please, please, please."

Gregg chuckled. "You can hear that Jimmy thinks it's a good idea. He goes to school at Pratt; it's right by the high school."

Ari assured Gregg, "I know where it is."

"He can stay for the after-school program. When you are finished for the day, I thought you could pick him up and walk to our house. It's only a couple of blocks. Then I'd drive you home when I get there."

"I ride my bike anyway. I could just ride home." Ari thought quickly. "That would be from four to seven, right?"

Gregg agreed. "What do you think? Want to help me out and make Jimmy very happy?"

Ari hesitated. Nevermore landed on her windowsill and tapped the glass. She took the sound to be an approval. "I'll have to ask Cedric, but I'm pretty sure it will be fine."

"Great!"

"Yay! She said yes! Right, Dad?" Jimmy's excitement bubbled over.

"Hush, Jimmy." Gregg returned to Ari. "Can you start this coming Wednesday?"

"Sure."

"If you could come by this weekend, Jimmy and I will show you the house and everything you might need to know. I'll talk to the school today so they know you'll be picking him up." He gave her the address, and they agree to meet Saturday afternoon.

Jimmy grabbed the phone and shouted his goodbye.

Ari stood in the middle of her room, grinning. Nevermore banged the glass and bobbed up and down. Ari waved to him and hurried down to tell Cedric and Nicole the plan.

Before bed, Ari opened the journal and using a pink pen, she wrote—, **"I am a strong, independent girl. I am not a victim of my past."**

She encircled the words with flowers and leaves.

Nicole will like that one. She closed the book and crawled under the covers.

***

The excitement among her classmates, that Angie's death had caused was replaced with new teenage drama.

Working two afternoons a week, the debate team, and regular classwork kept Ari busy. She still hung out with Cooper and Steve, but they were involved with sports, and she avoided going to the games.

The holidays came and went without incident.

In February, Ari helped Jimmy make valentines for his class. Gregg arrived home and admired their work. "Do you have plans for Valentine's?" he asked Ari.

"No, I thought Jimmy and I could make a cake or something."

Gregg shook his head, "That's not what I meant. A pretty girl like you, I figured you'd have a hot date."

Ari shook her head. "Not likely."

"Cooper likes you," Jimmy said. "I bet you could have a date with him."

"Cooper and I are friends," Ari explained.

Gregg raised his eyebrows in Ari's direction. "Cooper?"

"Cooper is cool!" Jimmy declared.

"He's a friend from school," Ari explained. "Sometimes we stop to watch the guys practice on the way home. Jimmy likes to talk to them."

"I'm going to be a baseball player." Jimmy swung an imaginary bat. "Just like Cooper."

"Careful, Sport. First, you need to finish kindergarten." Gregg grinned.

"I know, but Cooper said I can if I want to."

Ari and Gregg laughed at his excitement.

Ari turned to Jimmy. "Let's put this stuff away and then I need to get home."

With the cleanup done, Jimmy walked Ari to the door, hugged her, and waved as she mounted her bike and rode off.

He closed the door and said to his dad, "I love Ari. She's the best, right?"

"She is pretty darn great," Gregg agreed.

***

Ari parked her bike in the garage and entered the house through the kitchen. The murmur of voices reached her. She recognized Cedric and Nicole, but the others were unfamiliar.

"I'm home," she called out, plopping her backpack on a chair, and opening the refrigerator to get a soda.

"Ari," Cedric called from the living room, "come in here, please."

Ari's hand trembled. She set the soda can back down and shut the refrigerator door. *Apprehension, A-P-P-R-E-H-E-N-S-I-O-N, anticipation of future trouble or evil.* Ari closed her eyes for a second and steadied herself with a deep breath. *In through the nose. Out through the mouth.* "Be right there," she called.

Ari hesitated at the entry to the living room. Cedric and Nicole sat side by side on the sofa. A man and a woman, wearing suits, sat facing them. Cedric smiled at Ari. He patted the sofa. "Come sit here, Ari."

Ari kept her eyes away from the strangers and sat between Cedric and Nicole. *Police*, she thought. *What do they want now?*

Tthe woman spoke first. "Hi, Ari, I'm Detective Bower, and this is my partner, Detective Anders. We'd like to talk to you for a few minutes. Okay?"

Ari glanced at Cedric. He patted her leg and nodded encouragingly.

Ari turned her eyes to the detective.

"We just have a few questions, Ari," Detective Bower said.

Detective Anders opened a tiny notepad and clicked his pen.

Ari pushed her trembling hands under her legs, bit her lip, and counted to five. She managed a nod.

"Nothing to be afraid of, Ari," the policewoman said, smiling at her. "I've been the lead investigator into the death of your friend Angie Layton. I need a few more details before we can close the investigation."

"It was an accident," Ari blurted.

"Yes, it looks that way, but we need to be sure. Can you tell me about Angie?"

"What about her? I already told the police everything."

"I know, but specifically, was Angie getting along with her parents?"

Wow, I didn't expect that. She glanced at Nicole and then looked back to the detective. "Huh, yeah. Most of the time. I mean, they had the normal stuff, like cleaning her room and getting home on time. Her parents are really nice."

Bower gave a slight smile and nodded again.

Ari gulped. *One hundred, ninety-nine, ninety-eight, ninety-seven.*

Anders wrote something on his pad.

"How about Steve?" Bowers asked.

Ari frowned. "What about him?"

"Were they fighting about anything in the days before Angie's death?"

Ari shook her head.

Bowers continued, "Have you remembered anything unusual about that last night?"

Ari shook her head again.

"All right then. Thank you for talking to us." Bowers stood up.

Anders flipped his notebook closed and put his pen in his pocket. He spoke for the first time, "It's been ten months. We are closing this case. Angie's death will be recorded as an accident." He rose and looked down at Ari. "if you think of anything, you should contact either myself or Detective Bowers. Remember, there is no statute of limitations on murder. We can reopen this case at any time."

Cedric walked the detectives to the door.

Ari sat still, forcing herself not to tremble. *What did he mean by that? Was it a threat?*

Nicole smiled at her and said, "That was kind of scary, wasn't it?"

"A little," Ari admitted. "Steve didn't do anything wrong."

"Don't worry. It's over now," Nicole said. "How was Jimmy today?" she asked, changing the subject, and lightening the mood.

Ari's phone pinged. She pulled it out of her pocket. Cooper had typed, **Mom says I should go to the VDAY dance - want to come with?**

Ari ignored the message and returned the phone to her pocket. "I better do my homework," she said.

***

The following day, Ari found Cooper waiting for her at the bike racks. "You get my message?" he asked.

Ari nodded. "Sorry. It was a weird night. The cops were there."

"Again? What did they want this time?"

Ari averted her gaze and locked her bike to the rack. "Nothing new. They are closing the case."

"About time!" Cooper gave a low whistle. "Steve will be glad to hear that. So, what about the dance? My mom says I'm not doing enough. She's worried about my," Cooper hooked his fingers in quote signs, "social interaction patterns."

Ari laughed. "Sounds like she's been reading the parenting books."

"Yeah, she thinks I'm not interacting with my peer group in an appropriate manner."

"Shit! Does she really talk that way?"

Cooper shrugged. "Yep, she does. She thinks I should have a girlfriend."

"What about your dad?"

Cooper's voice dropped to a whisper. "He just calls me a faggot and tells me to straighten up."

"What a jerk!" Ari couldn't think of anything else to say. She caught his hand and held it as they walked toward the school. "Okay then. Let's go to this dumb dance together. It will shut up your parents and make Nicole happy. Deal?"

"Deal," Cooper agreed.

***

Ari listened carefully as the other girls gossiped about dresses and makeup. She talked to Cooper, and he suggested that she should wear something "hot".

"I don't even know what that means," Ari protested.

Cooper pulled up his Amazon account on his phone and searched for— "dress school dance". A weird assortment of dresses appeared on the screen. Quickly Cooper scrolled through the selections, pointing out possibilities.

Ari stopped him. "Okay, I got it. I'll have to go try some stuff on at the mall."

"Want me to come with?" Cooper asked.

"No, I think I'll ask Nicole."

"Really? Nicole—I thought you didn't like her."

"I don't *not* like her." Ari considered a moment. "I just think she's in my face too much, and if I ask her to go shopping, she'll be happy for a month."

Cooper laughed. "Devious move."

They slapped a high-five.

At dinner, Ari brought up the dance. She turned to Nicole and smiled. "I think I need to get a new dress for the dance. All my clothes are way wrong."

"Sure, we can do that," Nicole agreed. "Do you have anything in mind?"

Ari hesitated a second and then admitted, "I don't know what to wear. I think everyone else is wearing short dresses and really high shoes."

"Would you like me to go shopping with you?"

Ari hesitated, as if thinking it over.

Nicole observed Ari's hesitation and continued, "We could go to the mall tomorrow, and you could try on a few things and see what you like. Or, if you'd rather go with a girlfriend, I can give you a ride."

Ari diverted her gaze from Nicole's. *As if I had a girlfriend.* "I'd like you to shop with me, please," she murmured, keeping her eyes focused on the floor.

"Okay, it's a date. We'll make a day of it."

Later, Ari sat on her bed, fabricating a journal entry. She heard the rumble of Cedric's voice. She stood, and crossed to the door, opening it a crack to hear better.

"I think Ari reaching out to you is a very good sign. I was afraid she would never fully accept you."

Ari could hear the smile in Nicole's voice as she answered. "Ari is doing well. She's interacting with her classmates and is feeling quite confident in her own abilities. The fact that she accepted a date for the dance is a big step."

Gotcha! Ari thought. *Nicole has been reading my journal again. She's so easy to fool!*

Nicole continued. "She has the determination, logic, and resilience to solve her problems. Reaching out to me for help with her clothing choice proves how her trust levels have increased."

Ari pressed her fist to her mouth to cover her giggle. *Counselor talk! Adults are so unconscious.*

She returned to her bed and wrote an entry—, "**Nicole is so sweet. She's taking me shopping tomorrow. I'm sure she'll help me buy the perfect dress**".

Ari flipped the journal closed and picked up her history book.

***

Students crushed together on the dance floor, arms waving and feet stomping. Cooper whirled and waved with the rest of them. Ari managed to fake adequate dance moves. *Thank goodness Angie tried to teach me how to dance.* Cooper caught her hand and tugged her away from the other dancers.

He draped an arm over her shoulders, pulled her close, and whispered into her ear, "Thanks for coming with me tonight, Ari. You're the best."

"That's what Jimmy says." Ari laughed.

"The kid is right. Let's go get something to drink. Steve is over there with Marybeth." He gestured toward the far side of the room.

"Are they together?" Ari asked.

"She wishes." Cooper smirked. "Steve doesn't want a girl."

"You sure?" Ari kept her eyes on the couple. "They look like they are having fun."

"Steve's a good guy. He's always nice to everyone." He looked down at Ari. "We look like a couple, too. And you know we're not."

"True." She grinned at him. "Am I your beard?"

Cooper slapped at her. "Maybe."

They linked arms, laughing together as they joined Steve and Marybeth.

The following day, Ari wrote another entry—, "**The dance was SOOOOO fun. All the girls loved my dress, and Cooper said I looked beautiful.**" She drew a heart on the page, placed the journal on her desk and gave the cover a pat.

Morrigan landed on her windowsill and tapped the glass with her sharp beak.

Ari laughed. "Good morning to you, too. Meet me downstairs, and I'll give you some of my breakfast."

***

The friendship between Cooper and Ari grew stronger now that Ari knew he wasn't interested in anything but friendship with her. Ari soon trusted him enough to introduce him to the crows, and he admitted to his crush on Steve. They sat in Ari's backyard with a bag of sunflower seeds, feeding one seed at a time to Nevermore and Morrigan.

"Did you tell him?" Ari asked.

Cooper shook his head. "I like him, and what if he hates me when he finds out I like him 'that way'?"

Ari cocked her head and studied Cooper. "Maybe he likes you that way?" She stopped and considered a second before continuing, "I guess not. He was crazy about Angie."

Cooper nodded and pulled a sad face.

"Don't worry," Ari consoled him, "you're pretty cute. You'll go to college next year. There'll be lots of guys for you to meet."

"I guess," Cooper said. "What about you? Don't you want to date someone?"

Ari considered her answer and decided to tell the truth. "No."

"Why not? Everybody wants somebody."

"Not me."

"You went out with me before you knew I was gay." Cooper searched her face.

Ari laughed. "Not really. I went out with Angie and Steve so that Angie could fool her parents. You just happened to come along."

Cooper clutched at his chest and pretended to pull out a knife. He fell back on the ground. "That was like a year ago, and you haven't been out with anyone but Steve and me since. I don't believe you. There must be someone you like."

"I like Jimmy."

"He's what, five?" Cooper scoffed.

"I'll have you know Jimmy is almost six. Maybe I prefer younger men."

"Or," Cooper sat up, "maybe you prefer *older* men. Men like his dad. You spend a lot of time over there."

Ari blushed. "It's my job."

"I think the lady doth protest too much," Cooper teased.

"Shut up!" Ari slapped at him.

Nevermore squawked in protest. He flew into the air, turned, and dived toward Cooper's head. Cooper covered his head with his arms. "Hey! What the—?"

Nevermore landed next to Ari and cawed again and again.

Ari held out her arm. Nevermore accepted the perch. Ari gave him a sunflower seed.

Cooper dropped his arms. He grabbed a sunflower seed and extended it to Nevermore.

Nevermore turned his back on Cooper.

"I didn't know they were attack crows."

Ari lifted Nevermore higher. She stroked his head as she answered, "They aren't, but they are my friends and—" she stopped talking.

"And they don't like to see you upset, right?" Cooper asked.

"Exactly," Ari agreed.

***

Ari didn't want to admit that Cooper might be correct, but she knew that she liked talking to Gregg. He never acted like she was a kid. When he came home from work, he asked her what she thought of things, not just about school. He listened. Ari began fixing dinner on the days she stayed with Jimmy. Gregg insisted that she stay and eat with them.

Jimmy sat between them at the table and chattered. Gregg caught Ari's eye and smiled at his silliness. Ari smiled back and put more macaroni and cheese on Jimmy's plate.

Jimmy stopped eating and grinned. "Daddy," he said, looking very serious, "do you like Ari's cooking?"

Gregg nodded, his mouth full.

"Me, too." Jimmy put his fork down. "I think you should marry Ari so she can live with us."

Gregg and Ari gasped and stared at Jimmy.

Gregg recovered first. "I'm way too old to marry Ari."

"No, you're not," Jimmy insisted. "Mark's dad is way older. He looks like a grandpa."

"Ari is still in school. She's sixteen. I'm thirty-six."

"So what? Grandma says you need to fall in love, and I love Ari, so you should, too"

"When did Grandma say that?"

Jimmy shrugged and put a forkful of food in his mouth. "Before."

"Don't talk with your mouth full," Gregg admonished. He caught Ari's eye and smiled at her. To Jimmy, he said, "Ari is certainly pretty and sweet enough to marry, but I don't think it's a good idea."

Ari's stomach flipped at his words.

"Maybe when she finishes college."

Ari felt herself blush.

Jimmy considered. "Is that a long time?"

Ari managed to answer, "About six years."

"Too long," Jimmy said. "Try to get old faster, okay?"

Ari laughed. "Okay." She stood up and cleared her plate from the table. "Finish up, Jimmy. It's time for me to go home."

***

Ari daydreamed about Gregg at school and often dreamed about him at night. She experimented with her hair and makeup, attempting to make herself look older. Wednesdays and Thursdays, she chose her clothes carefully.

Cooper leaned against her locker at the end of the school day. His lazy grin lit up his face as Ari approached. "Lookin' good! Must be a Gregg day."

Ari twisted her combination, opened the locker, and grabbed her books before answering. "Mind your own business, Cooper." She slammed the locker shut and turned to walk away.

Cooper grabbed her arm. "Don't be that way, Ari."

Decamp, D-E-C-A-M-P. She shrugged off his hand. "Fuck off," she hissed.

"Can't," Cooper said cheerfully. "I promised Jimmy I'd help him with his fort today, remember?"

Ari rolled her eyes.

Cooper scooped her books from her arms and swung around to walk with Ari to Jimmy's school.

***

With Jimmy and Cooper occupied in the backyard, Ari took the opportunity to sit at Gregg's desk. She slid open the center drawer and ran her fingers over the pens and pencils. She lifted the mat and found a sticky note with a series of numbers written on it. *Probably a password,* she thought. She opened and closed each of the other drawers, discovering nothing of interest.

Ari checked the yard to be sure the boys were still busy and went into the master bedroom. The room was tidy, bed made, a stack of books on the bedside table along with a picture of Jimmy's mom. She moved to the adjoining bath. A single blue toothbrush and an electric razor lay on the vanity. The sink held a few short hairs. A bottle of Dolce & Gabbana's The One caught her eye. She opened the after-shave and daubed a bit on her wrist. It smelled like Gregg. Ari studied herself in the mirror as she brought her wrist to her nose. She noted the reflection of clothing in the mirror and turned to look behind the door. A pair of faded blue plaid pajama pants and a man's white T-shirt hung on the hook. Ari pressed them to her nose and inhaled deep-ly.

The back door banged shut. Ari dropped the shirt and hurried to the kitchen. "How's it going out there?" she asked the boys.

"Me and Cooper are working real hard," Jimmy said.

"Cooper and I," Ari corrected.

Jimmy ignored her. "We need some juice." Jimmy opened the re-frigerator and grabbed the orange juice.

Cooper extracted the bottle from his hands. "I'll pour. Show me where the glasses are."

Jimmy beamed at the attention.

The front door opened, and Gregg called out, "I'm home. Anybody here?"

"We're all in the kitchen," Jimmy yelled. "Cooper and me made a fort!" Jimmy rushed to Gregg and grabbed his hand. "Come see."

"Cooper and I," Gregg, Ari, and Cooper said at the same time.

Jimmy shrugged. "Sorry. Cooper and I made a fort. Come see, Dad."

"Hang on, sport. Let me put my stuff down." Gregg smiled at Ari. "Hi, Ari. Sounds like it's been a great day."

"You're early," Ari said. "I haven't even started dinner."

Jimmy clutched at Gregg's hand and tried to pull him to the yard. Gregg turned to Ari. "I was hoping you could stay late tonight. I need to go out for a few hours, and I don't have a sitter."

"Sure, as long as I'm home by eleven."

"You're the best, Ari." Gregg tapped her shoulder. "Tell Cedric I'll see that you have a ride home." He turned to Jimmy. "Okay, show me this fort."

Cooper stayed behind in the kitchen. Ari kept her eyes averted and busied herself putting the juice back in the refrigerator.

"Sounds like Gregg has a date," Cooper said.

"So what?"

"Nothing, just saying." Cooper drank his juice and put the glass in the sink. "I'm going to say goodbye to Jimmy and then head home. See you tomorrow."

Ari picked up the glass and opened the dishwasher, still not looking at Cooper. "See ya."

Jimmy yelled one last goodbye to Cooper as he barged into the kitchen. "Where's my dad going?" he asked.

Gregg answered the question as he, too, returned to the kitchen. "I'm going out to dinner with a friend."

"Can Ari and I come?" Jimmy asked.

"Not this time." Gregg smiled at Jimmy. "This is a grownup dinner. Ari is going to stay with you, and I think she'd be willing to order pizza—right Ari?"

"Hurray!" Jimmy shouted. "Get pep, pep, pepperoni with no yucky mushrooms."

"Please," Gregg reminded him.

"Please." Jimmy smiled at Ari.

Ari gave him a thumbs-up.

Gregg said, "I'm going to shower and change." He grabbed a beer from the refrigerator and left the kitchen.

Ari took a deep breath and blew it out. "Let's call for the pizza. Then you can watch a video while we wait."

Jimmy settled in front of the video, happy to be allowed additional screen time. Ari sat next to him but kept her eyes on the window, hoping to see the crows.

A spicy scent alerted Ari to Gregg's return, and she quickly pretended to be absorbed in the video.

"I won't be late," Gregg said, stooping to kiss Jimmy's head. "You be good for Ari."

"Dad, you smell," Jimmy said, wrinkling his nose.

"Too much?" Gregg asked Ari. "I haven't been on a date in a long time."

She shook her head. "No. It's good." Ari took in the way his pale blue shirt brought out the color of his eyes. "You look great," she managed to say. "Have fun."

The pizza arrived as Gregg exited. Jimmy grabbed the box and carried it back to the kitchen. Ari placed it on the breakfast bar and poured Jimmy a glass of milk.

"Yuck," he declared. "I need soda with pizza."

"No, you don't." Ari poured herself a glass of milk, too. "You know your dad doesn't allow soda for dinner."

Jimmy stuffed a large bite of pizza in his mouth and asked, "Who is he going to dinner with?"

"I have no idea." *Probably some tall, beautiful blonde.* "Don't talk with your mouth full. It's gross."

***

Later, with Jimmy asleep, Ari sat on the sofa and tried to concentrate on her homework. Instead, she found herself doodling hearts. "Stop it," she muttered. *There is no way he was going to take me out on a date. No matter what Cooper says. He doesn't like me that way.* She opened her chemistry book and looked at the assigned problem. *But maybe he does, and he just doesn't know it.*

She drew another heart and wrote "manipulate" inside it. *M-A-N-I-P-U-L-A-T-E, to manage or influence skillfully. It's not really manipulation; I just want to make him realize that I'm not too young for him to love.*

She forced herself to finish her homework and flipped on the TV just as Gregg walked in.

"Hi." He threw his keys in the bowl by the door and rubbed his hands over his head. "Whew," he exhaled loudly. "Dating is way too hard."

"Tell me about it," Ari agreed.

Gregg laughed. "You're so young and pretty. I bet it's not hard for you at all."

Ari's curiosity was piqued. "So, what happened?"

"Let me get a beer, and I'll tell you. Want anything?"

"No thanks." Ari took advantage of the few moments Gregg was gone to lick her lips, fluff her hair and place her schoolbooks out of sight.

Gregg returned and flopped down at the opposite end of the sofa. He lifted his feet onto the coffee table and took a deep pull on his beer.

Ari's stomach tightened. She ran the fingers of her right hand through her hair, lifting it and allowing it to fall into loose curls.

Gregg watched. "You have beautiful hair."

Ari's lips curved into a small smile. "Tell me about your date," she prompted.

Gregg took another pull on his beer. "Not much to tell, I'm afraid. I chose an Italian restaurant. She waited until we were seated to tell me she doesn't like Italian food."

Ari grimaced and shook her head. *I love Italian,* she thought.

"We didn't have anything to talk about, except work. Mostly she wanted to tell me about how terrible the last guy she dated was. All I could think of to talk about was Jimmy." Gregg finished his beer and picked at the label.

Ari waited.

"Then she told me she didn't see herself in a relationship with a guy that had a kid. I asked for the bill, and we were out of there before dessert. And, here I am, home before nine."

"I told you dating is hard." Ari reached out and patted his arm.

"Yeah, I wish everyone was as easy to talk to as you are, Ari." He rolled his beer bottle in his fingers and turned to smile at her. "As Jimmy likes to point out, you're the best."

***

"What are you concentrating on so hard?" Cooper flopped down next to Ari and tried to read her screen.

Ari covered her phone.

"Secrets?" Cooper reached for the phone.

Ari pulled it away. "None of your business." She slapped his hand.

"Now, I *really* want to know what you were looking at. Some dork on TikTok? What're you hiding, girl?"

"If you must know, I was researching how to flirt."

Cooper's eyes opened wide. "Huh?"

"I'm writing a paper on body language for my communications class."

Cooper cocked his head to one side and considered Ari's answer. "Right. I believe that like I believe in Santa. You're interested in some guy, aren't you?"

Ari shook her head.

Cooper waited, but when Ari stayed silent, he asked, "Still Gregg, huh?"

Ari nodded. "I know he likes me, and I see the way he looks at me, but —."

"The man has sense, Ari." Cooper shook his head. "Even if he's interested, he's way too old to start anything with you. He'd get in real trouble."

"Not if I want him to be my boyfriend."

"Leave the guy alone, Ari. If you want to have sex, pick on someone your own age."

"Coop! I just want him to like me back."

Cooper draped an arm around Ari and pulled her into a half-hug. "Girl, you need to relax. He likes you and he probably thinks you're cute, but he's never going to be stupid enough to date you. You're totally jailbait."

Ari bristled. "So, you think dating me is stupid?"

"Not what I said, and you know it. Come on. I'll walk you home."

Ari tucked her phone into her backpack and stood up. "No thanks. I've got my bike."

***

Ari stared at herself in the mirror. *No one is ever going to love me,* she thought. *Maybe if I put just a little oleander in Gregg's food, he'll get sick and I can take care of him. Then he'd have to love me.*

She shuddered and shook her head. "Stupid," she told her reflection. "He might die. Then where would I be?" *Jimmy would be so sad, and more than likely, someone would figure it out this time. Besides I promised Nevermore I wouldn't kill again.*

Later, Ari lay in bed imagining kissing Gregg, but Cooper's righteous indignation kept disrupting her fantasy. Her thoughts ran in circles: *Cooper needs to butt out of my life. But he's my only friend. So what, I don't need friends. If Cooper doesn't leave me alone, I'll kill him, too.*

Ari sat bolt upright in her bed. "Stop that!" she told herself. "What's wrong with me," she whispered into the darkness. "I can't kill anyone else. I'll get caught." *I need to get through high school. When I go away to college, no one will know anything about me.*

She reached for a notepad and wrote a list:

1. Stop working for Gregg—get a different job?
2. Avoid everyone—don't need them
3. Two more years of high school
4. Choose a college far away
5. Don't kill anyone—no matter what

Ari tore the list into tiny pieces, went into her bathroom, flushed them away, and returned to bed. She pulled her comforter up to her chin and counted herself to sleep. *One thousand, nine hundred and ninety-nine, nine hundred and ninety-eight, nine hundred and ninety-seven...*

***

Determined to make a change in her life, Ari considered her options and created a plan. She looked up the requirements for taking college classes while in high school and found that she could begin with a summer class.

Cooper thought she was crazy to give up summer vacation, but he approved of her determination to stop obsessing about Gregg.

Cedric was delighted that she wanted to challenge herself and quickly signed the necessary papers. However, telling Gregg and Jimmy that she would be too busy to continue caring for Jimmy two days a week was more difficult.

Jimmy cried, and Ari crossed her fingers behind her back and promised to still do things with him. Gregg hugged her and said how much they'd miss her. Ari fought back her tears.

Riding home, Ari felt more alone than ever. Nevermore and Morrigan swooped down and flew beside her.

***

CHAPTER SIX

Six for gold,

"If men had wings and bore black feathers, few of them would be clever enough to be crows." —Henry Ward Beecher

Taking college classes in the summer kept Ari busy and gave her the excuse she wanted so that she could avoid seeing Jimmy and Gregg.

Cooper and Steve left for college in August. Ari promised to stay in touch but knew she wouldn't.

In her junior year of high school, Ari avoided all school activities. She was at the college two days a week, and during the three days she spent at the high school, she kept to herself.

If her classmates thought about her at all, it was to consider her a loner —or, as Toby still taunted every chance he got, a loser.

Cedric and Nicole often told her how proud they were of her educational success. Cedric continued to worry about her lack of social interactions, and Ari assured him she was happy and busy. He chose to believe all was well.

At the end of junior year, Cedric rewarded Ari with a car, a small red Honda Civic.

Cooper and Steve arrived home for the summer, but Ari had signed up for two classes during the summer session and put off all their offers to spend time together.

She relished the independence her car gave her and delighted in driving to her summer classes instead of using public transportation. Cedric and Nicole had suggested that she take a break over the summer. However, Ari knew that classes and homework were the only things that filled her days and nights and had insisted that she wanted to get as many credits as possible completed before her high school graduation.

Early one morning, she pulled into the gas station and hopped out to fill the Civic's gas tank.

"Hey, pretty girl," a lazy voice drawled.

Ari glanced at the pickup that had pulled into the adjacent space. A guy was pumping gas, grinning at her. She took in his look: messy long hair, tight jeans, wife-beater, flip-flops.

Ari ignored him, inserted her cash card, and pulled the nozzle from its holder. She kept her back turned, pretending to concentrate on the gas as it filled her tank.

The pump clicked off. Ari removed the nozzle and turned to hang it back in its place. She stopped, frozen for a second, as she realized the guy was still there, leaning against his car, arms crossed, watching her. Her temper flared. "What are you, some kind of stalker?" she sneered.

"Nah. I was just enjoying the view." He grinned at her. "You've got a great ass."

Ari blushed.

"I'm Robin. Who are you?"

"None of your business," Ari snapped.

"Don't be that way." He held up his hands in surrender. "Take a chance. What have you got to lose?"

Ari slammed the nozzle into place and moved around her car to the driver's seat. She looked over the top of the vehicle and found him still watching, still slouched against his car.

Robin made a finger gun in her direction. "I'll be seeing you, Gorgeous."

Ari started her engine and drove off. "What a jerk."

She grinned at her reflection in the rearview mirror. "But he was pretty cute."

***

Summer session at the college was full of cute guys, all older, and all hanging out with friends. The other students ignored her. She looked for the guy from the gas station but didn't see him around the campus. When driving past the station, Ari always searched for the truck. She checked Facebook, Instagram and TikTok. There were too many guys named Robin. She didn't find him.

Her gas tank dropped to three-quarters full. Ari determined the Civic needed gas, so she returned to the station and filled her tank. She hoped to see Robin's truck. When it didn't appear, she decided to treat herself to a salted nut bar. The bell dinged as Ari pushed the door open. The clerk looked up.

"Hey, Sexy. I knew you'd be back." Robin smirked at Ari.

Ari flushed but managed to keep her voice even. "I'm just here for the gas and a PayDay."

Robin pointed toward the candy aisle. "Totally nuts," he said.

"Huh?" Ari looked confused.

"Old commercial. Guess you didn't see it."

Ari marched to the candy and took her time choosing her PayDay. She took a deep breath and held it. *One hundred, ninety-nine, ninety-eight, ninety-seven.* She exhaled through her nose. *Ninety-six, ninety-five, ninety-four, ninety-three.* She turned toward the checkout. Ari bit down on her inner lip to keep from grinning. *Yep, he's totally watching me.*

"Where are you headed, Beautiful?" Robin asked as he took her money.

"Not that it's any of your business, but I have a class at the college today."

"Oh, yeah?" Robin cocked an eyebrow. "It's summer vacation, girl. Time to have fun."

Fun, F-U-N, pleasure, enjoyment, entertaining, jollification. Ari accepted her change and turned to leave.

"At least tell me your name," Robin coaxed.

Ari turned back and considered him. *Kind of scruffy but cute.* "Ari," she answered.

"Nice." Robin tapped a drum roll on the counter. "Now we're getting somewhere. Come to the beach with me this afternoon."

"What beach?" Ari blurted out the question without thinking.

"River or lake, your choice. Meet me here when I get off work—at one. And we'll wartrundle."

Ari protested, "I don't know you." *And what the heck is wartrundle?*

"And, you never will know me if you don't hang with me."

Ari narrowed her eyes. *Why not?* "Maybe I will, and maybe I won't. I've got to get to class." She walked away, feeling Robin's gaze follow her. She waved without turning back.

"See you at one, Beautiful Ari."

Ari hurried to her car and drove away.

***

Unable to concentrate in class, Ari doodled and thought, *I'm almost seventeen. It's summer and everyone else is having fun. Cedric and Nicole are always after me to do something with my friends. Robin is not my friend, but maybe he could be.* The class ended. Ari closed her notebook and stuffed it in her bag. She glanced at the clock. *Noon. I'll just go home and put on a swimsuit, and then I'll decide.*

She avoided the gas station on the way home, parked in the driveway, entered her house, and found it silent. Then, relieved to have no need to explain, Ari hurried to her room and slipped into her bikini. She pulled on a pair of cutoffs and a T-shirt, checked that her ponytail was high and tight, grabbed a beach towel and her sunscreen and ran down the stairs.

Ari quickly wrote a note and placed it on the kitchen table. "Gone to the beach with friends. I'll be home by 10." The clock on the microwave flipped to 12:50. Ari pulled the door open and found Nevermore and Morrigan waiting on the lawn.

The birds cawed loudly at her approach.

"Sorry, guys, I can't talk right now. I've got a date."

Nevermore stalked behind Ari to the car and stood on the grass, cawing loudly, and shaking his head as she opened the door and slid in behind the steering wheel.

Ari laughed. "I'll tell you all about it when I get home."

Nevermore flew up to the tree, still muttering low caws and clicks while he watched Ari drive away.

***

Ari pulled into a parking space in front of the door at the gas station as Robin exited the store. He strolled to her window, gave her a solemn look, and raised an eyebrow. "You're late," he said.

Ari glanced at the clock. "Seven minutes."

"I'll forgive you this time, but don't let it happen again."

Ari laughed.

"Park your car out back. We'll go in my truck." Robin walked away.

Ari reversed out of the parking place and followed him to the back of the station. Robin didn't look at Ari. He strode to a well-polished, black pickup, unlocked the doors, and slid into the driver's seat. The engine roared to life, and music blasted from the truck's speakers. Ari quickly hopped out of her Civic, grabbed her beach bag, and hurried around to the passenger's side. Robin reached across the vehicle and pushed the door open. Ari seized the grab bar, crawled in, and shut the door.

***

Robin sped out of the gas station, ignored the stop sign, and gunned the engine to beat the oncoming traffic. Ari kept her eyes forward and did not comment. *He better not kill me on my first actual date!*

"So, Babe, river okay with you?" Robin reached over and placed his hand on Ari's bare leg.

She froze, unable to say anything. *Don't touch me. One hundred, ninety-nine, ninety-eight.*

"Reach over the seat and grab me a beer."

Ari turned sideways and blurted out, "You can't drink and drive."

"Of course I can. That's just a dumb rule for people who can't hold their booze."

He glanced over at Ari and gave her a grin.

She found herself grinning back. She unbuckled her seat belt and turned to kneel on the seat, reaching behind it for the cooler that was tucked there. Ari pulled out a dripping can of beer and handed it to Robin.

He expertly popped the tab with one hand and took a deep drink. "Get yourself one, too," he suggested.

Ari ignored the suggestion, turned around and sat down, twisting slightly to watch Robin. She refastened her seat belt and asked, "Why the river? Everybody goes to the lake."

"Exactly!" Robin saluted her with his can. "I want to get to know you, and for that, we need solitude."

Solitude, S-O-L-I-T-U-D-E, remoteness from habitations, absence of human activity.

Robin tipped his beer up and drained the can. He winked at Ari. "Surprised, college girl? Bet you didn't think I knew any big words." He dropped his empty can on the floor.

"Not exactly a big word," Ari protested.

"Oh, yeah? Tell me a big word, then."

Ari pondered for a moment. "How about tryst?"

Robin laughed and returned his warm hand to Ari's bare thigh. "Are you trying to tell me this is a secret meet-up?"

Ari blushed.

"How old are you, anyway?"

Ari hid her right hand and crossed her fingers. "Eighteen," she lied. *At least I will be in fourteen months.*

Robin squeezed her leg. "Grab me another beer."

Excitement caused Ari's heart to skip. *No fear,* she told herself. She took a deep breath and reached over the seat again.

They rode the rest of the short distance to the river without talking — Robin's hand on her thigh, one finger drawing small circles, and the radio blasting.

Ari's stomach fluttered with excitement. She felt like throwing up. *Is this love?*

Robin parked the truck and turned to Ari. "Come on, Babe. Let's get to know each other." He pushed open his door, got out and reached into the bed of the truck for a blanket. He looked back at Ari. "Carry this. I'll get the beer."

Grabbing her beach bag, Ari joined Robin. *I guess chivalry is dead.* She accepted the blanket and walked to the riverbank.

Robin pointed to a place back from the bank and under a tree. "Put the blanket over there, Babe."

"Let's sit closer to the water," Ari suggested.

"I like it under that tree." Robin pointed again. "Don't worry. I'll protect you from bears."

Ari laughed. "There aren't any bears around here."

She carried the blanket to the tree and spread it on the ground.

Robin plopped the cooler next to the blanket and sat. He lifted his hand to Ari. She took it, and he pulled her down beside him.

Robin pulled two beers from the cooler, popped the tabs, and handed one to Ari. "Here's to the most beautiful girl I've seen today." He tilted his can toward Ari's. She tapped her can against his and watched as he drank.

Ari lifted her can to her lips and took a swallow. Her eyes widened. She choked, spitting the beer on the ground. "Sorry, I don't usually drink beer," she muttered.

"Yeah, most chicks like that sweet, crappy wine." Robin grinned at her. "You'll get used to it. Just take small sips."

Ari sat on the blanket next to Robin and took a few small sips. She kept her eyes on the river and tried to ignore the flutter in her stomach. Then she took a large drink to calm herself.

Robin lifted his hand and idly twirled her ponytail around his finger.

Ari smiled slightly.

"There you go," Robin said. "Relax. I won't bite."

"I'm relaxed," Ari protested.

"Yeah, right," Robin teased. He finished his beer and stood. "Come on. Let's swim."

He toed off his shoes, pulled his T-shirt over his head and unbuckled his jeans.

Ari gulped.

Robin grinned. "Drink up before your beer gets warm."

Ari obeyed. Robin pulled her to her feet and watched as she removed her shorts to reveal her bikini.

"Nice." Robin's eyes roved over Ari, pausing on her breasts.

Ari wanted to cover herself. Her heart pounded, and she could feel herself blush.

Robin grabbed her hand. They ran together to the river's edge and plunged in.

After a few minutes of splashing about, Robin suggested a race to the opposite bank. Ari was a strong swimmer, but Robin was better, and he won easily. "Winner gets a kiss," he said.

"No bet, no prize," Ari laughed.

"Fair," Robin agreed. "Race you back? Winner gets a kiss."

Ari's stomach fluttered. She knew she was blushing. "Okay," she agreed and began swimming.

Robin caught up quickly and passed her with a grin. Ari slowed and readied herself for her first kiss. *I wish Angie could see this.*

Approaching the shore, Ari let her feet sink to the bottom and stayed submerged to her waist. She pulled at her bikini bottom to be sure it was in place, licked her lips, and walked through the water toward where Robin waited. Ari lifted her arms to wring the water from her hair.

Robin gave a low wolf whistle, his eyes on Ari's breasts. He stepped forward and ran one finger over her cleavage.

Ari gasped.

Robin whispered, "Come here, girl." He hooked his finger in her bikini and pulled her close.

Ari lifted her face and closed her eyes. She shivered.

Robin's lips pressed hard against her own. She felt his tongue pushing her lips apart. Their teeth clicked.

Robin pressed harder.

Ari tried to pull away, but Robin held her tight.

Ari opened her eyes and saw that Robin was watching her. She jerked back and broke contact with his mouth.

"What's wrong with you?" Robin grabbed her wrist and held her close. "You some kind of tease or what?"

Ari shook her head and fought back the tears that threatened to spill. *That was terrible, not nice at all.* She knew Robin could feel her shaking and tried to stop.

"Hey." His voice was soft now. Ari managed to look up and meet his eyes. "You sure you're eighteen?" he asked.

Divulge, D-I-V-U-L-G-E, to disclose or reveal something unknown. "I'm sure," Ari said firmly, "but it's kind of embarrassing to admit I've never kissed anyone before."

Robin gawked at her. "Never? Holy shit! Are you a virgin?"

Ari blushed and nodded.

"What the hell." Robin shook his head, slowly taking in her confession. He dropped his hand from her wrist and gently took her hand. "Come on. I think we need another beer."

Ari followed him to the blanket and accepted the beer. Robin drank deeply and at last pulled Ari close in a hug. He said, "Don't worry, Babe. I'll take care of you."

Ari relaxed and lifted her beer to her lips.

***

Ari sat in bed, propped against her pillows, her journal open in her lap. She doodled across the page, drawing lines and squiggles. *Robin is so sweet. I wish I could write about him.* She carefully crafted her entry for Nicole's eyes.

"Went to the river this afternoon. Swam all the way across in a race with a guy named Robin. He won."

She closed the journal, turned off her bedside lamp, and pulled her favorite pillow into her arms. Hugging it tightly, she whispered, "Good night, Robin," and kissed the pillow.

***

The following week, when she wasn't in class, Ari went to the gas station to be with Robin instead of spending her time studying and hanging out at home. He greeted her, each time, with a grin as he lifted the bar flap to allow her behind the counter. He always slid his hands into the back pockets of her jeans and pulled her close as he kissed her hello, even when there were customers. Ari blushed at the "Get a room" taunts, and Robin laughed at her embarrassment.

Cooper, home from college for the summer, called, suggesting they get together. They made a plan and Ari stopped at the gas station on the way to her class to tell Robin she'd be busy the rest of the day.

Robin shrugged. "Whatever. If you'd rather spend your time with some guy named Cooper, it's your choice, Babe."

"Don't be like that," Ari protested. "He's just a friend. I haven't seen him all year. We just want to talk."

"Do what you gotta do." Robin turned away and concentrated on straightening the cigarette display.

Ari started to protest, but a wave of hot anger swept away the feeling of rejection. "I will," she said, hen turned quickly and stormed out.

A loud caw interrupted her bitter thoughts. She looked to the roof of the gas station. Morrigan and Nevermore perched on the gutter. Nevermore bobbed his head, and they lifted off to fly lazy circles as Ari got in her car and drove away.

Ari choked back a sob and pounded her hand on the steering wheel. "Damn it," she muttered.

During class, Ari tried to concentrate and failed. Her stomach ached and her head pounded. She pulled her phone from her pocket and started to send a text to Cooper canceling their afternoon.

Hey. Not feeling— She stopped. *I'm not going to be like Stacy! No guy can tell me what to do.* She backspaced over the words, laid her phone on the tablet arm of her chair, and kept watch to see if a text came in from Robin.

***

When Ari exited the science building, she found Cooper lounging on the steps. He leaped to his feet and grinned. "Wow, girl! You slay!" Cooper held out his arms and Ari stepped in for a short, fierce hug.

"You look good, too." Ari moved backward and away, returning his wide grin with one of her own. "It's great to see you, Coop. College must be good."

Cooper flipped his hand back and forth in a "not sure" gesture. "Let's go to the quad. We can grab a cold drink and talk. I want to hear all about what it is that's keeping you so busy."

They found a spot away from the other students. "So," they spoke at the same time.

"Jinx, you owe me a soda," Cooper said quickly.

Ari laughed. "You already have one. Tell me about college. Only one more year and I'll go, too."

"I'd tell you it's great—that's what I say to everyone, but actually—" He sighed. "It's kind of weird."

"Really? Why?" Ari dropped down to the grass and crisscrossed her legs.

Cooper sat next to her and stayed silent a moment before saying, "Not sure how to explain it."

He plucked a blade of grass, placed it between his thumbs and blew a loud, sharp-sounding whistle.

Ari jumped.

Students turned to look.

Another student, somewhere on the quad, whistled back. Soon whistles echoed from every direction. Cooper blew again.

"Look what you started!" Ari said. She picked a blade and attempted to whistle, but she only produced a sputter and squeak.

Cooper laughed. He repositioned her thumbs and pulled her blade of grass taut. "Try it now."

Ari blew hard. A loud, screeching sound pierced the air. Ari laughed aloud and blew again. She was rewarded with only a tiny squeak. She dropped the grass and lay back with her arms folded beneath her head.

Cooper stretched out beside her on the ground. He rolled to his stomach and cradled his head in his arms with his face turned to look at Ari. "Steve joined a fraternity."

"I thought you pledged, too?"

"I was going to, but I don't fit in with that group."

"So, is that the weird part?"

"Nah, not really." Cooper stared up at the sky and considered his answer. "Actually, I don't know why I'm even there. I'm not like you and Steve." He turned back to look into Ari's eyes. "You guys are smart. I'm not."

"You're smart," Ari protested.

"I'm not dumb, but I don't like all the reading and writing about stuff that I'll never need to know."

Ari waited.

"I always wanted to be a policeman."

Ari caught her gasp before the sound could escape her lips. She took a deep breath and looked away. *One hundred, ninety-nine, ninety-eight, ninety-seven, ninety-six.*

"Surprised?"

Ari nodded. She sat up and wrapped her arms around her knees. "Wow!" she managed to say. "I had no idea."

"It's a great career." Cooper sounded defensive.

"It is," Ari agreed. "I'm just surprised." She turned to face her friend. "I think you should do it, if that's what you want."

"My dad will have a cow."

Crap, the only friend I have and he's going to be a cop. Ari forced a prickle of fear away and said, "You're nineteen. You can make your own choice."

"Sounds good, but it doesn't work that way at my house." Cooper plucked another piece of grass and split it lengthwise. "So, enough about me. What's new with you?"

Ari grinned. "Well, I'm pretty busy with classes."

"And? I don't believe that grin has anything to do with school," Cooper teased.

"Well, I did meet this guy that I kind of like. We're sort of going together."

"Tell all," Cooper demanded.

"His name is Robin. He's twenty, and he's adorable; he really gets me."

"Twenty?" Cooper gave a little whistle. "Did you meet him at the college?"

"No." Ari shook her head. "At the gas station."

Cooper considered her answer for a long moment before asking, "Uh, is it Robin Sharkey?"

Ari's eyes widened with surprise. She nodded. "Do you know him?"

"Sort of." Cooper kept his eyes on Ari as he said, "He was a year ahead of me at school until he dropped out in tenth grade. I didn't know he was still in town. He's kind of bad news, Ari."

Ari felt her anger rise. She swallowed hard and forced it away. "He's not bad news, Cooper. He's really sweet."

"Maybe?" Cooper cocked an eyebrow. "People can change, I guess. Does he know you're only sixteen?"

Ari shrugged. "He didn't ask," she lied. "And, anyway, I'll be seventeen in a week."

"Just be careful, Ari. I don't want you to get hurt."

***

Ari waved goodbye to Cooper as she pulled out of the parking lot. "That was interesting," she said to her reflection in the rearview mirror.

She turned her car toward the gas station. *I'll just say hi before I go home.*

Driving slowly past the station, Ari looked for Robin's truck. It wasn't parked in its usual space.

Ari flipped a U-turn and returned to the station. She pulled in and parked in front of the store, checked her hair in the rearview mirror, and went in. The woman behind the counter stuck her finger between two pages of a magazine and smiled at her, as she asked, "Can I help you, honey?"

"Ah, no, not really. I was just looking for Robin. I thought he was working tonight."

"Yeah, he was supposed to, but he called in sick or something."

"Oh." Ari blushed. She shoved her hands into the pockets of her shorts.

The woman's smile changed to a grin. "Want me to tell him you came by?"

"Uh, no. That's okay," Ari stammered. "Thanks, anyway."

She turned and fled.

Back in her car, Ari sent a message to Robin. **Hey, I'm on my way home, what's up?** She started the car and drove toward home, listening for the sound of an incoming text.

After answering Cedric's questions about how Cooper was doing at college, Ari escaped to her bedroom. She kept her phone close, hoping to hear from Robin. Finally, around midnight she dozed off with her phone still in her hand.

Ari woke the following day, checked her phone, and hurried out of the house to forestall talking to anyone. She drove the long way to the river, avoiding the gas station. Only one car was parked in the lot. Ari could see a couple inside as she drove past and parked at the far end. *No one I know.*

She checked her phone again: still nothing.

Ari opened the door and stepped out, slammed it behind herself, and clicked the locks shut with her key fob. The other car started, and Ari watched them drive off. *Alone again, naturally. Stacy used to sing that stupid song.* Ari blinked back tears.

The flutter of wings caught her attention.

Ari held out her arm to allow Morrigan to land.

She raised her arm and lifted Morrigan to her face. The crow clicked quietly and rubbed her head on Ari's cheek. Nevermore gave a low caw and landed on her shoulder. He, too, rubbed his head against Ari. "Hi, guys. You always come when I need you."

She kissed Morrigan on the head and moved her arm away to allow her to fly. Nevermore chirped and followed Morrigan into the air.

"Come on." Ari waved to the birds and started up the river path. The birds flew circles above her until they reached the flat rock. Ari sat down on the edge, her feet pressed against the sand and pebbles that lined the river. The crows settled beside her.

"I really like him, you know," Ari spoke softly. "And, I think he likes me. But now he's mad because I spent time with Cooper yesterday."

Nevermore shook his head and puffed his feathers. Then, he gave a hoarse raucous caw and paced a few steps away and back. Morrigan clicked nervously.

"Stacy always said there's plenty of fish in the sea."

Nevermore bobbed his head.

"I know, but I love him."

Nevermore croaked loudly. Morrigan cawed. The birds flew away and disappeared into the trees.

Ari picked up a stick and wrote Robin's name in the sand, followed by a line of question marks. She lay back on the rock and turned her head toward the hidden cemetery trees. Pulling her phone from her pocket, Ari rechecked her messages. *Shit!* Ari scuffled her feet over the loose sand, erasing Robin's name. She shoved her phone into her pocket, stood up, and walked back to her car. "I might as well study," she said.

***

Cedric noticed that Ari was at home more during the next few days and asked if everything was alright. She avoided the question with an excuse about assignments and spent her afternoon reading in the backyard. Cooper called, but she didn't answer. The week dragged past.

Finally, Ari sent one more text to Robin. **It's my bday. Want 2 celebrate with me?**

Her phone lit up almost at once with a string of emojis: birthday cake, party face, and a wrapped present. Ari grinned. *That's more like it. Persistence, P-E-R-S-I-S-T-E-N-C-E. Persistence conquers all. Benjamin Franklin was right.*

Ari went into the house to shower and get ready to meet Robin. *I knew he wouldn't stay mad at me.* She washed her hair and blew it out carefully so it would hang in soft waves, put on mascara and lipstick, and took her favorite sundress from the closet. She held the dress up to herself and considered it. *Nope, too much.* She exchanged the dress for a crop top and cut-off jeans.

A knock sounded on her bedroom door. "Yes?" Ari called.

"It's just me," Nicole answered.

Ari pulled on her shorts and top. "Come in."

"Hi," Nicole said, stepping inside. She smiled at Ari. "You look gorgeous. I'm glad you have plans for tonight. Cedric felt bad that he was out of town on your birthday."

"Not a problem. Like I told him, the presents and birthday dinner can wait until Saturday. He texted me this morning, so trust me, it's cool."

"Are you meeting Cooper and Steve?"

"No." Ari hesitated. "I'm meeting Robin. I think we're going to a movie, and then we'll grab some food."

"Why isn't he picking you up? I'd like to meet him."

Ari thought fast and improvised her excuse. "He has to work until seven. So if he drives over here, we'd be late to the movie."

Nicole nodded. "Okay. Have fun. You better take a sweatshirt for the movie. And, Happy Birthday."

Ari picked up her bag from the bed and buzzed Nicole's cheek as she passed her. "Thanks, Nicole. Don't wait up." She stopped in the doorway and winked. "It's my birthday!"

Nicole laughed.

***

Robin lifted the bar flap at the gas station to allow Ari behind the counter as if she'd been there every day. She leaned in for a kiss, but Robin didn't seem to notice. Instead, he turned his back and ignored her as he waited on customers and straightened the counter stock.

When they were alone, Ari moved to his side and laid her fingers on his arm. "I missed you," she said.

210 · TAMARA MERRILL

Robin turned to face her. He wasn't smiling. His eyes looked cold, and he didn't blink. Ari took a deep breath and started counting: *One hundred, ninety-nine, ninety-eight, ninety-seven.*

"I don't want my girl hanging out with other guys," he said.

My girl! Ari's heart skipped a beat. She forced herself to stay calm. "Cooper's not a guy. He's just my friend from school."

"Oh? He's a guy, alright." Robin turned away and fiddled with a display of key rings.

Ari flushed and ran her fingers through her hair, deciding if she dared tell Cooper's secret. *This is an emergency. He'll understand.* "Not that kind of guy. He's gay."

Robin turned back and studied her. "He tell you that?"

Ari stiffened. "Of course. Do you think I make stuff up?"

"Don't know, Babe." Robin leaned back against the counter and let his eyes roam over her. He lifted one eyebrow and grinned. "Come over here and show me you missed me."

Ari didn't hesitate. She smiled and closed the distance between them, slid her arms around Robin's waist, and nestled in, loving the feel of his hard body. She raised her lips for his kiss.

Robin stared down at her. "Don't ever go out with someone without asking me first," he said.

She started to protest but pushed the thought away. Ari nodded. "I'm sorry, Robin. It won't happen again."

Robin pulled her tight against him. He kissed her hard and fast. "It better not."

***

Robin's replacement arrived at seven. He grabbed a case of beer from the cooler and beckoned to Ari. "It's time you met the guys. Follow me to my house, and we'll celebrate your birthday in style."

Ari stayed close behind Robin's truck, not paying too much attention to where they were headed until he turned onto Crescent Drive, and she realized they were close to her old house. She shivered as memories of Jerry and Stacy and living alone flooded her thoughts. She pushed them away. *Not tonight. Not ever.*

Robin pulled onto the grass of a small cottage and waved Ari to park on the street. She locked her car, took a deep breath, and looked around. *I don't know anybody on this street. It'll be okay. No one remembers the bird girl anyway.*

A door slammed. Ari forced herself to concentrate. Robin had gone into the house without her. She hurried to catch up.

Ari pulled the screen door open, stepped in and looked around.

The house smelled of beer and dirty clothes. Empty beer cans sat on every surface. Somebody had shoved a couple of pizza boxes under a battered coffee table. Clothing hung from chair backs and lay piled on the floor.

I forgot about living like this. Ari felt a chill run down her spine. She bit her lip to refrain from commenting on the mess, shook away the memories, and hurried toward the sound of voices.

Robin and two other guys were in the filthy kitchen. Robin sat backwards, straddling a kitchen chair, with an open beer in his hand. He grabbed Ari's arm and pulled her to him. The wooden slats of the chair back struck Ari in the ribs. She flinched and inhaled sharply.

Robin ignored the sound. "These are my bros. Tank," he tipped the can to a small, skinny redhead perched on the edge of the counter, "and Tiny." This time the beer can gesture indicated a tall, heavily built guy with a shaved head and a scruffy beard.

Ari gave a small, shy smile. "Hi. I'm Ari."

Tank smiled back. Tiny belched loudly. Robin handed her his beer, and she took a large gulp.

"Let's go drink on the steps," Robin said, pulling two more beers from the case. "It's hotter than hell in here."

Ari put the rest of the beer in the refrigerator and followed the guys to the porch. For a moment, she thought about leaving, but she pushed the thought aside and quickly drank her beer then reached for a second.

They all sat on the porch steps—until the sun set. Tank and Tiny left for a bar. Everything grew pleasantly hazy. Robin ran his fingers through her hair and drew her close for sweet, long kisses.

He went into the house and turned on some music Ari didn't recognize.

Robin returned.

They sat close, Robin's arm draped over her shoulders, his fingers stroking her arm.

Ari relaxed. *This is how love feels.*

Robin's phone buzzed. He pulled it from his pocket and glanced at the message. He typed a quick reply. "Just the guys wanting me to join them for last call."

"Last call? What time is it?"

"About one." Robin crushed his can and tossed it into the yard.

Ari stood up and stretched, her arms high above her head. Her T-shirt rose up, exposing her firm stomach. Robin whistled softly, his eyes fastened on the exposed skin.

Ari dropped her arms. "I better get home," she said.

Robin's eyes traveled down her bare legs and back up. His eyes locked with Ari's. Tension sizzled between them.

Robin leaned forward, took her hand, and pulled her back down beside him on the step. He bent and kissed her.

Ari trembled.

His mouth tasted hot.

She relaxed into the kiss. Robin's insistent lips pressed harder, and her lips parted to accept his tongue. The kiss deepened.

Ari's stomach clenched. She broke away.

Robin stood, pulling Ari up and into his arms. He held her close and kissed her again. Ari melted against him. Every inch of her body craved to be closer.

Robin's warm hand cupped her face.

He circled her shoulders with his left arm, pulling her even closer, and lazily ran his right hand over her back, allowing it to drift lower and lower until he cupped her buttocks.

Ari trembled.

"Like that, baby?" Robin moved his lips to her throat and then nibbled on her ear.

His fingers traced the fringed bottom of Ari's shorts, skimming her upper thigh. "Hey, baby," he murmured, "let's go inside and get comfortable. We'll celebrate your birthday all night long."

Ari opened her eyes and pulled back.

Robin tightened his grip on her shoulders and tugged her tight against his body. His fingers stroked her bare legs in lazy circles.

Ari quivered as his stroking went higher and higher and moved to her inner thigh.

"You know you want me. I've been patient, but I need you, Ari."

"I can't sleep here. Nicole expects me home."

"Who said anything about sleeping?" Robin's fingers slipped under the edge of her shorts. "Are you still a silly little girl, or are you ready to be my woman?"

Ari thought she heard the crows cawing, but that was ridiculous. It was too late. She brushed the idea aside.

"I'll stay for a while, but I have to go home, or Nicole will call the cops."

***

Ari watched Robin as she struggled into her clothes. He slept, sprawled on his back, sheet pulled up to his waist, a scowl across his forehead. She wondered if she should wake him. Ari reached out and touched his foot. Robin groaned and turned over.

Ari picked up her bag and slid her feet into her sandals. She opened the bedroom door and left the house, closing the door quietly behind herself.

214 · TAMARA MERRILL

Ari took a deep breath. After the stale beer and unwashed clothing smell of Robin's house, the cool night air felt clean. Not wanting to disturb the silence with the beep from the fob, she used the key to unlock her car, started the engine, and drove away. It was almost three. The streets were empty.

Driving, Ari thought about the last hour. *That wasn't at all what I expected. Robin's place really stinks. If I am going to have sex with Robin again, he'll have to wash his sheets.*

Robin's kisses had been sweet and thrilling as he removed her clothing, then urgent and demanding when he climbed on top of her. The pain of his entry had made her cry out, but Robin hadn't stopped or even slowed down.

It all happened so fast! He was pissed about the blood and mad at me for crying. And then he fell asleep. Passed out, she admitted to herself.

Her stomach ached with a dull throbbing. Ari glanced down at her leg and saw the smear of blood. She'd tried to clean up in the bathroom but there hadn't been anything to wash with, not even a bar of soap. She shuddered and drove faster, anxious to take a hot shower and get into her bed, alone.

*****

Ari stared at herself in the mirror as she brushed her teeth. *Seventeen. I had sex last night with Robin.* A dark smudge caught her eye. She focused on her wrist. A bruise encircled her arm.

Preposterous, P-R-E-P-O-S-T-E-R-O-U-S. Contrary to who I am. I will never be like Stacy or Angie. She jammed her toothbrush into its holder and turned away from her reflection. *I promised myself that no guy would ever treat me like this.*

Pulling a long-sleeved T-shirt over her head, Ari heard her phone beep. Her heart jumped. She grabbed the phone. A message from Robin—**CU at work?**

He thinks everything is fine. Ari's fingers hesitated over the keys. She took a deep breath and typed **K**.

"I'm so stupid," she whispered. "Why did have sex last night?" She glared at herself and shook her head. "I need a morning-after pill."

She grabbed her purse and rushed out of the house. *If I hurry, I'll have time to stop at the drugstore and the gas station before class.*

***

At CVS, Ari held her head high and avoided eye contact as she purchased the pill and a bottle of water. In her car she stared at the package in her hand, steadied herself, and ripped it open. She swallowed the pill and followed it with a long drink of water.

Nevermore stood on the hood. He cawed loudly.

"Not now," Ari said and shooed him away.

She started her car and drove toward the gas station.

The crows followed, cawing loudly.

***

Robin pulled her in for a hard kiss.

Ari struggled against him.

He tightened his grip.

Ari pushed away. "Stop it."

"What's the matter with you. You're not a virgin anymore; no need to play hard-to-get. You already gave it away."

Ari heard laughter and whirled around. Tank and Tiny were by the chips, watching. Her thoughts froze. She flushed bright red and stammered an incoherent sound.

Robin laughed. "Go to school, little girl. Then meet us at the river. We'll bring the beer."

"What is wrong with you?' Ari screamed. "How could you tell your friends about last night?"

"No biggie." Robin shrugged.

"It is to me." Ari choked on the admission. She ran to the door and hurled it open.

Robin laughed "She'll be there. No way can she resist this." He made a rude pumping action with his hand.

Tank and Tiny laughed.

The door closed on the sound. Ari cringed, gulped in fresh air and steadied herself. "Asshole," she muttered as she strode to her car.

***

After parking her car in the student lot, Ari sat for a long moment, undecided if she wanted to see Robin ever again.

Glancing at the time, she realized that her science lab was underway. A white car whipped into the vacant space next to her own. *If there are five white cars in this parking lane, I'll meet Robin.* She pushed her door open, grabbed her bag and books and slammed the door shut.

And, if there are ten, I'll kill him.

Ari's anger solidified. She calmed and nodded to herself. *It's a plan.*

Walking toward the building, she counted the car next to her own. One.

Walked by two cars.

Spotted two white cars: two and three.

Passed a blue pickup. Found another white car and counted four, and across on the opposite side of the lane, five, six, seven.

A large SUV blocked her view down the lane. She quickened her steps. *More than halfway there.*

The lane curved. Eight, nine.

She could see the end. *No more white cars.*

A pickup swung into the lane and took the front-most space.

White! That makes ten! Ari pressed her hand to her chest. Her heart was pounding.

Okay, how should I do it?

***

Ari quickened her steps and hurried to her chemistry lab. The lecturer ignored her as she slipped into her seat and nodded to her lab partner. "What's the topic?" she whispered.

"Common acids, chapter ten."

"Thanks." Ari smiled and lifted her eyes to the screen where the instructor was flashing charts and pictures. She tried to focus but found herself thinking only of what to do about Robin. *Maybe this isn't a good idea.* Her sleeve pulled back, and she saw the bruise encircling her wrist. *He needs to be stopped. It's a good idea.*

The lecture portion ended, and the lab experiment was assigned: to measure and record the pH level of three acids using red cabbage water.

"Easy," her partner declared. "You grab three bottles of acid and our beaker of cabbage water, and I'll get the equipment."

"Okay." Ari gathered the acetic acid, hydrochloric acid, and sodium hydroxide from the front of the room and returned to her lab table. The experiments were easy and fun. They took turns doing the tests and recording the results. Ari was able to push Robin from her mind.

The lab ended. They cleaned their equipment and returned everything to the front of the classroom.

"Miss Blimm."

Ari startled and found the teacher standing beside her. "Yes?"

"I need a volunteer to replace the acid bottles in the cabinet. Since you were late, I think you'd be the perfect volunteer." He didn't smile.

"Sure, no problem." Ari stood up.

"Follow me." He spun on his heel and walked away.

Ari flipped him off. A few students snickered.

She followed him.

"This is the cabinet." He gestured to the tall, locked cupboard in the corner. "Those are the acids." He gestured again toward the small bottles the students had returned to the front table. "I will unlock the cabinet. You will place the bottles in the cabinet in alphabetical order.

When you are done, you will lock the cabinet and return the keys to my desk. Can you handle that?"

"Certainly." Ari smiled sweetly and looked directly into his eyes. "It will be my pleasure, sir."

He looked away and she saw his ears redden. He turned to the cabinet, unlocked the door, laid the keys on the counter next to the bottles, and left the room.

What a jerk!

Ari quickly began placing the small bottles back into the cupboard. CH_3COOH—acetic acid, HCI—hydrochloric acid. It went in a space next to a bottle of pale blue liquid, HCN—hydrocyanic acid—marked with a skull and crossbones. Ari slipped the HCN bottle into her pocket and quickly finished her task. NaOH—sodium hydroxide. *All done.*

She locked the cabinet and placed the keys in the center of the desk.

Ari felt the bulge of the small bottle in her pocket. She pulled out her phone to find out what it contained. *No! Don't use Google! They can trace a search.* She put the phone back in her pocket and flipped her chemistry book to the glossary. HCN—hydrogen and cyanide. She flipped to the referenced page and read the description:

Hydrogen cyanide, sometimes called prussic acid, is a chemical compound with the chemical formula HCN. It is a colorless, rapidly acting, extremely poisonous, and flammable liquid. It is know to have the odor of bitter almonds. A hydrogen cyanide concentration of 100–200 ppm in breathing air will kill a human within 10 to 60 minutes. A hydrogen cyanide concentration of 2000 ppm (about 2380 mg/m^3) will kill a human in about one minute. The toxic effect is caused by the action of the cyanide ion, which halts cellular respiration.

Perfect, now how do I get him to drink this stuff?

At once, the thought came. *In his beer. He'll never know.*

Ari covered her mouth so she wouldn't laugh aloud.

***

Ari returned home and parked her car in its usual space. The house was quiet. Nicole and Cedric were both at work. Ari changed into jeans and a long-sleeved camouflage T-shirt. She pulled her hair into a tight ponytail, put her phone and the small bottle of blue liquid into her pockets, got her bike and rode to the river.

Robin's truck was in the parking lot. Ari knew he'd wouldn't be at the public beach; he'd be up in the woods where they'd gone before. She rode past the parking lot and concealed her bike off the road in the dense undergrowth.

Nevermore and Morrigan landed in a tall pine tree.

"Go away," she whispered.

The birds stayed.

Ari cut through the woods and then crept up to the swimming hole Robin liked. Sure enough, he was there, but his friends weren't. Ari considered this a moment and then stepped out of the woods. "Where are the guys?" she asked.

Robin spun to face her. "Hi, Babe. You seemed kind of upset, so I told 'em to come later. After I'd had time to cool you down."

Ari wanted to hit him, but she forced herself to stay calm. "How much later?"

"Hour or so, why?"

"Just curious."

Robin tipped his beer up and drank it all. He dropped the can to the ground. "I'm going in. Grab a couple of beers and meet me down there."

Ari watched him walk away and dive under the water. Covering her hand with her T-shirt, she pulled a beer from the cooler, opened it, and dumped some onto the ground. She balanced the open can against the cooler and removed the blue liquid from her pocket.

She unscrewed the lid carefully and the faint odor of almonds filled her senses. *I wonder how much to use.* She shrugged and dumped it all into the beer. Re-screwed the top on the bottle and returned it to her pocket.

Robin was splashing back onto the shore. Carefully keeping her hand covered with her T-shirt, Ari picked up the beer and walked down to meet him.

He grinned at her and reached for the can. "Where's yours?"

"I want to swim out to the raft first."

Robin took a swig from the can.

Ari held her breath.

Robin looked at the label. "Hmm, tastes different." He took another long drink. "Nah, it's fine."

Ari let out her breath. "Drink up, and I'll race you to the raft," she said.

Robin tipped the can up and chugged the contents. He belched loudly and grinned at Ari.

Ari sat on a log and removed her shoes.

Robin threw the empty bottle aside and plunged into the water. "Last one there has to strip naked!" he shouted and started swimming.

Ari waited. *Nothing seems wrong; maybe there wasn't enough in the bottle.*

Robin reached the raft. He placed one hand on the ladder. It slipped off. He reached again and fell backwards.

Ari stood up.

She thought she heard voices and whirled around. It was only Nevermore and Morrigan clicking vehemently as they strutted behind her on the bank. She looked back at the raft.

Robin's head was gone now. The water was still.

Ari picked up the beer can taking care not to touch it with her bare fingers. She rinsed it out several times, sniffed to assure that there was no lingering almond odor, and dropped it near Robin's other empty can. She put on her shoes, walked away from the river, mounted her bike, and rode home.

Morrigan and Nevermore circled high into the cloudless sky and disappeared from sight.

***

Saturday afternoon, Ari and Nicole drove to the airport to pick up Cedric. Nicole stopped the car in front of the commuter terminal and jumped out to give him a hug and a kiss. Ari emerged from the front seat and avoided the couple as she crawled into the back seat. Cedric tossed his carry-on into the trunk and held the passenger-side door for Nicole as he gave her another light kiss.

He grinned at Ari. "Hey, birthday girl. Ready for a night out with the old folks?"

Ari managed a polite laugh.

Cedric settled behind the steering wheel and pulled into the traffic. Back on the highway, he caught Ari's eye in the rearview mirror. "Nicole tells me you had a big night out with your friends."

Ari shrugged and clenched her fingers into fists to keep them from shaking. "Sort of."

Nicole gave Cedric a tap on his leg and shook her head slightly.

What does that mean? Does she know I had sex with Robin? Ari bit her lip, pulled her scrunchie from her ponytail and finger-combed her hair. *One thousand, nine hundred and ninety-nine, nine hundred and ninety-eight, nine hundred and ninety-seven.*

"DiAngelo's still sound good for dinner?" Cedric asked.

"Perfect," Ari said. She kept her eyes on the view from the side window.

Nicole asked about Cedric's trip.

"It was great." Cedric began reciting the details of his meetings.

Ari stopped listening.

She drummed her fingers, silently, against her leg. *I wonder if anyone knows Robin is dead?* Ari's hands trembled. She shoved them under her legs. *Vindicate, V-I-N-D-I-C-A-T-E, defend, excuse, justify. He totally needed to be taken out before he hurt anyone else.*

Cedric's voice pulled her attention back to the moment. "Ari, did you want to invite anyone to join us for dinner tonight?"

"Ahh," Ari stammered, "I don't think so."

Nicole turned to look at Ari. "How about Robin? We'd like to meet him."

Ari shook her head. "I don't think we'll go out again."

Nicole nodded. "Okay. How about Cooper?"

Cooper would provide a distraction. Ari took her phone from her pocket. "Good idea," she agreed, and started texting.

Almost at once, Cooper replied. **LOVE TO - TIME?**

"Cooper's in. What time is our reservation, Cedric?"

"Tell him we'll pick him up at six forty-five, or he can meet us there at seven." Cedric reached over and squeezed Nicole's hand.

Ari pretended not to notice. She knew Nicole wanted to know why she wasn't going out with Robin again, but Ari was determined to avoid the subject.

***

The valet accepted Cedric's keys just as Cooper hurried up to the entrance and kissed Ari on the cheek, saying, "Happy Birthday." He shook hands with Cedric and greeted Nicole.

Ari and Cooper followed Cedric and Nicole into the restaurant.

DiAngelo's bustled with the usual Saturday-night dinner crowd. The smell of tomatoes and lemon mixed with oregano, basil, rosemary, and garlic hung in the air. Ari took a deep breath. Her tension eased. The events of yesterday afternoon faded, if only for the moment.

The talk at the table during dinner centered mostly around Ari's senior year and what college she would attend. "I'm hoping to get into Smith or Wellesley, but I applied to some others, too."

"Oh la la," Cooper gave a soft whistle. "I knew you were smart, but those are some serious schools. Aren't they both women only?"

Ari took a bite of her bread and nodded as she chewed.

Nicole laughed. "They both offer great educational opportunities for women, Cooper. It doesn't mean there is no chance to meet persons of the opposite sex."

Cooper flushed. "Got it." He smiled at Ari. "I was just surprised, I guess. I thought you were starting to date."

"Date, maybe," Ari said, "but I'm not obsessed with boys, like some people." She grinned at Cooper.

"I'm glad to hear it," Cedric interrupted. "You've plenty of time for all that."

Nicole took Ari's hand and smiled at her. "Be careful, but remember to have fun."

Ari pulled her hand back and picked up her napkin to pat her lips. *Does she know I had unprotected sex?*

Cooper cleared his throat and caught Ari's attention. He winked. *Does he know?*

Cedric pulled a small package from his pocket and handed it across the table. "Happy Birthday, Ari."

Ari opened the wrapping carefully to reveal a gold box. She lifted the lid and set aside the cotton pad, and gazed down at a gold chain with two charms attached to a loop.

Touching the charms carefully with the tip of her finger, Ari said, "Morrigan and Nevermore."

"Exactly!" Cedric grinned. "I hope you like it. I remember my mother saying every girl needs a few pieces of gold jewelry before she goes to college. So, I thought it was time to start your collection."

Nicole laughed and patted Cedric's arm.

Ari removed the necklace from its box and examined the crow charms, one on the wing and one strutting. She lifted her eyes to Cedric. "It's perfect. Thank you, Cedric."

Cooper stood and held out his hand. "Allow me to help you with that."

Ari relinquished the necklace and pulled her hair aside to give Cooper access. The chain was cool on her neck. She dropped her hair and ran her fingertips over the charms, feeling them warm to her touch.

Cedric nodded. "It looks lovely on you. So, who's ready for dessert?" He raised his hand to signal the waiter.

Cooper moved to return to his seat and waved at someone. Ari turned to look. It was Marybeth and Steve. She lifted her hand in greeting and said, "I didn't know they were dating."

Cooper shrugged. "It's just a summer thing."

The waiter placed a plate of tiramisù, garnished with a glowing candle, in front of Ari. "Happy Birthday, miss."

"Want me to sing?" Cooper teased.

"Don't you dare!" Ari leaned forward, made her wish, and blew out the candle.

The waiter served the others. The conversation turned to birthday wishes.

Steve and Marybeth stopped at the table. "Happy Birthday, Ari," Steve said, and then, "Did you guys hear about Robin?"

Cooper glanced quickly at Ari and then turned to Steve. "What about him?"

"They found his body this afternoon. In the river."

Nicole gasped.

Cedric frowned.

Ari held her breath and stared at her plate. So much for wishes. Ineluctable. I-N-E-L-U-C-T-A-B-L-E. Inevitable, unavoidable. She heard Cooper ask what happened and forced herself to look up and meet Steve's eyes.

"Looks like he was swimming alone and drowned. The cops say there will be a full investigation."

Nicole asked Ari, "Is that the same Robin you went out with on your birthday?" She picked up Ari's hand and squeezed it. "Oh. Honey. I'm so sorry."

Tears filled Ari's eyes and overflowed. *Think! Act normal.* Using her napkin, she dabbed at her eyes and admitted, "Maybe. Robin Sharky?"

Steve nodded.

Marybeth scurried around the table and threw her arms around Ari. "Oh, you poor thing. This is so sad!" She burst into sobs.

The waiter approached to see if he could help.

Nicole hurried to Ari and pulled her away from Marybeth. "We'll meet you at the car, Cedric." She kept her hand on Ari and guided her out of the restaurant.

Nicole handed the valet the claim and then pulled Ari into a hug.

Ari stiffened.

Nicole didn't let go. Instead, she murmured, "I know it's a terrible shock, and I don't know how you feel, but I'm here to help in any way I can."

She dropped her arms. "Here's Cedric and Cooper."

The valet arrived with the car.

Cooper opened Ari's door. "I'll call you later, okay?"

Ari nodded and ducked into the car.

***

Tears escaped from Ari's eyes. She swiped at them with the back of her hand. A wave of nausea threatened to overwhelm her. She swallowed hard.

The short ride home was accomplished in silence. Cedric pulled into the garage and turned off the engine. No one moved.

Ari watched Nicole and Cedric exchange a long look. She bit her lip and clenched her hands into tight fists.

"Ari." Cedric's voice was quiet but firm. He turned to look at her.

Ari held her breath. *This is it. He's going to send me away.* She lifted her eyes and forced herself to look at Cedric.

"Ari," he said again. "Is there anything you'd like to tell us about Robin?"

Ari burst into sobs.

Nicole exited the car and pulled Ari's door open. She reached in and tugged Ari into a tight hug.

Ari sobbed harder.

"It'll be okay," Nicole murmured over and over as she stroked Ari's hair.

Slowly, Ari's tears subsided. Nicole helped her climb out of the car and guided her into the house. Cedric followed.

Ari slumped down on a kitchen chair and cradled her head on her folded arms. She kept her head down as Cedric poured wine for himself and Nicole. When they, too, were seated at the table, Ari spoke without lifting her head. "I wasn't really dating Robin. I just met him at the gas station, and we went swimming and stuff."

"And, on your birthday?" Nicole prompted.

The doorbell rang.

Ari lifted her head.

Cedric carefully set his glass down and gazed at Ari. He rose and glanced out the window. "The police are here, Ari."

Ari's eyes widened in fear.

Cedric patted her shoulder as he passed behind her chair. "I'll talk to them first, but I'm sure they'll need to ask you about Robin."

Ari cleared her throat and nodded. "Okay." *Shit, shit, shit.* She reached for a tissue and blew her nose.

Nicole stretched her hand across the table.

Ari ignored Nicole's hand and concentrated on her breathing. *One thousand, nine hundred and ninety-nine, nine hundred and ninety-eight, nine hundred and ninety-seven...*

Cedric stepped back into the kitchen. "Ari, are you ready?"

She stood and followed him to the living room.

A man and a woman, both in uniform, stood in front of the fireplace, waiting. Ari glanced at them and quickly looked away. *Deep breaths,* she cautioned herself.

Cedric introduced Ari and suggested everyone sit down. He waved Ari to the sofa and sat beside her. Casually, he draped an arm over her shoulders and said, "Go ahead, Officer."

The man cleared his throat and nodded.

Ari gulped and thrust her hands under her legs to keep them still.

"No need to be afraid, Ari. We just have a few questions." He paused and waited for a response.

Ari stayed quiet.

Cedric squeezed her shoulders.

"I'm Detective Carson. We'd like you to tell us about your relationship with Robin Sharky."

Ari lifted her eyes from the carpet and managed to look directly at the policeman. "We didn't really have a relationship."

Carson shot a sideways look at his partner. He frowned at Ari. "Really?" He lifted one eyebrow. "Maybe you can tell us what you did have, then?"

Ari pulled her hands from under her legs and crossed her arms, hugging herself tightly. She drew in a shuddering breath and said, "I went to the river with him a few times, and then he got mad because I spent the day with Cooper."

"Cooper Adams?"

Ari nodded.

"Did that upset you, Ari?" the detective asked.

"Sort of." Ari took another deep breath. "I guess, but on my birthday, he asked me to come meet him at the gas station."

"And, you went to the movies," Nicole said from the doorway.

Ari whipped her head around and stared at Nicole. *Prevaricate, P-R-E-V-A-R-I-C-A-T-E, to speak falsely or misleadingly; deliberately create an incorrect impression; lie.* She looked back at the detective, caught his cold gaze, and froze. She held her breath. *One hundred, ninety-nine, ninety-eight, ninety-seven, ninety-six.*

Ari shifted her frightened gaze to the policewoman.

The woman nodded and smiled her encouragement.

Ari managed to say, "Ummmm. We didn't really go to a movie."

"Would you like some privacy, Ari?" the policewoman asked.

"She's seventeen!" Cedric exploded.

Detective Carson kept his eyes on Ari as he said, "Counselor, as you know, we have the right to question a minor with or without an adult, and the minor has the right to ask they be separated from any adult."

Ari caught her lower lip between her teeth and then let out a long sigh. "It's okay." She twisted her hands into a knot. "They can stay." She dropped her voice and muttered, "They're going to find out anyway."

Cedric's arm dropped from around her shoulders.

Ari closed her eyes. She felt the sofa cushion depress and opened her eyes to find herself sitting between Nicole and Cedric.

Nicole reached over and placed her hand on Ari's clenched fist. "It's okay. Just tell the truth."

Ari looked straight ahead, not making eye contact with anyone.

"I thought he really liked me. He said I was pretty. Then he got so mad and I knew I had to stop being so afraid of having sex or he'd find somebody else."

"Did he force you?" Cedric demanded.

Ari shook her head. "No, I decided to do it."

"Do what, Ari?" the policewoman asked.

"You know—have sex, whatever."

Nicole patted Ari's leg. "It's okay, Ari. Wanting to express your love with the sex act is perfectly normal."

Cedric stiffened and cleared his throat nervously. He didn't speak.

"It was gross!" Ari blurted.

The policewoman smiled slightly. "Start over, Ari. When was your birthday, and exactly what happened?"

"You already know what happened." Ari risked a glance at Cedric.

"We need you to tell us in your own words." The policewoman leaned back in her chair and waited.

"Last Thursday, my birthday was last Thursday. I sent Robin a text message asking if he wanted to celebrate with me."

"Did he answer?" Detective Carson asked.

Careful, he knows something. "Sort of. He sent me some emojis, so I went to the gas station to talk to him."

Carson nodded slightly.

"After I explained that Cooper is just my friend, I followed him to his house." Ari turned to Cedric. "I know you think that was dangerous, but I trusted Robin, and he wanted me to meet his roommates."

"Tim Kowalski and Arron Jones."

"I guess so. Robin called them Tank and Tiny."

"Okay." Carson wrote something in his notebook. "Then what happened?"

"We all sat on the porch and drank some beer. And, after a while, Tank and Tiny left. Robin and I made out, and he asked me to stay the night."

Ari paused. "Can I have a drink of water?"

Nicole jumped to her feet and hurried out of the room. Everyone sat in silence until she returned and handed Ari a glass.

Ari gulped the water. "After Robin went to sleep, I got up and drove home."

"You had a few beers. You went willingly into the house, and had sex with Robin, and then went home. Is that correct?"

Ari squirmed at the cold recitation of facts. Finally, she nodded and mumbled, "Yes."

"Then what happened on Friday?"

"Robin asked me to come to the gas station on my way to class."

"Are you in summer school?"

Nicole interrupted. "Ari is taking classes at the college."

"Ah." Carson wrote something in his notebook. "Did you go to the gas station?"

"Yes."

"What time was that?"

"About nine o'clock, I guess. Class starts at ten."

Carson waited for her to continue.

Ari looked at Cedric. He avoided her eyes. She turned back to the detective. "I stopped at the CVS first."

"Why?"

Ari stared at him defiantly. "I needed a morning-after pill."

Carson looked embarrassed.

Ari stifled a smile and looked at the policewoman as she continued. "Tiny and Tank were there. Robin wanted me to go with them to the river that afternoon. But," Ari brushed her eyes as if tears were threatening, "he'd told them that we'd had sex."

The policewoman nodded. "Did that make you angry?" she asked.

Ari nodded and rubbed at her eyes again. She counted to five. "Mad, but mostly hurt. I guess I realized right then what a jerk he is."

"Did you go to the river Friday afternoon?"

"No, I just came home after class."

"What time did you get home?"

"About twelve thirty, I think."

"Did anyone see you come home?"

"I don't know."

Carson wrote another note. "Did you see anyone on your way home?"

"I just drove here and parked in the drive, right where I always do."

"Ari was reading in her room when I got home at two," Nicole said.

"Got it." Carson studied his notebook. "Did you have any contact with Robin after Friday morning?"

Ari looked directly into the detective's eyes. "No, sir. I didn't text him, and he didn't text me."

"When did you learn that Robin was dead?"

"Tonight, at dinner. Just a little bit ago." Ari allowed tears to run down her face.

Nicole pulled her into a hug.

Cedric stood. "Is there anything else, Officer?"

"No, that's it. The kid was drunk and swimming alone. An accident waiting to happen. Thank you for your time."

Ari lifted her head from Nicole's shoulder and caught Cedric's look of uncertainty. *He's suspicious! I need to be careful.*

***

Seven for a secret, Never to be told.

"In many traditions, crows are messengers and close attention is paid to their actions. —*Robert Moss*

Summer classes ended, and Cooper texted to suggest one more meet-up before his departure for school. Ari declined.

An hour later, Cooper appeared at the door. Nicole invited him in. Ari was caught in the living room and couldn't deny that she was home, but as soon as Nicole was safely in another room, she turned on Cooper. "I told you I didn't want to see you. I don't need to talk about Robin, or sex, or my feelings, or any of that crap!"

Cooper raised his hands in surrender. "Whoa, girl. I just wanted to say goodbye."

"And check on me?"

"Okay, maybe. But mostly, I'm your friend, and this has all got to be making you think about Angie."

Ari grimaced. *Yeah, Angie, Stacy, and Jerry.*

Cooper gave her a little half-smile and cocked his head to the side. "And, I wanted to check on you."

Ari laughed at his admission. "Let's go outside."

She led the way to the kitchen and grabbed sodas from the refrigerator. As they settled at the picnic table, Morrigan and Nevermore set up a loud cawing and flew excited circles around the yard.

"Hang on a sec," Ari siad. "I gotta get them a snack."

The birds settled on the picnic table to wait.

Cooper reached out a gentle finger and Nevermore allowed him to stroke his head.

"So, what do you think," he asked the bird, "is she okay?"

Nevermore cawed loudly again and again.

"Yeah," Cooper agreed, "I don't think so either."

***

Cedric and Nicole watched Ari as she moved lethargically through the last days of summer. They discussed her withdrawal and when Ari refused to talk about Robin or her plans for senior year and college, Cedric suggested, one night at dinner, that she see a counselor.

Immediately angry, Ari bristled. She glared at Cedric and demanded, "Are you kidding me?"

"No, Ari." Cedric kept his voice calm. "I'm afraid I have to insist on this. I've called Alex Summers. He can see you next week."

"I'm not talking to that idiot!"

Cedric frowned. "I thought you liked him."

Ari rolled her eyes and clicked her tongue. "No, Cedric. I did not like him, and I won't talk to him again." She sighed. "I'm not crazy or suicidal. Why do I need to talk to anyone? I can handle this. It's just another dumb death."

"Exactly my point," Cedric said, reaching across the table and placing his hand on Ari's wrist. "It is another death."

What does he mean by that? Does he know I killed them?

She licked her lips and forced herself to make eye contact. "I know it's weird to have two friends die when you are still in high school, but it isn't just me. Everyone in our school knew Angie and Robin."

Nicole nodded. "That's true, Ari. I think I'll suggest that the whole high school should be offered grief counseling again. She's right, Cedric. They all need to process these sad deaths."

Cedric withdrew his hand from Ari's wrist and glared at Nicole. "Certainly, but it's Ari's mental health I care about."

He turned back to Ari. "As your guardian, it is my responsibility to protect and care for you."

Ari's upper lip curled in disgust. "Right! Don't worry, I'll be eighteen before you know it, and I'll be out of here."

She pushed her chair back and strode to the sink and stared out the window. *One hundred, ninety-nine, ninety-eight, ninety-seven, ninety-six, ninety-five.* She took in a trembling breath and turned back to face Cedric. *Concede, C-O-N-C-E-D-E, to make a concession; yield to pressure, admit defeat.* Ari nodded. "Okay, I'll talk to someone but not Alex."

"Good. Would you rather talk to a woman?" Cedric reddened. "I mean, maybe it would be easier to, um, you know, talk about stuff."

Stuff like murder? Ari stifled the thought. "Sure, maybe."

"Okay then, I'll set it up." He pushed his chair back from the table and stood. "How about some ice cream and a movie night."

"No thanks, I'm just going to go to my room and read." Ari managed to smile at Cedric and kept her back straight as she left the room.

***

Ari drove to the low redbrick building housing the offices of Sandra Madison and other health professionals. She slowed for the driveway, then changed her mind, and sped up, driving on until she reached the parking lot by the river. Ari parked at the far end of the lot, away from all the other cars. She rolled down her window, tipped her head back against the seat, and closed her eyes.

The sounds of splashing and laughter floated on the wind.

She knew she needed to drive back to the medical building and keep her appointment. Ari opened her eyes, rolled up her window, and climbed out of the car. *I'll just take a look.* She slammed the car door and quickly walked to the path that led upstream, away from the community beach and to where she'd been with Robin.

The remains of a takeout container and an empty drink cup littered the flat rock. Ari swept away, letting the trash fall on the rocky beach. She sat on the rock, pulled her knees up and wrapped her arms around them, staring out at the floating raft. From downstream, the laughter lifted, and something splashed loudly.

Leaves crunched behind her.

Ari turned. Detective Carson strode out of the woods.

Ari stumbled to her feet and took in a deep breath. *Tranquil, T-R-A-N-Q-U-I-L, free, unaffected by disturbing emotions. Keep it together!*

"Hey." He walked toward her. "I didn't expect to find you here. Are you looking for something?"

Ari smiled slightly. "Hi," she greeted the policeman. "No, I just—" Ari looked at the raft and then back to Carson. "Robin liked to swim to that raft."

He waited.

"Is this where you found him?" she asked.

"No. His body was found downstream, just the other side of the community beach."

"Oh, I guess I figured it would be up here because this is where we went swimming."

"We found his clothes, a cooler, and a few empty beer cans here."

Ari's face paled. She swayed on her feet.

Carson reached out a hand toward her. "Here, you better sit down."

Ari sat. She dropped her head into her hands and tried not to show how much she was trembling.

Carson's hand descended on her shoulder. "It's okay, kid," he said. "It's tough when someone you know dies."

Ari gulped. "But—what happened?"

Carson withdrew his hand. "Coroner says he was drunk and probably got a cramp. Good reason not to swim alone." He took a step away and focused on the river. "Your folks got you talking to anyone?"

"They want me to. I'm supposed to be there now." *Shut up, stop talking.*

"You ought to go. It'll help. This was just an accident, you know that, right? You made the right decision when you didn't meet him that afternoon. Guys like Robin are bad news."

Ari stood up. "I guess you're right. I better go." Ari took a step away and stopped. She glanced back. "Thanks."

"You're welcome, Ari. Stay safe."

Ari darted a look toward the cemetery trees and hurried down the trail back to her car.

She drove directly to the medical office, entered, and checked in. "I'm kind of late," she explained to the receptionist.

"It's okay. You take a seat, honey, and I'll find out if Dr. Madison can still see you."

"Thanks."

Ari walked over to the window and gazed at the parking lot. *I'll have to think of an excuse to tell Cedric if he finds out I was late.*

"Harriet Blimm."

Ari looked over her shoulder and took in the tall woman who'd called her name.

"Come on in. I'm Dr. Madison."

Ari followed the counselor through the door, down the hallway, and into a corner office full of light and bright paintings.

"Sit anywhere."

Ari chose a blue plaid wingback chair that was angled away from the desk and toward the window.

Dr. Madison settled herself on a matching sofa. "So, Harriet. I only have a few minutes, but let's get to know each other a bit. In our next session, we can start on time, and you can tell me how I can help."

Ari squirmed and then forced herself to sit still. "Sorry I was late," she mumbled.

"It's not always easy to come in. I get that." Dr. Madison opened a small notebook and picked up a pen. "Harriet is an unusual name. Are you named for someone?"

"Yeah. My grandmother, but I hate being called Harriet."

"I see. What should I call you, then?"

"Ari."

"Nice. Ari it is." She sat back and crossed her legs. The points of her blond bob fell forward over her cheeks as she tilted her head down to write in the notebook.

Ari pulled her sweater sleeves down over her hands and then shoved them under her legs. She studied the woman in front of her.

Dr. Madison sat quietly watching Ari.

As the silence grew uncomfortable, Ari turned her gaze to the window.

Still, the doctor stayed silent.

Ari squirmed in her seat. "Aren't you going to ask me questions?" she blurted.

"Perhaps you'd like to tell me why you are here."

Ari frowned. "Because I have to be."

"No, Ari. You agreed to be here, and I agreed to see if I could help you understand the deaths of your family and friends."

"I understand that—" Ari struggled to her feet and stood, her hands shaking and her heart pounding. She began again. "I don't want to talk about dead people."

"Then we won't talk about them until you are ready. Your guardian asked that we talk once a week." Dr. Madison stood and moved to the door. "I understand that you've just begun your senior year of high school. Our time is up today." She opened the door and smiled at Ari. "Perhaps next week we can talk about your classes and what you'd like to accomplish. How does that sound?"

"Fine, I guess." Ari shuffled toward the door, keeping her eyes down. As she passed the doctor, Ari murmured, "Thanks."

***

Ari pulled her journal from her bedside table drawer and flipped back to the beginning. She skimmed the entries, each one a carefully constructed lie. She flipped to the last entry, written the night of her birthday—: "**17 is just more of the same. I thought it would be different.**"

She took a purple pen from her desk, dated the page, and wrote—, "**Met Dr. Madison today.**" She drew a sad face and added a large, bold question mark.

Tucking the journal back into its place in the drawer, a flash of gold caught Ari's attention. She shifted the contents and found Stacy's gold bangle bracelet. Ari pulled it out and considered it carefully. She slipped it over her hand and felt the cool metal encircle her wrist. An image of Stacy making pancakes and laughing filled her mind.

Impatiently, Ari shoved the memory away and whipped off the bracelet. She buried it back in the bottom of the drawer and slammed the drawer closed.

Tomorrow I'll go back to the trees and add an "R." She turned off the light and pulled the blanket up to her chin.

***

The hours spent in Dr. Madison's office were nothing like her time with Alex Summers. Madison asked probing questions and then sat saying nothing, waiting for Ari to comment.

Ari hated it. Each week, driving to the office, she carefully chose a topic to talk about, and each week her plans were destroyed by a question from Madison.

As usual, the waiting room was empty when Ari arrived. At precisely 4:00 p.m., Dr. Madison opened her office door and invited her in. Ari responded to the therapist's greeting and slumped down in the chair she'd chosen as her own.

"Last week, we spoke about your indecision over college, and I asked that you make a pro-and-con list to help clarify your thoughts. How did that go?"

"Great. I brought it with me." Ari rummaged in her bag and pulled out a folded sheet of paper. She handed the paper to the doctor.

Dr. Madison unfolded the sheet and read the neatly printed headings. Each column was completely blank. She laughed and handed the paper back to Ari. "Not so great then. Any idea why this is so difficult?"

Ari looked out the window. Dr. Madison looked, too.

In the parking lot, a crow landed on her car. Ari smiled.

The doctor asked, "Do you like birds?"

"I'm not called Bird Girl for nothing."

"Who calls you Bird Girl?"

"The newspaper started it, but now it's just Toby Meyers and his gang." She faced Madison. "Go ahead. I know you want to ask how that makes me feel."

"Why do you think they call you that?" Dr. Madison asked instead.

Ari tipped her head and squinted her eyes a bit as she considered the doctor. "You know, because of the crows."

Madison waited. When Ari didn't continue, she prompted, "Tell me about the crows."

"I named them Morrigan and Nevermore."

Madison waited.

"I know, kind of lame, right?"

"Not at all. How did you choose the names?"

"Just liked them, I guess." Ari looked back at her car. The crow was still there. She knew it was Nevermore, there to give her the strength she needed to get through this session.

"Have you read 'The Raven'?" the doctor asked.

"Yes. I know what you are thinking. When the raven says 'nevermore,' Poe wanted to show that loss is part of life and that you can never hold onto those you love. I was only like eleven when I named the crows. Trust me, I wasn't that profound."

"Perhaps. Do you also know the meaning of Morrigan?"

"Yeah, 'phantom queen.' But I didn't know that either. My teacher was reading aloud about King Arthur and all that. And I thought Morrigan was a good name for a crow."

"They are both excellent names. How did you come to know two crows?"

Ari lifted her eyes and glared at the therapist, her jaw clenched. She pounded her thigh with her fist. "Don't pretend you don't know!"

Jumping to her feet, Ari strode to the window and slapped her hand against the glass.

Nevermore rose from the car and flew to the windowsill. He gave a loud caw and bobbed up and down.

Ari heard the therapist's sharp intake of breath. She touched her hand to the glass, gently this time. Nevermore cawed again and lifted off.

"I've never seen anything like that!" Dr. Madison said quietly.

Ari, calm now, turned back and studied the woman.

"That was Nevermore," she explained, and returned to her chair. "Didn't Cedric tell you about me when he set this up?"

"He told me that you have experienced several deaths, and he was worried about the stress this would cause you as you mature."

Ari laughed aloud. "That sounds like Cedric." She hesitated a moment, then continued, "The crows are my friends, especially Nevermore."

"I could see that." Dr. Madison looked toward the windowsill, but Nevermore didn't appear. "You said you met them when you were eleven—six years ago."

Ari nodded. "I found Morrigan on the porch with a broken wing. I fixed it and they stayed. You probably heard about it on the news."

"I only moved here three years ago. I've never heard about a girl that fixed a crow's broken wing."

"That's me. Bird Girl. I talk to crows."

"Sounds pretty cool."

"It is but—"

"But it sets you apart?"

"Not any more than being a girl with a dead mother and a guardian does."

Dr. Madison wrote something on her pad.

Ari snapped her lips closed and slid her hands under her legs. She bit her lower lip. "What did you just write?"

Dr. Madison handed Ari the pad. "A note to myself."

Ari looked down and read, "Death of mother?"

She handed the pad back.

"When I turn eighteen, in ten months, I'll be on my own again."

Dr. Madison waited.

Ari struggled with what to say. She pulled her legs up onto the chair and sat crisscross. She twisted a strand of hair tightly around her finger. "Cedric says I'll always have a home with him and Nicole." She looked directly at the doctor, took a deep breath, and whispered. "I don't know if I can believe him."

"Has Cedric done, or said, anything to make you doubt his word?"

"No, but he has to be nice to me. Jenks is watching."

"Jenks?"

"Mrs. Jenkins. She's my social worker. She writes a report on us every year. And, before you can ask, that doesn't feel good. I don't like to be watched all the time."

"Understood." Dr. Madison tapped her pencil on the pad. "Let's talk about your interests. Instead of where you would like to attend college, what would you like to study? Maybe that will make the choice easier."

Ari wiggled deeper into the chair. She untwisted the strand of hair from her finger and considered the question. "I like words and numbers. But I don't think I have a," she held up her hands and made quotes in the air, "career choice."

Dr. Madison smiled, "Tell me about words and numbers."

"They make sense," Ari said quickly. "They never change. You can trust them." She paused and sat up straighter, bringing her feet back to the floor. "You can't trust how people use words, but you always spell a word exactly the same."

"Who do you trust, Ari?"

No one. Ari looked directly at the therapist and lied. "I trust myself."

The doctor looked at the small clock on the table. "Time's up, Ari. Let's talk about that more next week."

***

By March, Ari refused the acceptance offer from Wellesley and accepted the offer from State College, where she declared herself a mathematics major.

Cooper, home for his spring break, looked at her in horror. "Mathematics! Are you nuts?"

"I like math," Ari said. "Cedric was surprised, too. But I think it was more that I chose to go to a state school instead of one of those fancy ones than that I chose math?"

"He has a point." Cooper shook his head. "You got accepted to Wellesly, so why not go?"

Ari fiddled with the silverware spread in front of her. "I need to stay here." She picked up a menu. "Let's order."

Cooper picked up his menu and pretended to consider the options.

He shook his head. "Glad it's you and not me. As soon as I graduate, I'm going into the Illinois State Police Academy."

"Did you tell your dad?"

Cooper shrugged. "No, but my mom knows, and I'm doing it. It doesn't matter what he thinks."

"So, you really are going to be a policeman?"

"Detective, I hope." He grinned. "Maybe someday I'll solve the mystery of Ari Blimm."

The waitress set their burgers on the table.

Ari took a large bite. *Time to end this friendship. He's too nosy.* She swallowed and said, "No mystery here. You already know all my secrets."

***

"Are you excited about graduation?" Dr. Madison asked as soon as Ari made herself comfortable in the blue plaid chair.

"Not really. I was going to skip the whole thing, but Nicole and Cedric were really disappointed, so I guess I'll go to the ceremony."

"Ceremonies are important. They often mark significant events and changes in our lives."

"Yeah, that's what Nicole said—it's a rite of passage or something."

"For many, high school graduations is the end of childhood."

Ari shook her head, "My childhood ended a long time ago."

"Can you tell me about that?"

Shit, I need to keep my mouth shut. Five hundred, four hundred ninety-nine, four hundred ninety-eight, four hundred ninety-seven. Ari took in a deep breath and said, "It's not important. Shit happens, and life goes on."

Dr. Madison remained silent, waiting.

She's like a damn spider in her web. Hoping I'll spill my secrets. What can I say that will satisfy her?

Ari stood and walked to the window. She looked out at the cold gray sky and rubbed her arms against the chill from the glass. With her back turned, she said thoughtfully, "I think my childhood ended the day Stacy took me away from my grandparents." Ari lifted her hand and pressed her palm on the cold glass. "Stacy made pancakes, but she wasn't ever a real mother."

She walked back to the chair, counting the steps. *One, two, three, four, five.*

Dr. Madison waited for Ari to sit down and compose herself before asking, "Tell me about the counting, Ari."

Ari flushed and clenched her fists in her lap. "I'm not OCD!"

Dr. Madison waited.

"I looked it up. I don't do stuff a certain number of times. I just like numbers."

"Do you count to stay calm?"

"Sometimes." Ari thought for a second. "Mostly, I guess, it gives me time to think."

"We call that a coping mechanism. I think you've discovered a method that works for you."

"So, is that good or bad?"

Dr. Madison shook her head, making her blond bob swing. "It's neither, Ari. It just is."

Ari nodded. "Sometimes," she hesitated and slipped her hands under her legs, "I think of a word and spell it." She paused again and continued. "It helps me think."

"That sounds like naming, which is a way to figure out what's really on your mind, why you are feeling the way you feel." She made a note on her pad and asked, "Can you name your feeling right now?"

Vigilant, V-I-G-I-L-A-N-T, wary, keenly watchful to detect danger. Ari pushed the thought away and said, "I was actually thinking about your hair. Do you think I'd look good in a bob?"

Dr. Madison pushed at her hair behind her ears and smiled. "You have lovely, dark, curly hair, Ari. Are you thinking of cutting it?"

Ari shrugged. *Safe, S-A-F-E, secure from danger.* "Maybe."

"You mentioned that your mother was never a real mother. Why do you think that?"

Not safe after all. Ari considered her answer and spoke carefully. "We lived in a lot of places, and she was gone a lot. Stacy was glad that I could take care of myself while she worked."

Ari pulled her legs tight together and folded her hands in her lap. "We moved here when I was in fourth grade. She let Jerry live at our house." Ari closed her eyes for a moment, opened them and allowed tears to escape. "He wasn't very nice."

Dr. Madison held out a tissue box. "Did he hurt you?"

"Sometimes, but he hit my mom more." Ari took a tissue and blew her nose. She bit down on her lower lip, let it go, and took a shuddering breath. "I was glad when he died." She tipped her head down and stared at the floor. "Stacy came home that day." After a long pause, she whispered, "I thought we'd be a real family forever." She lifted her head and looked at the doctor, "A family like everybody else."

"And, what happened?"

Ari's face remained completely blank as she answered. "She went away, and then she died."

"It is very difficult to lose your parents when you are young."

Ari looked away. Not as difficult as living with her, she thought.

"Did your mother like the crows?"

"Stacy was already gone when they came."

Dr. Madison flipped back a few pages of her notepad. "I thought you found them on your porch when you were eleven. Who were you living with?"

"It was just the crows and me. That's why the paper called me Bird Girl."

Dr. Madison struggled to keep her voice even. "Living alone must have been frightening."

Ari shrugged and looked toward the clock. "Sometimes it was." She stood and headed to the door. "But it was a long time ago. See you next week."

***

Eight for a wish,

"If there's a single lesson that life teaches us, it's that wishing
doesn't make it so."
— *Lev Grossman*, The Magicians

Ari stood at the kitchen sink, rinsing dishes, and handing them to
Nicole to put in the dishwasher. She kept her eyes averted and said,
"I've decided not to go to college."

Nicole stopped with a plate in her hand. Ari could hear her take in
a deep breath.

"But…" Nicole paused.

"I graduate next week. And, I have enough credits from the community college to get an AA."

Nicole bent to place the plate she was holding into the dishwasher.
"I thought you were looking forward to college."

Ari handed Nicole the last plate and turned off the tap.

Nicole closed the dishwasher and leaned against the counter. She
waited until Ari turned to look at her before asking, "What's really
going on?"

"It'll just be more of the same." Ari picked up a sponge and swiped
at the counter using fast circles. Her scrubbing slowed and came to a
stop. "I want to get a job and a place of my own."

"There isn't any hurry." Nicole held up a hand to forestall Ari's protest. "College is not like high school, Ari."

"Yeah, right." Ari rinsed the sponge and laid it in its dish. "You and Cedric should have a kid of your own. You don't need me hanging around."

Nicole reached toward Ari.

Ari stepped away.

"We're your family. We want you 'hanging around.'"

"When I'm eighteen, Cedric won't be my guardian anymore. I'll need to have my own place."

"No, you won't. You can live with us as long as you want."

"Says who?" Ari's voice quivered. She shoved her damp hands into her pockets to stop their shaking.

Catching only Ari's question as he entered the kitchen, Cedric asked, "Who says what?"

Ari pulled her hands from her pockets and clenched the edge of the sink.

Nicole answered. "I was just telling Ari this is her home. Her forever home."

"Well, of course." Cedric grinned at Ari. "We like having you around, and we always will."

Always, A-L-W-A-Y-S, in any event; at any time; if necessary. Ari kept her eyes focused on the kitchen floor.

***

In August, Ari turned eighteen and a week later, college classes began. It was different, she admitted to herself. No one recognized her. She watched the other students and quickly learned to blend in. She studied in the library, or at a secluded table in the student union, between classes. Most days, she didn't speak to anyone at all.

Then in her stats class, the students were assigned a team project. The teacher counted them off, just like in kindergarten, and Ari drew a six. She swallowed hard and walked to the center of the classroom, where the other three students who were also sixes had gathered.

"I'm Laurie," a tall blond girl introduced herself.

"Barb." A lanky redhead waved one hand.

"Ari."

"Lucas." A tall, thin, sandy-haired guy with dark-framed glasses grinned at the women. "Looks like I'm your token male."

Laurie and Barb laughed.

"Don't worry," Barb said. "We won't hurt you. Let's set up a study group. My roommate works evenings, so my apartment is empty after five or we could use the library."

"Your house sounds good," Laurie spoke up. "Then we can work as late as we want." Laurie turned to Lucas and Ari. "She lives pretty close. Does that work for you guys?"

Ari nodded.

Lucas shrugged. "Sure. I work on the weekend, Friday through Sunday nights. But any other night is fine."

"We need to choose a topic and get approval," Barb said. "Anybody got any good ideas?"

Ari considered the young woman who'd taken charge. Barb's red hair was pulled up in a messy ponytail. Her jeans and T-shirt were nothing special. She wasn't particularly pretty, but there was something about her. *Maybe the eyes,* Ari thought.

Ari opened her notepad. "How about something to do with movies or television shows?" she asked.

Laurie smiled at Ari as she responded, "Interesting. I'm a theater major, so that appeals to me."

Barb nodded and pulled a pen from her hair. She opened a notebook and held the pen poised to write. "We need a specific topic, or we won't be able to write a good hypothesis."

Barb turned to Ari and waited.

Ari thought a minute, and when no one else spoke, she said, "Um, how about popular movie genres among college students?"

"Male versus female?" Laurie winked at Lucas.

Barb shook her head, "Too easy."

Everyone looked at Ari.

She bit her lip. *Five, four, three, two, one.* "Aspects of a commercially successful movie?'

Lucas nodded. "Now we're getting somewhere. We could compare budgets, big-name actors, and stuff like that for the most commercially successful movies in the past three years."

Barb looked at Laurie and then Ari. They both nodded. "Okay, I'll write it up and hand it in for approval. First meeting Thursday at six thirty. Everybody share your numbers with me, and I'll text you my address."

She gave them all her number, and her phone dinged three times with their responses. She glanced at the phone and said, "All right! Come prepared to figure out the hypotheses." She held her hand up for a high-five, and they all slapped.

***

Sitting in the hairdresser's swivel chair, Ari had second thoughts about cutting her hair. She'd made the appointment determined to go short, but when asked how short, she hesitated.

The hairdresser smiled. "How about I cut off about six inches and bring it up to your shoulders. That'll give your hair a lot of bounce, and if you love it, we can go shorter, but if you hate it, it'll grow back in a few months."

Ari nodded. "Okay, do it." She watched as hanks of her thick, dark hair fell to the floor. Within minutes, her head felt lighter, and her eyes looked bigger.

The hairdresser caught Ari's eye in the mirror and winked. "Your boyfriend is going to love this new you," she said.

"I like it," Ari said, avoiding the boyfriend remark.

As Ari walked from the hairdresser to Dr. Madison's office, she glimpsed her reflection in a store window. *I look totally different; maybe I can be different, too.*

***

Dr. Madison looked surprised when she opened the office door for Ari.

"What do you think?" Ari asked, turning in a circle. "And don't ask me what I think."

Dr. Madison laughed. "It looks great, Ari. You have beautiful hair."

Ari blushed. "Thanks." She brushed past the doctor and settled into her customary chair.

"How was your week, Ari? What made you decide to cut your hair?"

"It just seemed like it was time for a change." Ari reached for her hair as if to twist it around her finger. Instead, she touched it and then placed her hands in her lap. "I wanted to look different."

"There is usually a direct correlation between what's happening on our heads and what's happening in our lives. By fearlessly cutting your hair, you are sending a message to yourself and others."

Ari pondered the doctor's words. "Maybe," she conceded. "I'm not sure what message I'm sending, though."

"Perhaps you want others to see you differently, too. To see the real you."

Ari dropped her eyes to her lap and twisted her fingers into a knot. *Nope, not that. I don't want anyone to see the real me.*

Dr. Madison waited a moment before continuing, "What else is going on, Ari?"

"I'm in a study group for my stats class. It's okay. A couple of other girls and a guy." Ari stopped twisting her fingers and looked up. "Lucas. The guy's name is Lucas. I think he likes me."

***

Ari found herself looking forward to her classes. They weren't more of the same after all. With all of her basic requirements done, her schedule was filled with only classes she enjoyed. For the first time, she felt like she fit in. Like no one was watching her and waiting for her to act weird.

When she'd first cut her hair, Lucas told her he loved her new look.

Barb and Laurie had agreed.

On campus, she noticed that people looked at her and smiled or called out a greeting. She found herself smiling and waving back.

"It's pretty strange," Ari told Nicole, "but since I cut my hair, I think people like me better."

"I'm sure they've always liked you," Nicole answered.

"Dr. Madison says cutting my hair is a sign that I want to rid myself of the past." Ari stopped and considered for a moment. "I think she might be right."

Ari glanced at the clock. "Oops! I better get dressed. Lucas will be here in a minute. I told him I'd help him with his Christmas shopping."

***

By the New Year, Ari and Lucas were considered a couple. Their class schedules were different, and Lucas had a weekend job, but they found time to be together. In her continuing sessions with Dr. Madison, Ari frequently talked about the fun she was having with Lucas.

Dr. Madison encouraged her to compare her feelings about Lucas to those she'd had for Robin.

"No comparison at all!" Ari declared. "Lucas is fun. We talk about everything. He's my best friend."

"Are you taking precautions?"

"Yech!" Ari jumped to her feet and crossed to the window. She kept her back turned as she continued. "Not that it's any of your business, but we aren't having sex."

Dr. Madison waited.

Ari spoke very quietly. "I told Lucas I wasn't ready, and he isn't pushing me."

"After your experience with Robin, it is understandable that you are cautious."

Ari spun around and glared at the doctor. "I might never have sex again."

"True, but unlikely. Tell me why you think that."

"Sex just screws people up."

"Sometimes, but not always." Dr. Madison clicked her pen shut and clipped it to her notebook.

Ari walked back to her chair and gathered her belongings. "I have a lot of fun with Lucas, and if I wanted to have sex with him, I would." She looked at the doctor and giggled. "So, it's true; you shrinks think that all mental health issues stem from sex."

"Not exactly, Ari. But the sex act involves powerful emotions. It's not so much whether you have sex with someone but why you have sex."

Ari smirked. "Very profound, Doc. I'll take that under consideration." She swept across the room and exited.

"Please do," Dr. Madison said to the closed door.

***

Ari stretched out on the spring grass, arms over her head, eyes closed, and waited for Lucas to join her. She heard the cawing of crows in the distance. *Damn it! Go away, Nevermore. Don't come now.*

Ari sat up and looked around.

Nevermore, followed closely by Morrigan, swooped down and flew low over her head.

"Go away," Ari whispered.

The birds made another pass, this time even closer to her head, and then disappeared.

"Damn, girl." Lucas plopped down on the grass and gave Ari a quick kiss. "I thought those crows were going to take your head off."

Ari managed a smile. "Crazy, right?"

"They probably just think you're as special as I do." Lucas leaned in for another kiss.

Ari kissed back but kept her eyes open to be sure the birds didn't return. *You have no idea how special those crows think I am.*

Lucas stretched out beside her and turned his head to gaze into Ari's eyes. "What are you thinking about so hard?" he asked.

Ari traced her finger across his lips. "I was thinking that I should invite you to dinner. Cedric and Nicole keep pestering me."

Lucas sat up and faced her. "Okay, when?"

Ari hesitated. She sat up and looked very sober.

"Will your parents bring out the baby pictures and tell embarrassing stories about you?"

"No." Ari dropped her eyes. "I can guarantee there will be no baby pictures."

"Too bad. I bet you were a really cute baby."

Ari kept her eyes on her lap as she twisted her fingers into a knot. *Ten, nine, eight, seven, six, five four three, two, one.*

She forced herself to look at Lucas and took in a deep breath.

"They aren't my parents."

Lucas didn't move.

"Cedric is my guardian. I've lived with him since I was twelve."

Lucas reached out and placed his large, warm hand over her fingers. He squeezed gently.

"What happened to your parents?"

Fact, F-A-C-T, something known to exist or to have happened. "My dad was gone, and my mom died."

"Wow! That must have been tough." Lucas pulled Ari in for a hug and held her close. "You are the smartest, prettiest, most amazing girl I've ever met. I'd like to meet Cedric and Nicole anytime you say."

***

Lucas, a perfect guest, arrived exactly at 6:00 p.m., carrying flowers for Nicole. He gave Ari a light kiss and shook hands firmly with Cedric.

Nicole shooed the men out to the yard to start the grill and gave Ari a thumbs-up.

Ari blushed.

"Everything's done in here. Help me carry the drinks to the patio."

At dinner, Ari sipped at her lemonade and watched Lucas as he explained about the added hours he'd be working this summer. "I'm one of five kids. So, it's pretty expensive to put us all through college. I have a scholarship, but," he shrugged, "you know, there's lots of other expenses. If I work full-time all summer, I only need to work part-time during the school year."

Cedric nodded his approval. "Ari tells us you're a math major, too. Do you know what you want to do with your degree?"

Lucas placed his fork on his plate and chewed slowly before answering. "Ultimately, I'd like to teach at the college level, but I'll need to work a few years before I can afford grad school. My favorite part, so far, is figuring out problems, so I'm thinking I'll look for work as a statistician in marketing."

He picked up his fork and resumed eating.

A loud cawing interrupted the conversation. Everyone looked toward the power line.

Ari's heart dropped into the pit of her stomach. *Crap!*

"Here come the birds." Cedric pointed. "They never miss a meal."

Nevermore landed on the grass and strutted toward Ari. Morrigan cawed again and again as she circled the yard and then settled on a chaise lounge.

"Wow," Lucas breathed out. "I've never seen crows come so close."

Nicole laughed and pointed at each crow in turn. "Meet Nevermore and Morrigan. Hasn't Ari told you about them?"

Ari glared at Nicole. "They're just stupid birds."

Nevermore squawked indignantly.

Cedric looked back and forth between Lucas and Ari. He rose from the table. "Come on, Nicole. Let's get dessert while these two talk."

Lucas shook his head slowly. "I should have known something was up when they flew so close to you last week. What's with the crows, Ari?"

"It's none of your business." Ari snapped her lips together and chewed her lower lip. "Just stop asking questions and leave me alone."

"Hey. It's cool. Just weird."

"I'm not weird!" Ari jumped to her feet.

Nevermore gave a warning crackle and jumped sideways to get out of her way.

Lucas stood and moved toward Ari, his hand outstretched. "I'm the one that should be mad. You're the one keeping secrets."

"Just leave." Ari pushed his hand away. "Go away, now!"

Lucas's arm dropped to his side. He looked at Ari, dumbstruck. His eyes turned black as he glared at her. "When you're ready to stop keeping secrets, call me."

He walked toward the gate, then stopped and turned to say, "Tell Nicole and Cedric I enjoyed myself until you went crazy."

Ari watched him leave and heard the gate slam. She looked down at Nevermore. "I'm not crazy." She sank down onto the chaise next to Morrigan. Nevermore flew to join them. Tears threatened and Ari pushed them away impatiently. "I'm not weird, and I'm not crazy."

Nevermore cooed softly and bumped his head on her leg. Ari stroked him.

**

This time when Ari answered the door and found Detective Carson on the front porch, she was completely surprised. Her mouth gaped open, and she began to tremble.

"Hey, Ari. May I come in? I just need to ask your parents a couple of questions."

"Guardians," Ari corrected automatically.

Cedric stepped into the entry hall to see who'd rung the bell after 10:00 p.m.. He stretched out his hand. "Detective, come on in. What brings you here?"

Cedric draped his arm around Ari's shoulders and gave her a little squeeze.

Carson stepped into the hall and preceded Cedric into the living room. Ari trailed after them, her stomach in a knot.

Revelation, R-E-V-E-L-A-T-I-O-N, the making known of something that was previously secret or unknown. Ari forced herself to breathe slowly. She saw Nicole hovering on the stairs and clenched her teeth together, trying not to seem afraid.

Cedric waved Carson to a seat. Then, pulling Ari down on the sofa next to him, he held her hand as he asked, "What's this about, Detective?"

"There's been an accident." Carson waited.

Ari and Cedric glanced at each other, and Cedric frowned slightly. They didn't speak.

Carson continued. "I understand Lucas Hunter was here tonight."

Cedric nodded. "For dinner, yes. He left early, about seven thirty, I think."

"Did you serve alcohol?"

"Of course not!" Cedric stiffened. "What kind of question is that?"

"Lucas crashed his car over on Abercrombie Road."

Ari gasped and covered her mouth with her hand. "Is he okay?"

"I'm afraid not. His seat belt wasn't fastened. Lucas died on the way to the hospital."

A sob escaped from Ari. "No!" she howled.

Nicole rushed into the room and wrapped Ari into a tight hug.

"That's dreadful." Cedric sank back down on the sofa and pulled Nicole and Ari close.

"There'll be a full autopsy, of course. If alcohol was involved, we'll know soon."

Cedric glared at Carson over Ari's head. Then he said, "If there was, he didn't get it here."

"Lucas doesn't drink," Ari blurted.

Carson turned his gaze to rest on Ari. "Was he upset when he left here?"

Ari nodded and scrubbed at the tears that were overflowing and running down her cheeks. "Sort of." She forced herself to face the detective. "We kind of had a fight."

Carson swept his glance between Ari and Cedric, waiting to see if Cedric would protest his questioning.

Ari continued, her voice trembling: "He thought I lied to him about the crows."

She looked at Cedric. "I didn't lie. I just never told him because people think it's weird."

"It's okay, Ari." Nicole rubbed Ari's back.

"But he's dead!" Ari sobbed.

"Honey, I know this is terrible, but it's not your fault."

Ari tucked her head into Nicole's neck and sobbed loudly.

"I'll be in touch," Carson said to Cedric and moved toward the door.

Cedric walked him out and returned to the living room doorway. He watched as Nicole continued to murmur and soothe Ari. Slowly, he crossed the room and sat next to Ari again.

***

Dr. Madison watched Ari pace the room, tapping her finger against her leg. "What's bothering you, Ari?"

Ari shook her head and stopped to stare out the window. She drew her shoulders up and back, straightening her spine. She closed her eyes and whispered, "Why does everyone die around me?"

Dr, Madison sat very still and waited.

Ari turned. "I didn't do anything. I liked Lucas."

"Sometimes bad things just happen, Ari." Madison kept her voice low and even. "When they do, we have to accept them and move on."

"It really was an accident, you know?"

"Yes, Ari. Accidents happen, and there is nothing we can do to change that. You did not cause this accident any more than you caused the other terrible deaths that have occurred in your life."

Ari turned back to the window. *Hazard, H-A-Z-A-R-D, an unavoidable danger or risk, even though often foreseeable. I'm a hazard.*

***

Cooper called as soon as he heard about Lucas's death. "Hey, girl," he greeted Ari. "I'm so sorry about Lucas."

"Thanks, Cooper." A sob escaped, and Ari forced herself to control her tears.

Concern filled Cooper's voice, "I'm worried about you, Ari."

Ari's anger flared. "I'm fine. It was just another dumb accident."

"I know," Cooper said slowly, "but it's a lot of accidents."

"What do you mean?" Ari felt goose bumps rise on her arms.

Well," Cooper remained cautious, "first Angie, and then Robin, and now Lucas."

And Jerry. And Stacy. That's five accidents.

Ari protested, "Accidents aren't my fault!"

"I didn't say they were, but it's a lot of deaths to be connected to any one person. Cops look for patterns, you know. I just want you to be safe."

***

Nine for a kiss,

"It's better to be unhappy alone than unhappy with someone."
—Marilyn Monroe

With Cooper's warning in mind, Ari withdrew from the social life she had established. Once again, people looked at her with sympathy, and she hated it. She overheard Barb speculating to Laurie that Lucas "must have been really upset to crash his car" and asking, "Do you think they had a fight?"

Ari withdrew further.

She signed up for the maximum course load in the second semester and then for a full load again in the summer.

Dr. Madison cautioned Ari that she should take time to grieve.

"I've grieved enough in my life," Ari declared. "I don't want to be sad anymore, ever." She crossed her legs and swung her foot gently back and forth. Her sandal slipped off and hit the floor with a thunk.

Madison made a note on her pad.

Ari lifted her eyebrow. "What in the world is worth writing about that? Or are you just making a grocery list for later?"

The doctor chuckled. "I wrote, 'Self-assurance has increased.'"

"Sorry, I hate not knowing what you write in your notes." Ari glanced down at her feet and slid the sandal back on. "I'm nineteen now. It seems pretty normal that my self-assurance is better."

Dr. Madison nodded and waited.

"I'll finish my BS in January. Then, I might apply for the master's program. Or I might take a job somewhere."

"What do you see as being the deciding factor in your choice?"

"Mostly, my age." Ari angled her legs to the side and smoothed her dress down over her knees. "I think I need the extra degree to get the job I want."

"What job is that?"

"I don't know. But I want a big salary and a kick-ass life. And, I probably have to be twenty-one to get that kind of job." She grinned at the therapist.

Dr. Madison laughed. "I have no doubt you'll accomplish whatever you set out to do, Ari."

She waited a minute before asking, "You haven't mentioned Nevermore and Morrigan lately. Do they still visit you?"

Ari blanched. "Nevermore comes sometimes, but I think Morrigan died or something." She shoved her hands under her legs and said, "Most crows only live about ten or twelve years."

"Oh, dear." Dr. Madison reached out to comfort Ari.

Ari leaped to her feet and crossed to the window. "Everything dies."

***

Life, therapy, and the study of mathematics had taught Ari to be a problem solver. She pushed emotion aside and approached everything in her life with careful judgment and analytical skills. Her internships and classes were chosen to complete her degree in the least possible time. She pushed all personal relationships aside and concentrated only on her goals.

The master's program proved challenging, but with no distractions, Ari sailed through the coursework and accepted a job fifty miles away that offered both an excellent starting salary and the possibility of advancement.

She made one last appointment with Dr. Madison.

When Ari was admitted to the office, she smiled confidently and said, "I've accepted the job I told you about. I start on the first of next month. I'm driving over next week to find an apartment. So, this will be my last appointment with you."

"Congratulation, Ari." Dr. Madison laid her notebook on the side table next to her chair. "Grief and loss will always be with you, but I'm confident you will succeed."

Ari curled her legs under herself and relaxed against the back of her chair. She looked around the room and then made eye contact with the doctor. "I know. Thanks, Doc. I'll miss these sessions."

"I'll miss working with you, too, Ari." She crossed her legs and looked more relaxed than Ari had ever seen her. "Tell me about your new job."

They chatted for a few minutes and then said goodbye.

Ari strode out of the office, head held high.

Dr. Madison watched from the window as Ari crossed the parking lot, one hand lifted in farewell.

Ari glanced up as she entered her car and gave a brief nod. *Way to go, Doc. More than three years of therapy, and you never even asked me if I knew what killed Jerry, Stacy, Angie, Robin or Lucas.*

She started her car and drove away.

***

When Ari had told Cedric and Nicole about her move, Nicole had suggested that she find an apartment with roommates. Instead, Ari found a small one-bedroom only a few miles from her office. She declined Nicole's help with choosing furniture. Instead, using part of the money her grandmother had left in trust, she furnished it quickly in one visit to IKEA. Linen, kitchen items, and a bookcase fit in her car. She arranged to have everything else delivered.

On the day of Ari's move-in, Cedric and Nicole rented a pickup and delivered her personal items from home, along with a bright red toaster and a box of groceries and cleaning supplies. As they carried things into the apartment, Cooper arrived with a money plant cradled in his arms. "What are you doing here?" Ari demanded.

"Hey," Cooper pretended to be hurt, "that's no way to greet a friend. Cedric said you were moving today, and I offered to help."

"Sorry," Ari muttered. "I didn't know you were coming."

He held out the plant to Ari. "You're forgiven. According to the florist, a money plant in your home will bring you prosperity and good luck. If you don't kill it."

"Very funny." Ari accepted the plant and set it on the kitchen counter. "Thanks for helping."

" No biggie. I only live about a mile from here. We're practically neighbors."

Ari rolled her eyes. *So much for starting over in a new place,* she thought. Forcing a smile, she said, "I hope you know how to use tools. All the furniture came in boxes."

Cooper kept everyone laughing as they struggled with the assembly, but Ari had a bed, a dresser, a table and chairs, a sofa, and a bookcase standing in place within a few hours.

Nicole offered to unpack the other items from IKEA, but Ari declined, saying, "Thanks, but I want to do it myself, so I know it's really my house."

Nicole gave her a side hug. "Makes sense." She looked around the apartment and then back to Ari. "We are so proud of you. It's kind of sad seeing you all grownup. I'm going to miss you."

"Me, too," Cedric grinned. "It'll be much too quiet with you gone."

"I'll come visit," Ari said. *But not very often,* she added to herself.

"Enough of that," Cedric declared. "Nicole, I'm starving. Call for some pizza, and I'll get the bottle of wine out of my car."

Ari looked at the three people gathered around her table, the only three people she could rely on. She thought about the cemetery trees with their carved initials. There were five now. Just yesterday, she'd stopped by the river to add another heart with an "L." Others might think Lucas's death was an accident, but she knew it was her fault. *Once a killer, always a killer,* she thought.

***

The sound of loud tapping woke Ari. She stretched and looked around the unfamiliar bedroom. The tapping came again. Ari sat up and looked toward the high window. The tapping grew louder. She pushed back the duvet and stumbled to the kitchen, yawning and stretching her arms over her head.

A crow stood on the kitchen windowsill, tapping on the glass.

"Nevermore!" Ari hurried to the window and pushed it open.

The crow stepped onto the inner sill and considered the room, tilting his head from side to side. Finally, he gave a loud caw.

"I take it you approve."

Nevermore bobbed his head.

"How did you find me?" Ari stroked his head with her finger.

Nevermore shook his wings and croaked a long series of rattles and clicks. He turned and walked to the outer sill, looked back, and lifted off.

Ari sighed, watching him rise into the clear morning air. She touched the two-crow necklace Cedric had given her on her seventeenth birthday and reached to close the window. A flutter of wings and loud happy caws stopped her movement. Nevermore landed again with another crow.

Ari laughed aloud. "Hello," she said, "you must be Nevermore's new mate."

Nevermore hopped from one foot to another and trilled a series of notes.

"Yes," Ari agreed, "she is very pretty."

Nevermore rubbed his head on Ari's bare arm. The new crow stepped closer and considered her.

"It is a pleasure to meet you, Veritas," Ari said formally. She pulled a bag of seeds from the cupboard, poured some into her cupped hand, and offered the seeds to the birds.

***

Ari's job consisted of statistical analysis of data for a large marketing firm. She found it fascinating. Following her usual pattern, she kept to herself at work and made no friends. She was polite and occasionally accepted an invitation to lunch with her coworkers. But she managed to avoid bar nights by pleading that she was busy with other events.

Cooper finished the police academy and joined the state police. He called to suggest a night on the town to celebrate.

Ari declined.

One Saturday afternoon, Cooper knocked on her door and Ari, caught off guard, invited him in.

"What are you doing here?" she asked.

Nevermore greeted him raucously from the open window.

"Yo, Nevermore," Cooper said. "Who's the new lady friend?" He stretched out his arm, and Nevermore hopped onto his wrist.

"Veritas," Ari answered. "And you didn't answer my question. Why are you here?"

Cooper avoided her question. "Veritas? What does that mean?"

"Goddess of Truth." She handed the bird a sunflower seed. "I told you I was busy."

"I didn't believe you." Cooper stroked Nevermore's back and grinned at Ari. "It's time you got a life. When was the last time you had any fun?"

"I have a life, and I have fun all the time," Ari protested.

"Fun? Like what kind of fun?"

"I run at the reservoir. I read, go to work, and I talk to Nevermore."

"Oh, yah! That sounds like what every red-blooded, twenty-one-year-old, beautiful girl does for fun."

Ari punched his arm. "Stop it! I like my life."

Cooper sobered. "I believe you. But come out with me tonight. There's a guy I want you to meet."

"A guy you like or a guy you want me to meet?"

"Jeff." Cooper's gaze turned dreamy. "A man I like."

"Ohh, a man! This sounds serious." Ari raised an eyebrow and blew a kiss at Cooper. "Okay, as long as you aren't trying to set me up, I'll meet you tonight. Tell me where and when."

***

Ari surveyed herself in the mirror. Her faded jeans were torn just enough, and her shiny silver camisole was tucked in tightly, accenting her small waist and high breasts. She brushed her short, dark hair until the curls lay flat around her ears, grabbed a faded jean jacket, pushed her phone, ID and credit card into her pockets, and headed for the door. Cooper was right; she needed to have some fun.

Nevermore squawked from the kitchen window. Ari turned back and waved to him. "Don't worry. I won't get in any trouble."

Music leaked into the street from the bar as Ari approached. She pulled open the door, and a blast of sound and flashing lights struck her. She paused and looked around. Spotting Cooper and a tall, good-looking, dark-haired man, she hurried to join them. Cooper pulled her in for a quick hug and introduced Jeff.

"Hi Ari," Jeff said smoothly. "What are you drinking? I'll get it for you."

"G & T, thanks."

Jeff moved out of earshot, and Cooper said, "So, what do you think?"

Ari scowled at Cooper. "He's cute, and he has good manners. I haven't even talked to him yet. But if you like him, I like him."

"I knew you would. He's a homicide detective already."

Homicide, H-O-M-I-C-I-D-E, the killing of one human being by another. Crap! Ari forced herself to smile. "Impressive," she managed to say as Jeff returned.

Ari accepted her drink from Jeff and took a deep gulp. "Let's dance," she said, moving onto the dance floor without waiting for an answer.

Soon Ari was swept up in the sound and movement. She danced away from Cooper and Jeff and then moved back to them. She finished her drink and accepted another, and then a third.

Cooper threw his arm around her and brought her close to say, "Told you, you needed to have fun!"

Ari bobbed her head to the music and grinned.

"We're leaving," Cooper said. "Don't do anything I wouldn't do." He took Jeff's hand and headed for the door. Glancing back over his shoulder he mouthed, "Call me tomorrow."

Ari gave him a thumbs-up and accepted another drink from a stranger.

"Who are you?" she asked.

"Your new best friend," the guy answered.

Ari giggled and allowed the stranger to hook his thumbs in her jean pockets and pull her in tight as they moved to the music.

The music soared, the lights swirled, voices rose in a crescendo of sound. Ari drank. Her head spun. She was aware of laughing and kissing and then she was outside walking with a guy. His arm wrapped around her waist holding her tight.

Ari stumbled to a stop and faced him. "Who are you?" she slurred.

"I'm your new best friend, remember?"

Ari giggled. "Yeah, I knew that." She pulled back again. "Where are we going?"

"I'm walking you home."

"Okay." Ari stopped. "Wait. I have a car."

"Sorry, babe. You're too drunk to drive. I'll take care of you."

Ari's head nodded and she wobbled on her feet. "Got it. Don't call me 'babe.'"

"No worries. Come on." He tugged at her hand and Ari followed.

He stopped in front of an apartment building and held onto Ari as he unlocked the door.

She giggled and allowed him to guide her into the building and into an elevator.

"This isn't my house," Ari protested, trying to straighten up.

"It's my house. We'll just have another drink and then I'll take you home."

Ari leaned on the wall of the elevator and closed her eyes. Her stomach churned and her eyes opened wide. She covered her mouth with her hand and swallowed hard. The elevator stopped and the feeling passed.

Her friend took her hand and led her into his apartment. Across the living room, Ari could see the lights of the city through a glass door.

"Pretty lights," she said.

"Maybe a little fresh air is a good idea, babe. Let's go out on the balcony."

"I told you. Don't call me 'babe.' I don't like it."

"Right. You said that. How come?"

"Robin called me that and I killed him."

"Whoa!" The man pushed the sliding glass door open and fresh air gushed into the room.

Ari stepped out on the balcony and looked down. The river flowed below them. The city lights danced across the water.

The man pressed his back against the railing and wrapped his arms around Ari. He kissed her, slipping his tongue into her eager mouth. When the kiss ended, he looked into her eyes and asked, "Did you kill the guy with love?"

Ari stiffened in his arms. "Kill what guy?"

The man laughed. "Robin, the guy that called you 'babe.'"

Ari sobered instantly. She tried to step away, but he held her tight. Ari demanded, "Do I look like a killer?"

He looked down at her, alerted by the change in her body language. His arms loosened. "You look like a beautiful woman."

He hoisted himself onto the railing and pulled her between his legs. His hands cupped her face. Ari's lips sought his and they kissed again. She raised her arms to his shoulders and pushed as hard as she could. He tumbled backward. A single, short expletive escaped before the sound of his body hitting the pavement below brought Ari to her senses.

Ari turned and fled the apartment. No one was in the hallway. It seemed completely quiet. She spotted the stairway sign and, ignoring the elevator, ran down four flights of stairs and exited the building into an alley. Everything was still quiet. No screaming. No sirens.

Ari slowed her pace and forced herself to breathe *One, two, three, four, five, six, seven, eight, nine, ten, eleven, twelve, thirteen, fourteen...* She refused to think about what she'd just done and counted her steps all the way back to a street she recognized.

Ari fished her cell phone out of her pocket and called an Uber.

***

All weekend, Ari watched the news and finally, on Sunday evening, a picture of the man she'd pushed appeared with a brief story of how Andrew Garland, age thirty-two, had fallen to his death from a balcony in the River Park area. The newscaster spoke briefly about the building having balcony railings that were only thirty inches high, less than current regulations required. The building owner was interviewed, and he insisted that all railings were posted with caution signs and that the building was currently being retrofitted with forty-two-inch-high guard railings. There was no mention of a suspicious death.

Ari let herself stop worrying. *No one can connect me to this guy. I didn't even know his name, and I'll never go back to that bar again.*

He was going to rape me anyway, she reasoned. *He deserved to die.*

Nevermore and Veritas arrived on the windowsill with a flurry of wings. Ari opened the window and pushed a dish of fruit toward the birds.

Nevermore shook his head and stared at Ari.

"I know," Ari said, "I promised I wouldn't kill anyone else, but sometimes it's the only way."

Nevermore rattled his disagreement from deep in his throat.

Ari stretched out her arm. He stepped on and walked up to her shoulder, where he nestled against her neck.

"I love you, too, Nevermore. I hope you never die."

***

Ten for a surprise you should be careful not to miss,

"Sometimes things become possible if we want them bad
enough." — T.S. Eliot

With the career of her choice well underway, Ari found herself
with too much time alone. She went to her local bar and became quasi
friends with Barry, the bartender. Guys offered to buy her a drink, but
she always refused, and when they insisted, she drank the free G & T
and left the bar quickly and alone.

She thought about trying to meet people using the dating apps others talked about. However, the idea of being in a sexual relationship
made her squeamish, and that seemed to be the main reason people
were using the apps. She just needed something to do. She joined a
gym, took a few classes, worked out on the equipment three times a
week, and always kept to herself. She listened to podcasts instead of
interacting with others.

Ari became a regular at the gym. The girl at the desk knew her
name, and other members said hello. She found herself waving back at
people who greeted her but steered clear of flirting or getting to know
anyone, man, or woman.

Wedding invitations for people she'd known in college became a regular thing. Ari declined them all until she received one from Cooper. He'd scribbled a note in addition to the formal invite:

Please come. My dad refuses to participate, but Jeff and I are very happy and would love to share our day with you.

Ari studied the note. *How do people decide they are in love? Sex I get. Some people need that, but living with someone, much less marrying them?* She shook her head and laid the invitation on the counter, poured herself a cup of coffee, and opened her laptop.

Nevermore tapped the window.

Ari cuddled the bird for a few minutes. "I suppose you think I should go to Cooper's wedding?"

Nevermore cocked his head, his bright black eyes watching her. Veritas landed on the windowsill. Nevermore flew from Ari's arm to the sill and joined his mate.

"You're probably right," Ari conceded. "I'll go. And I'll be friendly. I promise.

***

Ari stood alone, watching the happy couple circulate through the room, accepting hugs and congratulations from everyone. Someone touched her arm, and she turned to find Cooper's mom smiling at her.

"Hello, Ari. It's so good to see you again. Cedric tells me you are doing very well."

"Hi, Mrs. Adams." Ari smiled politely.

"Sometimes I don't know where time has gone. You kids are all so grown up now. I suppose it won't be long until we are attending your wedding." Mrs. Adams looked down at Ari's hand.

Ari laughed and lifted her bare left hand. "No time soon."

"You're a very pretty girl, Ari." Mrs. Adams patted Ari's arm. "What are you now? Two years younger than Cooper, so twenty-six?"

"Actually, twenty-five," Ari corrected.

"Well, no rush, but I'm sure Cedric and Nicole would like to see a grandchild."

"I don't even date," Ari admitted.

Mrs. Adams laughed. "I'm sure that's not true." She patted Ari's arm. "You just haven't met Mr. Right."

Cooper appeared behind his mother's back. He winked at Ari. "She's very particular, Mom. But don't worry—Jeff and I'll find her a perfect match."

Ari narrowed her eyes and shook her head, "I can find my own dates, thank you."

"Time's a-wasting, girl. You need to settle down." Jeff walked by, and Cooper caught his hand, pulling him into the conversation. "I was just telling Ari that if she doesn't fall in love soon, we'll have to find her the perfect mate."

Jeff laughed. "I apologize for this guy, Ari. Ignore him."

"I always do," Ari said. She kissed Cooper's cheek and drifted away. She accepted another glass of champagne and lifted it in a toast to the happy couple, but her mind was caught on the idea of love.

Perhaps, she thought, *it would be good to commit to someone, someone who would allow me to live a calm life, a life where I feel no need to escape by killing. Maybe I need someone like Cedric.* Ari lifted her glass and sipped as she looked at the other guests.

***

Ari stopped at her regular bar and settled herself at the far end where she could watch the other patrons. Barry acknowledged her entrance. "The usual?"

Ari nodded.

He fixed the drink and set it in front of her. "Always good to see you, Ari." Barry swiped at the counter with his bar rag. "What's making you look so serious tonight?"

"I came from a wedding." She picked up her glass. "I've been thinking about love and marriage," Ari admitted, taking a mouthful and swallowing carefully.

He laughed, "Yours or someone else's?"

When Ari didn't smile, he continued, "I didn't know you had a boyfriend. You never come in here with anyone."

Ari took another drink and set her glass carefully in the center of her coaster. She studied Barry and then shrugged. "I'm twenty-five; I have a good education and great job. But—" she held her glass out for a refill.

Barry stood still, his head cocked to the side, waiting for Ari to finish her statement.

Ari fiddled with a napkin and kept her eyes down as she said, "I haven't been out on a date in four years."

Barry took the empty glass, turned his back and fixed Ari another G & T. He set the fresh drink on a clean coaster and asked, "Why not?"

"Long, boring story." Ari looked through the clear liquid in her glass and watched the bar lights change shape.

"Pretty quiet in here tonight. I'll tell you my story if you tell me yours."

Ari bit her lower lip and smiled slightly. "You first."

***

"Where should I start?" He looked thoughtful for a long moment and then said, "My name isn't really Barry. It's Walter Barrett."

Ari laughed aloud.

"I know, it's an old man's name." He shrugged. "But what can you do? I was named after an uncle."

"I was named for my grandmother. So, I have an old name, too."

"Can't be worse than being a kid called Walter?"

Ari giggled. "Harriet."

Barry cocked his eyebrow. "I think we'll have to call that a draw." He glanced toward the other customers. "Be right back."

Ari watched him walk away. *He's a nice guy. Kind of old.* She sipped and waited.

"Okay, I'm back." Barry smiled at her. "So tell me why you haven't been on a date in four years."

Ari looked past Barry and considered her reflection in the bar mirror. *Truth or Dare?* She dropped her hands to her lap and twisted her fingers into a knot. *Half-truth, H-A-L-F-T-R-U-T-H, a statement that is only partly true, especially one intended to deceive, evade blame, or the like.*

"I guess I just thought I needed a break from the hassle." Then, turning her gaze back to Barry, she took a long pull of her drink and said, "Too many people in my life died."

Barry pulled a glass from the drying rack and began to polish it.

Ari drained her glass. "Like I said, it's a long story, and I have to go to work in the morning." She pulled her credit card from her pocket.

Barry waved it away. "Drinks are on me. I'll be waiting to hear the rest of your story."

Ari slipped off her bar stool. "Thanks."

"See you soon," Barry called after her.

Ari waved over her shoulder and kept walking.

***

On Friday, Ari went to the gym for a late spin class. She showered and redressed in skinny jeans, a black camisole, and her favorite oversized red hoodie. She added gel to her hair and combed it out as straight as possible, tucking the ends behind her ears. The receptionist gave her a thumbs-up when she passed the desk. "Looking good, Ari. Are you going somewhere special tonight?"

Ari smiled and shook her head.

She parked in her designated parking space at her apartment building and walked to the bar.

Barry waved when he saw her perched on her regular stool.

Ari lifted her hand in greeting. She felt a bubble of excitement. *I can make him fall in love with me,* she thought. *But do I want to try that again?*

A live band played classic rock. Ari quickly drank two large G & T's and watched the dancers in the bar mirror. The regulars knew enough to leave her alone. Twice strangers asked her to dance, but she refused each time without even a glance at the man asking.

Barry placed a third drink on the bar in front of her. She smiled her thanks but didn't try to speak over the band.

The band finished about one in the morning, and the crowd began to thin. Barry brought over a fourth drink. "I hope to hear more of your story tonight, Ari."

She smiled and took a sip, "Maybe, you will," she said. "After you tell me yours."

Barry chuckled. "Right, I forgot I was supposed to go first. Drink up. There's plenty more where that came from."

Ari giggled. She pressed her hand over her mouth to keep it in. *Drunk. Smashed. Wasted. Bombed. Hammered. D-R-U-N-K. I better slow down.* She stood and walked to the restroom, carefully placing one foot in front of the other, determined not to sway.

Back on her bar stool, Ari watched Barry as he made the last call, poured final drinks, chatted with patrons, and began the closing chores. At exactly two, he locked the door and flipped off the flashing open sign. He lowered the lights, poured himself a glass of whiskey and asked Ari if she was ready for another.

Ari, who'd been sipping slowly, picked up her glass and was surprised to find it empty. She said, "Yes, please."

"So polite," Barry teased. He placed a fresh cocktail in front of Ari, lifted the bar flap and sat down next to her. "Are you always such a good girl?"

Ari lifted her glass to her lips and touched the rim with her tongue. She arched an eyebrow. "Except when I'm not." She winked and took a drink.

"Tell me about that?" He lifted his glass and swirled the amber liquid. The single cube of ice clinked against the side. "Tell me the worst thing you ever did?"

"I killed my mother." Ari answered without thinking. She sobered instantly, aware of what she'd said.

Barry froze, his drink touching his lip.

Fear throbbed through Ari, and she stammered to change her statement. "I mean, I didn't kill her, but when she died, I didn't care."

Barry took a long drink and said slowly, "When did this happen?"

"A long time ago. I was eleven. She left me alone and went out and got drunk. Somebody killed her in an alley."

"You poor kid." Barry placed his hand over hers.

Ari forced herself not to pull away. *Shut up, shut up, shut up,* she counseled herself.

"Where was your dad?"

"Gone. It was just my mom and me."

"Did they put you in foster care?"

"I don't want to talk about all that." She pulled her hand away and used it to lift her drink to her mouth. "It makes me sad. Tell me your story. Do you own this bar?"

Barry stayed quiet a long minute.

Ari felt panic rising and forced it back. *What is he thinking?* She pretended to take another sip from her glass.

At last, Barry cleared his throat and refocused on Ari. "My story really is pretty boring. I was a kid, then a soldier. Became a cop. Got married. Drank a lot. Got divorced. And now I'm a bartender in this place." He lifted his glass to his lips and finished the whiskey.

She lost track of what he was saying, the words—became a cop—echoed in her mind. Ari forced herself to concentrate on Barry. She smiled and touched his arm. "That was a very brief version of your life. I'd like to hear the whole story. Why aren't you a cop now?"

"I was asked to turn in my badge." Barry stood. "I was fired for drinking on duty."

"That must have been tough." Ari searched for something to ask that would change the subject. "Do you have children?"

Barry went behind the bar and refilled his glass. He leaned on the bar and considered his answer. Finally, he said, "Not that I know about." He smiled grimly. "I'm forty-two-years-old. I could be your dad for all I know."

"I don't think that's likely. You would have only been seventeen when I was born."

"Those were wild times, Ari."

"Like what kind of wild times?"

"I ran with a bad crowd. I skipped school all the time. Used a lot of drugs. Had a lot of unprotected sex."

A cold chill ran down Ari's spine. She remembered her grandmother telling her about Stacy. "My mom was fifteen when I was born," Ari blurted.

Barry nodded. "I was one of the lucky ones. I got arrested. The judge said I had to join the army or go to jail. The army was good to me. It straightened me out. I quit using drugs, and I stopped drinking." He held up his glass of whiskey. "At least I quit drinking for a while."

Ari saluted him with her glass, and they drank in silence.

"I need to lock up, Ari. Will you be okay to get home?"

Ari nodded. "It's just a couple of blocks. I'm walking."

"Hang on. This will only take a minute. I'll walk you there."

Ari agreed and waited until Barry's work was done. They walked side by side, neither saying much. Barry took her hand and held it gently when they reached her building. "You're easy to talk to, Ari." He leaned forward and kissed her forehead. "I still haven't heard your story. Next time you can tell me about that necklace you wear. Okay?"

Ari nodded.

"Good night."

Ari punched in the code and opened the door. "Good night, Barry." She closed the door and leaned against it, feeling the room spin. *I have to be more careful. Did I tell him too much?*

***

Despite her fear that she'd revealed too much, Ari was drawn back to the bar. Barry greeted her with a casual wave and brought her a drink. *Maybe it was all right.*

By midnight, only the two of them remained in the bar. Barry locked the door and turned down the lights. He freshened Ari's G & T and poured himself a whiskey.

"How's life going, Ari?" he asked, making himself comfortable on a bar stool.

Ari searched for something to say. "I started running in the morning instead of going to the gym so often."

"Oh, yeah. The fresh air is good. I run down by City Park most days. It's exactly four miles to circle that little lake in the middle." Barry took a drink and held his glass in his hand as he swiveled toward Ari. "You should try it sometime. It's a nice run."

"Maybe I will." Ari turned her head and caught his measuring glance. "What's up, Barry? You've been looking at me funny ever since I got here."

"Well—" Barry took a deep pull on his whiskey and set the glass down carefully. "I've been wondering about a couple of things. That necklace you wear, is it two crows?"

Ari nodded.

"Pretty unusual. Why crows?"

Ari frowned. Her hand rose to her throat. "It was a present. I like birds, especially crows." She moved her hand to cover the charms.

Barry turned his glass in circles. When he spoke, it was almost a whisper. "You said your mom died when you were eleven. So, fourteen years ago?"

Divulge, D-I-V-U-L-G-E, tell nothing. Ari nodded. She watched Barry in the mirror. *What is he thinking? Why is he asking this? What does he know?* She sipped her drink and waited.

"Back then, I was still a cop, but I was drinking a lot, and I hung out in a sleazy bar over in Granville." He met Ari's eyes in the mirror.

Ari stayed still and didn't look away. Her hands trembled. She pressed them flat on the bar, hoping he hadn't noticed.

Barry picked up his glass. Realizing it was empty, he stood and reached over the bar to retrieve the whiskey bottle.

Ari stood, too. "I'll be right back," she said, and headed toward the ladies' room.

She pushed the door open and stepped through. The lights were very bright after the dim bar. Ari closed her eyes and leaned against the door. *One hundred, ninety-nine, ninety-eight, ninety-seven, ninety-six, ninety-five.* She forced her breathing to slow and pushed the fear away. *He knows something. I need to be ready.* She looked around the bathroom, hoping for an escape or a weapon.

Spying a closet door, she opened it. There was nothing inside but cleaning supplies, paper towels, toilet paper, and refills for the tampon machine. She stood on her tiptoes and peered into the top shelf. Pushed far to the back, Ari found an open box of rat poison. She pulled her hoodie sleeve down over her hand, pulled the box forward and removed the foil-sealed pack she found inside. She pushed the empty box back into the corner of the shelf and placed the pack in her pocket. *I just want to be ready. I won't kill him unless I have to.*

Ari washed her hands and left the restroom.

Barry had replenished her glass along with his own. Ari resumed her place at the bar, took a sip of her fresh drink, and smiled her thanks.

"So, you were telling me your story," she prompted.

Barry nodded. "Actually, your story the other night reminded me about that bar and a woman that was killed a couple of blocks from there. The strange thing was, this Stacy was someone I'd known when

I was a kid. We talked some about the old days. She never mentioned she had a kid, but the story was all over the news when they found her body. It turned out she had a little girl who was living alone with some birds."

Ari stayed very still, waiting for him to continue.

"The newspapers didn't report the names, of course, but they called that kid, The Bird Girl. Is that you, Ari? Are you Stacy Blimm's daughter?"

Ari shut her eyes. The lights from the neon signs danced behind her closed lids. Bile rose in her mouth. She swallowed hard to keep from throwing up.

Ari opened her eyes and whispered, "Yes."

"Did the cops ever arrest anyone for her murder?"

Ari shook her head.

Barry finished his drink and poured another. "You're like a ghost from my past, Ari. When I first heard about the kid, I thought she might be my daughter."

The color drained from Ari's face. "You don't have to worry about that. Stacy always told me my father was dead."

"Stacy never paid much attention to the truth, did she?"

Ari had to agree. "That's true enough. But," she added, "my grandmother told me Stacy had a lot of boyfriends."

"Did you live with your grandmother after Stacy died?"

Ari crossed her fingers under the bar. "Mostly. She's dead now, too."

"The old lady leave you any money? Stacy always said she had a bunch."

Ari shook her head. "No. There wasn't any money." She downed her drink and stood. "I'd better get going. Let you lock up."

"Hang around. It'll only take a few minutes. Then, I'll walk you home."

Ari sat back down.

He poured another full glass of whiskey, took a sip, picked up Ari's empty glass, and moved to the bar sink, leaving his drink in front of Ari. She slipped her hand into her pocket and lifted the flap on the foil packet of poison.

Barry spoke without turning around. "Ari, how did that guy that was taking care of you die?"

"Jerry?" Ari's voice trembled. "He fell down the stairs. How do you know about Jerry?"

Barry faced her. "I was a policeman, remember. I read the reports on you after Stacy died."

"If you thought I was your kid, why didn't you say something?"

"I was still pretty young, and I had enough problems without taking on more, but it kind of haunted me, you know. If that kid were mine, I should have stepped up and claimed her even if she had killed that guy like some people thought."

Barry turned back to the sink and plunged Ari's glass up and down in the soapy water.

Ari took the poison from her pocket and dumped it in his glass of whiskey. It formed a pile of crystals in the bottom.

Barry lifted the glass from the soapy water and dunked it up and down in the rinse water.

Ari grabbed a cocktail straw and stirred the whiskey.

Barry swished the glass through the sanitizer water and placed it in the drain rack.

Ari dropped the straw on the floor. She slid off her barstool and hung her purse over her shoulder. She started for the door. "I'll let myself out, Barry. See you tomorrow."

"Hey, kid—"

Ari turned to look at Barry. He had his glass in his hand.

"For what it's worth, I would have been a lousy dad." He downed the glass of whiskey, turned back to the sinks and swished his empty glass in the soapy water.

Ari opened the door and walked out into the rain. Pulling her hood up, she ducked her head and walked the few blocks home. Safely back in her apartment, Ari put on pajamas, washed her face, and brushed her teeth. Before getting into bed, she opened her jewelry box and pulled out the gold bangle bracelet. She carried it to the light and examined it for the first time in years. The faint engraving was still intact, and now she could read it easily: SB&WB. The small silver-framed picture lay face up in the jewelry box. She studied the image. *Maybe he was my father, but he would have told someone about Jerry and Stacy. I had to kill him.*

Ari turned the picture facedown, put the bracelet back in the box, climbed into bed and turned out the light.

***

Eleven for health,

"Far too many people are looking for the right person instead of trying to be the right person." —*Gloria Steinem*

When the news broke about Walter Barrett's suicide, Ari pretended to be as surprised as the bar's other patrons. "He was such a nice guy." She agreed. Then she shook her head no when others asked if she's had any hint that he was unhappy in his life.

During the next few months, Ari accepted a promotion at work, moved to a new apartment in a different neighborhood, and changed her gym. She spent her evenings reading every book she could find on serial killers and brain chemistry. Nothing she read seemed to fit her feelings of justification. Obviously, it was wrong to kill but, was it really? The people she'd had to kill had all needed to die. However, she promised herself not to do it again, no matter what.

At work, Ari met Cari, an account executive, and for the first time since Angie, she had a best friend. Cari was a couple of years older, unattached, and not looking for a permanent man in her life. The women often met for drinks after work. Soon the drinks became shopping and an occasional movie night.

Cari approached her in the coffee room at work and suggested a double date with her current crush, Brad, and his friend from New

York. "I've never met Brad's friend, but Brad is a lot of fun, and this guy is his friend, so how bad can he be? Drinks and then dinner at Mirabella on Friday? Does that sound good to you?"

"You know I love that place! It'll give me a chance to wear the new dress I bought last week." Ari grinned. "Just tell me where and when." She tossed her used coffee cup in the trash. "I'll be there."

***

Ari slipped the black silk sheath over her head and pulled it down over her curves. She closed the side zipper and felt the cool, slippery fabric encase her body. The dress fit perfectly. Stepping into strappy, black silk, stilettos she surveyed her look in the mirror. *Stacy would have killed for a dress like this.* Draping her gold, two-crow necklace around her throat, she watched the shiny birds settle in place between her breasts. Ari added a pair of simple gold hoop earrings, fluffed her hair, and picked up her clutch.

Nevermore settled on the bedroom windowsill with Veritas.

Ari opened the window and greeted the birds. "Did you want to see me in my new dress?" She spun in a slow circle.

Nevermore cawed loudly and bobbed back and forth.

"Thanks. It's the most expensive dress I've ever owned."

Veritas clicked her approval.

Ari laid her clutch on the bed and stroked the birds. "I was just thinking about Stacy. Did you know I'm older than my mother was when she died?"

Nevermore clicked softly.

"I'm not sad. I just was thinking." She held out her arm, and Nevermore hopped on. Ari raised him to her lips and kissed his head. "Please don't ever die."

Nevermore rattled deep in his chest and bumped his head against her cheek.

"You're right." She lowered her arm. Nevermore stepped back to the windowsill. "No more thinking. I look great, and tonight is going to be fun."

***

Both men rose to their feet when Ari entered the restaurant. Cari hugged Ari and introduced her. Bradley Saunders was everything Cari had said: handsome, well dressed, with impeccable manners and bedroom eyes. In any other setting, his friend Eric would have been equally impressive, but next to Brad, he was a pale copy.

They ordered cocktails and allowed the conversation to meander. Ari tried to listen to Eric, but her eyes kept drifting to Brad. Finally, Eric caught her eye and said, "Don't worry about it. Everyone falls in love with Brad. I'm used to it. Been that way since we were in preschool together."

His acceptance caught Ari's full attention. "I'm sure that's not true," she said.

"Oh, yes. It's true. Why do you think I became a psychiatrist?"

Ari laughed, suddenly aware that this might be a very nice man. She picked up her glass and tipped it in his direction. "Here's to difficult childhoods."

Eric touched his glass to hers. "Mine and my clients."

Happiness bubbled up in Ari. *He's funny and smart,* she thought. "Tell me about your practice. Do you have a specialty?"

Eric gave Ari a quizzical look. "Sounds like you know something about psychiatry."

"Not really." She felt herself blush. "I took a bunch of classes, and I read a lot. The brain is fascinating." She watched Eric's eyes as she took a sip from her glass. *He looks kind.*

He waited, and when she didn't continue, he said, "Enough about my job. Cari says you're wicked smart. What are you interested in besides the brain?"

***

Over dinner, the four clicked liked couples who'd known each other forever. Brad extravagantly complimented the girls and flirted openly with both of them. Ari laughed at him and made it clear she preferred Eric. Brad pretended to pout. Cari soothed his ego. By dessert, there was no doubt that the evening was a roaring success.

As Brad gave the valet his keys, Eric turned to Ari. "I hate to see the evening end. Can I talk you into a nightcap?"

Behind Eric's back, Cari gave Ari two thumbs up.

Ari nodded. "There is a piano bar just around the corner. How does that sound?"

"Perfect." Eric reached for her hand. Ari allowed him to take it.

Cari kissed her on the cheek and whispered, "Have fun. Call me tomorrow."

***

It was the perfect relationship. Eric lived a thousand miles away. He made no demands on Ari, and, in return, she made none on him. Instead, they flirted by text and late-night calls. Every six weeks, Eric flew into town for a weekend visit.

He always reserved a hotel room around the corner from the piano bar. They met there and thought of it as their place. On the fourth weekend visit, Eric asked about meeting Cedric and Nicole. "We've been dating a while now, and I'd like to meet your family."

Ari flinched and blurted out, "Why?"

Eric placed his hand over hers. "I'm not trying to rush anything, but I really like you, and I'd like to spend more time with you. Also, I think your parents will be more comfortable with you coming to visit me in New York if they know me."

Ari pulled her hand back and sat up very straight. She looked Eric directly in the eye but kept one hand tucked under her leg so he couldn't see that she was trembling. "First, I'm an adult. Second, we've been out—in person—exactly five times, counting tonight. And third, my parents are dead."

Eric's mouth opened, but he didn't speak.

"You don't really know anything about me."

"I feel like an idiot," Eric said. "You're important to me, Ari. I don't take knowing you for granted, and I'd like to get to know you better." He ran his hand over his face and added, "I was hoping you'd come to New York so that we can explore this relationship."

Shrink talk. Ari dropped her eyes to the table and considered what she wanted to say. *Maybe it's okay to tell him about her childhood. Not everything, but—* Ari pushed her chair back and stood up. She held out her hand to Eric. "Come on. There's someone I want you meet."

Eric didn't ask any questions. He stood and walked with her out of the bar.

***

On the short ride to Ari's apartment, they stayed mostly quiet. Ari parked and Eric followed her into the elevator and then into the apartment. Ari watched him look around and wondered what he was thinking, but she didn't ask.

Ari crossed the room and opened the balcony door. She stepped out and lifted her arm. With a flutter of wings and a loud caw, Nevermore flew to her and landed on her outstretched arm. Veritas circled the patio once and landed on her shoulder.

Eric gasped.

Ari turned to face him. "I'd like you to meet my friends, Nevermore," he bobbed up and down, "and his mate, Veritas."

"Wow!" Eric was dumbfounded. "I've never seen anything like that. How did you tame them?"

"They are my family and my friends; I didn't have to tame them. Nevermore and his original mate, Morrigan, came to live with me when I was eleven."

"They've stayed all this time?" Eric stepped out on the balcony and shook his head in wonder. "That is the coolest thing I've ever heard."

He held out his hand to Nevermore, who turned his back and rattled. Eric stood still, shaking his head in disbelief. "You really are amazing and wonderful, Ari."

Ari stroked Nevermore's head and clicked to him. Nevermore clicked back. "Make yourself comfortable on the sofa. I need to give the crows their dinner, and then I'll tell you about the rest of my family."

Ari opened a bottle of wine, poured them each a glass, and settled herself in a chair across from Eric. "This is pretty weird," Ari said. "I'm not sure why I wanted you to meet Nevermore. Most people have no idea I live with crows."

Eric's lips quirked up in a wry smile. "I think it was a test. Did I pass?"

"You did," Ari admitted. "Do you still want to get to know me better?"

"I do." Eric watched her over the rim of his glass. "Will the birds be okay if you come to visit me in New York?"

"They don't need me to feed them, and if I'm gone long, Cedric will check on them."

"Who is Cedric?"

"Cedric was my guardian. I lived with him and his wife until I graduated from college." *Trust, T-R-U-S-T, to rely upon or place confidence in someone. Why do I trust this man?* Ari shook the thought away and took the plunge.

She told Eric the abbreviated version of her childhood and her life now.

Eric moved next to her and hugged her against his side. Ari forced herself to relax into his embrace and lifted her lips for his kiss.

Nevermore tapped loudly on the glass, and Ari moved away.

"He's very protective," she said. "Bring your wine out on the balcony and get to know him."

"It must have been hard to have a boyfriend with Nevermore on guard."

Ari laughed. "I haven't dated much. I've never been in love. It always seems so complicated."

Eric laughed. "It can be complicated, but it is also fun."

"So, you've been in love?"

"I have many times. My first love was my preschool teacher."

"Tell me more."

The mood lightened. They spent a pleasant hour talking. Nevermore stayed on Ari's shoulder, but Veritas moved to the arm of Eric's chair and allowed him to stroke her head.

***

Eric returned to New York, and Ari reached out to Cooper and Jeff. "He wants to get serious," she admitted.

Cooper frowned in mock horror. "What a terrible man!" He studied Ari, "Unless the sex is bad."

Ari blushed.

"I knew it!" Cooper clapped his hands together. "You haven't been to bed with him, have you?"

Jeff looked surprised. "Seriously?"

"You're not a virgin, are you?" Cooper asked.

"I'm not," Ari said, "but that's none of your business."

Jeff came to Ari's defense. "Yeah, Coop, leave her alone."

"Eric wants me to come to New York and—"

"And, if you do, sex is involved," Cooper finished her statement. "If you like this guy, I say go for it. You'll never know if you love him until you spend actual time together."

"I know, but what if it's bad?"

"Then you get on a plane and come home, girl. Besides, there's always the chance that it will be good." He winked at Jeff. "You'll never know until you try."

When Ari told Cari she was taking a Friday and Monday off and going to visit Eric, Cari squealed in delight. "I knew it. You two are so cute together. I think I hear wedding bells."

"What about you and Brad?" Ari asked, to change the subject. "I haven't heard anything about him for a while."

Cari shrugged. "That's over. But I met a new guy last night."

Ari laughed and listened to Cari spin a tale about her new love interest.

***

Nicole and Cedric agreed to look in on the crows while she was out of town, and Cedric offered to give Ari a ride to the airport.

"Nicole told me not to ask questions," Cedric admitted as he drove toward the airport, "but who is this guy? I know you've been seeing him for a while. We'd like to meet him."

Ari pulled on her hair and twisted a curl around her finger.

Cedric smiled. "You have always done that when you're nervous."

"I guess so." Ari dropped her hair. "Eric is a really nice person. He says he loves me, but I'm not sure I know how to be in love with anyone."

"No one does, Ari. It just happens. You've had a couple of bad experiences, but don't let that stop you. Take your time. You'll know if it's right, I promise."

Ari felt tears gather. She blinked them away. "How did you know you were in love with Nicole?"

Cedric thought a moment. "I was a forty-year-old bachelor when you came to live with me. I never expected to marry or have children. But when I saw how much Nicole cared about you, I realized that I wanted a family. And, then over time, I knew I loved Nicole and that she loved me. It wasn't love at first sight. I didn't hear bells ringing or anything. I just knew it was good."

Ari nodded. "If this weekend works, I'll bring Eric over to visit."

Cedric swung the car into the drop-off lane. Ari leaned over and kissed his cheek. "Thanks, Cedric. For everything." She grabbed her bag and hurried into the terminal.

***

Twelve for wealth,

"Never marry at all, Dorian. Men marry because they are tired,
women, because they are curious: both are disappointed."
—*Oscar Wilde*

Ari put her analytical math skills to good use. Using the hypothesis
that she would marry Eric, she set out to test her conclusion. Ari created a spreadsheet listing the pros and cons of marriage to anyone, and
Eric specifically. Next, she examined her personality traits versus
what she believed to be his and found few matches. All of her studies
of the brain had convinced her that highly analytical, competitive,
emotionally contained personalities like herself were often attracted to
empathetic, nurturing types like Eric. The pros outweighed the cons.
She wanted to live a normal life with no more killing.

Ari deleted the spreadsheet from her computer and called Eric.

"Hi, sweetheart." His voice, as always, sounded happy. "I didn't
expect to hear from you tonight. Is everything okay?"

Ari cleared her throat. "Um, yes."

Nevermore tapped the glass patio door and clicked his encouragement.

"I've been thinking a lot about moving our relationship to the next
level." She paused and could hear Eric breathing. "I talked to them at

work today, and I can work remotely if you still want me to come to New York."

"I want to marry you and spend the rest of my life loving you." Eric's happiness exploded. "Yes, please come as soon as possible. Tomorrow?"

Ari laughed. She could feel herself grinning. It felt good to make someone so happy. "Not tomorrow, silly. I have to arrange things at work and tell Cedric and Nicole."

"Okay, when?"

"Soon, I promise."

***

Ari invited Cedric and Nicole to dinner at her apartment to tell them her news. "We both really like Eric, Ari," Cedric declared solemnly. "He's older, but I know that he loves you."

"Only seven years older. That's not so much. I told him everything about my childhood." *Except that I murder people who treat me wrong.* "He likes the crows even though they don't like him."

"I want you to be happy, Ari. You deserve it." Cedric lifted his glass in a toast. "To our daughter. We love you."

Ari wiped tears from her eyes and gave them both hugs. "Now," she said briskly, "I gave notice on the apartment, and I've listed the furniture I'm not taking. There's just one problem. I have to tell Nevermore and Veritas that I'm moving far away. It's almost a thousand miles, and I don't think they will be able to find me in New York. It will break my heart to leave them."

"Well, that's no way to start a new life!" Nicole exclaimed. "Buy a big cage and take them with you."

Ari clapped her hands. "Do you think that's possible? What if they hate the city?"

Nicole laughed at her fears. "If Eric's place has a balcony, they'll adjust. Those crows would die without you."

Ari smiled. *If the crows are with me, I can do anything, even get married.* "Okay, then I guess I'm moving to New York."

It took a month before Ari hooked a U-Haul to the back of her car and drove the five days it took to reach New York. She stopped every three hours to let the birds out of the cage that took up her whole back seat. Each time she watched them spiral high and disappear, her heart pounded until they returned, cawing and happy to be back.

Eric had cleaned out his second bedroom and furnished it with a sofa bed and a desk so that Ari could have an office of her own. "I hardly ever work at home," he explained, "and when I do, I can use the dining room table. If we have company overnight, they can use the sofa bed. Is that okay, darling?"

"Perfect. It looks like you've thought of everything."

"Was it presumptuous?"

"Not at all. I have boxes of books and things to make this room my own. If anyone was presumptuous, it would be me, bringing a cage of birds with me."

The cage was the first thing Eric and his friend Allen unloaded. Nevermore made his rattling noise but kept it down, almost as if he knew they didn't want to draw attention to the big cage with two crows that were moving in. They carried it to the balcony and set it down carefully. When Ari unlatched the door and propped it open the birds stayed inside.

"Won't they fly away?" Allen asked.

"They aren't pets," Ari said. "They are free to roam."

"But you brought them all this way. Don't you want to keep them safe?"

Ari smiled. She poked her finger through the spokes of the cage and stroked Nevermore's head. "He can take care of himself, his mate and even me. Come on, let's get the U-Haul unloaded before we get a parking ticket."

***

Within hours the crows took to New York. They roamed far and wide but returned to the balcony to roost each night. Ari loved New York, too. She felt completely free as she wandered the city, visiting museums, parks, and galleries. Ari had been afraid that she wouldn't like living with someone, but Eric was gone from 9:00 a.m. to 7:00 p.m., and it was almost like dating. She often thought that life wold be perfect if only Eric didn't want to have sex so often.

After a couple of months of living together, they agreed to marry. Ari called Cedric and Nicole, who were delighted. Eric bought her a beautiful ring, and they made plans for a city hall ceremony.

One night as they lay side by side, Eric playing with her fingers and Ari watching shadows on the ceiling, Eric said softly, "Ari, I think we need to talk about our physical relationship."

Shrink talk! Ari snapped, "If you mean sex life, Eric, say sex life!"

Eric turned on his side and propped himself up so he could watch Ari's face.

Ari stayed still and kept her eyes on the ceiling.

"I love you, Ari. I want you to be happy in every way, and I know that you find sex uncomfortable."

Ari bit back a nasty retort.

"We need to talk about this. Or if you'd like to talk to someone else, that's okay, but the physical part of love is crucial for everyone's well-being."

Ari's anger flashed in her eyes. She sat up and glared down at Eric. "I don't need a shrink! I've been there, done that, and I'm fine. I just don't get what all the hullabaloo is about."

"I want to please you, Ari."

"Don't you mean *you* want *me* to please *you*? If you don't like sex with me, you can leave." *Desertion, D-E-S-E-R-T-I-O-N, the act of deserting, especially of one's partner without consent.*

Eric placed his hand on Ari's back and stroked slow circles between her shoulder blades. "I don't want to leave. Please talk to me and tell me what's wrong. If something bad happened to you in the past, you can tell me."

Ari threw the blankets aside and stomped to the window. On the balcony, Nevermore stirred and looked back at her, his eyes bright with understanding. Ari shivered. She pressed her hand to the glass. Nevermore bobbed his head.

Ari turned back toward the bed. "It's always the girl's fault, you know." She picked her robe up from the chair and slipped into it. "No one ever believes that sometimes bad things just happen."

Eric waited.

Ari moved to the mirror. She could see Eric sitting on the bed. *Confession, C-O-N-F-E-S-S-I-O-N, acknowledgment or disclosure of sin or sinfulness.* "When I was ten, Stacy left me with a man named Jerry. He was mean, and I was afraid of him." She watched Eric's features rearrange themselves into a look of concern.

"Did he hurt you?" Eric asked.

"You mean did he rape me?" Ari shook her head. "He came into my room at night and touched me. I didn't make him stop."

"You were just a child. It was not your fault."

"Not the sex part, I know that." Ari took a deep breath.

"What part, then? What was your fault?"

Ari didn't turn around. She kept her eyes on his reflection. "The part where I killed him."

Eric blinked. His look of concern was replaced with one of horror. "Surely, that's not true."

At last, Ari faced him. She nodded. "It's true."

"Ari, whatever happened, I know you are not capable of murder." He stood and crossed the room, wrapping his arms around Ari.

Ari laid her head on Eric's shoulder and pushed aside the memory of his look of revulsion when she'd confessed.

"Let's not talk about anything else tonight." Eric tipped her chin up, cupped her face, and kissed her. "Would you like a cup of tea?"

Ari nodded and followed him to the kitchen.

***

Eric left for his office in the morning, and Ari settled at her desk. Instead of working, she Googled "Is confession good for the soul?" The question turned up 51,600,000 results. She skimmed down the page to "Does confession make you feel better?" and read: "Any type of open and truthful disclosure reduces stress and helps individuals come to terms with their behavior."

"Bullshit!" She closed the search. "Confessing didn't lower my stress." *It was a stupid mistake. I saw the way he looked at me.* She logged into her work screen and forced herself to concentrate.

Eric called to say he'd be late, so Ari poured herself a glass of wine and turned on a movie. When he came in, he kissed her, asked about her day, and excused himself to go to bed.

It didn't feel right. Ari waited until the house was quiet. She went to the kitchen, poured another glass of wine, and opened Eric's briefcase. His planner lay on top of a stack of computer printouts. Ari lifted the planner out and set it aside. The top paper was a printout of her LinkedIn profile.

Ari removed the stack of pages and settled at the breakfast bar. She took a deep gulp of her wine and leafed through the pile. The newspaper stories about the bird girl were followed by police reports about Jerry's death and then the reports about Stacy's death. *How did he get those?* Beneath the police reports was a printout of the newspaper's front page, with her picture, when she won the spelling bee. Ari studied herself and smiled a bit. "I loved that red hoodie," she said, tracing her hand over the picture. The court order placing her in Cedric's care and a few notes from Mrs. Jenks were stapled together. Her high school graduation picture with a list of honors appeared to have been copied from the yearbook. And at the bottom, more police reports: Angie and Robin. Nothing else. He hadn't found everything, but he had seen too much.

A noise alerted her. Ari spun around to find Eric in the doorway. "Did you spend all day researching me?" she demanded. "Does it make you happy to learn about my freaky life?"

"You know I'd never hurt you, Ari. If you'd been honest about all of this, I wouldn't have felt compelled to search for answers."

"Answers! Right, you think these papers give you answers? You think they tell you who I am?"

Eric hadn't moved from the doorway. He watched her carefully.

"I think," he said slowly, "that they tell me that you have experienced a great deal of trauma and have been surrounded by a lot of death."

"My life before I met you is none of your business."

"Perhaps not for the ordinary person on the street, but I thought we were going to marry and create a family together. I want to help you. I was trying to understand."

Ari poured more wine into her glass. "So, what do you understand now, Eric? What conclusions have you drawn?"

"I want you to explain these deaths to me, Ari. I can see why you feel responsible for Jerry, but why hide the rest from me?"

Ari ignored the question. She carefully pushed the printouts into a neat pile. Then, keeping her eyes on the stack, she asked, "Do you want me to leave?"

"No, Ari. I made an appointment for you with a colleague of mine for tomorrow morning. I want you to talk to him."

Ari shook her head and shoved her trembling hands under her legs. "I've already talked to a therapist."

"I know, but this time you need to tell the truth, the whole truth. What you say in therapy is completely confidential. He won't tell anyone else—not me, not the police."

Shit, shit, shit. Ari nodded. "Okay, I'll go once."

"Thank you." Eric smiled for the first time. "Let's not talk tonight. Come lie down with me and try to sleep." He held out his hand.

Ari took it. Slid off the stool and followed him to the bedroom.

They lay side by side without speaking. Eric drifted to sleep, but Ari stayed awake. *There is only one way out of this. I have to kill him or myself. He knows too much.*

In the morning, Eric made coffee while Ari showered and dressed. Then, they walked in silence to his car. "John's office is in Brooklyn," Eric said, starting the engine.

Ari nodded. She looked straight ahead.

Eric maneuvered the car through the Manhattan traffic, took the E-ZPass lane and entered the Brooklyn-Battery tunnel. He stayed in the right-hand lane and accelerated past the thirty-mile-per-hour limit.

Ari watched the walls flash by.

She glanced at Eric. He was looking straight ahead.

She watched her hand shoot out, grab the wheel and twist it to the right. "I'm sorry, Eric," she said.

Eric fought her, trying to pull the wheel to the left.

The car scraped against the wall.

Ari let go.

Eric overcompensated. The car spun to the left.

Horns blasted.

Something huge hit the car.

Ari screamed.

***

"Over here. This one's alive." Ari opened her eyes into a bright light. "It's okay. Just stay still. We got you." She closed her eyes. Men shouted. Horns honked. A siren wailed and stopped. Car doors opened and closed. Ari felt herself lifted. She opened her eyes. "It's okay, Miss. There's been an accident. We're going to take you to the hospital."

"Eric?" she whispered.

"He the driver?"

"Yes."

"Sorry, miss. He didn't make it."

Ari closed her eyes again.

A blood pressure cuff tightened on her arm, and she felt the poke of a needle. She opened her eyes again and looked at the EMT.

He smiled at her. "Don't worry. You're okay. You have a gash on your forehead and maybe a couple of broken bones, but nothing serious. You were lucky. The car's a total loss."

***

Patched up and tucked into a hospital bed, Ari drifted on the pain meds. A nurse came in to check her vitals and said, "There is a policeman here that wants to talk to you. Do you feel up to it?"

"Okay." Her voice sounded funny, and she struggled to clear her throat. The nurse stuck a straw in a water glass and brought it to Ari's lips. She sipped.

"Better?"

Ari nodded.

"I'll tell him you're ready." She patted Ari's foot as she left the room.

"Harriet Blimm?" The policeman came to her bedside with his hat tucked under his arm.

Ari tried to turn her head to smile. She winced at the pain it caused. "Ari," she whispered.

"Sorry, didn't get that?"

"People call me Ari," she said louder.

"Got it. Can you tell me what happened?"

"I don't remember much." She cleared her throat again. "Can you give me some water?"

"Sure." He held the straw to her lips.

"Eric was driving, and I was just watching the wall go by." She paused. "Then the car was spinning, and horns were honking, and we hit something big."

"Were you fighting or talking or—?"

"No. Just driving. Maybe we were talking, but I'm sure we weren't arguing."

"Where were you going?"

"To see a friend of Eric's in Brooklyn. He's a psychiatrist, too. We're going to get married, and he was going to talk to us about that."

"John Lindberg?"

"Yes. How did you know that?"

"Dr. Cohen's planner was in the car."

Planner? Printouts? Ari stopped breathing for a second.

"The car behind you said that your car jerked to the right and bounced off the wall. Do you remember that?"

Ari lifted her hand and stared at the cast that covered her arm. "I think so. It made a horrible sound. I screamed. Eric jerked the wheel back the other way, and we hit something."

The policeman nodded. "Actually, he overcorrected, and a semi T-boned the driver's side."

Tears leaked from Ari's eyes.

He handed her a Kleenex.

"You're lucky you survived with so few injuries. Our best guess is that the driver looked at you and pulled to the right. It happens all the time. People don't realize that the car follows the way the driver looks, and that tunnel is narrow. On the open road, things would have been different."

He reached into his shirt pocket and handed her a card. "Dr. Cohen's ID shows you as his next of kin. The car is a total loss, but you can pick up any personal items that were in the vehicle at this address. The hospital will give you the stuff that came in with his body." He laid the card on the tray table.

"Thank you," Ari said, and allowed her tears to flow.

He turned to leave and stopped short as Cedric and Nicole burst into the room. They brushed past him. Cedric took in the uniform and stopped. "Everything okay, Officer?"

"Just routine. Accidents happen in that tunnel."

***

When Ari was ready for release from the hospital, Cedric picked her up and delivered her to Eric's apartment. While he drove around looking for a parking space, Ari accepted condolences from the doorman and hurried to the elevator. She let herself in. The crows immediately set up a clamor, but Ari ignored them and rushed to the kitchen. The stack of printouts was right where she had left it. Ari swept them up, dropped them in the trash compactor and pushed the button.

"That's done," Ari declared, dusting her hands together. She dropped her purse on the counter and hurried to greet the birds.

Cedric and Nicole urged her to come home with them to mend, but Ari insisted she was fine alone. "If you can stay long enough to help me figure out who I need to call and how to make arrangements, then I'll have a better idea of what comes next."

They readily agreed. Cedric went through Eric's planner and found his attorney's number. Ari asked him to make the call. When he hung up, Cedric explained that Eric had taken care of almost everything. "Did you know that he had no family?" he asked Ari.

"Yes. His parents were killed in a plane crash, and his brother died of an overdose." Ari wiped away a tear. "I think that was why Eric became a psychiatrist."

"Grayson will take care of the arrangements for the cremation and would like to see you tomorrow. I told him you were injured, so he offered to come here in the morning, about eleven. Okay?"

Ari nodded and sank into the sofa.

Nicole pressed her hand to Ari's forehead as if checking for a fever. "You look exhausted. Can I get you anything?"

"No, I just need to rest." Ari swung her legs up onto the sofa and closed her eyes.

Nicole slipped off Ari's shoes and covered her with a blanket.

***

306 · TAMARA MERRILL

Grayson turned out to be a man about Cedric's age. He greeted Ari with a kiss on the cheek. "I'm so sorry to meet you under these circumstances. Eric's death has come as a terrible shock."

Ari felt her hands tremble and clasped them together tightly. She nodded.

Cedric stepped in. "Make yourself comfortable." He took Ari's arm and walked with her behind the attorney. "Would you like to speak alone?" he asked Grayson.

"That would be up to Ari." Grayson settled into a chair and placed his briefcase on the coffee table.

"Please stay," she said. Cedric pulled Ari down next to him on the sofa. He wrapped an arm around her shoulder.

Grayson got right down to business. "Eric was very excited about the upcoming nuptials. As soon as you two set the date, he updated his will and other documents. As you know, Eric had no other surviving relatives. He made a few bequests to charitable organizations, but the majority of the estate will transfer directly to you as his primary beneficiary."

"May I ask what the estate entails?" Cedric asked, leaning forward.

"After all expenses are paid, I believe you will receive a few hundred thousand dollars and, of course, this property."

Ari gasped. "This apartment? I thought Eric rented it. We were talking about where we would buy a house."

"Oh no." Grayson clasped his hands together. "The apartment is yours. If you'd like, I can inform the homeowners' board and transfer any HOA bills, utilities, et cetera into your name."

Ari sat dumbfounded. *I should have waited. He did love me. Or, maybe he just didn't have time to take me off the will.* Tears rolled down her cheeks. She swiped at her eyes and then burst into sobs. *I'm safe. I never have to kill again.*

***

Ari attended the cremation along with Cedric, Nicole, and Grayson. She'd considered notifying Brad, but she had no idea where he lived, or how to reach him.

Ari sorted through Eric's office, removing any personal items, and looking carefully to ensure there were no records of his search for her information. Then she turned the task of notifying clients and closing the practice over to his receptionist and Grayson.

Cedric and Nicole left for home. Ari called her office and gave notice. She wanted a job, but she'd look for something in New York, something different, something where no one knew her.

Alone in the apartment, Ari opened the doors to the balcony and allowed Nevermore and Veritas to come in and out at will. She laughed and told Nevermore, "Maybe I am the crazy bird girl after all."

Nevermore cawed loudly and shook his head.

"You're right. I'm not crazy, but I am your bird girl."

Nevermore clicked and cawed.

"I know. We are safe now. I had to kill those people, but I promise, I'll never kill again."

Nevermore hopped back and forth, rattling his advice.

"Yes, I'll be very careful not to get involved with anyone."

Nevermore cawed his agreement, flew to her shoulder and rubbed his head on her cheek.

***

Thirteen beware it's the devil himself.

"Finding two crows, however, means good luck. Three crows mean health, and four crows mean wealth. Yet spotting five crows means sickness is coming and witnessing six crows means death is nearby." —*Zuzana Starovecka*

Ari sat at the hotel bar, nursing a tall G & T, folding a cocktail napkin into squares, smaller and smaller.

The bartender caught her eye and smiled. "Need anything?"

She shook her head and took a long sip of her cocktail.

"Harriet Blimm!" A deep voice interrupted her thoughts, and she swung around, still clasping her drink. "Alive and well and as beautiful as ever, I see."

She stared at the uniform, her heart pumping. *What the fuck?*

The policeman's face split in a wide grin. "You don't recognize me, do you, Hairy Fairy?"

Shit. Ari shook her head and studied him to gain a moment. *Toby Meyers! He's a policeman now?*

"I'm a little insulted that you don't remember me." He raised an eyebrow. "My friends say I haven't changed a bit."

"Good grief! Toby Meyers—ah—hey, Toby!" Ari forced herself to smile, turned back to the bar, and set her glass precisely in the middle of her coaster. "Wow! Talk about a blast from the past."

Ari shot a look at the bartender. He was watching them closely. She smiled wryly and cocked an eyebrow. The bartender responded by moving closer.

"Can I help you, Officer?" he asked. He folded his bar rag and set it on the counter beneath the bar.

"I don't think so." Toby gave Ari the nasty grin she remembered from school. "Unless," he said slowly, watching her closely, "my friend here is giving you a hard time."

Toby moved to stand next to Ari.

She forced herself not to squirm as he invaded her space. *Still a bully, then.*

"I didn't know you were back in town."

Ari didn't respond.

"You moving back?"

Ari shook her head. "No, I live in New York. I'm just here for Cedric's funeral."

"I'd heard about that." Toby sounded contrite. "He was a good guy."

"Yes, he was." Ari reached for her glass and took a long drink.

The bartender interrupted, "Can I get you anything, Officer?"

Toby kept his focus on Ari. "Still talking to birds?"

Ari scowled but otherwise didn't react.

Toby tried again. "Killed anyone lately?"

Asshole. "That wasn't funny in high school, and it's not funny now." Ari looked directly into Toby's eyes and watched as he processed her response.

Toby held up his hands in mock surrender. "Sorry," he jeered, "you never could take a joke." The radio on his shoulder squawked. He touched one of its buttons. "Gotta go, but I'll be watching you." He gave a two-fingered salute and strode toward the door.

Ari kept her eyes on the bar and drew in a deep, shaky breath. *One hundred, ninety-nine, ninety-eight, ninety-seven, ninety-six, ninety-five.*

The bartender replaced her empty glass with a fresh G & T.

"On the house," he said.

Ari smiled. "Thanks."

The bartender held out his hand. "I'm Gary."

Ari extended her hand and touched his fingertips. "Ari."

"Charming fellow," Gary said. "What'd you ever do to him?"

Ari tilted her glass in a mock toast and took a long swallow. "It's a long, boring story. He's just a bully from my past." *A bully I need to get rid of.* Ari finished her G & T. "Thanks again for the drink."

Gary grinned. "Anything for a damsel in distress."

Ari walked to her rental car, keeping alert to be sure Toby wasn't watching her. *All I need is to have him pull me over.*

***

Cedric had been respected in the community, and the funeral was well attended. Back at the house, Ari stood next to Nicole, smiling politely as people she didn't remember commented over and over again on how proud Cedric had been of her success and then asked if she were married yet.

Cooper and Jeff each hugged her, and Cooper whispered in her ear, "I need to talk to you about something."

Ari murmured, "I'll find you in a minute."

Giving Nicole another hug, Ari excused herself and went looking for Cooper. She found him on the back patio, leaning against the wall, staring into the yard. He straightened as she approached. "How are you holding up?" he asked.

"Sad, I guess. Cedric was always good to me. My grandmother made the right choice when she named him my guardian."

"I was surprised to hear of his death. Was he sick?"

Ari shook her head. "No. It was a massive heart attack. Friday night, he seemed fine, and on Saturday, he was gone. Nicole said he'd never had any heart trouble before."

"It was lucky you were home for the weekend."

"I guess. I was just here because Nicole asked me to help plan Cedric's retirement party." Ari shaded her eyes and looked into the trees, half expecting to see Nevermore and Veritas.

"Ari."

His somber tone caused her to turn and look at Cooper.

"Toby Meyers has been stirring things up at the station house. He's suggesting you killed Cedric."

Ari's mouth fell open. "Why? Why in the world would he say that?"

"He's an ass. You know that. But he keeps talking about all the deaths that occurred in your life when you were a kid. He told the captain that it just seemed highly unlikely that Cedric died of natural causes."

"Shit. What is wrong with that guy? I never killed anyone." *Except for Jerry, Stacy, Angie, Robin, Lucas, Andrew, Barry, and Eric.* "There was a full autopsy on Cedric. Nicole said that they did a tox screen and everything. It was a heart attack."

"I know, but you need to be aware that Toby is still the same jerk he was in middle school. He had a crush on you then and I think he still does. He won't leave you alone until he gets your attention."

"That's not going to happen. I'm going back to New York the day after tomorrow. He'll forget about me again."

"I hope so." Cooper took Ari's hand and gave it a squeeze. "You can always count on me for help. You know that, right?"

Ari nodded.

"Let's go find Jeff. We'll get a drink and tell happy stories about our youth and about Cedric."

Ari allowed herself to be pulled along.

Dr. Madison approached and beamed at Ari. "It's good to see you, despite the circumstances. You look very well."

"Thank you." Ari smiled. "You look the same. Did I ever thank you for all your help?"

"No thanks needed, Ari. Watching from the distance as you matured and developed into your own self-confident person was all I needed."

Ari laughed and covered her mouth.

For a moment, Dr. Madison caught a glimpse of the seventeen-year-old she'd treated. "How's Nevermore?" she asked.

"He came with me to New York. He and Veritas roost on the balcony of my apartment." Ari's eyes lit up. "He's still my best friend. We talk every day."

"It's an astonishing relationship you two share. Because of you, I've learned a lot about crows. Nevermore must be over eighteen-years-old now."

"He's very healthy." Ari realized she sounded defensive, and she quickly changed her tone. "There are crows that live to thirty and there's one documented case of a crow living to fifty-nine."

"Goodness, I didn't realize that. I hope he lives a long time."

"Me, too. Excuse me for a moment. I think Nicole needs me."

As Ari walked away. Dr. Madison murmured to herself, "The injured child is always just inside." She watched Ari cross the room and stoop to hear what Nicole needed. "But she's doing well, I think."

"Did you say something, ma'am?" a waiter stopped to see if the woman needed anything.

"No, dear. Just talking to myself."

People began to leave, and again Ari stood by Nicole's side, accepting condolences and promises to stay in touch.

The catering crew cleaned up the house and departed.

Ari and Nicole sat alone in the living room.

Nicole tipped her head back against the sofa cushion and closed her eyes. "I'm going to go up to bed, Ari." She stretched and opened her eyes. "Why don't you call Cooper and spend the evening with him."

"I don't think so." Ari slipped off her heels and bent to pick them up. "I think I'll go back to the hotel and change into my running clothes. A run will do me good. I need to clear my head."

Nicole stood and walked toward the stairs. "Okay. I'll see you in the morning." She placed her hand on the banister and turned to look at Ari. "Cedric loved you like his own daughter, Ari. He always said that no matter what, Ari's tough, and she'll be okay."

Ari nodded; the lump in her throat seemed too large to speak around.

"Lock the door on your way out, dear."

***

Ari drove to her hotel, changed into dark running clothes, and re-turned to the hotel bar. Gary greeted her entrance with a wave and asked, "Can I get you something?"

Ari slid onto a bar stool. "Sure. How about a martini, very dry and a little dirty. Extra olives, please."

"You got it."

Ari placed her elbows on the bar, lowered her head, and massaged her neck.

"You okay?" Gary asked, placing the drink, and a tiny bowl of ol-ives, in front of her.

"I am," Ari said. "It was a hard day, but yeah, I'm okay." She lifted the glass and sipped. "Nice," she said.

"That creepy policeman was in here looking for you a little while ago. I told him you hadn't been in tonight. He said he'd be back."

Ari took another drink, not sure what to say.

Gary kept his eyes on her. "If you don't want to talk to him, you can leave, and I'll cover for you. Tell him I still haven't seen you."

"Thanks," Ari said, "but he's just a bully that likes to remind me of what a misfit I was when I was a kid. It's always better to face a bully than to run."

"Too late anyway. He's coming in now. I'll be right here if you need me." Gary lifted a glass out of the drying rack and polished it.

Ari lifted her eyes to the mirror and saw Toby, hand on his gun, surveying the bar. He recognized her and approached. Ari dropped her eyes to her napkin and read the joke printed there: "Not to get technical, but according to chemistry, alcohol is a solution." She smiled.

"Something funny, Bird Girl?"

"Nothing you'd understand. If I remember right, English was never your favorite subject."

"Where've you been all day?"

"Officer Meyers, I don't believe that's any of your business. However, if you'd really like to know, I was attending the funeral and reception for Cedric Danvers. You may remember he was my guardian, the man I consider my father. Most of this city's elite were in attendance."

Gary cocked an eyebrow in her direction, amused by her insult.

"You always thought you were so smart, Hairy Fairy, but my dad swore you killed that Jerry guy and I believe him."

Ari turned slowly and faced Toby directly. "Officer Meyers, you are harassing me in front of a witness." She nodded toward Gary. "Do you think that's a good idea?"

Toby's hand caressed his gun. He glared at Ari. "Just remember I'm watching you, smartass."

Ari finished her martini and handed the glass to Gary. "May I have another, please."

"Drunk and disorderly," Toby said.

"I don't think so." Gary pulled his phone from his pocket.

"Just teasing her—don't get your panties in a knot, buster. This woman is not nearly as pretty and sweet as she looks."

"Why, Toby Meyers, I think you just called me pretty and sweet." Ari laughed. "I guess there's a first time for everything."

"You're still a bitch. And one of these days, I'm going to prove my dad right. There is no statute of limitations on murder, Bird Girl." He turned and stomped away.

Gary set her new martini on the bar and crossed his arms. "Okay, it's none of my business, but that guy's crazy. Are you sure you don't want me to report him?"

Ari shook her head slowly.

"Okay, but what was all that stuff about murder?"

Sometimes the truth is the only way out. Ari took a gulp of her drink and braced herself. Then, she asked, "Did you grow up in this town?"

Gary shook his head. "Moved here about six months ago."

"I grew up here, and some bad stuff happened when I was young. My mom had some drug and alcohol problems. She left me with the guy, Jerry, that Toby was talking about. One night he fell down the stairs and broke his neck. I was ten. Nobody ever thought I killed him except Toby. He's been raving about it for twenty years. Most people in town ignore him."

"How'd he ever get to be a cop?"

"His dad was the police chief for years. I guess it's all in who you know."

"Wow, that's crazy." Gary thought a moment. "Why's he call you Bird Girl?"

"I used to have a pet crow."

"Cool." He held up the gin bottle. "Ready for another one?"

"No thanks. It's been a long day. I was going to go for a run, but I think I'll just go to bed." Ari stood and pushed her glass to Gary. "You make a great martini. Good night."

"Night."

Ari walked away. She thought she felt Gary watching her, but he was wiping down the bar, eyes focused on his bar cloth, when she glanced back.

She summoned the elevator and stepped inside. She gazed at her reflection in the brass panel. "Just one more time. Toby has to die."

The doors opened on the tenth floor. Ari pushed the button for the garage and rode the elevator back down.

ACKNOWLEDGMENTS

Writing a book is a solitary endeavor at the best of times. Writing during the pandemic lockdowns was even more so. My writing group, who met on ZOOM, provided excellent support and encouragement. In addition, writing this book would not have been possible without the understanding of friends—you know who you are—who listened to be me discuss bizarre ways to murder ad nauseam. A special thanks to JR Strayve JR, Theresa Banks, Teresa Espaniola, and Frederick Zarndt who are not afraid to eat my cooking. To my wonderful editor, Lisa Wolff, who made this book sing. Thank you for your hard work, and your kind words. And last but not least, I want to thank the internet for the astonishing amount of information available about ways to murder. Without the help of search engines, I would have no idea about the number of poisons available to us all.

ABOUT THE AUTHOR

Tamara Merrill is the author of the Amazon bestselling books, Shadows In Our Bones and The Augustus Family Trilogy. Her work has been published in fourteen anthologies, numerous magazines, and online publications.

She fell in love with books at a very early age—all books, any genre. She reads incessantly and perhaps, as Louise May Alcott said, "She is too fond of books, and it has turned her brain." While reading may keep her from writing every day, it is also why she writes. Reading the Betsy-Tacy books by Maud Hart Lovelace caused her to proclaim herself an author and resulted in her first published work, in the American Girl magazine, when she was nine years old.

Tamara enjoys writing in many genres, including short stories, literary fiction, historical fiction, humor, nonfiction technical manuals, and how-to articles. You might expect that she would blog, but she seldom does.

Tamara finds writing inspiration anywhere and everywhere. The book you hold in your hand grew out of her interest in crows and their significance in mythology and folklore. The crow is a highly intelligent bird capable of social interaction. Perhaps it's true that Nevermore told Tamara this story.

Tamara currently resides in Coronado, California and Wickenburg, Arizona. She is available to speak at book clubs, writers and readers events,` and teaches writing skills in the adult education system.

Learn more about Tamara at: www.tamaramerrill.com.

Follow her on Facebook, TamaraMerrillAuthor or Instagram @tmerrillauthor

CPSIA information can be obtained
at www.ICGtesting.com
Printed in the USA
BVHW030025030322
R13235300001B/R132353PG630416BVX00009B/9

9 781733 855549